THE COTTON CHRONICLES
VOLUME ONE:
A PLANTING SEASON

A COTTON PROFESSIONAL PRESS
PUBLICATION

OTHER BOOKS BY BETTY COTTON MCMURTRY:

THE COTTON CHRONICLES VOLUME TWO:
A GROWING SEASON (DUE MAY 2018)

THE COTTON CHRONICLES VOLUME THREE:
A HARVEST SEASON (DUE OCTOBER 2018)

THE COTTON CHRONICLES VOLUME FOUR:
A FALLOW SEASON (DUE MAY 2019)

OTHER BOOKS BY FORD MCMURTRY:

COTTON FIELDS

CARDIAC CATS: THE GREATEST FOOTBALL STORY NEVER
TOLD (DUE SEPTEMBER 2018)

A Planting Season
The Cotton Chronicles: Volume One

BETTY COTTON MCMURTRY

And

FORD MCMURTRY

DEDICATION

To all of the people who have supported me throughout this endeavor, especially my wonderful children, Mary and Ford.—Betty

To my family and friends for their undying support.--Ford

ACKNOWLEDGMENTS

My children, Meme and Ford, helped me every step of the way; serving as my co-writers, proofreaders, and editors. Thank you to my family for allowing me to devote the time needed to bring this novel to fruition. Thanks to Cheryl O'Leary, Sarah Platt, and Lois George, without whom this book would lack its current depth of character and context. Thank you to Tony Morris and The Ossabaw Island Writer's Retreat. I attended the Spring 2017 retreat with an idea for a story in my head and 30 pages of sophomoric writing which turned into the novel you are holding in your hands. Thanks to the Alabama Writers' Conclave for your mentorship and support. Thank you to Judy and Craig Johnson for your encouragement and mentorship as I navigated through learning the writing and publishing process. Last, I would be remiss if I did not mention my faithful muse, Missy the dog. --Betty 2017

I echo Betty's thoughts above. Also, a special thanks to Dr. Michael Turner at Santa Fe College in Gainesville, Florida who set the writing bar higher than I thought I could achieve. To our Advanced Readers Sherry Shearer, Jeanelle Kalka, Bobbi Neely, Sabrina Odom, and Nancy Bryan, thank you for your priceless candor and feedback. Finally, thank you to my mother Betty for allowing me to walk alongside her on this journey. I will forever be indebted.

Author's Note: This is a work of fiction. Outside of actual historical figures, any resemblance to persons living or dead is purely coincidental.

Cover Photo Credit:
United States Library of Congress FSA/OWI Collection

PROLOGUE

In 1929, the American Stock Market crashed; and fortunes, businesses, and farms were lost. For most wage earners, there were no jobs. Individuals and entire families faced hardship for which there seemed to be no relief. Many lived on the streets or in their cars, depending on private charities that operated soup kitchens. Facing a miserable existence with no end in sight, many sought refuge in the open spaces of the American far west. After traveling westward as far as their cars and legs would take them, these brave souls started their new lives where they were arguably no better off than before. Entire families were admitted to work camps where they were abused by camp bosses who charged inflated prices for the most basic of essentials. Regardless of the circumstances, most workers stayed and fought to be chosen for the privilege of working for pennies a day from till to can't.

Unlike urban dwellers, farmers of the rural South and some parts of the Midwest, with fairer weather and tillable soil, were less impacted. With hard work, determination, and a little luck, their efforts produced a bounty from the earth which became the currency of their communities as they sold, traded, or bartered for their livelihood. In spite of the terrible conditions in many parts of the country, the farmers fared better. They were known to be frugal and had saved for a lifetime.

This is the story of one such family and their neighbors who were planted in the clay loam and sandy soils of the Deep South and whose gritty determination allowed them to thrive where others failed.

CHAPTER 1

With each delicate step, the shadows cast by the loblolly pines danced across the dusty dirt road in front of Olivia Turner. A light breeze wafted through the trees, causing them to gently sway against the setting May sun. She knew she had been gone too long. Her blue chintz dress ruffled in the breeze and she avoided tripping over its hem as she picked up her pace. Despite being nearly a mile away, her house was in view now. As she rounded a bend, she crossed the drainage ditch at the edge of the hard-packed roadway and made her way to the white fence that bordered the grazing pasture for Papa's horses.

Beyond the pasture, she could see field hands dragging boards to smooth the surface around the newly constructed circle track Papa had built to train thoroughbreds. Olivia felt the ground shake and heard a familiar noise from her left. Two trotters, Butterscotch and Taffy, approached the fence to greet her. They nickered as they pranced proudly along the fence line. Breaking off a lump of rock candy, she allowed each to take a piece from her outstretched palm. She rubbed them on their velvety noses and playfully patted them on their jowls. Then she started home. Her short legs on her nearly five-foot frame slowed her pace, so she began to jog lightly to close the distance home.

Although Olivia was the tallest of the four Turner girls, she was viewed by most as a petite young woman blessed with a stunning natural beauty. Because of her small frame and demure disposition, some would say she appeared frail with ivory skin, long dark brown eyelashes, and sky blue eyes. Olivia's wavy hair was the color of corn silk and fell softly onto her petite shoulders.

When she approached the long driveway to the Turner farm, she slowed to a brisk walk and glanced longingly at the last slivers of sunlight piercing the South Alabama skyline. "At least you get a break!" she admonished the sun. "I'm forever ablaze under Papa's watchful eyes." She put her head down to finish walking the last quarter mile up the hill to the main house.

As she reached the front yard, she could see Papa seated in his rocker on the porch, his pipe glowing in an orange hue that nearly matched the sunset as he drew an extended puff. She stepped onto the porch and stopped beside him, while looking down at her feet.

Papa spoke in a Scottish brogue, "Olivia, am I to assume that you have lost your ability to tell time?"

Olivia had learned that the best way to avoid riling Papa was to use Ann as a part of any excuse. "Why Papa, don't you remember? You told me not to come home without ribbon to finish the dress that Ann needs for her party tomorrow. It took time to find the exact shade she wanted." Olivia hid her sly grin and walked toward the door.

"Humph," he grunted, "Well, okay then."

Although he was proud of his daughter's work ethic, Papa drew on his pipe and cajoled. "Get yourself inside and see what help Gussie needs with dinner." He took another puff from his pipe as Olivia scurried through the doorway and into the darkened interior of the house.

.....

Walt and Annie Turner lived on a three thousand acre farm dubbed "High Point," about seven miles outside the town of High Springs in Geneva County, Alabama. They were of Dutch and Scottish lineages, and Walt was known as an influential farmer, businessman, and power broker in local and state politics. In addition to his farming operations, he owned and operated a lumber mill, and he bred and sold Angus bulls and thoroughbreds.

As a result, he was well-traveled throughout the Southeast and was also notoriously known to some to be a regular jackass when it came to business deals. A farrier Walt had bested in a deal after cutthroat negotiations once remarked Walt, "could squeeze six pennies from a nickel."

The shadow he cast in the community was broad, but his influence on his own family was even more pronounced, as he ruled it with an iron fist. When Papa spoke, all listened and obeyed without question. Annie, ever the loving wife, deferred to his judgment on most matters. She was frail and weak, having delivered nine living children. Walt realized early on that in equestrian terms, Annie was a "thoroughbred" who could have been married to the finest of stallions but who had somehow become smitten with this grade horse.

At High Point, appropriately named because it was the highest point in Geneva County, the main house was situated on a hill where it was visible for more than a mile. The structure was massive with large columns framing a view of ceiling to floor windows across the front, and a wrap-around porch. Behind the house were the canning shed, smoke house, and clothes washing area where large pots were hung over fire pits. Rows of pecan trees flanked the perimeter of the parcel of land on which the house stood. A white picket fence separated the grounds of the house from those of the barns and paddocks that housed livestock. Adjacent to the acres of crops were the "Quarters," the living spaces for Negro families and itinerant share croppers. The yard consisted of rolling terraces covered with wild flowers, landscaped flowering shrubs, and trees. Walt had worked tirelessly to build the home where Annie could be happy.

MCMURTRY

CHAPTER 2

Annie McGee Turner was born in 1873. All who knew her remarked upon her beauty and refinement. Her father Michael owned a successful mercantile and provided well for his wife and three daughters, Pearl, Rebecca, and Annie. The McGee's loved horses and Walt was more than willing to sell them the best he had.

It was on one of his first deliveries Walt became aware of Annie's existence. He had come to deliver a pair of trotters when he spotted her as she sat upon her Bay horse, tall and proud in the saddle. She gazed straight ahead, seemingly ignoring him as her reddish curls gently nuzzled her smooth, pale neckline. Her rose colored cheeks were beacons and her emerald green eyes turned to him and met his briefly before she turned away.

He felt the blood rush to his head and his cheeks matched hers in color. His heart sank to his stomach, and he realized he was smitten with this girl. He prophetically thought to himself, "I must have her." For the first time in Walt's life, he had only one goal: to rope Annie McGee into marriage and take her back to Alabama.

.....

As the months passed, Michael observed Walt while suspecting his interest in Annie. Although he feared the potential outcome, he invited him to supper to satisfy his own self-serving need to connect with his fellow countryman. The house boy Anthony rang a tiny bell signifying it was time for dinner to be served and they all moved toward the dining room.

"Take this seat." Michael ceremoniously took his place at the head of the table and directed Walt to a seat on his right where Annie was seated between her two sisters. While it was considered an honor to be seated at the right of the host, Michael had an ulterior motive: to minimize Walt's ability to engage in conversation with Annie.

He had not, however, anticipated their silent communications as they exchanged coy glances throughout the meal. Michael was consumed with much chagrin. He had counted on an evening with Walt's recounting engaging anecdotes of his far-flung travels, but Walt thought of a different type of engagement. His mind was elsewhere; at least two chairs away.

Michael watched the two exchange glances and his emotions stirred. He enjoyed Walt's company but the thought of Walt's courting his beloved Annie was more than he could handle. She was, after all, a debutante with numerous suitable prospects in the local community. And, he thought, she certainly was not reared to be a farmer's wife.

He envisioned Annie as a thoroughbred being led down the aisle at her wedding by a donkey and he chuckled. Why couldn't Walt see himself as wholly unsuitable to take on a wife of Annie's social status!

He would not enjoy the task he saw he must undertake, but the time had come to have a meeting of the minds regarding his expectations for Annie. What he had to say to Walt might hurt his feelings but it was essential that Walt abandon his ill-conceived plans to be betrothed to Annie.

As quickly as they finished the dessert course, Michael ushered Walt outside and away from the house. As they walked to the stables, he produced two cigars. After pausing briefly to light them, their talk of maintaining a healthy stable of horses continued. Although Michael had been involved with the care of horses throughout his life, he eagerly listened to Walt's counsel on the subject.

Pointing to a pair of horses, Walt said, "These are trotters and they need room to run. You have to give them long straightaways in order for them to achieve their stride and there isn't enough acreage on your property to create a mile run. Since I have not seen a mile track anywhere around here, have you given thought as to how you intend to maintain their stamina for competition at the track?"

Michael thought but did not answer. Walt continued. "Are your plans to run and sire them or will you consider selling them in the future?"

Michael discussed his plans in detail and Walt conceded that they were well thought out. Then Walt, never one to forego a business opportunity, seized his chance.

"Michael, I've talked to several businessmen here in the community and I've found that all hold you in high regard. I don't mean to impose upon your hospitality by bringing up business, but if you will permit I have a question." He paused and Michael nodded for him to continue.

"Given your satisfaction with the horses I have brought you, would you feel comfortable steering me toward any of your associates who might be in the market to buy my horses or cattle? I am eager to branch out into new markets and I would welcome the chance to have reason to return here."

Michael clamped tightly on his cigar. He could see it coming a country mile away. He flicked away the snake-like ash with a snap of his wrist. Although he knew that what he had to say would damage their friendship, the time to act was now. He extinguished the end of the stubby cigar and rested both arms on the top of the fence railing. In a firm but not abrasive voice he answered.

"Walt, there is probably some help that I could give you, but I am not going to do so." Michael paused. He knew he must continue but he dreaded what he had to say. Walt turned to face Michael squarely.

"Well Michael, I don't…," Walt murmured. Michael knew of Walt's temper. He knew if he did not tread lightly, the two would end up in a shouting match, or worse.

"Walt, I intend to stop your contacts with Annie. I'm asking you now to forestall future efforts to court her. If you don't agree, I'll have no alternative but to forbid her to see you. Of course, you understand that if it comes to that, it will also regrettably be the end of our horse trading days."

Michael's words stung like a bush full of briars and Walt winced as he could not muster a reply. Michael sensed he was getting through, and although he was fond of Walt, his intuition as a former boxer drove him to go on the offensive to land the knockout blow.

"Hear me, Walt, and understand that I mean what I say. I will not tolerate your thoughts of marriage to her."

Walt wobbled in response and staggered briefly on his feet. Michael's barbs landed in combination and Walt had no defense. He had expected some pushback, but he hoped Michael would eventually concede as he often did in their other negotiations. The fight was afoot.

Walt's pride sometimes got the better of him as he assumed himself to be the equal of any man, no matter the size, in any battle. In this situation, however, he had too much at stake from both a personal and business perspective. He was on the ropes. His instinct was to fight; he also knew this was a battle with Michael over Annie that he would not win today. He had never thrown in the towel, but he knew he had to concede at this time if there were ever to be a chance for him with Annie.

"I must live and fight another day," he thought.

For once, Walt, the master storyteller, was at a loss. He stepped closer to Michael and found himself toe to toe. "Says you," he uttered in a low pitched grunt.

The very thing that Michael liked about Walt, his brazenness, was the thing that most angered him in this moment. He saw Walt's failure to concede on his request not to pursue Annie as a test of wills and he raised his voice.

"Yes, says I," Michael responded, trying desperately to find the words to help Walt understand why such an arrangement would never work. He found none. His voice leveled out, but his desperation became more evident with each rise and fall of his chest.

"Walt, for God's sake, can't you see she is not suitable for you. Why can you not understand this?" He continued before Walt could respond. "Walt, I stand here before a pair of thoroughbred trotters that you have brought me. You should understand more than others the importance of maintaining their pure blood lines if you expect to continue the line with healthy offspring. Boarding and breeding them with inferior breeds serves only to water down the line."

Walt knew exactly what Michael was saying. He did not need to use analogies. "I'm not good enough, huh?"

"Don't take it that way, Walt. Can't you see what I am trying to tell you? We both know that if the roles were reversed, you would not allow it for your daughter." Walt nodded his head in acknowledgement. He could not argue this point. Michael continued.

"Annie is my 'thoroughbred.' She has been reared to live the life of her social standing. To expect her to live as a farmer's wife, especially the wife of one with so little to offer her is to breed a Morgan to a grade horse. Walt, I cannot make any stronger argument against your pursuit of Annie."

The insult pummeled Walt and bruised his ego. His chest swelled with indignation and his cheeks boiled a crimson red, the color of a branding iron ready to meet virgin cowhide. He felt rage inside and he exercised all his restraint to resist the urge to strike Michael. With so much at stake, he backed off, slumped slightly, and spoke.

"You knew how to hurt me using my love of horses against me. I cannot refute your analogy, and I understand your concern for Annie's welfare. But, you are wrong Michael. I am not a grade horse. I am a winner at everything I attempt. According to your standards, I am not a rich man. You don't seem to consider, though, that against insurmountable odds I have achieved success as a farmer and businessman. No draft horse could have had the character and fortitude to accomplish what I have. More to the point, I intend to become very wealthy. Who knows? Perhaps one day I will own your farm."

Michael quietly absorbed Walt's perspective.

"Know, too," Walt continued, "that I'll do what is necessary to give Annie the life that she dreams of." He paused to catch his breath, "I tell you as a man, neither you nor anyone else will stop me. I swear it."

Michael understood he was powerless against the likes of a man as determined as Walt Turner. "Damn fire all to hell," Michael croaked as he shook his head and walked toward the house.

So it was that Miss Annie McGee became Mrs. Walt Turner. Shortly thereafter, he took her to Geneva County to plant their seeds and begin their lives together on the farm.

MCMURTRY

CHAPTER 3

It was nearly April, 1894, by the time Walt and Annie arrived by horse-drawn wagon to High Springs, Alabama. He spurred on the horses pulling the wagon loaded with trunks of Annie's belongings and a few pieces of furniture. Walt was worried that Annie would find High Springs much different from her home town because of its small size.

"Walt, I'm curious about this place that you call home. How big is High Springs? Does it have an opera house? What about the shops?" Walt knew that a mere description of High Springs did not do it justice so he urged her to wait until they arrived so that she could formulate her own opinion.

"Honestly, Annie, I am at a loss to put into words the charm of High Springs. It would be better if you see it so that you can appreciate its size and character for yourself."

As they entered the town square, she was pleasantly surprised to discover a quaint village. "Just a lap," thought Walt. "And then it's off to the farm." They slowed near a church which, he pointed out, had been erected on land that he and his family had donated. They passed the train depot and entered the main square a few minutes later.

Passing the cotton broker, Walt pointed toward the center of the square consisting of a grassy area with park benches, varieties of trees, and flowers in well-manicured beds. "Annie, notice the covered structure there. That gazebo is large enough to hold a four piece band. Why, it's the centerpiece for our annual Independence Day festivities and you won't find anything like it for forty miles. It's a real gem!"

Annie, unimpressed, did not want to hurt Walt's feelings so she dutifully expressed her delight with the prospects of High Springs' July Fourth celebrations. She folded her gloves in her lap so as to stave off a remark about the absence of an opera house.

Walt continued, oblivious to her lack of engagement to the tour. "When we come to town on Saturdays, you'll find this square a hub of activity. Most of us farmers, along with the townspeople, assemble here to socialize after we take care of our shopping and other business matters. It's a real who's who of Geneva County. I know you will cultivate a multitude of friends from these Saturday excursions."

Annie stared at the nearly empty square and replied, "To be sure, I will."

As they continued on 2nd Street, Walt pointed out a building on his right that occupied almost the entire side of the block on the south side of the square. The First National Bank was easily the tallest structure in High Springs. At three stories, it sat in sharp contrast to the wooden buildings nearby. Annie pointed past the bank to the end of the block.

"Walt is that building a …, she paused to find the right description…, a restaurant?"

Walt looked at the building wedged beside the bank and on the corner. "Yes dear. That is Dallon's Diner. It serves the finest food in town. Mr. Dallon has a boy bring up fresh oysters from Apalachicola Bay every other day when they are in season. I'll bring you to town in a few weeks to try them." Annie nodded in agreement though her downcast eyes reflected her disbelief that she would care in the least for anything carved out of some hard shell.

As they reached Main Street, Walt turned left and pointed out the office and clinic of Dr. Charles James, situated on the east side of the square along with Jerrell's drug dispensary.

"You know a lot of towns our size cannot boast of its own medical clinic equipped as well as a hospital in larger towns. I don't know how he was able to afford the building and all of the equipment, but we are really fortunate that Dr. James moved here to be closer to his aging mother.

As they turned left onto 1st Street, Walt prattled on while pointing out different landmarks. They passed the post office, and cotton broker, and Mr. Adkins' mercantile situated opposite the bank. As Annie's eyes strained to see the small signs, she noted Kelly's Barber Shop and Gates Farm Supply and Feed Store. Mercifully, she realized they had circumnavigated the square and were heading out of town toward home.

After a few blocks, Walt steered his team into the livery and exchanged his horses for the final leg to High Point. Annie wondered about this.

"Walt, how far is it to the farm?"

"Oh, we are about seven miles from the outskirts of town. These nags have been pulling this load since our last stop in Camilla, Georgia, and they are worn plum out. They've done their good deed for us and it is time for them to have their rest. I'll rotate a few of my horses from the livery to

High Point. It will only take a minute and then we'll be on our way."

Shortly, they pulled out of the livery and to a warehouse across the street.

"What now, Walt?"

In anticipation of his upcoming nuptials, Walt had installed several ice boxes in the kitchen. He would pick up a block because he was not going to chance it. He wanted to ensure that his new bride had all the comforts of home for their honeymoon.

With fresh horses for the final leg, the wagon lurched out of the ice plant back toward the square. He skirted the business district and turned right toward the homes that made up the residential section of the town. The homes ranged from modest to stately but they all had one thing in common: they were well maintained. With their hedges and blooming flowers, Annie found her initial view replicated many times over at the sites of the various homes along the road. After four to five blocks, the houses became further and further apart and the skyline became awash in farm land. Walt turned the wagon west toward High Point.

The team pressed on and after about two miles, the sign for the Turner Lumber Mill appeared on the left side of the road. Walt slowed to turn in but Annie objected.

"The farm?" she asked meekly.

"Of course," Walt answered, "You must be tired."

As High Point loomed on the horizon, Annie rested her head on Walt's shoulder and she tried to imagine what life lay before her. She hoped she would find happiness on the farm. Although she was wary of this new lifestyle, she couldn't wait to start their family and Walt was eager to oblige his young bride. As they turned into the steep dirt driveway, Annie marveled at the glistening rays of sun bouncing off the stream that ran through the valley below them. The view was mesmerizing. As the sun set, so ended one chapter of Annie's life as another began.

MCMURTRY

CHAPTER 4

Within the first year of their marriage, Annie became pregnant and delivered their first son, Thomas, in 1895. Her pregnancy was not an easy one and her adjustment to farm life had been even more difficult. She quickly found she was unable to manage the daily requirements characteristic of a thriving farm: cooking, ironing, canning and butchering.

Walt became concerned. Each time he returned from one of his trips, he observed changes in Annie's demeanor and her continued withdrawal from social interactions. Although she attended church services, as soon as the last song ended and the minister said his last prayer, she beat a hasty retreat. She refused social invitations and had no interest in entertaining in their home. He had to face the truth. Running the household was too much for her; and Walt, ever the loving husband, consoled her.

"Annie, it is unimportant to me whether you manage the house and kitchen. What is important is your happiness. Won't you please stop trying to handle these mundane tasks that some of our women in the Quarters can assume?"

Annie, recognizing that she was ill-equipped to handle the load, agreed. But, she could not escape her own thoughts of how she met and fell in love with Walt despite her father's objections.

She thought to herself, "I've made a mistake in not adhering to my father's counsel. I refused to listen when he tried to convince me of the disparity between Walt and me. I understood Papa's logic, but he was unable to understand that he could not dissuade me from marrying Walt. From the first time I spotted him watching me when I sat atop my horse, I knew he was the one."

She recalled how her father had spoken of the little man with the big horses and she was quickly intrigued. When their eyes met for the first time, she was taken back to the time when she rode her first horse. The fear, mixed with the anticipation of the ride, made her stomach flip and she felt the same with Walt. The feeling was only magnified when her father invited Walt into their home for dinner.

Try as she might to observe the rules of etiquette, she could not keep her eyes off Walt. Michael McGee put her sisters between them but it did not prevent their stealing several glances during the saying of Grace and throughout the meal. The zenith of the evening, and perhaps the moment that sealed her fate to become Mrs. Walt Turner occurred when her father pulled Walt into the foyer and left him there while he retrieved cigars from his study.

Carrying dishes to the back porch for washing, Annie noticed Walt standing alone and she seized the opportunity. The look of surprise on Walt's face was one she would cherish forever. She grasped his hand and pulled him into the parlor, and embraced him. "Whatever you do," Annie pleaded, "don't let daddy back you down. If you want me, I am yours, Walt Turner." Before Walt could react, she was gone. Walt knew in that moment nothing would stop him.

....

Annie's misery and depression continued to increase with each pregnancy. From the time of her marriage in 1894 until the birth of Ann in 1912, she was pregnant almost every two years. These pregnancies, including six miscarriages, drastically affected her health. As a result, she was bed ridden much of each day. Walt spent time that he could ill afford at his wife's side encouraging her and attempting to find ways to overcome her acute depression.

One afternoon, after returning from High Springs, Walt shared with Annie messages from several townspeople. "You are going to have to go with me next time. Carolyn Gates threatened me within an inch of my life if I didn't bring you to visit, and several ladies in our church spoke of your unfulfilled promises of visits. They made it clear they were going to hold me to bringing you to call on them. At the mercantile, Miss Metcalf asked about our children. She sends her kindest regards and her wish for your improved health. You know, Annie, people are drawn to you. I don't know a single soul that is not taken with you once they meet you. I am so proud of you."

Annie acknowledged the greetings but was resolved in her intentions of not leaving the farm for any social events. Walt soon became desperate. Nothing he tried worked and he was at his wits end. It broke his heart to see Annie so utterly unhappy. More than once Michael's warning in the barn so many years ago echoed in Walt's head.

"Son, a thoroughbred can never be mated to a grade horse. Surely you must know that."

Had Michael been right? Would his selfish love of Annie and his pairing of his grade lineage to her champion bloodline ultimately destroy her? Walt slept feverishly for several weeks as he contemplated what he had done.

At last, he knew he must act. The next day he entered her bedroom and was struck by the darkness within. Only a hint of bright sunlight escaped the heavy, tightly drawn shades.

"Goodness Annie, don't you want me to open these curtains and let you enjoy the bright sun-filled day?" Walt thought to himself, "No wonder Annie feels depressed!"

The darkness of the room hung like a cloud over all within. He sat down beside her on the bed, drew her into his embrace and brought her face up to his.

"Annie, please talk to me. What can I do to help you? Name it! Don't you know that you are more important to me than my very own life? Please help me. Tell me what it will take to make you happy again."

Annie smiled at him broadly. He was the man who had showed her his love and devotion every day since she had her first glimpse of him from the back of her Bay mare. How she wished she could be the woman he deserved. She ran her fingers across his lips and stilled them.

"Walt, you have provided all that I could possibly want in our dear children, as well as financial security. You can't do more. Yes, I am unhappy but not with you. I am a failure as your wife, and I don't know how to change this. I am like a horse that has run its last race and I have nothing more to give. I fear another pregnancy, yet I welcome you in my bed. Moreover, I need your tender love."

She pressed her lips against his cheek and held them there. The warmth from his skin coursed through her cheeks and down to her neck. Her scalp tingled. She gathered all the strength she could muster, rose from the bed, and forced herself to dress. She was eager to see the new horses, and a visit with Carolyn would be a treat. She stopped at the kitchen to ensure that Gussie had things under control while she was away.

"Missus Annie, you knows you can depend on me. Go ahead with Mr. Walt and don't worry 'bout things in this here kitchen."

Walt awaited her on the front porch. "Annie, you have no idea how happy I am that you are with me. We'll see the horses and then we'll go to High Springs. I don't want to tire you so I'll drop you at Carolyn's house while I take care of some business with William." Together, they set out in the horse drawn wagon for the seven mile trip to High Springs.

.....

When they arrived, Carolyn welcomed them and insisted that Walt not rush with his business. "Annie and I have so much to catch up on so take your time. If she tires before you return, I'll have her lie down to recover. In the meantime, we'll gossip like schoolgirls along with our tea." Walt took his leave and Carolyn turned her attention to her friend. She was keenly perceptive and in a matter of minutes, found Annie reluctant to converse with her.

"Annie, I know you too well and I can't help but feel that there is something wrong with you. Forgive me if you feel I am prying, but I have subscribed to one axiom throughout my life. A problem shared is only half a problem. Won't you let me help you lessen the burden I sense you carry alone?" Carolyn sat back in her chair praying earnestly that Annie would trust her enough to share her load.

After an uncomfortable silence, tears streamed down Annie's face. Carolyn fetched a handkerchief which Annie gingerly took from her. Then she began to pour out her sorrow and unhappiness.

"I have reached the end of my endurance. Do you know about Ruth's sickness?"

"No," replied Carolyn. "What has happened?"

Annie shared with her all her sadness and anxieties that she could not share with Walt because it would hurt him too much. Although she knew that he would try, nothing he could do would change her circumstances.

"Sometimes I despair because we are unable to keep Ruth well. Since her premature birth, she has been frail. At a young age, she was diagnosed with rheumatic fever and for nearly a year she was bedridden and unable to attend school. For the next two years she required constant care. I suffered a miscarriage during this time, but even with this I provided most of her care throughout the day and night. The damage to her heart restricts what she can do and even now she is in bed with an ailment. We have just learned from Dr. James that again she needs constant attention and rest for the next several months. I am worn out physically caring for her."

Carolyn interrupted. "Annie, can Walt arrange for one of the colored women from your Quarters to relieve you?"

Annie smiled. "Walt already took care of this a while back when he arranged for Gussie to handle most of our cooking. She also looks after Ruth during the day. Florabell, her daughter, stays with Ruth at night."

"Has it helped you? Are you feeling better?"

"No, I am more stressed because of my father's recent death. His business was failing and he literally worked himself to death trying to save it. I know my mother needed me but I was not well and my health was too fragile to make the long journey. Now, Walt expects me to get better and I have not. Actually, I am getting worse." Annie paused, and then continued, "I am depressed. Every time I look at myself in the mirror I see an ugly woman who is aged far beyond her years and one who has none of the youthful vitality her husband once admired."

Carolyn sat in silence as she digested Annie's painful recitation. She was concerned about Annie's state of mind.

"Without any hope of reprieve, I have kept to my room to shield Walt and the girls from my further decline."

Carolyn was both shocked and saddened. "In all you say, the love you have for your family is evident. How can you think of keeping yourself from them?"

Annie stood and walked about, clearly agitated. "I can't find any other answer. I have sunk into this deep, dark hole, and I can find no way to escape."

Carolyn was frightened for her friend. She didn't have to be a physician to recognize what Annie intimated. There was an underlying message that touched upon Annie's permanent escape, and she faced a dreadful dilemma. Annie expected their conversation to be between them, not to be shared with anyone, but Carolyn would have to share it. She had no choice. The question was how and when?

When Walt returned to fetch Annie, Carolyn wanted to pull him aside to speak to him of her concern about Annie's mental state, but no opportunity presented itself. She realized she would have to depend on her husband William to arrange for a meeting at a later date.

A few days later when Walt came to pick up supplies, Carolyn summoned him to the stock room to share the salient points of her conversation with Annie. Walt listened closely, and offered his insights.

"I have suspected what you say, but I had not realized the gravity of her depression. Some time ago I was forced to accept the fact that Annie could not be burdened with running our household. It was just too much. So I set about relieving her of the cooking, and I had Olivia take over the management of most household chores. All these changes have not been enough. For months I have agonized over her poor health and desperately looked for ways to minimize her feelings of inadequacy, but I have not been successful."

Carolyn offered her sympathies and Walt thanked her for her loving concern, said goodbye, and headed for home, leaving his purchases behind.

As the horses' hooves slapped the dusty road, the wagon rocked gently from side to side and Walt's mind drifted off as he thought of his options. There must be some way to bring his beloved Annie back from her emotional death!

CHAPTER 5

For some time, Walt had observed Olivia as she went about her daily chores. Among his children, she, alone, was capable of completing multiple chores on time, and of responding to his demanding attention to detail. As Annie's condition continued to deteriorate, his sense of urgency to find relief for her increased and he looked upon Olivia as his last best hope.

Walt was amazed at his daughter's ability, of her efficiency to organize her workload so that nothing was left wanting. He marveled that she never complained. "Yes," he thought, "Olivia will be the savior of our family. She will enable Annie to regain her life."

.....

It was an unusually warm afternoon and Walt caught Annie sitting at her window peeking around the heavy shades.

"What are you watching, dear?" he asked.

Annie was pensive as she answered. "Just the wind in the trees; I often dream that I'm a ball of fluff and that the wind can carry me away from my failures as a wife."

Walt lowered his head and then sat beside her. "I've been thinking," he offered. "It's time for you to step back from your responsibilities here at High Point. You need to take on more social responsibilities in High Springs. The interaction with Carolyn Gates and the ladies at the church would do you good." He placed his hand over hers and squeezed it gently. "I need to make you the queen of Geneva County just like I promised your father I would."

"Oh Walt," she exclaimed, "as much as I would enjoy that, there's no one to take on my responsibilities here at High Point. I can't just …."

Walt interrupted. "I have it planned," he said. "I have found your surrogate." He went on to share what he had observed in Olivia. Annie agreed with his assessment, but she could not agree with his assigning

Olivia the household responsibilities at such a young age.

"Walt, she's only ten years old," Annie argued.

"I know that, but she is aged far beyond her years," Walt retorted.

"But it could hurt her schooling and her social standing. If you persist in this, our Olivia will be seen as nothing more than our housekeeper. As such she'll not attract many, if any, suitors."

"This is not necessarily true." Walt countered. "After all, she's the daughter of Walt Turner. This, alone, should be sufficient for serious suitors, the ones who value a fine young woman who has proven her worth and has no qualms about hard work."

Annie loathed the idea. She knew, too, that Olivia would accept Walt's edict without question. While it hurt her deeply to realize Olivia would likely have no opportunity to enjoy her childhood, she accepted that Walt was right. If this was the way it had to be, then Olivia was the best candidate to continue her schooling at an exceptional level while maintaining their household. Thus in 1916, at the tender age of ten, Olivia became the sole heir to Annie's household duties at High Point.

.....

That evening Walt sat in the kitchen with Olivia and he explained that Mama was very ill and needed help with household chores. Olivia, much to her character, was eager to help.

"What can I do to help Mama?" she asked.

He went over the list of things that would become Olivia's responsibility. He laid out a carefully planned itinerary for her to ensure that she could maintain the balance between her responsibilities at home and her schoolwork. Olivia was dumbfounded at the magnitude of the workload she was to assume. However, she voiced no objection.

"It sure seems like a lot, Papa," she replied as she held the list of tasks. "But I will find a way to get everything done on time. I won't let you or Mama down. I promise."

.....

Over the next few months, Olivia was frustrated as she worked to accomplish the myriad of tasks and keep up with her studies. No matter how hard she tried, it was nearly impossible to satisfy Papa. Of all her siblings, Olivia was most like Annie as to her sweet nature and refined ways; but unlike her mother, she owned a definitive strength and drive. Some might say that she had a stubborn streak a mile wide as she would not allow Papa to browbeat her with his constant trivial complaints. His inequitable treatment of her became clear over time, and caused a question to plague her.

"How was it that she, alone, was singled out to assume these household responsibilities?" It would have been easy for her to become resentful and bitter, but she did not. Rather, Olivia matured into a strong and nurturing individual. She was governed mostly by her desire that Mama regain her strength and vitality. Olivia could not know that the determined resolve built over the next few years would be what sustained her throughout her life.

....

Papa's feelings on education were generally more progressive than others of the time. It was not common for most farmers' children to be educated beyond middle school because the families could not afford to lose the time in the fields. As soon as a boy could read, write, and 'figger,' he knew enough to be a good farmer. By the end of the third or fourth grade, most boys could meet those requirements.

Olivia toiled, and as the years passed, her innate nurturing interests blossomed into helping others outside the family. On one occasion, Miss Metcalf encouraged her to consider college. Troy State Normal College was only 70 miles away and offered curriculums in both teacher education and nursing. Olivia was intrigued; and a few weeks later, she posted a letter with her application.

It was not long before news arrived of her acceptance and her being awarded a scholarship for the fall term of 1925. Olivia was ecstatic. She was nineteen years old and at last the time had come for her to escape her life of servitude. She had done her part to support her family for nine years. The only thing standing in her way was her mustering the strength to tell Papa. As expected, he chastised her.

"How can you be so selfish as to leave when your family needs you? The matter is closed. I don't want to hear you speak of going to college again. Is this clear?"

His attitude was beyond her understanding and Olivia grew angry.

Education beyond high school seemed to be manageable for all of her siblings, but not for her. Olivia remained steadfast in her efforts to convince him.

"Papa, every time one of the boys or Ruth has left the farm for college you promised that I, too, would have an opportunity to pursue my nurse's training. You've told me time and again that it was not the right time because of Mama's health."

Papa interrupted, "I know what I said, and I meant it. I just needed time to find someone that I could hire to take over for you. Confound it, Olivia, with my worry over your Mama, and the demands of the farm and my business, I couldn't find anyone. Do you think I am not still trying? There is no question about it, you are going to have to stay here a while longer. I will not discuss this further with you. Be on your way."

CHAPTER 6

By 1929, the Turner family had sprouted roots in different directions. As each son graduated college, he was gifted 40 acres of farmland. Thomas and James elected to build homesteads and work their acreage. Harry apprenticed as a cotton broker, and, with Walt's backing, acquired an interest in the nearby brokerage house. Jerry, now 28, married the only child of a Louisiana sugar cane plantation owner.

While the others got on with their lives with little fanfare, Jim stood out as the thoroughbred of the Turner family. He stood resolute as he defied Papa's insistence that he accept his 40-acre plot and remain on the farm. Although a loyal son, he had ambition beyond farm life, and he firmly, but respectfully rejected Papa's attempts to control his life. Even so, he was a constant fixture at High Point when he could make the time.

It was during these visits that Jim's bond with Olivia grew stronger. Less than a year younger, Jim was the sibling most like Olivia as they shared a love of books and helping others. On his travels, he scoured book stores in larger cities and brought home every textbook on medicine he could find, and together, they devoured the information inside. His goal was to become a doctor and, perhaps, one day, a pilot. As much as he was like Olivia, he regarded her as far superior to him in her intellect and he recognized her to be the smartest of the family.

The injustice of Papa's use of Olivia's work ethic and family loyalty troubled him. He wanted desperately to help her improve her lot. With each of his visits, his anger escalated as he watched Olivia work without any assistance from either of their younger sisters.

After he was accepted into medical school at the University of Alabama, Jim, now 21, returned to High Springs a few weeks before reporting for the first day of classes. From the moment he arrived, he was acutely aware of the same attitude and behavior of his father and his siblings toward Olivia. Resolved to atone for his inability to help her in the past, Jim's opportunity came one evening before he left to meet friends for a movie. He found Olivia alone in the kitchen and approached her.

"Olivia, things cannot go on as they are for much longer if you ever expect to become a nurse or have some life of your own. You are twenty-two years old and you don't date. You have no friends. Rather, you work all the time either at home or for others. You've become a recluse on this farm."

Olivia continued drying the dishes without looking up. She doted on her brother and she knew that she would begin crying if she looked at him.

He continued, "Why? No, Olivia, don't respond. I know the answer. Papa has burdened you with the responsibilities for our family for years. Since you were a child, you have been required to perform the duties of an adult woman and it's just not fair!" he exclaimed.

"Shhh," she responded, "Papa will hear you."

Jim, quietly now, "You were the valedictorian of your class. When are you going to break away to pursue your own dreams? When are you going to stop being a wet nurse for the rest of the family and become a nurse on your own?"

"Jim, I understand what you are saying. Papa does not intend for me to leave the farm. I know how proud he is of you and of the other boys and your accomplishments, just as I know that he has little interest in Beth and me. He realizes Ruth is like Mama and cannot survive life on a farm, especially considering her lengthy illness that still drains her strength. Although several years passed before Ruth was strong enough, Papa set aside funds for her education, and she is now nearly ready to graduate. My lot is to toil here to support everyone else. Beth isn't afraid to get her hands dirty to help around the farm and she will find her own way with one of the town boys who will choose a wife who can work a farm."

Jim knew that Olivia was right. Beth had always preferred shadowing her brothers around the farm. She loved working with the animals and tending the garden, and detested inside work.

"And, of course, there's Ann," Olivia stopped short. She didn't need to say anything further; Jim nodded in agreement.

"So what about you, Olivia," Jim asked. "What will become of you?"

As their eyes met, the air in the kitchen grew heavy. "I have waited more than four years to use my scholarship. And, you are right. If I wait any longer it will not be there, and I will be doomed to live out my life here on this farm working as an unpaid housekeeper."

Olivia bent to wipe the table, "This is what Papa intends for me but I will not let it happen. Beth still lives at home, and Ann has one more year of high school. It is time for her to begin to assume some of the responsibilities Papa has given me. She is capable of handling her school work as well as some household chores."

Jim's laugh interrupted Olivia, "Ha! I should have known that you had made plans, and that you would not be thwarted as to your goal for nurse's training. You know that Papa is not going to agree to this and will certainly not provide funds for you. What do you intend to do?"

"I don't know," she said. "When I graduated high school, I made plans to attend nursing school but because Mama had just suffered a miscarriage, Papa said no." Olivia spun on her heels, tapping on the table for Jim to join her there. "Papa told me I couldn't leave right then but he promised to hire someone to permanently take over the running of the household as soon as Mama was better. I agreed to stay until he could make such arrangements."

Jim leaned forward, "Olivia, we both know that Papa never tried to hire anyone."

"I know," Olivia said softly. "He is such a penny pincher and besides, why would he when he had me? I tried to bring it up over the following months but he became enraged when I raised the subject. Two years ago, I finally faced the fact that Papa would never help me."

Jim could see the hurt in Olivia's eyes. He hated his father for treating Olivia so callously, and in the same moment, he felt swallowed by the guilt that he had been given so many opportunities. He took Olivia's petite hands in his own. "I'm so sorry, Olivia," his voice nearly breaking.

"No," she said pulling away. "I will not have you feel sorry for me. I have made my plans and now I am going to follow through with them."

Jim, pulling back from her asked, "How?"

Olivia leaned forward. Her tears had turned to determination and it showed around the corners of her blue eyes. "I have known that it is up to me to find a way and for the last year and a half, I have taken in sewing and mending for others while Papa was away on trips. I bought chickens and kept them behind Gussie's shack in the Quarters so Papa wouldn't know about them. I saved the money from the sale of their eggs, and I've put aside every penny for the time when I could go to college. I knew that if I were able to complete nurse's training, I could be free of this bondage."

Jim was amazed. "Perhaps Olivia was more like their father than either recognized," he thought. They talked until the kitchen fires flickered into ashes. Jim, woefully late and his movie already nearly over, left hurriedly to meet his friends. He pushed the starter button on the reliable 1912 Brockway pickup truck and sped off into the night with the rear end bouncing off the ground as he crossed the wagon ruts leading out of the main yard. He felt relieved that his beloved Olivia would soon be free of her bonds of servitude.

Olivia joined Beth and Ann as they prepared for bed. Beth's sunny disposition always made her feel better. She was a little envious of Beth's ability to have a life outside the home. It was a life Olivia hoped she, herself, would soon come to know. She would miss Beth as well as Ann's antics with her frequent male visitors. Too, she would miss this home where she had lived for twenty-two years. But, she would not miss the demands of Papa and the hopelessness she often felt.

Reflecting upon her upcoming departure and the changes that would come, Olivia was saddened. She was unable to share her plans with Beth and Ann until she first faced Papa. She prepared for bed with some anxiety about the outcome of her decision.

CHAPTER 7

Olivia awoke eager for the day to pass, for she and Jim planned to meet in the afternoon to confront Papa together with her decision. The two had agreed that the Turner family would get along without her. Papa would arrange for Mama's care as well as household management. Everyone else, except Ann, would manage for themselves and she would not worry about them as she planned her departure. Both she and Jim were troubled about Ann.

Increasingly, she demonstrated a "wild streak" and a willful disregard for Papa's or anyone else's authority. As his favorite, he was wrapped around her little finger, and he rarely, if ever, punished her no matter how unacceptable her antics. When the rare moment presented itself, Olivia tried to subtly warn Papa that Ann was becoming the subject of unseemly gossip in town and being received in a negative light by her peers and their mothers. Papa would hear none of it.

"They are just jealous of my precious Ann," he said as he forbade her to further criticize Ann.

As time passed, Ann's behavior continued to deteriorate. Often, when she came home from an outing with John Ward, Olivia noticed her sister's disheveled appearance and her carefree attitude toward intimacy between girls and boys in her class. Olivia reminded her of the cost of a bad reputation, but Ann paid no attention. Olivia hoped, against the odds, that Ann would mature before she reaped the trouble that she appeared to be sowing.

Olivia dressed quickly and went downstairs where Papa sat quietly at the kitchen table. He raised his head and she saw his tears.

"Sheriff Miller has just left," he said, voice breaking. "Jim was killed in an automobile accident late last night." Olivia rushed to Papa's side and embraced him with her petite arms gripping his barrel chest tightly.

"It cannot be true! Jim cannot be dead," she thought. Her cheeks grew warm and acid laced saliva pooled at the back of her throat. The dusty blue clapboard kitchen walls seemed to close in around her.

Olivia drew back from Papa and her eyes and nose dripped with sadness. Aside from Mama, Jim was dearest to her. While her heart ached, she ruefully accepted that she would have little time to mourn his passing. While Papa, Mama, and her siblings would pause to mourn, she knew that she would be expected to take care of the wake, funeral, and the sundry tasks associated with preparing the house for a multitude of visitors. She knew the family members, save Mama, would get through Jim's funeral and on with their lives with little disruption. She feared his death would push Mama's health and mental state into further decline.

She broke her embrace with Papa and sat at the table across from him. His head was bowed and he looked down into his hands. Olivia stared at the tablecloth in front of him. There was a stain from last night's dinner preparation she had missed, but her thoughts wandered as she was reminded again of hers and Jim's conversation just the night before, sitting in these very same chairs.

She raised her head as though he were beside her, "Jim, what do I do now?" she thought. "On top of the sadness that Mama will experience at your death do I dare heap more worry? Do I dare approach Papa now with the plans you and I shared? I am filled with sorrow and confusion. What should I do?"

Olivia listened as though she expected an answer. Her lips curled as she realized the futility of an imaginary discourse with her departed brother. She was on her own and she now had to face Papa alone with her decision. With all his bluster of strength and ability to handle whatever came his way, she knew Papa loved all of them dearly. He would, however, not be happy with what she was going to tell him.

The timing was horrible. She knew that and she pressed her lips together as she plotted how to raise the subject. Olivia witnessed a deep sorrow in Papa for the first time in her memory. Her heart fluttered as she stepped to the precipice of her fear of telling Papa her news. She stood and moved to the wash basin near the window. She peered out over the rows of corn in the field as she plotted her next steps.

Jim's declaration from the night before echoed in her ears. "Olivia, if you don't do it now, you will never escape!" She felt his spirit within her, encouraging her to go forward. As he had insisted, she had the strength to fashion her destiny. All she needed now was to muster her strength. It was now or never! She turned to find an empty chair.

"Agh," she gasped as she turned back to the counter top and braced herself over the wash basin, gripping it firmly with both hands. Today would not be the day. She went off to find her sisters to tell them of the horrible tragedy that had befallen the family.

.....

Over the next few days, Olivia's energy was devoted to making sure that her brother was laid to rest properly. Family and other visitors were in and out of the Turner household all through the day and many came at night to "sit up" with his body before interment. Mama suffered silently just as Olivia had feared and was unable to leave her bed until the final church service and the subsequent burial. The boys took care of Walt's business ventures as he spent much of his time consoling Mama.

By Sunday, activities at High Point returned to normal, and as expected, Olivia was left alone to grieve without sympathy. In happier moments, her excitement at the prospect of joining Ruth at college provided some relief. It was now two and a half weeks before the fall term commenced at Troy State Normal College, and she could wait no longer to tell Papa of her decision. On Monday morning at breakfast, she told Papa of her plans.

"Papa," Olivia said, her voice quivering in anticipation, "I've made a decision that I know you will not agree with."

"What now? You're not still thinking of learning to drive the truck are you? It is so unladylike for a woman to drive. I'll not allow it." He drained the last of the milk from his glass and gaveled the glass back to the table.

"No, Papa," Olivia continued, "I'm not thinking of learning to drive." She paused as she threw caution to the wind. "I've been accepted into college and I'm going to leave for the start of the fall term in two weeks."

Papa shoved his chair away from the table. He looked as though he would strike her as he pulled himself up to his full height. "You dare think about leaving when we have just buried your brother? Are you so selfish that you would even consider leaving knowing how this would affect your Mama?" The veins in his face and hands rose like tree roots breaking through hardpan soil. His voice reached a crescendo.

"Truly, I have raised an ungrateful daughter and this is the thanks I get for all I have provided you." His hands curled into fists. "Go about your business. Wake your sisters and prepare them breakfast. You need to decide how you'll manage the household over the next few days while we all get back to our normal schedules." He emphasized each word as he declared, "I will not tolerate any further discussion about your absurd idea of leaving."

Olivia's eyes fell earthward and the kitchen floor shook as his footfalls retreated toward the back porch. She felt fire building and rising within her with every step. Olivia possessed a well-managed stubborn streak most folks knew nothing about and without warning in this moment it erupted. She squared her shoulders, raced ahead, and stepped around Papa to cut him off.

"Papa, you are not going to intimidate me any longer." Walt recoiled; he had never before heard that tone from her. "You never had any intention of helping me go to school. Although you have used me as an unpaid servant, you will not anymore. You will not stand in my way."

Walt attempted to shove her aside without comment, but Olivia remained unyielding. "If you think that you can, then you fail to understand how I am prepared to act!"

Walt's eyes looked squarely into hers. "What are you going to do?"

"I don't know for sure, Papa, but I have some ideas. You are held in high regard by many and I am sure their opinions will change quickly when I share with them your behavior toward me."

Walt stared at her, mouth agape.

"Today is a day of reckoning, Papa. Don't underestimate me. If you persist in holding me here, I'll share my story of the injustices that you have wrought in my case." Her eyes narrowed. "Your businesses will dry up like peaches left on the branch to die once I inform them of your lack of honor and the worthless nature of your word."

"You wouldn't," Walt proclaimed, nearly coming out of his spats.

"Oh wouldn't I? You may not think so, but I am capable of doing whatever it takes to share my plight with anyone who'll listen. Papa, if you don't honor your long standing promise, I'll share with each of them your treatment of me. Decide now!"

Walt's eyes bulged and his body shook with his fury. His breath came out as incoherent snorts. He shook his head from side to side as though he could shake off her attacks. He had always ruled his household and all within it with an iron fist. Other than Jim's refusal to farm his 40 acre plot, not one of his nine children had ever dared cross him. Now, he was being forced to concede to Olivia's ultimatum from which he knew she would not retreat. Walt sighed and slumped over grasping a nearby chair as it seemed he could not stand under the weight of Olivia's resolve.

"I will allow you to leave for school, but I will not finance any part of it. You will be on your own. Do you hear me?"

Olivia nodded her head and left the kitchen. She had stared down Papa, but there was little satisfaction in her victory for there was no Jim to share her news, and no one else really cared. She would manage to get through these next few weeks and then she would leave in spite of the obstacles she knew Papa would create for her.

MCMURTRY

CHAPTER 8

As the days ticked by, Olivia's thoughts returned to her confrontation with Papa. He had conceded to her demands and she was emboldened by the prospects of having arrived at her opportunity. Her time left at High Point was short, and she visited with Mama as much as she could. She knew Mama would miss their afternoon visits with Olivia entering her mother's room singing and bearing a tray of hot tea and biscuits. Mama never partook of the tea, or the biscuits for that matter, and she certainly didn't talk much. But, behind the shades of sorrow and depression that covered Mama's eyes, Olivia knew that Mama looked forward to seeing her smiling face every afternoon. Olivia was a beacon of light in an otherwise dark existence.

Olivia's plans for the fall term were coming together. As she checked off her last few items before leaving, she came to a startling realization. She had no way to get to Troy. Surprisingly, it was Ann who came to the rescue. John planned to take Ann for a Saturday excursion and at Ann's suggestion; he agreed to drive the 70 miles to deliver Olivia to Troy.

.....

Olivia awoke filled with anticipation as she prepared to embark on the next phase of her life. After packing, she spent the morning sitting with Mama at her bedside. She offered to get her up and out to the porch for fresh air, but as usual, she wasn't up to the task. Olivia felt a genuine joy and she wanted Mama to share in it. She promised to write weekly to tell her how she fared at school.

The morning passed quickly, and around noon Beth helped Olivia move her travel cases to the front porch to await John's arrival. His reputation for having a wild streak preceded him, and Olivia wondered at the wisdom of Papa's allowing Ann to spend hours in his company without a chaperone. She sat in Papa's rocking chair taking in the scenery of the blooming flowers and smells of the farm one last time. A smile crept into the corners of her petite mouth. She could not remember the last time she had smiled.

The peaceful sounds of the farm were interrupted by the cacophony of an automobile lumbering up the steep hill to the main house. His 1928 Ford Model A lurched forward as he punched the gas and its engine gasped for air. John's inexperience behind the wheel, combined with the vehicle's weight and limited horsepower, proved a challenge the Ford barely matched. It bounced over the cavernous wagon wheel ruts in the driveway and into the main yard. As it rolled to a rest, the engine sputtered and stopped, as if sighing in relief.

The doors opened and John and Ann spilled out. Ann pushed past Olivia, buttoning her blouse and adjusting her brassiere as she ran into the house. Her lipstick was smeared and Olivia gritted her teeth and fumed silently as she carried her cases down the porch steps. John paced restlessly as he intently examined the mud overspray on the candy apple colored body and black fenders of the sedan. He ignored her as she loaded the travel cases and climbed into the back seat.

Olivia's eyes wandered over to the heap of yellow and silver metal and wood piled in the side yard. The hulking wreck of Jim's damaged truck sat motionless on its side. The roof was nearly gone, severely crushed where workers pulled it from the ditch where the drunk driver pushed it. Olivia could still see the massive clumps of sod plowed up near the windshield on the driver's side. She blotted away a few tears as she imagined the violent end he must have suffered. She struggled to clear the lump in her throat, but her thoughts were interrupted by the slamming of the car doors. Soon, they were on their way.

.....

The hum of the engine and wind noise drowned out most of the whispered conversation from the front seat. As the miles ticked by, Olivia drifted into a daze as the wind caressed her face. The late summer air was warm and smelled of honeysuckle. Ann giggled and John pulled her closer to him. Neither one seemed to give her presence a second thought. Olivia was resigned to being regarded as a piece of freight to be picked up and delivered without incident.

The campus gates drew closer. In less than twenty minutes, Olivia found herself deposited on the steps of Peak Hall where she would spend the next three and a half years. She watched the dust covered rear of the '28 Ford disappear into the crowd of students hurrying to find their dorms. As she stood, dwarfed by the towering academic buildings, Olivia was overcome with a sense of both wonder and freedom. Her thoughts drifted back to her last conversation with Jim. She would control her own destiny and not be deterred. He would be proud of her. She would ensure it.

MCMURTRY

CHAPTER 9

The weeks passed quickly and Olivia thrived in her new environment. Although she missed Mama and Beth, she was happy to be pursuing her dream. She listened to the nightly radio broadcasts of the events of the Great Crash in October 1929. Much airtime was devoted to the effect it was having upon the general population, and dire circumstances were described in minute detail. Living as she had, in a closed rural farming community in the South, did not equip Olivia with an understanding of the national situation.

Based on letters from Beth, it was difficult for her to equate the radio announcements with the world at High Point because few in Geneva County appeared to have changed their lifestyles. Beth reported that, to the contrary, most families she knew continued to work their farms and operate their businesses. While she had heard the radio reports of widespread closing of factories and the unemployment in other parts of the country, there had been only a small decline in production at the cannery.

She also said that while Papa's business was still good, he was away less frequently now. As was usually the case, it appeared that his horse and breeding businesses had slowed as winter approached. Other than that, Beth had not discerned any changes in the farming operations or in the lumber mill production. Financially, the family was doing just fine.

Olivia could not know that in a very short time many in her community, including her family, would suffer to one degree or another throughout the years of "The Great Depression."

.....

In December, after completing her exams and recording five "A's" and one "B," Olivia settled in for her first holiday away from home. Although she missed Mama and Beth terribly, she did not plan to travel back to High Point for Christmas due to her financial situation and her reluctance to face Papa who she feared would not allow her to return to school.

With the campus nearly devoid of students who had gone home for the holidays, Olivia spent her idle time mending aprons for the cafeteria and completing sewing jobs she picked up from fellow students. She fashioned a makeshift Christmas tree from a mop handle, twine, and pine tree branches. Paper napkins scavenged from the dining hall were folded into various shapes as decorations. Atop the "tree" sat an angel made from stuffed silk stockings.

As she gathered some mending to return to several students before they left for the holidays, there was a knock at the door. She was summoned to the Dean's office and as she entered, Papa awaited her, standing impatiently, hat in hand.

"Hello Papa," she said meekly. She prayed that the visit did not portend something wrong with Mama. She stepped forward to greet him with a hug, but he did not return the gesture.

"Olivia, it is time for you to come home with me now. Dean Warner will take care of shipping your belongings. Let us go. Now."

"Papa! What? Why?" she asked.

Papa pounded a fist on the desk and ordered her to do as she was told. She was going home with him that day, and that was final. Olivia was overcome with anger and despair.

"How could this be," she thought aloud. She did not move as she took stock of what was happening.

Dean Warner cleared his throat. "Do you two need a moment? I can take my leave and…."

Walt stepped toward him. "What you need to do, kind sir, is prepare the documents for my daughter's withdrawal from her classes. Do it now!"

Dean Warner scurried around his desk and disappeared into the foyer. "Where would he find someone to prepare the documents on holiday break?" he wondered.

Walt grabbed Olivia's arm and reined her up short toward the door. She jerked her arm away from him defiantly.

"Papa, I am twenty-three years old, and I am old enough to make my own decisions. I am not leaving school," she continued, her voice rising. "You have provided no support for me since I enrolled and you cannot just simply show up and demand that I leave school. Do you understand that you have no authority over me? Go home and leave me alone!"

Walt, taken aback by Olivia's newly found independence, bowed his head. He looked tired and defeated. His voice pleading now, tears filled his eyes. "Haven't you hurt this family enough? Because you delayed his leaving, Jim was at that cross roads when the drunk ran a stop sign and now he is dead.

Olivia was taken aback. "No Papa. Don't you lay that at my feet. Not Jim's death. It wasn't...." Tears began to flow as her voice cracked and she fell to her knees sobbing into her coat sleeves.

Walt continued, "You have abandoned us all, including your Mama. If you will not return for your siblings and me, Olivia, will you forsake your Mama by not returning for her? I will await your answer outside." Walt donned his hat, turned, and exited the office, leaving Olivia kneeling on the marble floor.

Anger overtook her sorrow and Olivia rose and chased after her father. She could not fathom the words he used. They cut to the bone. Was it true? Was she responsible for her brother's death? She had never considered that possibility. The events of the past three months raced through her mind as it swam in confusion. Perhaps Papa was right. Perhaps everything he said was true. If so, how ungrateful she had been as a daughter and sister to her family.

Walt turned to meet her. "Your mother is not well," he said, his lower lip trembling. "She needs you desperately." His cracking voice penetrated her anger and her heart was crushed.

Olivia knew she could not deny Mama's need. Within twenty minutes she stood in front of the Model T stake bed truck with bags in hand. She took in the buildings silhouetted against the gray December sky and bid them a silent farewell. Then she climbed into the passenger's seat and closed the door. Tears eroded the thin makeup on her round face as the twenty horsepower engine roared to life. They completed the journey back to Geneva County in silence.

.....

The holidays of 1929 were a blur for Olivia. She tried but found it difficult to find joy in being home. She spent weeks going through the motions of her daily chores. Mama was much better now but Olivia was still overcome with the hopelessness of her own situation and its finality.

Each day she looked upon the sunrise with a desperate plea to God to help her get through that day and the others to follow. She would live out her life on the farm, and would watch as each of her siblings went about their lives as they chose. Her life had come full circle. She imagined that this was the way it was supposed to end. She was back where she belonged.

CHAPTER 10

The spring of 1930 roared in like a lion. March winds whipped several trees down around the main house and one shack was destroyed in the Quarters. There was, however, a happiness that abounded at High Point through the season and into the summer months.

After graduating from college and becoming a school teacher, Ruth, at age 30, married a preacher and moved several hundred miles away. Thomas, James and Jerry, along with their families, made it their practice to share Sunday dinners together at High Point. Beth continued to live at home as did most unmarried women of her generation, and seemed to be content to work in the office at the cannery. She, like Olivia, led a more solitary life, having few friends and virtually no male suitors.

Ann, at seventeen, ended her junior year of high school and continued her carefree ways. To Olivia's displeasure, she continued to divide her time between John Ward and Paul Gunderson, the son of the local bank president. The thought of Ann's promiscuity angered Olivia. She saw through John's nice boy façade and knew that his intentions with Ann were far from honorable.

Paul seemed to be the quieter and more polite of the two. He carried a quiet confidence and of the two boys, Olivia felt that he was the one most likely to be able to curb Ann's hard ways. "Maybe she has met her match in him," Olivia thought. "It certainly would be good for her to have at least one male in her life that she could not control."

While the Turners continued to live better than most of their farming neighbors, they began to feel the adverse effects of the Depression as it oozed into Geneva County. Times were tight and Walt urged the entire family to be as frugal as possible.

His restrictions did not seem to apply to Ann though. Papa yearned for her to attract a suitable young man. Any man who could further the Turner line would do, and Papa did not deny her money for new clothes to achieve this objective. Furthermore, he expected Olivia to use her skills as a seamstress to dress Ann consistent with her place in the community. One benefit of her fitting sessions was that they afforded Olivia the opportunity to interact with Ann uninterrupted. She deftly used these situations to try to steer Ann away from trouble.

Ann teetered to and fro as she carelessly balanced herself on the stool in the parlor. "Sit still you," Olivia chided as she adjusted a hem and turned her attention to the neckline. "It's apparent that you enjoy considerable popularity at school. You are asked to attend many functions and …,"

Ann wasn't about to be lectured by her spinster sister. "You nag and nag me about who I date and about protecting my reputation. Will you ever stop? Just because you were never popular, it doesn't mean that I cannot be. Unlike you, I am going to find a suitable beau. I'll be known as a belle about town and I will get off this wretched farm. I'll not be known as a 'Farm Filly' any longer."

Olivia seethed at Ann's notion that her family was held in lower regard than others because of their farming background. They were by any measure a success story for the times.

"This dress is for the end of summer dance and it sets the stage for the entire coming school year. It's the first look we girls get to see which boys have sprouted into men over the summer. Of course, the boys are eager to see which girls have sprouted bosoms." Ann chuckled and Olivia shook her head in disbelief. Not to be deterred, Ann continued.

"Fortunately, I've never had to worry about that," she said as she adjusted her ample breasts in her brassiere. "I've been blessed with these since eighth grade. How else do you think I became so popular with the older boys?"

"You're impossible, you know?" Olivia remarked. "I've never heard such talk as that. You know the reputations of both John and Paul are deplorable. Please promise me that you will not drink alcohol with them. It is not ladylike and your behavior must not bring shame to you or to this family. Do you understand?"

"Stop trying to mother hen me."

Olivia knew her sister well and, unlike Papa, she held her ground. "Ann, if you cannot give me your solemn promise on this, I'll tell Papa that you should not be allowed to attend the dance. Do I make myself clear?"

"Oh Olivia, you are such a stick in the mud. You never have any fun!

You could be so pretty if you just smiled and took a little effort with yourself."

Olivia blushed, "Well, thank…."

Ann interrupted, "You know, I feel pity that no suitor has ever offered for you. You're just a lost cause. Anyone that might have been interested in you is either married or planning to be. I shall marry either Paul or John and not end up trapped under Papa's thumb like you."

Olivia winced; she knew Ann's assessment was correct. Although she regarded Ann as a selfish, immature brat whose beauty was overshadowed by her mean-spirited nature, she conceded that Ann was right. She was trapped in this life of domestic servitude with no way out. Once any suitor discovered her responsibilities at High Point, they ceased calling. No one wanted to call socially upon the maid. Her spirit was dealt a killing blow. She dropped the needles and thread, hung her head in despair and retreated to her bedroom.

As she lay in bed, Olivia fretted over her inability to convince Ann that once she lost her reputation there would be nothing she could do to restore it. She had witnessed the downfall of some girls in the community and it was never a pretty sight, seeing them shunned by the entire town. On top of that, no respectable man would consider for a wife a girl known to be promiscuous. Such a girl was considered "damaged goods." Olivia was generally one to find the good in all the people that she met. She was not, however, fond of John Ward.

Aside from their drive to Troy, they had crossed paths many times during his frequent stops at High Point to call on Ann. He was genuinely charming to Ann and Beth, but he was brusque with her. She suspected he acted in an ill manner toward her because he knew that she saw through his beguiling demeanor. She also knew that he regarded her as a challenge to overcome. Predictably, their strained relationship sat like a simmering pot. Without attention, it was destined to boil over into a frothy mess. Olivia's thoughts were interrupted when Beth burst into their bedroom.

"Olivia, I saw Ann with Papa. What's put a bee in her bonnet?"

Olivia sat up in bed to answer while pushing aside her quilt. "She's mad because I threatened to tell him what I know about Paul and John unless she conducts herself in a more ladylike manner," replied Olivia.

Beth grimaced. "Not you, too? Have I told you about the two young girls who left a party because of John's and Paul's unwanted advances?

Although the girls complained to their parents, nothing was done to either boy because both girls' fathers worked for Mr. Ward and the fathers knew that saying anything could cost them their jobs. I have tried to warn Ann about those boys, but she turns a deaf ear. She doesn't want to hear the truth."

"Beth, Ann is so intent on being popular that I fear the outcome of her association with either one." She continued, "If you can believe it, the gossip is that both have had flings with older women." Beth listened intently. They concluded that Ann was blind to the truth and was deaf to their warnings. Frustrated, neither knew what to do to reach her inner sensibilities. "It will take a calamity," Olivia said. "That's the only thing that will make that child grow up." Beth nodded in agreement.

.....

As the summer of 1930 drew to a close, the crops grew flush with every rising and setting of the sun. The fields were abuzz with hired men who moved to and fro like ants on a hill. Their movements, while seemingly random at times, were perfectly choreographed with a determined purpose. Planting season had ended and the growing season was in full effect. Soon, it would be time to reap the rewards for the long hours they had put in over the grueling summer months. As the sun baked the crops in the fields, farmers hoped their efforts yielded a bountiful harvest. In many ways, parents experienced the same cycle of growth with their children. Only time would tell if the attention given in the planting season would bring forth honorable and productive adults during the harvest season.

.....

Olivia particularly dreaded John's visits. Ann had confided in him that her sister had spoken to Papa about his influence on her, and he set out to make her life miserable. One afternoon, as he waited in the yard for Ann, Olivia happened by carrying a pan of soapy water.

"Hello Olivia. I see that you have your arms full. I would offer to help but you look like you have the window washing under control."

Olivia nodded and smiled briefly as she continued on her way.

"You know, Olivia, my parents have an opening for a domestic at

High Bluff. Your training here as a house maid has prepared you well. If you like, I can put in a good word for you. I'm sure you would cherish the opportunity to work for my Mother and to see me nearly every day!" Olivia did not respond, but John could tell he had struck a blow to her ego.

"What did you say? No? Okay. Just let me know if you change your mind."

Olivia had reached her limit with this brash boy. "You won't live to see that day," she responded as she poured the dishpan of water on the ground causing it to splash onto his shoes.

"Hey! Watch it," he said as he stepped back. "You'll get yours. You just wait."

Olivia knew John's taunts were those of an immature boy, but his remarks about her position as a domestic hit too close to home. The worst part was that it rang true. She was a de facto servant for her family. Satisfied with having soaked John's shoes and pants legs, she was determined to keep her eye on the larger picture: keeping Ann out of trouble.

It was clear to Olivia that John and Paul planned to have their fun with Ann now and discard her in favor of college-aged girls when they left for school. She was confident that by the time they came home for Christmas, both boys would have found girls from families more socially placed and suitable as future wives. If she could shield Ann for just a few more weeks, she would gladly endure whatever ridicule John Ward chose to lay on her.

CHAPTER 11

Later that evening, Olivia sat on the porch snapping beans and she wondered why John chose to be so ornery. "It is unfortunate that he is so immature," she thought. Olivia knew the Ward family did not lack for money, but they did woefully lack standing in the elite social strata of Geneva County. They were the "new rich" and as such weren't accorded the respect of the established families. Their social situation was compounded by Judy Ward's off-putting personality and her husband's suspect business undertakings. If they were not all entirely illegal, some were certainly not ethical. Others, of course, went beyond the pale.

.....

Over the years, Robert Ward had accumulated, at the expense of his friends and neighbors, many tracts of land within Geneva County as well as three large farming operations in South Alabama and North Florida. When a landowner was unable to get a bank loan, he would often come to Ward Enterprises out of desperation. With cash to lend in short supply, his was the only game in town and Robert Ward knew a full house hand when he held it. Not only did he charge interest rates that many regarded as usury, he also did not extend deadlines to repay them.

The general consensus in the community was that he "cheated" his friends and "crushed" his adversaries without regard to any conventional civil courtesy. When they were unable to repay their debts, the land put up as collateral became his. Allegations of crooked land grabs were bad enough, but in a time when drinking was illegal due to Prohibition, rumors circulated about his ownership of clandestine night clubs throughout Northwest Florida which served the three staples of the degenerates of the day: bookmaking, booze, and broads.

America was ten years into Prohibition which forbade the manufacture and sale of alcohol countrywide. As a result, a cottage industry of small batch moonshiners sprung up overnight to meet the needs of those with a thirst for the Devil's Juice. Gambling, bookmaking, and sex were an industry all unto their own and many men, like Robert Ward, were eager to forge their fortunes.

Robert Ward's nightclubs bristled with a constant influx of young women who entered through the front door and lived and worked upstairs while barrels of libations came in through the back door. The "juke joints," as they were known, provided an untraceable revenue stream to fund the centerpiece of the Ward business empire, cattle ranching.

In response to the rapid settlement of Florida to the south and the need for beef to supply the troops in The Great War, Robert Ward had invested wisely in land and ranching in the 'Teens. Bolstered by several well-funded investors, it was only a matter of time before he edged them out of the picture with some creative bookkeeping and "unfortunate losses" to the cattle due to sickness and predators. Robert Ward had a manner about him that caused business partners to trust him far more than they should have, and Judy was a master at cooking the books.

Soon, one snag emerged in his scheme: Florida taxes. Faced with bills from overzealous Florida taxation authorities, Robert Ward stumbled upon an ingenious idea on a night when one of his herds escaped through an open gate at a Florida ranch.

"Move 'em out," he thought. The ruse, as those in the know described it, involved covertly loading livestock on trucks and moving them to pastures at nearby farms when he got "inside information" of impending visits by tax assessors. Although he managed to move the cattle fairly quickly when needed, due to the shear logistics of moving a thousand head of cattle, he had several close calls which prompted his adoption of a new strategy.

On a whim, he established sole ownership in a company that built a railroad spur from High Springs to Geneva, Dothan, and Tallahassee on the Southern Railway Line. From a logistical standpoint, it afforded him a vehicle to move cattle across state lines without drawing suspicion from the wrong people. It also provided him the opportunity to move cattle in two days as opposed to two weeks. The beauty of the plan though, and one that he hadn't fully anticipated, was that as the sole stockholder he set the carriage rates for transportation of people, mail, and goods along the spur. Local farmers near High Springs depended on this spur for transporting produce and livestock to Dothan where it was sold or transported on to Montgomery and points east and west.

Although almost completely by accident, Robert Ward had succeeded in cornering the local railway market and became widely regarded as a shrewd businessman who generated wealth at the expense of many. As an owner of one of the largest farms in the county, director for the Community National Bank, and chairman of the local school board, he was everywhere. Very little went on in High Springs in which he and Judy were not involved.

His reach also stretched beyond the county line into the rest of Alabama and Florida. His political influence was felt statewide due to the substantial campaign contributions he made toward the purchase of favor and consideration. Because of his business practices, Robert and Judy Ward were the source of many rumors which they did nothing to silence. As a result, many snubbed the couple socially.

Judy desperately sought to pierce the iron ring that prevented her inclusion into the closed social cliques. Much to her annoyance, she learned her "new money" that allowed her to live lavishly at her farm at High Bluff and make substantial contributions to her church did not assure social acceptance in certain groups.

"I'll be accepted one way or another, even if I have to marry into the right social circle," Judy thought. Ensuring her son John married into a well-established family became her primary mission in life. Even if it was to the detriment of their daughter, Evelyn.

CHAPTER 12

John Ward differed from his parents as to his standing in the community. He was idolized as a fine specimen of the male gender. At 6 foot, 3 inches tall, he was a giant of a young man. His high school athletic career had caught the eyes of many college football coaches and he had been offered a scholarship to attend the University of Alabama, but when it was suddenly withdrawn without explanation, he accepted another offer to play for Coach Robert Neyland at the University of Tennessee.

John's olive complexion, jet black hair, and piercing brown eyes engendered him the nickname "Handsome Devil." All agreed that he was a good looking young man who possessed an abundance of charm. Some might have said it was an overabundance.

In spite of his popularity, he was essentially a loner with only Paul Gunderson being considered more than a marginal acquaintance. They seemed to get along swimmingly and they were similar as to their likes and dislikes, but certainly not as to their personalities. Whereas John's nature was abrasive, Paul's was kind. For John, there was only one person for whom he truly cared: his sister Evelyn who was twelve years younger than he and who had recently celebrated her sixth birthday.

.....

In August 1930, as Ann prepared to enter her senior year of high school and Paul and John were within a few days of leaving for college, John stopped by High Point to call on Ann for an evening of fun. Olivia greeted him cordially at the door and explained that Ann had not returned from a farewell party for one of her girlfriends. He asked her to let Ann know he would return for her later that evening. Unbeknownst to Olivia, Ann had already set a date with Paul and was not at home when John returned. As she met him at the door that evening, she dutifully explained Ann's absence. John was floored.

John's thoughts drifted back. The friendship between the boys had always been fluid but over the preceding weeks it had taken a nasty turn when Paul shared his attraction to Ann was more than a dalliance. He genuinely enjoyed her company. John persisted in his objections and Paul would have none of it.

"I think I may actually like Ann as a girlfriend," Paul said. "She annoys the tar out of me sometimes, but she is the prettiest girl at school and she is spunky. I like her spontaneous nature and I don't have to talk much. I like that."

Now, John stood before Olivia looking for Ann who was out with Paul. Although she had chores, Olivia recognized his embarrassment and disappointment and decided to turn the tables on him. Her nature was not to carry a grudge, but John's catty remarks equating her to a house maid had long stuck in her craw. "This," she thought, "is a perfect opportunity for this boy to get a dose of his own medicine."

She drew out her explanation of Ann's whereabouts so as to twist the proverbial knife in his gut. She made her first stab as an aside that Ann would probably not be back until late. She landed her second thrust with an innocent question laced with bitter weed.

"He is your best friend, isn't he?" She asked with a coy smile, "I'm surprised he didn't tell you." She let the comment simmer for a moment. John looked on in disbelief. Sensing the timing was right, she went in for the kill. "Oh," she said, "Ann did leave a message. Let's see, as I recall she said to tell you the early bird gets the worm and the late one gets nothing."

John became more shaken and pushed past Olivia into the house. "I'll just wait for them in here," he said.

"Suit yourself, Mister," she said sarcastically, motioning toward the parlor.

John turned and followed her closely. He was furious with Ann, but he knew what Olivia was doing and he did not want to give her the satisfaction of knowing that she had bested him. Olivia turned, surprised. "What do you think you are doing?"

He smiled broadly, "I am keeping you company. Is it so rare for you to have a male want to keep you company?"

Olivia shook her head in disbelief. She desperately wanted John to leave and stop pestering her, and she said as much. He dismissed her objections with a laugh and plopped himself into a chair at the kitchen table. What was she to do for the next three hours until Ann returned? She was alone in the house and trapped by John's presence.

Beth and Papa were out. He was not expected home from a business trip until the morning and Mama was in bed. The competitiveness in Olivia had been awakened. Although she knew that he was "baiting" her, she had been taken aback by his brash and hurtful statements. Perhaps it was best to simply ignore him. With luck, he would grow weary and leave.

John leaned back on two legs of a chair, all the while maintaining a disjointed conversation. He rambled on about the challenges that he would face in keeping up his grades and playing football. Olivia ignored him save a few grunts to acknowledge the breaks in his soliloquy. Abruptly, John faced Olivia. Sandwiched between talking about football and what a cad Paul was for asking Ann out, he struck a note that caught Olivia's attention.

"I have observed what goes on around here and what is expected of you. How do you handle the constant pressure your father places on you?" He leaned closer to the table. "I cannot achieve all that my parents expect and I hate myself for it."

Olivia all too clearly understood how he felt. Surprisingly, she felt her disdain for him thawing. She moved to sit beside him at the table and listened. She patiently offered him a few suggestions as to how to deal with his parents, but soon reality set in. She was late in feeding a newborn calf and had no more time for trivial chatter. She pushed back from the table and did her best to usher John toward the door.

"Ann may not be home anytime soon. I am busy here and cannot spare another minute to entertain you. Why don't you come back tomorrow?" She stopped at the hall tree to get her wrap, and then opened the door for him to leave. John did not move.

"A calf you say? Do you mind if I watch while you feed it?"

She was taken by surprise. While she preferred that he leave, she could not ignore the thawing of her distaste for him. "Okay," she said, "but only for a few minutes. I've been up since four thirty this morning and I am tired." They walked side by side to the barn about 60 yards from the house. As they arrived, John opened the gate for her and ceremoniously waved her inside. Olivia blushed slightly and thanked him kindly.

Getting the calf to take the bottle was time consuming. Olivia held its head in her lap and forced the bottle in its mouth while she struggled to keep it still. Sensing her frustration, John intervened.

"Hey, can I try?"

"Sure you can, but please be gentle."

The gentleness he demonstrated in handling the orphaned calf did not reflect his generally hard personality. Even more remarkable was that for more than an hour, John had ceased his disparaging comments. To the contrary, he remarked several times on how much he admired her spirit and all that she did for her family.

"You know," he said, "It's really unfair that all of the work falls on you here at the farm. If I were your father, I'd make the others help. You deserve it."

His words brought tears to her eyes and for the first time in a long while, Olivia let her frustrations and unhappiness show. John set the bottle aside and took her in his arms to comfort her. At first she resisted, but as she felt the strength in his grip she relaxed, and then she clung to him. For the first time in her life, she felt the compassion of another person. She marveled at how it made her feel. His warmth was a balm to her feelings of unworthiness and inadequacy.

He bent to kiss her and although everything in her mind said no, she did not resist the awkwardness of the situation. They lay back together in the hay and he kissed her neck softly as he lifted her skirt. Olivia's mind wandered and she thought only of the tingling in her scalp and hair mixed with the aroma of fresh hay around them. She felt the warmth of his breath on her chest and she succumbed.

As quickly as it began, it was over. He pushed himself from Olivia, fastened his clothing, and left without looking back. Olivia heard a car crank in the distance and as the sound of the motor disappeared into the August evening, she felt disgust with the realization that she had been seduced by the very same cruel boy from whom she had been protecting Ann. It was her fault. She was older, and she knew better.

"He should consider the theater as a career," she thought. He had put on a grand performance in creating a persona crafted to break down her guard and overcome her reserve. The lectures she gave Ann about John and Paul echoed in her ear. As she put her clothing to rights, she knew nothing could erase what had happened. How would she tell Ann? She couldn't. It would be a dying secret. So acute was her shame and embarrassment at being taken in by John's charms that she prayed their paths would not cross before he left for school in a few days.

CHAPTER 13

Ann was a brat and an opportunist who took advantage of her father's partiality for his youngest daughter. There was virtually nothing that he would not do for her. Papa planned for her to graduate high school, go to college, and become a teacher like Ruth. She, however, had different plans. She would attend college, but only as a means of finding a suitor from a prominent family of old money, such as the Gundersons.

While she had little interest in getting an education, she had even less interest in the hardship those in her family would endure in order for her to go to college. She was confident Papa would manage. Although she knew times were tight, Papa had never allowed her to want for anything and she secretly suspected that if it became necessary, Papa would use the money he had reserved for Olivia's education to pay for her college.

Ann was more than a pretty face. She was a master at manipulation to get what she wanted. As she prepared herself to meet a prospective husband, she plotted how she could gain control of the estate at High Point. Ann made her intention clear one morning when she thought she was alone with Papa. Olivia, polishing silver in the next room, overheard Ann launch her campaign.

"Papa, I am thrilled to start college. I can imagine what it will be like to marry and have a husband who can work with you to run your businesses. I know he will be smart and he will be able to take over the farming operation here and make it bigger and better."

"Hmmmph," Walt grunted. "You think some young buck can come in here and push me out, do you?"

"Why no, Papa," she countered, "I just know that having someone continue your work would allow you more time to train your horses. I know that is your first love and it would make me happy beyond all hope if I were able to make that happen for you, Papa." She leaned in and kissed him gently on the cheek and then sat on his lap. "This place is too quiet; it needs the noise of children, and I can't wait to move back here and have a bushel of children right here at High Point for you and Mama to spoil."

Papa, ever the doting father when it came to matters concerning Ann, nodded in agreement. "You better have some boys then," he added, "There's a lot of labor to be done around here."

"It's working," she thought. "I'll soon be the Duchess of High Point."

They sat quietly for a few minutes then, from nowhere, "Papa, what do you think of the Gunderson family? I think I may want to marry their son Paul. Of course, you'll have to make sure I have what is expected if I am to fit into their social circle."

Papa told her he understood the requirements and assured her that he would not fail her.

.....

Annie Turner's background adequately equipped her to pass on to her daughters the rules of etiquette and deportment. All of which, when incorporated into their behavior, produced young women of refinement. Mama's determination to instill proper behavior in each of her girls was important for Ann. In spite of her flighty ways and questionable behavior, she was prepared to utilize her training to achieve her objectives. In preparation for Ann's receiving suitors, her mother had taken the steps to ensure that the main house at High Point was representative of the lifestyle in which they wished to portray themselves.

The home was furnished with expensive furniture, china, crystal and silverware which painted a picture of excellent taste. Visitors to High Point were profoundly impressed with the ambiance she had created, and Ann planned to use her upbringing and surroundings as a means to lure a prospective husband.

One night when she and Olivia were alone in the kitchen, Ann shared her plans with her sister. "I'm going to do it, you know," she declared.

"What's that?"

"Marry Paul," she answered. "I've enjoyed the last few times I have been with him very much. I can see us walking down the aisle right now. I can't wait for us to make you an aunt."

"Whoa there, Ann. Just hold your horses. If you know what is good for you, there won't be any babies at High Point for quite some time. I think Papa would ring both of our necks if you came home expecting right now. You haven't…."

"No! I'm still pure in that way, but not because those rowdy boys aren't trying."

"Well I am relieved you have been hearing my pleas for you to protect your reputation and that you have found someone that you love."

"Love? I never said I loved anyone. Where did you get that silly idea? I'm not in love with either Paul or John; however, each has a promising future with their fathers' businesses. And more importantly, both will have resources so I won't have to reduce my lifestyle as a newlywed."

Olivia did not comment. There was nothing to say. Ann would not become less selfish or less spoiled with any wisdom she could impart to her, and Ann certainly would never put another's feelings before her own. Olivia pitied her and feared for the heartbreaks Ann would surely experience one day.

.....

Over the last few weeks of September, the mornings had begun to turn cooler and this Sunday was no different. Ann wrapped her shawl around her shoulders and went downstairs to find coffee to warm her, but there was none to be found. Mama, as usual, was in her room "recovering" from her latest malady. Papa was in Georgia delivering horses, and Beth was still in bed. There was no other sign of life in the house so she decided to go back to bed for a brief sleep before church.

As she approached the stairs, she noticed the parlor doors were ajar. She peeked in and found Olivia bundled in a quilt, lying on the settee. Her skin appeared even more pearl-like than usual; she was downright pale. Beside her a milking pail rested within arm's reach.

"Creeps, what's that smell?"

Olivia knew Ann meant the acrid stench emitting from the pail. It tickled her nose and stung the back of her throat. Although repulsed by the odor, Ann moved closer to her feverish sister.

"Olivia, you don't look well." Ann had never seen Olivia nap during the day. "I don't know if this is the right time or not, but are you able to make me breakfast?"

"I'm fine, Ann. I must just have a bug." Olivia lurched toward the pail and a stream of vomit rang against the side. "I just seem to be a little dizzy. I'll bring up coffee in a few minutes." Olivia gathered her quilt and bucket and made her way to the kitchen.

"Okay, but don't take too long. It's cold in this house!" Ann scampered up the stairs to her waiting bed.

A month had passed before Olivia knew she was expecting. Once she overcame her initial shock, she wondered, "What am I to do?" Once Papa found out, he would throw her out. She was sure of it. Somehow she had to delay discovery as long as possible. Beth and Ann would figure it out when she didn't have her monthly "visitor," and she had to count on them to keep her secret. "No sense dragging it out with them," she thought. Today, she would share the biggest secret of her life with her sisters.

As Olivia entered the room bearing a tray with coffee, Ann poked Beth and turned over to greet Olivia. "Did you have to milk the cow for cream?" she asked smartly.

Olivia moved more confidently now. Placing the tray on the side table, she squared to face her sisters. "Beth and Ann, I have something to share with you, but first you must swear to keep what I tell you in secret. May I count on you?" Both nodded affirmatively. "Soon you are going to be aunts. I am expecting." The girls stared at her with disbelief. Both had the same question.

"Olivia, how could you be expecting?" Beth asked.

They knew she had no beau. In fact, neither could remember the last time a gentleman had called on her.

"Is this a joke?" Ann asked.

"How can this be?" echoed Beth.

"It's an immaculate conception," chirped Ann. Both waited for the punch line that did not come.

"I'm going to have a baby," Olivia said solemnly, "and I want you both to be the first to know."

They pulled her close and smothered her with hugs.

"Well, when is the wedding," asked Beth.

With a trembling voice Olivia spoke. "There will be no wedding. My baby's father doesn't even know I am expecting, and it wouldn't matter if he did, he would not marry me. I am alone in this."

Quickly, the gleeful cheers stopped as if the oxygen were sucked from the room. Olivia seized the moment.

"I desperately need you both to promise not to divulge this to Papa.

When he finds out, I know he will send me away from here."

Beth and Ann stared at Olivia in silence. Neither doubted what Papa would do once he found out about Olivia or the consequences to them if they kept her secret.

.....

For the next two months Olivia ran the household while taking on every outside job she could find to increase her savings. She sewed dresses and tutored several of the girls in Ann's class in French. In spite of her having no prior teaching experience, the girls made remarkable improvement causing other families to seek out her services. But, she could only tutor when Papa was out of town. She worried he would discover her condition.

Each day she worried that Beth or Ann would inadvertently do or say something that would expose her secret. It was fortunate that Papa paid her no attention as long as she kept meals on the table and the household running smoothly. Although she suffered from morning sickness and retched at the smell of cooking, she hid it well. It was a blessing that she remained nearly invisible to Papa, thereby delaying his discovery.

.....

By Thanksgiving 1930, Olivia was at wits end. Her belly was expanding as were her breasts. Her clothes were too tight, and it was difficult to hide her expanding middle. Soon her bulky aprons would not afford her cover. In desperation, she bound her breasts with straps made from flour sacks and attempted to do the same with her waist and stomach. For the longest time, Olivia had prayed asking God to strengthen Mama so she could be up and about the house. She was thankful now He had not answered these prayers. There was no question, had Mama been with her in the kitchen or downstairs for meals, she would have immediately discovered Olivia's secret.

Each day presented new challenges for Olivia to overcome and her mind raced with thoughts about her soon to be born baby. How unfair it was that an innocent child would come into this world and through no fault of its own, be looked upon with disdain by all. As these thoughts assailed her, she experienced a change in her thinking.

Heretofore, she thought of her pregnancy as happening to someone other than herself. Not once had she connected to the baby inside her. How could she? She carried a child not born of love, but rather, born out of lust. Like a lightning bolt, Olivia felt a forceful need to protect her child; she felt love for her baby. A peace came over her as her anxiety evaporated and she became fully reconciled to her fate.

CHAPTER 14

As fall inched toward winter, life on the farm altered little. Beth and Ann were anxious. They waited with a degree of dread for the time when Papa would surely find out about Olivia's situation. Both feared the consequences Olivia, as well as themselves, faced if they failed in keeping her secret from Papa.

The scuttlebutt in town was John and Paul had returned home for their holiday break. Ann rode with Beth to High Springs where she hoped for a chance meeting with Paul. She expected him to visit her as soon as he got home, but she had not heard from him and was as miffed with his ignoring her as she was perplexed.

Ann left Beth at the mercantile and stepped into Jerrell's Drugs looking for Paul. He was nowhere to be found but she heard giggling and saw Laura, Dorothy and Betsy seated at a table. Laura waved and shushed the table as the others nervously turned to greet her. Ann ordered a Coca Cola at the soda fountain and waited for it to arrive. It was evident the girls shared some juicy gossip, and she could not wait to get caught up on the news.

Unbeknownst to her, the girls resented her haughty attitude. They endured her ongoing prattle of her plans for a future with Paul, while making fun of her behind her back. She had become a pathetic joke and her antics had worn thin with them.

Smiling a toothy grin, Laura pulled over an open chair.

"What did I miss?" Ann asked.

There was a pronounced silence as the girls eyed each other. Dorothy, a short, dumpy brunette, pulled back her hair from her face, cupped her hands, and quietly mouthed "Paul" to Ann.

"Paul." Betsy chimed in an uncomfortably loud voice, "Have you seen him since he got home?"

"Well no, not yet," answered Ann. "But I'm sure that it is just…."

Betsy interrupted, "He's got a girl with him."

There was silence at the table as the girls turned in admonishment at Betsy's direct approach.

"What?" Betsy exclaimed, "It is not like she's not going to find out sooner or later." She turned to Ann. "Wouldn't you rather hear it from us than from one of the old ladies at church?"

Ann averted her eyes while fighting back the tears. While it was always a possibility that he might meet someone at college, she had never allowed herself to imagine it would actually happen so soon. Ann righted herself in her chair. She was determined not to show her disappointment.

"Come on, Ann. Did you really expect to become Mrs. Paul Gunderson?" Betsy asked.

"Betsy," Dorothy exclaimed, "What in the name of Sam Hill are you doing? Stop it this instant."

Betsy turned to Laura for sympathy. "Well," she whispered, "it's true." Laura took Betsy firmly by the arm and led her toward the rest room. "Ouch! You're hurting me!" Betsy shrieked.

Ann was barely able to hold back a tear and Dorothy could tell how the news hurt her.

"I'm sorry that you had to hear this," Dorothy said. "The skinny is that they are to become engaged very soon."

"Oh?" Ann retorted, composing herself. "This is old news. I knew about this several weeks ago and I understand that she is charming. I wish them both nothing but the best. I am really glad he has found someone to help him get over his disappointment of learning that John Ward and I have become especially close."

Dorothy's jaw hung agape at Ann's incredulous statement.

Ann seized the opportunity to take her leave before Laura and Betsy returned. "John and I are going engagement ring shopping shortly. According to him, it will be the biggest engagement ring that High Springs has ever seen." With that, she arose quickly and exited the store.

Ann waited around the corner and out of sight for Beth. She absorbed what she had just heard and thought, "How did he dare do this to her?" While she was not in love with Paul, he represented her way off the farm and into an elite social circle. The thought of his betrayal both angered and frustrated her. But, she remembered what Papa always said: "where there is a will there is a way." John, after all, was still available.

.....

Back at High Point, Ann and Beth met Olivia carrying a load of laundry.

"I suppose you have heard that Paul is home from college and has brought a girl to meet his family. Now, it seems I'll need to change my options for getting off the farm. It will have to be John Ward and I'm okay with this because, to be honest, I really never could decide between them." Olivia lowered the overflowing basket to the floor as Ann continued.

"John is not a bad second choice. I always have a good time with him."

Olivia glanced at Beth who returned her look of mortification. Olivia picked up the laundry and exited the foyer with Ann following close behind her.

"John has shared with me his father's plans for him to return to High Springs after college."

"Ann, I don't think anyone questions what Mr. Ward plans for his son. It concerns me, though, that the Ward family does not seem to be a very happy one."

"Well they may not be as happy as some, but that won't bother me because of their wealth. That is what counts. I plan to invite him for supper soon to meet Papa. Do you think you can try to be civil to him for a change?"

Olivia was at a loss for words. She was expecting his child, and Ann was planning to marry him. She had to be careful now. Any response out of the ordinary could tip off Ann and the others.

"Well, Ann, if this is what you think will make you happy, I will support you. But, as I have warned you, John, as a potential husband, is a real risk. He is self-centered and you should be careful."

"Oh, Olivia, you have never understood him. He is a 'mama's boy,' but the right person can change him and I aim to be that person."

"You may change your opinion once you get to know the real John Ward," Olivia cautioned. "He's a charmer on the outside but you don't know what lurks in his heart."

Ann became defensive. "How can you appreciate the facets of John's character that endear him to me? You don't know him!"

"You are wrong, Ann! I have seen for myself his lack of honor and respect for you and others. What aspect of his 'honorable' character did he display when he brought you home from a date with your clothes in disorder and your lipstick smeared? I don't know what happened, but I do know those are not actions of an honorable person. Are these the facets of his character that you suggest I don't understand? Honestly, Ann, you are making a mistake."

"Olivia, you are such a prude. Since I have put a lot on the line to keep your little secret, you must do this for me. I intend that John will never forget this dinner or this night!"

Olivia's heart was full and she had an unquiet mind. It was not just that she feared for Ann, but that she did not know how she could face John after their last encounter. Every time she thought of how he looked at her as he left her lying in the hay, she felt acute disgust with what she had permitted him to do. She had no intention of ever divulging him as the father of her child, and it repulsed her to think he would soon become her brother-in-law.

CHAPTER 15

Walt was determined to do his part to engender himself to the young man. After all, it would not be a bad thing to have a son-in-law with a powerful father such as Robert Ward. Much less, one who controlled a railroad line spur Walt planned to use for transporting his crops and horses.

Throughout the evening, Walt behaved as the consummate host, encouraging John to relate his experiences at college and talk about his family. Ann was beside herself with joy as the evening moved along without incident. Even Olivia noticed that the two men had taken a liking to each other. "I'm sure it will be brandy and cigars in the parlor after dinner," she thought.

Ann wasn't mad with Paul in the least. She had witnessed many high school relationships fall apart when the boy left for college leaving the girlfriend behind. It was only natural that they would meet and court young ladies of social distinction whose parents could afford to send them off to school. In most cases, they married their college sweethearts. In some, however, the boy returned home after a few years to reclaim his lost love. Time would tell if Paul would have another opportunity to compete for Ann's affections.

Compete was the right word for it. It was nothing more than a game to her, a horse race between the boys to win her affection. Now, faced with one jockey out of the running, Ann would rig the race to ensure that John would not return to school without committing to her. Although she did not doubt his interest in her, she did not discount the obstacle his mother, Judy Ward, represented. John had shared his mother's concerns about his marrying the "right" kind of girl more than once. Ann acknowledged that neither she nor her family measured up to Judy's expectations.

Although Walt Turner was a successful farmer and wielded some power in local and state politics, the Turners were not a socially prominent family. They did not move in the social circles of John's parents; but then again, John's parents weren't exactly movers and shakers. Sure, Mr. Ward had many prosperous business dealings all over the Southeast and they were well received at many social events, but Mrs. Ward's querulous attitude proved to be a liability for them. How could Ann live with herself if she married into a dead end relationship that did not grant her the social standing that she desperately desired?

From the time he arrived and throughout the meal, John never formally acknowledged Olivia. Although he stole glances at her several times, their eyes did not meet nor did he address her. He did his best to seem disinterested in her, but the twitch of his hands gave him away. He was as uncomfortable in Olivia's presence as she was in his. Their secret tied them together with an invisible twine. His facial expressions captured his anxiety, and his inability to look her in the eyes spoke volumes of the unexplained guilt he felt. His tension increased and he was baffled at his own feelings.

In the past, John never felt guilt concerning his bad behavior. Now, however, he did and as much as he could not understand it, he despised it. He tried to attribute his odd feeling of guilt to his fear that Olivia would expose their secret. "It is folly," he thought. "She would never expose herself to the shame of their dalliance."

Walt, aware of an unnatural lull in conversation, broached the subject of John's parents.

"John, I understand that your father served in the Great War in France and that your family did not settle in High Springs until his return from Europe. Do you have memories of this time in your life?"

"Yes, sir. I remember much of the time that my mother and I spent in Oak Grove, Alabama while my father was away. She was the headmistress for the local post office, and I spent many a day helping her in the mail room. To make ends meet, she conducted a thriving loan business."

"So is your entire family steeped in successful business ventures?" Walt asked.

"Yes. Although some, like my Uncle Seth who is an accomplished physician in Birmingham, made their fortunes elsewhere. He provided the initial funds for the business my mother started. She possesses a real knack for financial matters and singlehandedly orchestrated the purchase of the foreclosure of the Chambers farm near High Bluff and two more nearby farms. My father will tell you that her prudent attention to business matters in his absence created many opportunities for him after the war."

"I am duly impressed," Walt remarked. "The Turner women are all content to sit in the lap of luxury and allow the menfolk to provide for their every need. They would not know a stock from a stable."

Olivia's ears perked up and she bit her lip at Papa's remarks. She alone had handled the farming operation at High Point since she was eleven years old. Without her shrewd planning, Papa would never have had the resources to expand the lumber mill and horse and cattle operations. Like the good daughter that she was, she kept her eyes focused on her plate and pushed her food around until it was time to serve the next course.

"You know for a woman alone with a young child to care for, my mother did extremely well. My father picked up where she left off upon his return. To be honest, I sometimes feel oppressed with the weight of their expectations of me. I just don't share their same love of business."

John became aware that he was droning on and Ann nervously shifted in her seat. She knew John had been the valedictorian of his class, but she wondered if he were lazy. She certainly hoped not.

John continued, "Oh, forgive me for carrying on for such a long time. I've shared much more than is in good form."

Walt empathetically reassured John, "I have thoroughly enjoyed our chat and would welcome hearing more of your family next time." Walt took a sip of his wine and realized Olivia and Gussie had cleared their plates and that it was time for dessert. Knowing how Ann regarded John, Walt treaded lightly but firmly. He had some concerns about John and the Wards and he could not pass up the opportunity to probe a little deeper to see if he could shake loose more details of Robert Ward's business ventures.

"John, I must tell you that I have the utmost respect for your father; however, I like many others in our community, wonder at his business undertakings. Some of the men I have business dealings with, as well as fellow elders in our church, have expressed concerns about your father's seemingly lack of compassion for those with whom he deals. Some in the community, who have lost their businesses or land to him, consider him to be ruthless. If you were to run his businesses one day, how would you manage through the trying times? Are you a man of honor or not?"

John could not respond to Walt's cutting remarks. He had often heard the scuttlebutt around High Springs concerning his father and he wondered if he were by nature incapable of empathy and compassion. While Walt impatiently waited for his response, he tapped his pipe on the table and thumbed his fingers. The sound of the pipe hitting the mahogany table echoed in John's ears and it seemed to grow louder like a bell tolling John's death. He was near panic now. "Does he know about Olivia?" he wondered.

"Yes, I am," he finally responded. "I am a man of honor. Or at least I hope I am."

"Well I'm glad to hear that. I just wish that you had not taken so long to come to that conclusion." They both laughed nervously.

A sense of relief overtook John as he realized that Olivia had not shared their sordid encounter in the barn. His thoughts turned to Ann. He knew that she had ideas in her head about them that would never come to fruition. This did not mean that he would forego spending time with her in the last few days he was home. He recognized her desperation now that Paul was beyond her reach, and he would play along and enjoy all that she might offer, but he would not jeopardize his future plans, none of which included her.

Olivia was anxious to serve dessert and have the men retire to the parlor. When Papa paused, she spoke.

"Shall we enjoy dessert and coffee next?" As Olivia stood, she felt a sharp pain in her abdomen and became dizzy. The room spun and she struggled to right herself, but could not stand. She fell. Walt stood with his mouth agape. His pipe fell to the table with a whack.

"Olivia, what are you doing?" Walt demanded. "Beth, get Gussie and a cold rag for Olivia's face."

Walt stood over Olivia and in a loud and threatening voice demanded that someone tell him what the hell was going on. At a time when the attention should have been on Ann, Olivia was taking the spotlight. "How selfish of her," he thought.

Beth arrived with the cloth and handed it to Papa who sneered as he mopped Olivia's brow. Beth reacted with disgust at her father's attitude and blurted out, "Well, I guess a woman who is expecting and who has worked herself to the point of exhaustion may faint."

Ann, close behind, shrieked, "Oh shit."

Walt, beside himself, pulled Beth around to face him.

"What you said is not true. It is impossible. Olivia cannot be expecting." He prided himself on controlling every facet of life at High Point, and this fiasco, as he would refer to it later, was not a part of his plan. The more he thought, the more agitated he became. Walt pulled

Beth's face up to his.

"Why do you lie? What basis do you have for what you have alleged? Tell me now."

Ann continued to rub Olivia's wrists and wipe her face. Olivia was coming back to consciousness but when she heard Papa's angry voice, she did not dare open her eyes. In low tones Beth addressed Ann.

"We cannot keep Olivia's secret any longer Ann. Tell Papa. You must." Ann looked up and stammered uncertainly.

"Papa, it is true, Olivia is expecting. She swore us to secrecy until she could find a way to tell you."

Lying still with her eyes tightly shut, Olivia knew that from this moment on her relationship with Papa would change forever. She had one consolation: only one other person knew the identity of the baby's father; and with any luck, they would manage to keep that a secret for a little while longer.

Despair overtook Olivia. Approaching the age of twenty-four, she was a woman who had valued a virtuous life who knew right from wrong. Yet, she had succumbed to John's lustful advances. Now, her plight was that of an "old maid" who was destined to remain on her father's farm without any escape.

Walt's anger hung over his daughters like a heavy fog, and like a horn booming from the mist, he pointed to Ann and Beth and bellowed.

"You two have dared to withhold from me what you knew about Olivia's condition. You have aided her in deceiving me and in forestalling her punishment that I shall mete out this very evening. You have betrayed your mother and me at the request of one not worthy of remaining a member of this family. Look upon her now as she lies there. She no longer has any standing in this household. Do I make myself clear?" Both girls trembled. "I will deal with you both later, and I promise you your punishment will be commensurate with your deplorable deceit."

Olivia knew that she must end her charade and sat up feebly while searching for an explanation for Papa. None came to her. John had initiated the scenario leading to his taking her virginity, but she knew Papa would find her guilty because she did not exercise her judgment to stop his advances. He would look upon her as an adult who succumbed to the immature desires of an eighteen year-old boy!

"Who fathered this bastard child?" Walt demanded.

Olivia hid her face in her hands and Papa promptly pried them open. She pulled back as she recoiled in fear of being struck by him. She knew that John's presence was the only thing that saved her from suffering a physical blow. The girls clung together and cried inconsolably.

John quickly rose from the table. As he did, his eyes briefly met Olivia's and a look passed between them telegraphing the truth. He shook his head with a stern look signaling Olivia that she must not implicate him, and he addressed Walt.

"Please, everyone, do not disturb yourselves on my account. It is best that I leave to provide you all your privacy. I assure you that what has transpired this evening will not be divulged to anyone by me. Mr. Turner, I appreciate your hospitality. Goodnight."

Having witnessed Walt Turner's display of temper and his rough physical treatment of Beth and Olivia, John hastened to leave. He hoped that his look to Olivia was sufficient to warn her not to involve him, but he could not be sure. He made his way toward the door.

Walt was an excellent negotiator, in part because of his ability to tell an adversary's position by his expression as well as his hand and eye movements. At the poker table, he had taken many a hand with a losing one because he was able to decipher his opponent's tells. He noted John's twitching, and right away his voice had raised several octaves. But, he thought, the most telling sign was "the creep." John's neck had begun to turn red at his collar and the blood was slowly coming to the surface from his neckline up into his jaws and cheeks.

"That's a gambler who is bluffing," Walt thought. "And he has gone all in with my daughter!" He called to John. "Wait, young man. Do not leave this house."

John broke into a run, stopping only to open the front door.

Walt then turned, "Olivia, you refuse to name the father of the child you carry but your eyes betray you. John Ward is the father! Is he not?"

"Oh my God," John thought as he reached the bottom of the steps. "How did this happen?" He jumped into his car and quickly engaged the engine. As he sped from the yard, he called back.

"Olivia, you set them straight. I have no place in my life for you or a baby. Don't try to saddle me with your problem."

Walt turned to Olivia and shook her violently until she slumped and fell to the floor. He had backed down to her desire to attend college, but a baby? That was out of the question. He spewed vulgar and hurtful language and heaped scorn upon her as he stood over her. She thought of speaking, but she had not seen Papa this angry in years and frankly, she was terrified. She remained there until he jerked her up violently by her hair.

"Go upstairs now and pack only your clothes. I want you ready to leave with me right away. High Point is no longer your home, and we are not your family."

"But, Papa, I will need to retrieve my money I earned from sewing and selling my eggs from my cigar box in the kitchen.

"You have no money, Olivia. Anything you made while living under my roof belongs to me. That money should go to pay household expenses. Get on with packing now and do not tarry for even a moment. You have embarrassed this family for too long already tonight." Then, he loosened his grip and hurried away.

Beth and Ann gathered Olivia and ushered her upstairs. Faced with the prospects of Paul having a new girlfriend, and now John having fathered a child with her older sister, Ann lashed out relentlessly at Olivia as they walked.

"This is your fault. How could you have seduced John? He is five years younger than you. What were you thinking? I know that you have no hopes of anything more for your life, but does that give you the right to destroy my chances for a life beyond this place? You are worse than the common whores at the roadhouse in Esto. At least they do not seduce young boys and neither do they end up with bastard children that no one will acknowledge. I hate you Olivia!"

Beth moved between them to shield Olivia from Ann's vitriol. "I'll share with Mama all that has happened to you. I'll find out where Papa is taking you and find a way to get you help. Don't ever forget that I love you, sister," she whispered.

MCMURTRY

CHAPTER 16

Olivia gathered a few items of clothing and the Bible Mama had given her. She stuffed a hair brush and a few other odds and ends into the small suitcase and pillow covering that she would take with her. As she passed, Ann continued reading a magazine and did not look up or bid farewell to Olivia.

Beth followed Olivia downstairs and at the bottom landing she stopped and caught Olivia's arm. "I will try my best to find a way to see you, but until then, this will be our farewell." Beth and Olivia embraced before Papa ushered her to his truck.

Olivia pleaded, "Please, Papa, let me see Mama and say goodbye." Walt would have none of it. His face turned red and his nostrils flared, as he took deep breaths in his effort to restrain himself from striking her as he shoved her into the passenger's seat.

"You have no Mama or any other family member here. Do you understand? By your actions you have forfeited all of this. I consider you nothing more than a bag of dung that I have to rid this family of, and I'll not allow you to upset her." He slammed the door causing the glass window to rattle in its frame.

"Where are you taking me?" she pleaded.

He did not answer. As the Model T truck turned sharply to exit the driveway, she saw Beth standing on the porch. The glow of the gas lanterns highlighted the tears streaming down her face. Soon, they were on the main road and the chill of the night air whistled around the windshield and doors. Papa did not speak as he drove intently with both hands on the wheel. He presented an odd silhouette as his diminutive frame sat up close to the steering wheel so that he could reach the foot pedals for the gas and brakes.

Olivia felt profoundly alone. Life as she knew it had ended. Ruth was not strong enough to go against the dictates of Papa; and Jim, the only sibling who had the courage to stand up to him, was dead. As for her brothers, none would help because they feared the loss of their farms if they went against Papa.

She was groggy from her fainting spell but her head was clearing, and she wondered again where Papa was taking her. As the moonlit landscape rushed past her window, she began to form a short list of destinations. There was a women's home in Dothan that took in destitute ladies whose husbands had died in the war or who had gone west seeking employment during the Crash. Both were unlikely places at this time of night.

The truck leaned heavily as Papa slowed and turned right onto Highway 41without stopping. As he accelerated past Capps Road, she saw the Dr. Pepper billboard and recognized her surroundings. "Oh no," she thought. "We must be headed to the Ward's house at High Bluff." Although she had passed the Ward farm dozens of times on her way from High Springs to Enterprise, she had never stopped there.

"Papa, where are we going? Papa, answer me! Are we going to the Ward's?"

There was no response as they lumbered onward. As they passed Iroquois Road, she could see the dim lights of the Chambers farm off to the right. Sixty seconds later, the intersection at Highway 167 was upon them and Walt didn't stop as he double clutched the gears through the stop sign. Then, he downshifted abruptly and turned into the driveway leading up to the Wards' homestead stopping directly behind John's '28 Ford sedan. Its warm engine emitted an eerie fog that dissipated into the darkness. Although it was late, lights were shinning throughout the main house.

As Walt exited the truck, he motioned for Olivia to stay put. He walked across the sandy area that served as a driveway at the front left side of the house. A white cat crossed his path as he climbed the wide wooden steps to the front porch. As he grasped the screen door, it opened much more easily that he anticipated and it slammed against the wooden clapboards. Walt ignored the bell hanging on the frame in favor of a few firm strikes to the door with his closed fist.

At last, he saw movement in the house and a short, heavyset figure in a purple dress and apron appeared at the door. From the truck, Olivia saw the front door open. Backlit by the interior lighting stood a colored woman named Flora Jackson who Olivia recognized from her visits to the mercantile in town. She stood a little over five feet tall and weighed 180 pounds. Her hair was tied back with a blue handkerchief and a white apron nearly covered her large breasts and the front of her purple dress. Walt addressed her firmly before she could greet him.

"I am Walt Turner, and I am here to see Robert Ward."

"I know who you are, Mister Turner. Can I tell Mr. Ward what your business is at this late hour?"

Walt responded angrily, "I have urgent business and that is all you need to know. Go and fetch him now! Now!"

Flora disappeared for a few minutes before Robert Ward appeared. "Walt Turner, what in blue blazes are you doing at my front door at this time of night? Whatever business you have to discuss can wait until tomorrow."

Walt pushed his way past him into the house. "Your son, John, is the reason for this visit, and the business I have with you and him will not wait until tomorrow."

Suddenly remembering his manners, Walt removed his brown Homburg hat and held it closely to his chest covering his tightly buttoned vest and white shirt. His fingers tapped nervously in unison around the brim. "I have learned tonight your son is the father of my daughter Olivia's unborn baby. Are you aware of this?"

Robert blinked his eyes and his head tilted. As he processed what he was hearing, his thoughts were interrupted.

"I do not raise whores in my home. My family and I will have nothing more to do with her. She's your problem now. What say you?" Walt's grip on the Homburg tightened as he awaited a response.

"Walt Turner, you have come into my home uninvited and made serious charges against my son. Yet, you have offered no proof. Before I can consider what you have said, I need to talk to my son to get his side of things. You may bring Olivia inside from the night air. I shall return shortly."

Walt had no interest in further discussion. "I have told you all that you need to know. As for Olivia, the cold air will do her good. The fires of hell will greet her soon enough to warm her as atonement for her perverted sins. Be quick about your talk."

After what seemed an eternity, Robert returned with John. "Mr. Turner, I have spoken with John and he admits that he was a victim of Olivia's womanly charms when she seduced him in your barn in August. But, he claims that the child is not his. He says that she must have other lovers and one of them must certainly be the father." Walt bristled at the thought.

"However," Robert continued. "My son has frequently been known to bend the truth to suit his own agenda, so I would like, with your permission, to speak to Olivia." Robert moved toward the front door. Walt remained motionless with a look of sheer disgust on his face. He nodded curtly in agreement. Robert donned a wool overcoat and descended the wooden steps into the yard.

As the screen door slammed behind him, Walt called out, "It doesn't matter what she says. It will not change anything I have already told you. You must decide how you will handle this fact. Are you an honorable man or a scoundrel like your son?"

As Robert approached the rusty yellow truck, the sand crunched under his shoes like loose snow. Olivia tentatively opened the passenger's side door. His voice was low and gentle.

"Olivia, I'm John's father. You may call me Robert." He squatted on his haunches so that he was eye level with the petite girl. "Your father is upset and you're tired and afraid, but I need to understand what is going on here."

Olivia's blue eyes sparkled in the moonlight as they met his.

"I understand that you have named John as the father of the unborn child that you carry. Is this so?"

"Mister Ward, John is the father of my baby, and that is the truth. I do not mean to besmirch your family name but I am here today because, in my efforts to protect my younger sister from his beguiling ways, I fell prey to his scheming lies."

Olivia breathed deeply and related how Ann and Paul Gunderson had betrayed John's trust and how he had seduced her to get back at them. "I'm very sorry, Mister Ward," she continued, "I was weak and I did not stop it before it happened."

"I understand now. Thank you for your honesty," he said as he helped her from the cab. "It is evident that you cannot go home. Will you accept a bed in my home tonight?"

"No," she said, "I should only trouble you for a place in the barn. I'm sure I would not be welcomed by John in the house."

"Nonsense," Robert exclaimed, "you will come inside as our guest. You are carrying our grandchild."

Walt stood on the porch out of earshot of the truck. His anger had turned melancholic now and his rage turned to disappointment as he thought of how dependable Olivia had been for their family only to betray them in such a public manner. He didn't know how he would tell Annie that Olivia would never return. She would be heartbroken but that would be a conversation for another day. He silently cursed Olivia for her selfishness. "Who will take care of Ann now?" he wondered.

Robert slipped his overcoat around Olivia to shield her from the night air and they slowly made their way up the wide steps to the porch. As they arrived at the top, Olivia addressed her father.

"Papa, I have told Mr. Ward the truth about my situation, and I have stated that I expect nothing from John or the Wards…."

Before Olivia could say more, Walt descended the steps, jerked open the truck door, and tossed her pillowcase and suitcase to the ground. "Fair enough," Walt exclaimed as he entered the cab, started the engine, and prepared to leave.

Looking at her with disgust, he let out the clutch, launching sand and intermittent clods of grass from the yard, and sped away. As the sound of the engine melted into the night, Olivia was certain that her life had changed. As Robert escorted Olivia inside, Flora retrieved her belongings and carried them inside.

Quiet returned to the Ward yard. On the corner of the porch behind a swing, a diminutive figure sat quietly, observing and soaking in the conversation. As the Model T truck disappeared into the November evening, its dim red taillights reflected across the yard giving off an eerie reddish glow. Quietly, the figure disappeared into the shadows under the house. Inside, a clock chimed midnight.

CHAPTER 17

Flora took the pillowcase and pasteboard suitcase containing Olivia's earthly belongings to the kitchen. She passed John's mother, Judy in the hallway talking to John but neither spoke. Judy saw the suitcase, clutched John by the arm, and quickened their pace until they reached the parlor. John explained the happenings of the evening to his mother.

"She passed out during dinner and then awoke rambling nonsense. The truth is Olivia doesn't know who her baby's father is. She has named me because she is either jealous of Ann's affection toward me or she sees it as a way off the farm. She's very smart. Trust me, Mother. You don't know what she is capable of."

Robert and Olivia entered the parlor. Judy was livid and it showed in her posture and in the red hue of her face.

"Robert Ward! What do you mean bringing this whore into our home? Her very presence blackens decent people. Get her out of here this very minute!" She turned her attention to Olivia and continued. "How old are you, woman? How base you are to trap a mere child into an unthinkable relationship. The likes of you will not ruin his life. I will ensure that."

Olivia knew that Mrs. Ward was angry at them both and she felt bad for John. Yes, he had charmed her into his embrace, but their current situation was certainly more than either of them could have imagined when they lay in the hay in the barn on that warm summer night. Mrs. Ward was standing over her now with her finger angrily poking Olivia's chest.

"Your claim is a lie. Do you understand me? I know what you are up to young lady and you will not gain a respectable name by entrapping my son. I won't have it." She turned to Robert. "Get this liar out of our home and let us be done with her ridiculous assertions."

Robert took Olivia's arm and led her out of the parlor and down the wood paneled hallway to his study. Olivia's senses were awakened by the smell of leather books and chairs as well as a slight aroma of cherry tobacco which reminded her of the brand Papa smoked.

As they entered the room, Robert released his kind but firm grip on her arm and she fell over into an overstuffed chair. The cool leather surface was a surprising, but welcome, relief. She still felt the effects of her passing out at dinner and she was exhausted. She tilted her head back to catch her breath and admired the marvelously sculpted ceiling. Perfect squares were bordered by pearly beads and an eagle motif capped off every corner. She heard a scraping noise and sat up to see Robert drag a wooden chair around the oak desk and deposit it beside her. He adjusted the wool coat around her shoulders and sat down.

"Now," he said, "let's start at the beginning.

After a half hour, Robert cracked the study door, stepped out into the hall, and summoned Flora. "Yes sir, Mister Robert. What can I be doing for you?"

Robert replied quietly, "Bring John and his mother to join Olivia and me in the study."

Soon the 'clip, clip, clip' of Judy's suede leather heels on the smooth wooden floor boards echoed in the hall, followed by John's heavy footfalls. Judy cast a disparaging look at Olivia who sat forward in the chair with her eyes cast downward. Although Olivia dared not look at Judy, she stole a glance at John. His athletic frame seemed to have shrunk into that of a child as he stood behind his mother, eyes down and his hands resting limply in his pockets.

Robert stepped between Olivia and Judy. His jaw clenched and his eyes narrowed. He knew he would have to be firm with his family because Judy had proven grossly protective of John in the past. Tonight, their son would learn a valuable lesson in accountability.

"Judy, I understand how overwhelmed that you must feel in just now learning that you are about to become a grandmother. Considering how you have learned of this, I can understand your outrage. But it is time for us all to face and accept reality. No matter how much anyone denies it, I am firmly convinced that our son is the father of Olivia's baby."

Robert slid into the chair behind his desk while Judy stood silently with her fingers interlaced in front of her at her waist. Her eyes burned as she looked at him directly.

"Tomorrow John will marry Olivia. I will not allow a grandchild of mine to be born a bastard."

"How can you know that Olivia carries John's child?" she asked. "Can't you see how cunning she is? Can you not see through this ploy to marry into our family to gain her a name? How could you force your son to marry this...," and turning back to Olivia she finished, "harlot?"

Robert was taken aback. It hurt him that Judy could be so averse to doing the right thing. He had never before noticed the streak of hardness in her. Placing both hands firmly on the desk he faced her squarely.

"My decision is made and will not change." He pushed back from the desk. "We can discuss how we have failed to raise an honorable son at a later date." He opened the study door. "Flora," he called. "Please prepare John and his mother's Sunday best clothes. We will leave early in the morning for Camilla, Georgia. Judy, show Olivia to our guest room. We have a busy day tomorrow." He then retired to his bedroom for the evening.

.....

As he stood in front of his dresser, Robert loosened his tie and was surprised at the sweat that had accumulated under his collar. He had become angry with Judy for one of the few times in their relationship and he fought the urge to feel guilty for the manner in which he had spoken to her. The thought passed quickly as his attention turned to the minutia of the details that lay ahead of him for the coming day.

He would call on his long-time friend George Johnson. Once a war buddy, George was now a highly respected judge living in Georgia. "If anyone can sort this mess out," he thought, "George will be the one."

.....

Meanwhile, back in the study, Judy looked at Olivia with malevolence. Her face was flushed and her lips compressed as she scowled at her and considered the ruin that she had placed at the feet of the Ward family.

"I shall never forgive you for what you have done to my son. I am not like my husband; I am not fooled for one minute by your demure posture. You will never be welcome in our home. You are best put outside with the dogs but that in and of itself would be an insult to the dogs.

Follow me, Jezebel."

Judy led her down the hallway toward the kitchen, pausing to pluck a quilt from the top shelf of a closet and throwing it at Olivia's feet. Olivia observed the patchwork design and had an odd feeling as she found herself more curious as to the intricacies of the design than what was to become of her. She followed Judy into the kitchen, but before she could orient herself to the layout, she found herself standing in the dark. Moonlight filtered through the window panes softly illuminating the floor. She needed a chamber pot in the worst way but she dared not go off in search of one at this hour. Before sleep overcame her, she pondered what tomorrow would hold.

.....

Walt Turner sat in his truck at the foot of the driveway at High Point for over an hour. He could not bear to go inside. What would he say to Annie? He had acted in anger; he had over-reacted, to be even more precise. He thumbed the bowl on his pipe. Its embers had long ago died but the aroma of burnt Granger tobacco lingered.

He was a broken man. He had lost his wife to severe depression and she was a shell of her former self. He had lost a beloved son to an accident, and now he had disowned his most dependable daughter. To go through these things in the space of a little over a year was nearly more than he could handle. The world he ruled with a tight fist was crumbling around him.

He dried his eyes and stiffened his lip. He would tell Annie and try to help her understand why having a baby at High Point did no one any good, especially Ann. She would be their focus now. They must help her find a suitable husband so that she did not become the spinster that Olivia had become. The livelihood of High Point and all of Walt's businesses depended on diversifying his interests and expanding his domain. Matching Ann to a suitable partner would go a long way toward achieving this goal, and Walt was determined to see it through.

"Annie will understand," he thought. "She must."

CHAPTER 18

"Morning Miss Olivia."

Olivia awoke to a crowing rooster and Flora standing over her. She wiped the sleep from her eyes, rose, and folded her quilt. Instinctively, she put it back in the closet from whence it came.

"Flora, I have not had much to eat in the past two days, and I am hungry. Is there something I may have?" Flora handed her a ham biscuit wrapped in a cloth napkin.

Olivia smiled for the first time in days and thanked her. "I must relieve myself first and then I should bathe and change my clothing." Flora understood how angry Judy would be if she were kept waiting, but she sympathized with Olivia.

"I'll show you the facilities where you can relieve youself, but you best not take time to bathe and change clothes. Missus Judy will be fearsome mad if you ain't ready to leave on time and I'll be the one she blames."

Olivia followed Flora to the porch on the back side of the house. The cold wind bit her face, but it was a welcome relief to wash away the last 24 hours of denigration that had been heaped upon her.

"This here is where the colored folks wash up," Flora said. "But it gonna have to do for now." Olivia pulled back a curtain to reveal a chair with a bucket under it. It was crude but she was grateful to relieve herself. She was preparing to change clothes when Flora arrived in a tizzy.

"They's back and awaiting for you. Ifn you knows what's good for you, chile, you won't delay no more."

She wore only the thin dress she was wearing at supper the night before. Flora handed her a light sweater that was far too big and Robert's wool overcoat. Olivia pulled them on hurriedly as Flora cautioned, "Stay warm, chile, or you'll catch yore death of cold."

From the porch, Olivia could see that the Wards were already waiting in the car. John was sitting in the far corner of the back seat behind his father and Judy sat up front. She entered the opened back door, greeting everyone warily. Robert nodded. He steered past the house and onto the highway. The hum of the engine offset the silence in the cabin and no one talked for the next sixteen miles. He slowed at the intersection of Highway

84, and as he turned right to head into Dothan he shared the purpose for their trip.

"Olivia, it is best that you and John be married right away. I have a dear friend in Georgia who is a judge and he will make all of the necessary arrangements to ensure that it is accomplished as discreetly as possible."

Olivia sat with eyes cast downward to the floorboard, thinking of Mama, Papa, and Beth. She never imagined a scenario where she would be married without them by her side. She wondered how John felt. He seemed so disinterested. Sadness overcame her. Within a few hours, she would become Mrs. John Ward and he would become an unwilling husband and soon-to-be father. As they passed through Dothan, Judy was already getting restless. Robert sensed this and he turned to her.

"It's about three hours from here. I am confident that George will perform the wedding ceremony forthwith and we should be back in High Bluff by early evening."

Judy stared mindlessly out the window as the last few buildings in Dothan melted away behind her. They drove past peanut fields on either side as far as the eye could see, and Olivia mentally recited her favorite Bible verses to calm herself. John gently snored, his head against the side window. Robert thumbed the wheel as he tapped out a whimsical tune in his head.

After a short time, they arrived in Camilla and stopped in front of the courthouse. Robert and Judy, with John in tow, ascended the steps quickly, leaving Olivia behind. She hurried to catch up with them in the biting cold. They arrived outside Judge George Johnson's office and Robert motioned for them to remain seated on a hall bench while he went in to make the necessary arrangements. As he entered the Judge's chambers, George Johnson rose to greet him.

"Robert, it is so good to see you after all this time!"

"You haven't changed a bit," Robert replied, ignoring the forty pounds his friend had packed on in the last twenty some odd years. Robert briefly recounted what he had told the judge on the phone.

"Don't you worry, Robert, I understand the delicacy of this matter and I am pleased to assist you. I'll need to arrange for a marriage license to enable me to perform the ceremony. Thankfully she is of legal age and I will not need to secure her parents' consent. It should all be prepared within an hour."

Robert nodded thankfully. He was embarrassed for his son's unseemly behavior that led to the necessity of a "shotgun" wedding, but he was relieved that his friend could handle the details as quietly as possible. Given his penchant for stretching his business associates over a barrel, he was none too pleased to give anyone ammunition to use against him.

"Fetch your wife and son, along with his soon-to-be bride and wait for me. It is certainly not a day conducive to sitting in a drafty hallway."

The judge took his leave and Robert ushered in the trio. John and Olivia took their seats on opposite ends of an eight foot bench while Judy pulled Robert aside. "I cannot abide the idea that I'll be associated with her. You must not do this, Robert. For the love of God, stop this farce before it is too late! We should simply set her up in another town somewhere. Isn't that best for everyone?"

Robert stood with mouth agape.

"Look at them," she said, motioning to the pair on the bench. "They can't stand the sight of each other. Let us leave now and end this tragedy!"

Robert was angry that Judy so easily could abandon their unborn grandchild. "But now," he thought, "was not the time to push the issue."

Soon, he returned and summoned them to join him. As they entered his chambers, Judge Johnson presided behind a large oak desk. They listened as the judge's voice took on the deep baritone of authority.

"Everything is in order for the marriage to take place," he said nodding to the couple. "John and Olivia, if you will stand, we can begin." His attention turned to Robert and Judy. "Robert, will you and Mrs. Ward stand as witnesses and attest as such on the marriage certificate?" Before Robert could respond, Judy turned to him. Tears and anger were evident in her eyes as her voice rose.

"I will not be a witness to this farce of a marriage. I can't stop this abomination, but I don't have to agree to it. Find someone else."

The squeaking of his high back chair pierced the uneasy quiet in the chamber as the judge turned to face Robert. His left hand reached for an imaginary gavel but there was none. He certainly would have hammered her quiet in the courtroom. He waited patiently for Robert to speak, but was met with a wall of awkward silence.

"Robert, I am aware of the peculiar nature of this union, but I must say that I am reluctant to proceed over Mrs. Ward's strong objections." He shuffled some papers together as he thought for a moment. An idea came to him and his forehead relaxed as he turned to the young couple.

"John and, Olivia, it is my understanding that you are both of legal age, and as such, it is your decision as to whether I should continue with…," he glanced at Judy, "this 'farce.' What say you both?" He leaned forward on his desk with his arms crossed.

"Ye… Yes," Olivia spoke quietly.

"Yes…," John said softly.

"But…" Judy exclaimed before she was cut off by Robert's elbow to her side.

"It's their choice," he whispered sternly.

Judy thought to interject, but her shortness of breath and the piercing pain in her ribs convinced her otherwise. She nodded her coerced approval and Robert did the same. The judge sat back in his chair.

In a measured voice he said, "Then by the power vested in me by the Great State of Georgia, I pronounce you man and wife. Robert, I'll take care of the witnesses later. John and Olivia, you are married. May God bless you. You will surely need it."

Robert was relieved that John understood his obligation. Acknowledging the precarious situation in which he had placed his friend, Robert shepherded them toward the door where he stopped and turned back. "Please accept my deepest apologies, George. You cannot know how much I appreciate your help on behalf of John and Olivia."

Ahead of them lay the painfully awkward trip home. As they entered the car, Judy clutched Olivia by her upper arm and whispered menacingly, "Do not ever let me hear you refer to yourself as a Ward. You will never be a Ward. Ever!" Olivia's piercing blue eyes returned a fiery stare.

.....

It was early evening when they arrived in High Bluff and everyone independently dreaded what lay ahead. Judy had steadfastly argued, among other things, that Olivia could not stay in the main house. Although he felt strongly to the contrary, Robert reluctantly gave up on his demand that Olivia take up residence in the guest room. Judy had another idea and although he cringed at the thought, he hoped against all odds that Olivia's living in close proximity would help Judy overcome her hatred for her. "It's a battle for another day," he thought.

Judy and John disappeared into the house, and Robert pulled Olivia aside. "I know you are hungry and are anxious to prepare yourself for bed. Until we can come to a more suitable arrangement, you will live in a place in the Quarters. It's not much, but it is better than the driveway where I found you last night. Give me some time and I'll figure something out. I'm sorry."

Every sizable farming operation had an area reserved for the colored folks that worked in the fields or as domestic servants in the main house. It was rare, but occasionally a down and out white itinerant family might work during harvest time and be allowed to live in one of the run down shacks for a few months.

In this case, Judy sought to reduce Olivia's standing in the community to that of the lowest of the low. By placing her in a shack in complete disrepair and barely sufficient to keep out wild animals, Judy intended to mark her as a bonded servant without any resources or any hopes of rising above her allotted station.

Olivia's jaw clenched. "I shall be regarded as no more than hired help," she thought. "Judy Ward will not intimidate me; I will not permit such to happen. No sooner did I escape my de facto indentured servitude at High Point than I have landed in the fire at High Bluff. Such is life." She bowed her head and offered a silent prayer that God would give her the strength to endure the indignities heaped upon her. The feeling of hunger escaped her for the moment. It was time to move onward.

Robert struggled to find comforting words, but he found none. He could tell that she was profoundly hurt at the news of where she would live and he was determined to get her settled and remove himself from the constant reminder of the injustice of her situation.

Abruptly, he took her hand and led her down a rutted pathway to her new home. In the moonlight, he surveyed the rotten boards and leaking roof of the shanty and acknowledged to himself that it was at best uninhabitable by anyone's standards. He felt like a cad, but he was powerless against Judy at this time. As he stopped to open the door, Olivia took the quilt, lamp and matches that he carried for her, pushed by him, and opened the door herself. It rattled on one hinge as it closed behind her.

"I've got it from here."

Robert heard the latch lock from within and he began the unenviable journey back to the main house. He still had Judy to face before the day was over and he did not relish hearing her attacks on Olivia. Although he loved his wife, he resented her cruel ways. As he thought of Olivia, he lamented Judy's treatment of this young woman who was obviously a fighter and who was worthy of their respect.

As her eyes adjusted to the dim interior, Olivia soaked in the bleakness of her surroundings. The small pot belly stove stood bare in the center of the room. The kindling and wood box bore only sheathes of straw. A mouse scurried away from her as she moved about inspecting what lay beneath the randomly discarded boards and debris. The wind whistled through the holes in the roof and walls as well as through broken window panes.

"This will do nicely," she thought. "They won't lick a Turner. I'll show them." She folded the quilt into a pallet and curled up in a corner shielded from the draft. Her eyelids grew heavy and sleep came quickly to feed her exhaustion.

.....

Robert Ward did not sleep all night. As daylight peeked through the shades in his study, he twirled a fountain pen in circles on its base. The Parker Duofold desk set before him had been a gift from the Southern Railroad executives as a thank you for his support of the High Springs to Dothan spur. With his management of the line, profits soared in an otherwise dour economy.

Like Walt Turner, Robert was exemplary at squeezing the most out of those who could least afford it. He found himself arriving at the realization that Olivia had much of Walt Turner's determination in her. He cringed at the thought that he had somehow failed to instill the same qualities in his son. John was smart, but he lacked drive and it burned Robert to the core that Judy had convinced their son that he was not responsible for anything connected with Olivia or the baby that she carried.

He heard heavy footsteps in the hallway as John carried his suitcases to the car for his trip to college. Robert's arms and legs felt like they were filled with lead. He could not bring himself to face his errant son. "As strange as it sounds," he thought, "I feel closer to Olivia than my own son. I hope she can save that boy one day." The air splintered with the sound of the Ford's motor as it exited the yard. Robert could not wait for this year to end. Surely 1931 would hold better prospects for his family.

CHAPTER 19

Olivia awoke to the sounds and the smells of farm life. For a moment, she imagined herself at High Point. She was stiff from the lengthy car ride and her slumber on the dirt floor. Her stomach, back, and arms ached from her pregnancy. She pushed herself up to see the light filtering through the window and around the door frame. The golden beams crossed paths with the slivers of light piercing the cottage walls.

"This place is filthy and there is no cook stove, ice box, or furniture. I don't even have any bedding. No place to go but up from here."

She needed to relieve herself so she set out to find the community outhouse. When it did not become immediately apparent, the urge overcame her and she squatted behind the shack. "Now to find some food," she thought.

By this time of day, the Quarters were devoid of people. They were off in the fields or at the main house going about their daily chores. Moving between two shacks, Olivia almost bowled over Flora who was out of breath.

"Honey chile, where you been? I looked for you all over dis place. Missus Judy is a looking for you at the main house. Come on now. Let's git you up there without no delay."

Olivia surveyed her dirty clothes with dismay. She had no way of bathing or changing and she rather suspected that Judy would revel in her discomfort. She ran her slender fingers through her hair to get it out of her eyes and dutifully followed Flora into the main house. "Dignity," she thought. "No one can take my dignity. Not even Judy Ward."

Arriving at the big house, Olivia walked slightly ahead of Flora. As they approached the dining room, the aroma of coffee and freshly grilled sausage links lingered under her nose and her stomach growled in anticipation. She had lost count of the hours since she had eaten anything of substance. Olivia stopped in her tracks as she met Judy's cold, beady eyes, devoid of warmth. Olivia moved toward a chair at the side of the table.

"What are you doing, girl?" Judy asked with hands on hips.

"Oh you foolish, foolish girl, you thought you were going to have breakfast with the family?" Judy laughed. "Not today. Not ever…." The words hung in the air as Olivia, nearly starving, attempted to digest them. "You'll have your breakfast in the Quarters like the colored folks do. You'll be fed based on the work you accomplish. And," Judy paused, "you haven't done any work yet so we better get you started."

Olivia felt the spit boil at the back of her throat. She knew that she had reached her brink. She thought of Mama and their last moments together the day before she left High Point. Calmness came over her. A piece of paper being waved in her face brought her attention back to the moment. She snapped her neck back and tried to focus her eyes on the writing, but it was fruitless.

"The only reason you are here is because my husband has been taken in by your guile. He's no less gullible than our son when it comes to your charms. Just know that I despise the necessity of enduring your presence."

Olivia took the paper from Judy and read the first line: Weekly Chores. Scanning the list, she noted each item: cooking, cleaning, washing and ironing. She dropped the paper on the table.

"I ran my father's household for years, and I know that these duties cannot be accomplished in a work week unless there are at least four competent people assigned individual tasks. Which of these is meant for me?"

"All of them, Miss Turner. You are an unwanted person who should earn her keep if she hopes to remain here. Of course, you can always go back to 'Low Point' as I believe they are calling it these days."

The reference to Papa's farm stung and Olivia turned to go. "Might as well get started with this sentence," she said flippantly.

Judy stopped her. "Your father has disowned you and forbidden your family to associate with you. As far as I am concerned you are a scheming woman who plotted to secure a place in a respectable family and a name for your baby. I will see to it that you regret naming John as the father. I pray that you never deliver your bastard child."

Olivia stared in disbelief. Was it possible that Judy Ward prayed for her to lose her baby? "Mrs. Ward, are you so cruel and heartless that you would create this impossible list of duties to be completed by me alone, which would ultimately cause me to lose my baby?"

Silence echoed throughout the house. Lines had been drawn and there was nothing more to be said. Olivia accepted that her mother-in-law despised her and wanted to exclude her from John's life, but to hear her blatantly express her wish for the death of her baby was more than she could comprehend. She was filled with a fear she could not dispel. She hung her head to hide the tears that threatened to flow. Olivia gathered her resolve, and calmly raised her head to meet Judy's eyes.

"I'll not let you kill me or my baby. Try what you may, but in the end you will fail. I may be down, but I'll never be out. Papa taught me that there is nothing more dangerous than a wounded and cornered animal, and I am both. You've made sure of that. You have been warned."

Blood surged through Olivia's veins. For the first time since she returned home from college, she felt alive and in control of her life. She made her way back down the rutted path to the Quarters. As she entered her shack, she nearly stumbled over her suitcase and pillow case with her personal belongings. "Clean clothes," she thought. "Finally!" As she unpacked her meager belongings, she began to process the events which had just taken place.

In less than an hour, she had learned more about Judy Ward's character than she could have discovered in a lifetime. Olivia knew that if she and her baby were to survive, she would have to plan carefully. Many of the folks in the Quarters frequented town on business for the Wards. They would tell their friends about the new girl at High Bluff, and Judy's treatment of Olivia would provide ample fodder for their gossip. She also imagined the disdain that would be felt for Robert and his businesses once people in High Springs learned of her plight.

The gossip about Judy in High Springs was already rampant, and Olivia was not oblivious to what she had heard. Judy Ward desperately hoped to be included in the most exclusive of social circles. Therein lay Olivia's opening. Surely Judy Ward would not persist in her insensitive cruelty at the risk of losing standing as a genteel woman within the community. Time would tell, but Olivia firmed her resolve. She would be ready to act.

.....

After bathing and changing into clean clothes, Olivia answered a knock at the door. Flora entered with two large colored men behind her.

"Honey chile, Mister Robert done told me to bring you a bed and some furniture. My boys has come to hep you." Flora stepped aside as the two boys, in their early twenties, brought in a bed frame and mattress, small table, two chairs, and a dresser. Then Isaac, the older boy, returned with a wooden crate containing various household linens and utensils. Olivia was delighted to see a cooking pot and a tea kettle on top of the heap. A cup of tea would do her wonders as she adjusted to her new surroundings. Olivia instinctively reached out to hug Flora who blushed and embraced her warmly.

"It's gonna be alright chile. We's gonna look after you rightly. Don't you worry none, you got family here with us." The boys left and Flora turned to follow them. "Oh," she said, "I don't know what come over her but Missus Judy done said you can have whatever you can harvest out of the truck garden. It ain't been tended since the last family moved on from here, but there will be some sprouts in the spring ifn you tend it in the next few months. Ask Joe here to hep you 'cause he's good at dat. I'll pick you up a few things when I goes to High Springs tomorrow."

Flora and the boys left and Olivia set out to arrange her furniture in the shack. As she moved about, she had an overwhelming feeling that she was being watched. "Impossible," she thought. "There's no one here but me." She heard a noise against the outside wall and saw a shadow through a gaping crack the size of her hand. She ran to the door and thrust it open but it was too late. Her "visitor" was gone. She braced her door that night and sleep came slowly. "As God is my witness, Judy Ward will not intimidate me; not even with imaginary ghosts outside my door."

.....

Over the next few days, Olivia settled into the routine of her duties. Isaac and Joe patched the holes in the walls and roof. Frank fashioned a wooden floor out of pine beams over the dirt floor. And a new door that didn't sag on one hinge was a welcome sight. Frank made sure that her woodpile and kindling bucket were full. The pine and oak sticks yielded a glowing stove that served her well to keep the December cold and stiff winds at bay.

She spent her days diligently working her way through her list of chores and successfully avoiding Judy. "I'll not give her any opportunities to belittle me and distract me from my work at hand," she thought. At night Olivia preferred to spend time sitting with the colored folks as they sang spiritual songs and told stories of their ancestors until the campfire embers dimmed and the flames died out. She was most impressed by the sense of community and giving between the families. They had adopted her as one of their own, and she welcomed their love and affection. She and her baby were truly among family.

As Olivia walked back home, Flora called to her. The portly woman was carrying a large croaker sack stuffed to the brim. Olivia opened the bundle to discover a pile of flour sacks.

"You said that you could sew me some pillows for my boys ifn you had needles and threads," Flora said, handing her a leather zippered pouch containing sewing implements.

"Why yes, I certainly can."

Olivia's cheeks felt flush. She had been praying for a way to generate money to get some supplies but she had yet to come up with a solution. She was grateful for all that those in the Quarters had done to help her. She hugged Flora tightly.

"I'll have pillows for you tomorrow," she said. As the door shut behind her, she dropped to her knees to thank God. She worked late into the night and awoke the next morning surrounded by needles, thread, scrap flour sacks, and four pillows. She gathered them and made her way through the Quarters to Flora's house.

.....

Flora and Frank enjoyed their positions of authority with the Wards and they benefitted most by having a house that was substantially better built than the shacks in the Quarters. Flora maintained the Ward's household staff and marshaled the activities therein, and Frank oversaw the farm workers to maximize production. Together, they lived in a house with multiple rooms and indoor plumbing. They had earned these perks by their hard work, loyalty, and a little luck.

Frank proved his worth quickly when he demonstrated a remarkable skill at predicting unannounced visits to the Florida farms by the state taxing authority. Based on his instincts, Ward Enterprises was able to avoid three such visits in less than a year. As a result, Robert relied on Frank to advise him as to the timing for likely visits to ensure that hundreds of cattle were moved from fields in Florida a few miles north over the state line into Alabama.

Beside himself with curiosity, Robert had inquired many times as to just how exactly Frank managed to pull off his predictions with one hundred –percent accuracy. Frank always smiled and responded that it was the Lord's work that helped him know.

What Robert would never come to know was that Frank's definition of the "Lord's work" involved a distant cousin, aptly named Lord Jackson, who worked as a janitor in the state tax office in Tallahassee. By rummaging through the waste paper baskets and calendars on the desks of the appropriate staff members, he was able to pin down precise dates and managed to get Frank warning in advance of the revenuers' trips west to the Florida panhandle.

.....

As Olivia climbed the steps to the rear porch at Flora and Joe's, she was met by Joe and Isaac who were on their way to the woodshop where they made and repaired furniture. Their skill was remarkable, considering they had received no formal training. Robert sold the fruits of their labor as far away as Montgomery and Mobile, while paying the boys pennies on the dollar for their efforts, but they did not complain. Their lot in life was much better than the other young men struggling to survive in the Quarters. As Olivia reached for the door, Joe stopped and held the door for her to enter.

"Momma's expectin' you inside. Go on in now," he said politely. Olivia was duly impressed with the interior. They had made the most of scraps of wood and cloth to make their home both comfortable and appealing. Their efforts were made possible by the generosity of Robert Ward who had donated the excess materials from each of the projects that Frank and his sons had undertaken around the main house.

Most who knew Flora understood that there was no middle ground as far as she was concerned. She either liked you, or she had no use for you. It was fortunate for Olivia that she had heard all that had transpired on the night Olivia came to High Bluff. Flora felt a genuine compassion for her. She knew, better than most, Judy Ward's capacity for cruel behavior and she would help Olivia as best she could to get through the trying times she knew were ahead of her.

Flora beckoned Olivia to follow her into the tiny kitchen. She took a pan of biscuits, fried eggs and sausage from the potbelly stove and put them on a plate for her. A mason jar of goat milk quickly followed.

As Olivia finished eating, there was a knock at the screen door. In sauntered a little white girl of about five or six years of age by Olivia's estimation. She wore a calico dress which framed her petite figure. She sported brown hair, cut in a bowl shape, and big brown eyes.

"Miss Olivia, this is John's baby sister, Evelyn."

The girl shifted behind Flora's apron, smiled sheepishly and mumbled something incoherent.

"Oh, I's sorry girl," Flora laughed. "You ain't no baby." Evelyn looked around the kitchen as if searching for something. Ever watchful, Flora noticed quickly.

"Now Evelyn, you knows I don't have no corn pone patties till tonight. Git on outta here right now and I'll save you one for later."

"Two," the little girl cried. "I will need me two."

"Well listen to you gettin' too big for your britches! Okay, I'll save you two."

Evelyn grinned and winked at Olivia. As quickly as she appeared, the child vanished into the morning sunlight. Flora wiped her hands on her flour sack apron and then examined the pillows.

"Chile, these here are so purty. You did 'em last night?" Flora asked in disbelief.

"Yes, I did. I had a little trouble with the seams because it was so dark, but I can fix them if you need me to."

Flora continued to inspect her handiwork. "You is real talented. Us coloreds here in the Quarters ain't got a pot to pee in but I believe you can make some good money in town with these here pillows. Can you make anything else?"

"Yes, I can make rugs from the sacks, and quilts too if I have enough cloth, thread, and batting material."

"Oh chile, I needs me some rugs. I'll get yore materials when I goes to market tomorrow. Missus Ward allowed for me to pick up any necessities you might be needing. I ain't gonna lie, that sho nuf didn't sound like Missus Judy, but I ain't gonna argue with her 'bout dat."

Olivia smiled slyly. Could her warning to Judy have gotten through to her? Perhaps not, but either way, she felt stronger and emboldened.

.....

A relaxed demeanor hung over High Bluff. Robert and Judy were on their way to Tallahassee to call on their political connections there and along the way, they planned to check in on their string of juke joints in the Florida panhandle. Judy kept a watchful eye over the books and when sales of illegal alcohol slipped, a surprise visit with an accounting of cash usually rectified the problem.

While they were away, Olivia finished the rugs for Flora and her handiwork was the talk of the Quarters. Due to the regimen of regular food and rest, Olivia looked and felt better than she had in months. As she sat on the steps to the back porch at the main house waiting for the laundry to dry. She took advantage of the time to nibble on a snack of one of Flora's corn pone patties.

Out of the corner of her eye, she saw a shadow lurking at the side of the house. She leaned forward to look closer and heard a loud bark followed by a high pitched squeal. Evelyn dashed from her hiding place. Rufus, one of the Ward's yard dogs, chased her from behind, barking and nipping at her heels. Evelyn scampered up to the porch and hid behind Olivia.

"That there's a mean 'un," Evelyn said as she pointed to Rufus who was standing at the foot of the steps and panting in the midday sun.

"Really? I think he just wants you to play with him."

"Play with him?" Evelyn looked inquisitively. "How do you play with a dog? Ain't they just for scaring off foxes and hunting with Daddy and John? You don't play with them, do ya?"

"Just give him some attention. Throw a stick for him to fetch and he'll be your friend for life."

Evelyn jumped down and grabbed a stick from the yard. "You mean like this?"

Olivia nodded and Evelyn tossed the stick as far as she could. Rufus retrieved it and promptly plopped down in the sandy yard and continued panting.

"Like I said, you don't play with them."

Olivia chuckled. "No, I guess you don't."

They both laughed in unison. Evelyn moved back up on the porch and took a seat beside her. Olivia smiled and pinched off two fingers worth of corn pone which Evelyn accepted.

"You remembered that I like these, didn't you?"

It was evident that she was both bashful and lonely. "Evelyn, I am so glad I met you. I didn't really know you were here until a few days ago."

"Well, I knew you."

Olivia was surprised. "What do you mean?"

"I mean I have seen you since that night that your daddy brought you here. I saw the whole thing from behind the rocker on the porch."

Olivia sighed in relief. "And let me guess, you have been peeking through the cracks in my house?"

"Well..." Evelyn answered shyly. "I didn't mean you no harm. I just ain't got nobody to play with here and I wanted to see if you would play with me."

Olivia smiled. "It sounds like to me that maybe you and Rufus have more in common than you bargained for. You both need a friend."

"Will you be my friend?" Evelyn asked in anticipation.

"Of course I will. You know, Evelyn, I have chores to do while Flora is gone. If you stay, I'll let you help me."

Evelyn could barely contain her excitement. Later that afternoon, Flora returned from High Springs with a wagon full of supplies for the main house and a few "necessities" for Olivia and several others in the Quarters. As she stopped the wagon near the back door to unload the sacks and boxes, she saw Olivia and Evelyn returning from the laundry line with wicker baskets full of folded clothes.

"I see you gots youself a hepper there." Flora laughed.

"She's a good one even for a seven year old."

"Seven and a half!" Evelyn chimed in.

"She's cheap too. She works for corn pone!" Olivia and Flora laughed in unison. Even Frank chuckled from the front of the wagon.

.....

Over the next few weeks, Olivia and Evelyn spent most of their waking time together. Evelyn listened intently as Olivia instructed her in the nuances of becoming a proper young lady. One area Olivia insisted that she focus on was her grammar.

"Evelyn, I've heard everyone in your family speak and they are all quite educated. Yet, I hear you speak in the slang of the Quarters more often than not. I want you to concentrate on eliminating words such as 'ain't' from your vocabulary." Evelyn promised that she would try her best.

"Olivia, why don't you eat with the rest of the family inside the house?" Evelyn asked as they sat on the back porch one night.

"Well...," Olivia started to answer, but went no further realizing that she was on dangerous ground here. She felt she owed her protégé an answer, but perhaps it would be better if the truth came later.

"You sure ask a lot of questions, little rabbit."

Evelyn giggled, "I'm not a rabbit!"

"Well," Olivia laughed in return, "you're my little rabbit."

Evelyn's eyes opened wide. "Well if I'm a rabbit, you must be Olivia Cottontail. I'll just call you Cotton for short."

"That's fine Evelyn. It will be our little secret."

.....

One afternoon as they walked to the hen house, Olivia noticed a puzzled look on Evelyn's face. "What's wrong, Rabbit?" Olivia asked.

"Olivia, why are you the only white person who lives in the Quarters? I thought only Niggers lived there."

"Oh no!" exclaimed Olivia, "That's not a nice word. You don't call anyone that. Where in the world did you hear that?"

Evelyn stammered. "At the peanut mill. I ... I... I heard the man there ask Daddy how many Niggers he had picking for him."

"Evelyn," Olivia said grasping her hands, "most polite people either call them Negroes or colored people. I know this is hard for you to understand, but a long time ago people like Flora and Joe were owned by white people. It was wrong then and it is wrong now to call them names. They may have a different skin color but they are flesh and blood, God fearing people just like you and me." Evelyn looked on with wonder. "Can you promise me that you won't ever use that slur again?"

"Yes, Olivia," she nodded.

"Good girl."

"There's one thing I don't understand, Olivia. Did my Mama hire you to work for us?"

"Rabbit, why do you ask these things?"

Evelyn shrugged in response. "I'm just curious is all. Nobody ever tells me nothin'. That's why I gotta sneak around; so I can find out stuff."

Olivia grinned. "The truth is that I needed a place to stay and your parents graciously allowed me to live in that abandoned shack in the Quarters in exchange for helping out around the farm. It needs a lot of work, but I know I can do it with yours and Flora's help."

Evelyn's wonderment and curiosity was often ignored by her parents and Olivia committed herself to devoting time to answering her seemingly endless barrage of questions. She hoped her explanations to her inquisitive protégé had satisfied her needs to understand her unique place in the world.

.....

Olivia was getting into a routine. Save for seeing Papa, Mama, and the girls, she sometimes felt that she had never left High Point. She missed Gussie, but Flora had proven to be more than a friend and mentor to her and had treated her like a member of her own family. Fortunately, Judy had been spending a lot of time in High Springs, Geneva, and Dothan in an effort to raise her social standing.

With Judy away, Olivia was able to spend more time improving her shack. Although she had no stove for baking, only the hook over her fireplace, Olivia used heated stacks of bricks to form a crude oven. In it, she baked small loaves of bread and cakes. She also developed a friendly rapport with the stable hands who eagerly collected discarded burlap feed bags for her. After a few weeks, she had enough bags to complete a braided rug to cover the floor and its cracks. The different colored writing on each bag made the rug appear to be variegated and added a warm beauty to the room.

As she sat admiring her work, she felt a need to thank Joe and Isaac for all they had done for her. They had demonstrated special skills in wood working and carpentry, but as was common in the Quarters, they had no formal education and could not read. Olivia had experience in tutoring so when the time was right, she approached Flora.

"Flora, the boys have done so much for me and I have been unable to repay them properly. Yes, I've baked them a few cakes when I have had extra ingredients but that just doesn't seem to be enough. I know that neither can read nor write. Do you think they would have an interest in learning to do so and allow me to teach them?"

Flora could not believe her ears. Her eyes met Olivia's and she hugged her tightly.

"Oh Lordy Mercy, chile, you don't know how long I has dreamed of my boys' being able to read." She shook her head. "But chile, you know how dangerous it is for you to talk 'bout dat? There's white mens around here that don't want us colored folks to read or write."

Olivia nodded, "I know Flora, but the Wards certainly don't feel that way and as long as we keep it private, I know Isaac and Joe will enjoy learning that there is a big world out there that they have no clue about."

"I don't have to ask; I know they be loving to read. Us coloreds ain't been allowed to go to school and there was none of us who could teach 'em. But girl, you has to know that this must be a secret at all costs. A colored boy in Slocomb be done got hisself roughed up when some mens catch him with a book. It weren't even his'n. He was carrying it to a neighbor's house for a white lady. Promise me, Olivia. Promise me that you be keepin' this here a secret. They's gonna be so happy. When can they start?"

Thereafter, they spent two evenings a week in the back of their shop with Olivia, huddled around a kerosene lamp. Joe and Isaac were dedicated in their studies and in a matter of eight weeks, they were reading with a modicum of proficiency from the grade school reading primers salvaged by Flora from John's closet.

By the New Year, the boys were writing complete sentences and could read and understand the waste newspaper they used to stain furniture in the shop. Given the repressive climate toward Negroes in the South at the time, they were careful not to share their newfound skills with anyone lest they be branded as "uppity" for their efforts to better themselves.

CHAPTER 20

Olivia was nearly halfway through her pregnancy now, and her most pressing concern was how she would raise enough money to care for her baby. Her flour sack rugs and pillows had been a big hit with everyone in the Quarters. The problem was that she couldn't get everything she needed via barter and there wasn't much cash money to be had amongst the residents there. Most worked in exchange for food and shelter, so she had to find a way to sell to local farmers. For many years, she had shopped for Papa and Mama at Mr. Adkins' mercantile. With the Depression deepening, she noted that he had begun accepting hand crafted items in trade. "Perhaps Mr. Adkins will stock my cakes and rugs," she thought.

Olivia had been well known in High Springs for her chocolate cake which regularly took first prize at the annual Independence Day baking contest. If Flora would allow her to use her kitchen, she could easily produce eight cakes a day. Olivia approached Flora with her plan.

"Oh Lawdy," Flora remarked. "You knows that I be heppin' you any ways I can but Missus Judy gonna know sumpin's up ifn you be using my kitchen all the time. Lemme talk to Mister Robert and see ifn we can work sumpin out for you, Sugar." Judy had been held at bay for the past few months and Olivia did not want to do anything to draw her wrath. Until she could generate some cash to buy staples like flour and sugar, and solve the oven issue, cake baking would have to wait.

.....

A few days later, Olivia heard the farm truck stop outside her shack. Joe and Isaac backed up near the door and hopped out smiling toothy white grins from ear to ear.

"You aren't going to believe this," Joe laughed. Olivia was intrigued but she was even more impressed with Joe's recently refined speech. She noted how much he had improved his use of proper English as a result of their study sessions and it warmed her heart. Isaac climbed on the back of the truck and pulled off a tarpaulin to reveal a cast iron, wood burning cook stove.

"A cooking stove!" she exclaimed. "Is it. . . Is it for me?"

"Yes," said Joe. "Mister Robert took it out of the house on a farm that just foreclosed. He said a little birdie told him you might need one."

Over the next few days, Olivia burned through a healthy stack of wood. Flora came through with some badly needed staples and the stove burned steadily as Olivia honed in on the exact cooking time needed to produce the perfect cake. Her helper, Evelyn, was never far from her side and she only mildly complained at being relegated to wood-fetching duty. At one point, after careful instruction, she had been promoted to head batter mixer but she was quickly reprimanded and summarily demoted.

"You're eating more batter than is going in the cake pan," Olivia admonished.

"Well, I can't help it. It's so good," she smiled sheepishly.

As promised, Joe and Isaac received the first finished cake and they hurried off to share their newly found bounty with Flora and Frank. Olivia surveyed her "bakery" and nodded to herself that she was ready to undertake baking for Mr. Adkins. Now to convince him of that!

Later that night, Flora appeared at her door. Frank and the boys had devoured the entire cake for dinner and all agreed that it was the best that had ever caressed their palates. They planned to go into town the next day. Flora hoped to get Judy's permission to have Olivia accompany them. At first, Judy resisted. Flora agreed with her that if Olivia was seen in town in the company of the Negroes working at High Bluff, it might be an embarrassment for her. Then, Flora saw Judy's expression change as an idea struck her.

"Yes, Flora," she agreed. "It might do Olivia some good to get into town for a change. Please be sure that she makes the rounds to all of your stops and that all of the shopkeepers know that she is my newest domestic and that she has full authority to charge whatever staples are needed for the farm."

"Yes'um Missus Judy. I'll be sure that they be knowin' she be having yore full authority. I'll say it jus like dat." Flora couldn't believe their luck. In her attempt to publicly humiliate Olivia within the community, Judy Ward did not fully understand the license that she had just granted her.

.....

The ride from High Bluff into High Springs was two and a half bumpy miles in the back of the wagon. But, it sure beat walking. As they entered the town square, Joe pulled over on a side street behind Jerrell's Drugs to allow the ladies to disembark. Flora handed Olivia Mrs. Ward's list of supplies and then she went off on her own while Olivia went in to see Mr. Adkins. Joe was parched from the trip and set off in search of the coloreds' water fountain to quench his thirst; then he returned to the wagon to wait for them.

"Hello, Olivia," Mr. Adkins called from behind the counter. "It has been some time since I have seen you and I thought you might have been sick."

"I've been helping out at the Ward farm for the past few weeks." While Mr. Adkins took a minute to absorb what she said, Olivia continued. "Mr. Adkins," I understand you are open to bartering for goods and I wanted to see if you were interested in these rugs I have made. Everyone who sees them loves them and I have a few left over for sale or trade."

He examined one of the rugs closely and remarked, "Olivia, you have created an eye-catching design and I am impressed at the way you have cut the color variations. There is no doubt that rugs like these will be gone as quickly as I put them on the shelf." He took two from her and placed them on the other side of the counter. "These are going home to Mrs. Adkins tonight," he smiled. "I'll take all that you have today. I hope to see more of them from you in the future."

"I know you prefer cash, but if possible, I'd like to trade for basil, thyme, rosemary, dill, and mint plants to start my herb garden."

"That's fine. I'll have my boy bring them around from the back for you. Except for cash, trade is better than the alternative. I don't know if some of these charge accounts will ever be paid off," he said. "These are good people caught in bad times. I just can't face God on Sunday after I've refused a farmer who needs to charge a bag of seed. It is especially true when I know that it is their last best chance to feed their family. Is there anything else you need?"

"There is one other thing," she said sheepishly. "I know you have a demand for freshly baked cakes and the ones you used to get from Dothan or Geneva were often stale by the time they arrive. Mrs. Adkins always enjoys the cakes I have baked for the church socials. Will you take a chance on allowing me to supply them for you? I promise I will not let you down."

A bell over the doorway announced two customers entering the store. As he moved over to greet them, he turned and nodded to her in agreement. "Olivia, don't leave until I am finished here. I'll be back with you shortly to finalize our agreement."

Olivia could barely contain herself as she digested his remarks. Quickly, she figured the cost to make the cakes and what she thought customers would be willing to pay for them. Understanding the mix of clientele that frequented the mercantile was helpful. She knew she would need to make a few basic cakes that were affordable to the general shopper and mix in a few special occasion cakes to the buyer who had the money but not the time to drive to Dothan or Geneva. By the time Mr. Adkins returned, she had formulated an entire menu as well as the pricing for each. He readily agreed and she promised to bake five chocolate cakes and deliver them a few days later.

"Thank you for trusting me, Mr. Adkins. I won't let you down."

"You are welcome, Olivia. Please give your mother my regards when you see her. We've missed her at church lately."

"I will," whispered Olivia as she closed the door behind her. "Oh Mama," she thought. "I hope you are not ill again."

Shortly, Flora arrived with her packages and Mr. Adkins' helper, a young boy about eleven years old, came around from the back of the building with a tray of plants for Olivia. Together Olivia and Flora set out to find Joe and the wagon to head home.

.....

The December weather was too cold to put plants in the ground just yet, so Olivia started them in a bed so that in the spring they would be ready to transplant to the small plot she had tilled near the back door. When Evelyn got home from school, she hurried down the rutted path to the Quarters to see Olivia. She was intrigued with the herbs which were much smaller than the corn and other crops grown on the farm.

"Olivia, I want to help!"

"Sure, Rabbit, you can water them daily. It's a very important job and you must do exactly as I instruct lest they get too much water and die."

Evelyn proved to be a competent assistant and Olivia grew to love her as if she were one of her own siblings. For the first time in her life, Evelyn felt noticed and her sense of self-worth soared. She hoped to one day grow up to be just like Olivia.

.....

Between her exhaustive efforts to complete Judy's extensive list, Olivia rose early and went to bed late as she worked to cut and braid rugs. Isaac made clandestine runs into town each week so that Olivia could keep her promise to deliver her cakes on time.

Mr. Adkins was pleased, and as a result, he placed a standing order for five cakes a week. She bartered for more sewing supplies, and soon, she had two requests for winter outfits from ladies in town. She had long worried that she would not have enough money to buy diapers, blankets, and baby clothes, but her business with the mercantile was proving to provide more than she needed and she was able to put away some money into a coffee can as savings.

As often as she could, Olivia spent time helping Joe and Isaac to become more literate. They soaked up her instruction and soon they were ready for more. She decided that the Bible would serve to expand their knowledge of proper English in a way much different than the primers.

Her Bible was one of the few possessions that she stuffed into her pillow covering during the final frantic and hurried moments of her last night at High Point. Mama had presented it to her when she was seven years old and it provided solace in her lonely life after the fires dimmed in the Quarters each night. Every evening, she set aside a few minutes to read from it and thanked God for His blessings. As Olivia prepared to retire for the evening, she was at peace and found joy with the expectation of the birth of her child. God was good.

.....

Flora appeared at Olivia's door with troubling news. John would be returning from college for Christmas break soon.

"I expected him to come back," she said. "But I am sure that John and his mother have no plans for our paths to cross while he is here. To be honest, that suits me fine. I'm very concerned that she may catch on to the help Joe and Isaac have been giving me and I am afraid of what she would do to them. You know she does all in her power to make my life hard and I cannot risk having your sons do anything to cause her anger to be directed at them."

"You be probably right, chile. You better plan on stayin' down low ifn you can while he's here. It's probably best for everyone that way. Don't you worry none about Missus Judy. Do you think she knows all that goes on 'round here? There is not a soul in these here Quarters dat would tell her 'bout the hep you get from us. All us colored folks knows you be a fine woman who goes out of her way to lend a hand to anyones of us needin' it."

"You have been kinder to me than my own family. All of you are God's children and I love each of you as if you were my own."

"Oh chile," Flora groaned. "You gonna make me cry." Flora smiled and patted Olivia on the back. "Don't worry chile; we gonna get through this birthing together. You gonna see. You can count on us here to hep you."

.....

Olivia's pregnancy progressed into her third trimester. Her legs and feet began to swell so that her shoes pained her as she went about her chores. Pumping and hauling buckets of water to the wash tubs caused her back to ache and prevented her from sleeping at night. It was a miserable existence.

Despite the acceptance of those in the Quarters, Olivia was lonely and so she kept busy to pass the time. More and more she became aware of the truth of Judy's words. She was truly alone.

Regardless of the respect of Flora and the others working around her, a palpable distance existed due to the likelihood that Judy might notice anyone's interactions with her and exile them from the farm. Flora was the only person who ever had a conversation with her in public. Judy never spoke to her, and Robert was cautious not to let Judy know of his behind the scenes efforts to make Olivia's life more bearable.

Evelyn, on the other hand, found a way to spend time in Olivia's company nearly every day. Often, Evelyn followed Olivia back to the

Quarters carrying with her a small pail of water to meet Olivia's household needs. She deposited it on the table and lingered to share tidbits of whatever had happened that day at school.

Olivia recognized how lonely Evelyn was and how even at the age of seven, she still craved attention and any expression of love. Neither of her parents appeared to have time for her and she was mostly left in the care of Flora. Evelyn loved to talk about her older brother John, but little did she know of his connection to Olivia.

Evelyn, like every child her age, was eager for Christmas to arrive. "Olivia, you know it is just a few days until John comes home for Christmas and I can hardly wait. He sent me a post card with a note reminding me that I needed to be good if I expect Santa Claus to visit. Don't laugh. He just doesn't realize that I know about Santa Claus."

"Well you better not tell him, Rabbit. If you do, you will likely find nothing under the tree on Christmas morning!"

"Oh no!" she shrieked. "My lips are sealed."

Olivia never let on to Evelyn that her brother was her husband, or that Evelyn would be an aunt in a few months. She refrained from any discussion of her relationship to the Ward family.

"He said that he will be home this weekend," Evelyn added.

Olivia's heart sank. She had not seen John since they had returned from Georgia, and Evelyn's news wrecked the peace that Olivia had achieved over the last month. That night, Olivia was unable to sleep as she agonized over John's imminent visit. What would the Wards expect of her? Her answer came soon enough. The day before he was to arrive home, Judy summoned her to the main house.

"Olivia, John will be home tomorrow. You are to remain in your shack until he leaves in two weeks. I have arranged for some of the colored girls in the Quarters to handle your chores. Do not set foot around this house." Judy insisted that Olivia repeat her instructions, and then added, "Understand that I will not tolerate any deviation from these instructions I have given you."

Olivia's relief was acute. She would be spared any unpleasant encounter with John, but she had not considered how Evelyn would react.

.....

119

Christmas had always been a joyous time for Olivia. With so many siblings, the preparation of the family celebration of Jesus' birth took on all of the trappings of a traveling circus. Jim and one of the brothers found and cut a massive tree from the woods. As usual, Papa oversaw its erection in the parlor and the girls festively decorated it. The air was filled with the smells of baked goods, and gaily wrapped packages anchored the tree skirting.

Olivia was deeply saddened when she realized that all of this was going on without her as she sat alone in her shack. "I will not be a stick in the mud," she thought. She intended to celebrate the birth of Jesus as she always had, even if it was on a much smaller scale. She enlisted the help of Flora to gather red berries and she made them into decorations for a tiny sapling she had transplanted into a wash pot and adopted as her Christmas tree.

She found some discarded Christmas wrapping paper embossed with stars, candles and angels in a shed behind the back porch and made ornaments from the paper. When she finished, she sat back in her rocking chair and gave thanks for what little she had. "You've come a long way from sleeping on a quilt in the Ward's kitchen," she thought.

Nearly two months had passed since she had been thrust here. In this time, she had made a home out of not much more than a lean-to and found a way to provide for her baby's basic needs. On this Christmas Eve 1930, she hummed a Christmas carol that she had sung many times with her sisters. So engrossed was she in her song that she did not hear the knock on her door or the entrance of her visitors.

CHAPTER 21

Olivia turned to find Evelyn standing in the doorway. "Look who has come to visit," she said as John stepped inside behind her. The December cold followed him like a frigid cape around his shoulders and she noticed the vapor from his warm breath evaporate into the warm interior of the shack. Evelyn rushed across the knotty pine floorboards to embrace her.

"Merry Christmas, Cotton!" she exclaimed as she held out a small package with Olivia's name written on it in charcoal pencil. Olivia stared blankly at John. "Look who I've brought to meet you. Forgive him; he is shy meeting new people for the first time."

John feigned helplessness as he shrugged his shoulders and mouthed, "I'm sorry." Olivia shook her head in disbelief. She had just begun to feel at ease with her situation and now the one person she never wanted to see again was standing in front of her. Feeling the weight of the silence, John managed a weak hello.

"Oh, Cotton!" Evelyn exclaimed and turned to John. "That's my nickname for Olivia because her hair is as fine as a cottontail rabbit," she whispered. "She calls me Rabbit," she giggled. "Cotton, I wanted you to meet my big brother John. He's always in school, at a game, or with a girl so I don't get to see him much but he's the best brother ever!" Olivia managed a weak smile and a nod. John gained his composure.

"Thank you for introducing us, Evelyn, but we should be going now. Mother and Dad will not want us to be away for very long on Christmas Eve. Tell Olivia goodbye." He had been home for three days and no one had mentioned Olivia. His mother had assured him that she would take care of the situation with her and that he was not to worry. "Goodnight, Olivia," he said as he firmly grasped Evelyn's hand and turned to leave.

Olivia interrupted their departure. "Evelyn, it was really nice of you to stop by. Thank you for the present," she said as she laid it on the table and reached to retrieve a small package. She handed it to Evelyn who pulled away from John as her eyes grew as big as saucers. "Merry Christmas,

Rabbit," she whispered. "I think you best get back before your parents send out someone to find you two."

John recognized the look of happiness on Evelyn's face as he took her hand again and led her out into the December night. Evelyn's "surprise" had upset him more than he would have imagined and for a moment, he had a bout with his conscience. Olivia sat in a lonely shack away from her family on Christmas Eve because he had wiled her with his charms. She was a good woman who had been able to survive on her own in spite of all that she suffered from their families and him. A fleeting thought passed through his mind: "This is my wife, and she carries my baby. Will I ever escape the consequences of my actions?"

.....

Olivia shivered and put another log on the fire. She missed her siblings and Mama, and tears ran down her cheeks as she considered the years to come and the attendant loneliness she would endure. But in the midst of her reflections upon what her future held, she acknowledged that in a few months, she would have her child; she would not face another holiday alone.

There was a knock at her door. She gasped, worried that John may have returned. "Who is it?" she called out. She was relieved to hear a familiar voice. Barely managing to withstand her excitement, Olivia flung open the door and Beth rushed to hug her.

"Oh Beth, I am so glad to see you. Aren't you afraid that Papa will find out that you have come?"

Beth, with tears in her eyes, turned to lift a package from the doorway and presented it to Olivia.

"We have had a hard time keeping this from Papa," she said. "But we have succeeded and now you have a present for your baby." Olivia looked in disbelief. "This," Beth whispered softly, "is from Mama." She held up a blanket and a fruitcake. "She wanted you to have it because she knows how much you enjoy this treat each Christmas." The girls hugged and Olivia cleared out a spot at the table for Beth to sit down.

"How are you, Sister?" Beth asked. "Tell me how you have fared."

Olivia relayed what had transpired in the past months and how she had been able to cobble together a semblance of a life in the Quarters and how good the residents there had been to her. Beth was aware of the marriage via Ann who could not resist telling her about Olivia's "selfishness" in stealing Ann's soon-to-be husband.

"And John?" Beth asked.

"He's nowhere in the picture," Olivia answered. "He takes no responsibility for his actions and his mother has forbidden me or anyone else to acknowledge our legal ties. Essentially, I'm a widow."

"I'm so sorry, Sister," Beth said soothingly. "I wish that Papa could understand what happened and allow you to come home to us. We miss you terribly but Papa has promised a similar fate if any of us are caught reaching out to you to help you in any way."

Olivia attempted to relieve Beth's unhappiness over her situation. She yearned to convince Beth that she would be alright. Beth hugged her and promised that she would return as soon as she could.

"Olivia," she asked. "What plans have you made regarding the birth of your baby?"

"None, so far."

"Janie Green is the wife of one of the sharecroppers at an adjacent farm and she has served as midwife to most of the local women. I will reach out to her to advise her of your situation."

"Oh Beth, you should not...," Beth put her index finger to Olivia's lips. "Shhh, Olivia it will be done."

Beth handed Olivia the money she would need to secure Janie's services. Olivia hugged her and vowed that she would get Flora to contact Janie to make arrangements for the delivery. Beth needed to hurry on her way. She had dropped Ann at the church for the evening services and would have to be there when they were over. She dared not let Ann know of her visit lest she tell Papa.

Olivia watched her make her way up the path to the roadway where she had parked and she waved a final goodbye. In the background, Olivia heard "Silent Night" wafting through the Quarters in joyful celebration of Jesus' birth. She held her hand aloft a few extra seconds as Beth's car sped off into the night. She was resigned to the fact that Beth could not risk a return visit.

CHAPTER 22

The New Year of 1931 came with Olivia growing in her pregnancy. As time allowed in the evenings, she prepared a few simple dresses for herself from flour sacks, along with blankets and smocks for the baby.

As spring bloomed, she noticed that she was having more difficulty completing her chores at the main house. Her increased size made it difficult to wash, iron, milk, and haul feed and water for the cows. Tub after tub of clean water was required for the washing. Pumping water for four tubs and a wash pot meant filling the wash pot and each tub twice. Her hands were swollen and ached so it was difficult for her to hold the pump handle firmly enough to produce a steady stream of water.

At the end of each day, she experienced fierce pains throughout her body. More than once, she had spotted blood in her underclothes. She dreaded a miscarriage and shared her fears with Flora who contacted Janie Green to let her know of Olivia's deteriorating health. Within two hours, Flora returned with an herbal tea mixture, which, Janie insisted, along with propping up her feet, would reduce the pain and swelling. Olivia diligently followed Janie's instructions and found welcomed relief.

"We's got to take better care of you," Flora cautioned. "This baby gonna be here 'fore we knows it." Olivia nodded in agreement and promised that she would make an effort to exert herself less. In the back of her mind, she knew that Judy Ward would soon double down on her promise to prevent a baby from being born at High Bluff.

"Over my dead body," Olivia thought.

.....

About a month before the baby was due, Olivia was sick all night. As the first rays of light appeared in the morning sky, Olivia dressed and trudged to the main house to start the ironing before she needed to milk and tend to the cows.

As she bent over to place the solid metal irons on the hearth, she felt a distinct wetness around her legs and she lifted her dress to reveal fresh blood in a puddle at her feet. A sharp pain pierced her midsection and she bent double and felt as though she would faint. She overcame the urge to vomit and rushed to mop up the blood.

Robert nearly collided with her as he was heading out to work. Seeing the calamity before him, he called out for Flora to help. Together, they were able to move her to the window seat where she could recline.

"Flora, what is wrong with her?" he asked nervously. "Is she dying?"

Flora cursed and said Olivia was about to lose the baby and if they were not careful, they might lose her as well. She was so enraged at the sight of Olivia's condition that she spoke before she thought. "Mister Robert, sir, it's no wonder that Miss Olivia is in this here condition what with Missus Judy has been pushing her to do every day. She ain't even giving the girl time to eat or rest. Just push, push, push all the time. Anybody's be seeing Miss Olivia was in a bad way, but not Missus Judy. No sir. Not nohow."

Robert nodded, obviously embarrassed by Judy's lack of care and compassion for Olivia.

"Mister Robert," Flora asked. "How come Missus Judy is so hateful toward this girl? She done told Olivia that it was the Lord's punishment that she be bringing a bastard chile into the world." Robert cradled Olivia in his arms as Flora applied pressure to stop the bleeding. "We all saw it," she continued. "But we couldn't do nothin 'cause Missus Judy done told us colored folks that there would be a heap of bad trouble if anyones tried to hep her."

Robert looked at Flora in disbelief. Surely Judy was not so cruel as to inflict Olivia with duties detrimental to her and the baby. Or, was she? If so, it would stop today! But first, Olivia needed attention now.

"Flora, isn't Janie Green the midwife that helps out with all of the farms around here? Please rush to find her. There's no time to fetch the doctor; he will arrive too late." Flora showed Robert where to apply the pressure and handed him fresh towels. As she departed, Robert called to her, "Flora, hurry!"

.....

Although it seemed hours had passed before Janie appeared, it was actually about forty-five minutes. Janie told Flora what she needed to do to assist her and the two of them worked for more than an hour to prevent Olivia's miscarriage. Instead, the two women helped her deliver a healthy baby girl.

When Robert looked at his granddaughter, he saw a strong individual who touched his heart. He knew that she was legitimate, but because of the timing of her birth and her conception without love, he feared that some would treat her with disdain, resentment, and rejection throughout her lifetime. He resolved to do what he could to ease her life. "She should not," he thought, "endure the scorn that Olivia had been saddled with under Judy's thumb."

"Olivia, what will you name her?" Robert asked tenderly.

She marveled at Kate's beauty and loved her more with every waking moment. "Her name is Katherine, but I plan to call her Kate for short. It is a strong name for what I imagine will be a strong girl."

"That's a beautiful name for a beautiful girl, Olivia. Kate it is."

.....

Judy Ward returned home, and hearing a commotion in the kitchen, she made her way there to investigate. What she saw before her would be replayed in the darkest corners of her mind for many years to come. It could not be! Olivia held the newborn baby in her arms as Robert sat beside her with an expression of delight mixed with concern. Upon seeing Judy in the doorway, Robert rose and marched her by the arm to his study. "Now," he said, "I know what has been going on behind my back and it is time for you and John to come to an understanding with me."

.....

Robert left Judy in the study to absorb his directives: John was to be held accountable for his actions, and beginning immediately, he was to withdraw from classes and return to High Bluff. Additionally, provided Olivia would have him, he was to begin his life as a father and a husband living as a family with her in the Quarters. Judy, for her part, was to be supportive of their marriage in every way. Anything short of that, Robert promised, she would regret.

When Dr. James arrived, he joined Robert to check on Olivia and Kate who had been moved to a guest bedroom together. Dr. James recommended bed rest for the next three weeks for Olivia. Kate, he said, was premature by several weeks but she was strong. Robert was relieved but, because of Olivia's condition, he determined that John would care for them both. He would need to grow up fast to take on these responsibilities. Would he become the man that Robert hoped he could admire as a son? Time would tell.

.....

Olivia detested her stay in the Ward home and she was determined to push herself to return to self-sufficiency as soon as possible. Fortunately, Judy had stayed away and after a relatively quiet week in the main house, Olivia insisted that she felt well enough to move back to her shack. Robert visited daily to check on her and Kate. He reveled in the experience of having a baby at High Bluff again. He had been so busy traveling to oversee his business ventures that he had missed most of Evelyn's upbringing. To his disappointment, Judy never visited them.

"Olivia," he began. "John will be home soon. Have you thought about how you and he will raise Kate together?"

"John has made it plain that he has no interest in me or Kate. I doubt seriously that I will even see him while he is home on break."

"He is withdrawing from college and will be home in a few days. Mrs. Ward and I have decided that it is time for him to assume the role he has shirked for far too long: that of husband and father." Robert paused to gather his thoughts. "He will need to move in with you and Kate so that you may live as a family. I will make arrangements for him to have a job to provide for you both."

Olivia was floored. "I…," she stammered. "I don't know what to say except that I was partially to blame for what happened between John and me. I was the older and I should have thwarted John's advances in the barn. I do not and have never desired a relationship with John as a wife or as a father to Kate; I am certain that he feels the same way."

"Olivia," he interrupted. "John must accept the consequences of his actions and become a man."

"Mr. Ward, you must reconsider your decision! I will not have John live here under this roof to live out some pretend marriage. I cannot do it. I will not do it!"

Robert put his hands on his hips. "Olivia, there will be no further discussion." He turned and walked away.

Olivia was distraught and she prayed. "Lord, please do not forsake me in my time of need," she called out loudly. "Please Lord, guide me and give me the strength to endure, protect, and provide for my beautiful Kate. Amen."

She was so engrossed in her petition to God for His blessing that she did not hear the rustling of small feet outside her window. Evelyn ran to her hiding place under the porch and cried silently as she realized that Olivia and the rest of her family had been keeping a very big secret from her.

.....

The hum of the Ford's engine and grinding of the gears echoed across High Bluff signaling John's arrival. Robert walked from his study to the front door where Judy had already positioned herself. She rushed ahead of him taking John by the arm as she nervously engaged him in idle chatter.

"Dammit," Robert thought. "She's not going to make this easy." He stepped in front of the pair to block their retreat as his outstretched hand landed firmly on John's chest. Although John outweighed him, Robert halted him dead in his tracks. "We need to talk, son."

"Uh…, maybe later."

"No, son," Robert said firmly. "We are going to talk now." Robert grasped him firmly by the nape of the neck and guided him toward his study.

"Dad?" he exclaimed. "What is going on?"

"You are about to become a man, son. Come hell or high water, by God, you are going to become a man today." As they entered the study John lost his balance and stumbled as Robert directed him toward a chair. Judy lurked in the hallway outside, but she dared not enter. Robert sat on the edge of his desk looking down at his son.

"This is the time for you to listen for a change. Your mother and I have come to an understanding and today, so will you. There will be no discussion or deviation from what I am about to tell you."

John lowered his head in disbelief. Mother's letter had warned him that his father was at wits end. Although she had promised to secure his divorce prior to the baby's birth, he knew now that she had failed. John braced himself for what was to come.

.....

Flora had been standing at the kitchen sink in the main house skinning a chicken destined to swim in a sea of dumplings when she heard the automobile's gears grind as it turned into the driveway.

"Oh Lawdy," she thought. "Missus Olivia gonna have to know that John is here and theys gonna be a ruckus real soon." She slipped out the back screen door and made her way to the Quarters to warn Olivia of his arrival. After a short search, she found her in the barn milking a cow.

"He's here."

"I heard his auto," she answered.

"You gonna be okay, chile?" Olivia nodded affirmatively. The two hugged and went their separate ways to wait. Life at High Bluff was about to change for everyone.

"You bests lay low, chile. I'll come back and check on you later today."

"Thank you, Flora," she said softly. "You've been kinder to me than anyone in my life."

CHAPTER 23

Robert Ward did not rise to become the influential businessman he was by being timid. Rather, he did so because he had a keen sense of timing and he acted at just the right time to achieve the most favorable outcome. Somehow, he thought, he had mistimed his actions in bringing up his only son. Perhaps he had relied too much on Judy to shape him into a man. He had been shaped alright; shaped into a self-centered and egotistical jerk that cared for no one more than he cared for himself. He was smart, popular, and athletic; and before Robert knew it, John had the town of High Springs in the palm of his hand.

"I pulled back," Robert thought. "I pulled back instead of taking charge when I should have. I never made that mistake in business and it sickens me to think that I have done so in rearing my son. It's not too late though. I will fix it now."

Robert stood firmly with his hands clasping the leading edge of his desk as he spoke with authority.

"John, you know my feelings concerning your behavior with Olivia Turner. There is no doubt in my mind that the child she gave birth to is your child – my granddaughter. I am beyond disappointed in you, son. While I cannot undo what we have done to foster the uncaring nature that you have, I can make you become a man who will take responsibility for his actions."

John bristled at the notion of his father's disappointment.

"So here we find ourselves in quite the dilemma," Robert continued. "You have a child and a wife who wants nothing to do with you. Olivia has made it clear she only wants a place to stay until she can get on her feet." Robert paused.

"Dad, I made a mistake. That is all. I do not need nor do I want the responsibilities of a wife and child. I have my future plans to consider…."

"What plans?" Robert interrupted.

"I have become quite fond of Margo Brown, a young woman I met at school. Her family is one with the type of standing that will advance my opportunities for business after college."

Robert could not believe his ears. "Had the boy not heard a word he had said?" he thought as he paced the room.

"Dad, I suggest that you accept Olivia's wish to be left alone and see to it that she has funds to support herself until she finds work. Then you can arrange for my divorce." John stood up to leave, but Robert turned to block his exit.

"Not so fast, son. Because of your selfishness, you have caused a respectable young lady to suffer unnecessarily. Her father has driven her from her home, and her mother and siblings have been forbidden to visit or communicate with her. To top it off, her reputation in the community and in her church has been ruined." John was visibly dejected. "Don't hang your head son. This isn't going away. You've made your bed and now you are going to lie in it."

"Dad, I'm not . . ." John was interrupted in mid-sentence by a firm slap to the face.

"You're damn right you're not!" John stumbled backward from the blow as a welt in the shape of a hand quickly rose on his left check. He was speechless; his father had never struck him or his mother in anger before.

"I'm going to tell you what you're going to do, son. You're going to follow my instructions to the very letter or I will mete out to you the same fate that Olivia has met with her family. Do not misunderstand me; it is you and me now. Your mother is not going to save you. You will not be returning to college; you are a man with a family now and as such, you need to find a job that will support the three of you. Until you can earn enough to pay for decent housing, if Olivia will have you under her roof, you may live with her and Kate in the Quarters. I will sell your car to offset your rent and I will allow you to use the farm truck when needed. As for work, there is an opening for a school bus driver, and you should consider it. That's it son. This is the life that you have made for yourself."

John looked at his father in disbelief. The term "bus driver" echoed in his ears. It was unthinkable that he would suffer the ridicule he knew would be forthcoming from many of the students with whom he had been classmates just a year ago.

Anxiety crept up John's spine. His toes and fingers tingled and he felt emptiness in his stomach. John panicked. He shoved his father aside and burst out of the room. As he passed his mother seated in the hallway, he called out to her. "Mother, you must fix this. No Ward will ever be a bus driver. I'm going to Paul's beach house with his family for a few weeks and then I will spend time with Margo's family in the mountains."

"Wait son," she shouted as she dug into her purse and withdrew a stack of greenbacks secured in a paper wrapper. "Your father has closed your bank account and you will need this." He hugged her briefly, picked up his luggage, and made a hasty retreat to his car and drove away.

.....

Despite Robert's demand that John take up residence with her, nothing could have been further from her desires. She loathed John. She knew that Robert expected her to work miracles with him but she was reticent to try. There was nothing she or anyone else could do to squeeze any redemption out of him.

Instead of focusing on fixing John, Olivia was determined to work harder to become self-supporting with one purpose in mind: find another place to live and get away from the Quarters before she was forced to concede to Robert's plan of having her live as husband and wife with John. "That," she thought, "would be my undoing if it were to come to fruition."

MCMURTRY

CHAPTER 24

The Florida state line was nearly in sight now and John whistled mindlessly as he drove with his left arm trailing in the slipstream on the side of the door. He was 25 or so miles into his 160 mile trip to the Gunderson's beach home. He hoped to enjoy the sandy paradise with Paul before he journeyed on to Raleigh for a two-week mountain vacation with Margo Brown and her family.

John spotted a wagon halfway up the hill in front of him. "Damn farmers are always taking up the road," he thought. Maneuvering into the left hand lane, he sped up to forty miles an hour as he crested the hill. Nearly halfway around the wagon, a vehicle topped the hill in front of him. John jerked the wheel to the right to avoid a collision.

"Watch where you're going, idiot," John exclaimed looking back over his shoulder. As he resumed his course, he noted that his knuckles were white from his grip on the wheel. "You have to relax or you're going to die a young man," he chuckled as he sped along.

.....

The next ten days passed quickly and John was glad to have the debacle with his father behind him. As he packed his bags and bid his farewells, he reflected on the activities of the prior week.

In addition to sunning themselves on the sugar white sand by day, he and Paul blew off steam at night by visiting several local nightclubs featuring gambling, illegal liquor, and girls. John took note of the amount of money changing hands behind the bar and opined that he might want to own a place of his own like this one day. "There's money to be made here. I hope my father won't be a prude and object," he thought. Little did he know Ward Enterprises was already one step ahead of him.

That would be a discussion for another time. In the interim, John was eager to rekindle his relationship with the girl he saw himself spending the rest of his life with.

.....

Within weeks of arriving at college, John had managed to capture the interest of one of the top beauties on campus, Margo Brown. She was a pledge of the most prestigious sorority, and it was common knowledge that she came from a prominent family in Georgia. Not only was she beautiful, she was smart and everyone enjoyed being around her.

John knew immediately that she was the one for him and he amazed himself that he never sought to behave in any way that would reflect poorly upon her reputation. Somehow, he knew that she would bring out all that was good in him. He was happy to be with her and only her and his thoughts often drifted to the "what ifs." What if they were married? What if they had children?

For her part, Margo was as smitten with John as he with her, and she wrote to her family describing her care for a football player they would soon come to know. Noting the seriousness of their daughter's ongoing correspondence with them prompted them to visit her during homecoming week.

.....

After meeting John for a brief time on Friday afternoon and at Sunday morning church services, Lamar Brown wanted to observe the young man up close and personally so he conceded that it was a fine idea for Margo to invite John to join them at their cabin in North Carolina.

The Browns were delighted with their daughter's choice. The two made a handsome couple and they concluded that she had chosen wisely. They were convinced that John had sufficient backing from his family to provide a pleasing life for Margo. It would not be too long before they had a son-in-law.

Only once during his visit with Margo did John consider Olivia and Kate. It never occurred to him that it was immoral for him to lead Margo and her parents on as to a possible future with him. To the contrary, he behaved as a young man smitten with her and he pronounced his intentions as being serious. In his mind, Olivia and Kate were mere inconveniences and he refused to face the reality of his situation.

He held onto a slim hope that his mother would find a way to eliminate these inconveniences. But as he lay in bed on his last night there, he acknowledged the truth of his situation. His father would prevail and Olivia and Kate would not be gone from his life when he returned to High Bluff. How had fate been so unkind to him?

.....

It had been a month since John arrived home from college and left in a rush for the beach the same day. Now, he was home and ready to put the matter of Olivia and her baby behind him. It was nearly eight o'clock as he pulled into the side yard by the main house. The long drive left him hungry so he left his bags in the car and set out to find Flora in hopes of her rustling something up for him. As he cut across the yard toward the main house, Flora appeared and approached him with Isaac and Joe following behind.

"Welcome back, Mister John," Flora called out. "Mister Robert is in Dothan and Missus Judy be in High Springs preparing for the July 4th celebration tomorrow. He done give me instructions for you and you best be coming with me."

"Uh, okay," John stammered. "What's this all about?" He followed the trio past the barn and down the rutted path toward the Quarters. "Where are we going?"

As they rounded the corner to Olivia's shack, John saw his clothing packed and stacked under an eave. "You need to read this here note," Flora commanded. "It's s'posed to explain everything."

John opened the folded paper and mouthed the words as he read them. "John...," he read. Scanning further down the page he stopped. "You are no longer welcome to live in the main house...."

"What the hell?" he thought as he continued reading.

He could not believe his eyes. It went on to suggest that he work out an arrangement with Olivia for his living with her and Kate in the Quarters. His father's note was clear. To receive any sort of support from his family, John would need to convince Olivia to live as Mrs. John Ward and as the mother of his daughter. If he failed to convince her, he and his belongings would be removed from High Bluff and he would be left to fend for himself on his own. John was visibly shaken and could barely contain his emotions as he read the last line.

"Your job as a bus driver will begin the second week of August and the job at the cannery this weekend. Your Father."

John was infuriated. He returned to the main house and started the Ford. Shortly, he was on the road toward High Springs to locate his mother.

.....

Judy Ward watched the arrival of her son from the gazebo in the center of the High Springs town square. The timing could not have been better for her as she was losing a debate over which color bunting to use around the gazebo. As John approached angrily, she embraced him and cautioned him to keep his voice down.

"The flowers have ears," she said softly. They moved over to a nearby bench.

"What are you going to do about this note from Dad?"

Judy shrugged lightly and frowned. "Nothing, son. There is absolutely nothing that I can do. Your father is in complete control of your life and your finances now. I cautioned you against pushing him too far and you ignored my advice. Now we must both learn to live within his guidelines."

"Surely Olivia will want no part of having me at her side. Thank God that woman hates me. This will be resolved by morning."

As he drove toward High Bluff, he faced a startling fact. It was Olivia who now held power over his future and he was at her mercy. Upon arriving, he proceeded directly to the Quarters in search of her.

.....

Walt Turner sat in his rocker by the fireplace in the parlor. Summer was in full swing and the logs lay idle before him. He slowly rocked back and forth. He had recently abandoned his pipe in favor of plug tobacco and a rivulet of spittle tracked from the corner of his mouth to his neck. As he leaned over and plunked a wad of spit into the brass container beside him, it rang out with a hollow thud. He felt a presence beside him and looked up to see his beloved Annie.

"What brings you downstairs on such a lovely summer evening?"

"I haven't seen much of you lately," she answered, grasping his hand. "I thought I might best check in on you to make sure you don't have a new little filly down here." She smiled a frail but warm smile.

"Annie, you know that you're the only filly for me. Once I experienced the champion bloodline, others will always pale in comparison." Annie blushed and rubbed his arm.

"Walt, when will enough be enough?"

Walt looked at her with wonder.

"What do you mean dear?"

"You know what I mean, Walt. Don't make me ask."

"I just can't," he replied. "It goes agin' everything I was brought up to believe and everything we have taught our children about being God fearing and living a good life."

"I know, Walt, but tomorrow is Independence Day and all of our children will be here, except one. You know that my daddy was hard headed like you, and yet he found his way to put his feelings aside to allow our courtship and marriage. Look how we've prospered, and the family we've built together. Sometimes Walt, even though they mean best, papas can be wrong."

"Hmmmph," Walt grunted in dismay. As he leaned over and expelled the plug into the brass spittoon, his eyes met Annie's and he was captivated by them just as he had been the first time he saw her on her horse at Michael's stables. Tears formed in both eyes and his heart shattered.

"I'm weak and tired and don't know how much more of this sadness I can take, Walt. It's time to let bygones be bygones." She paused and kissed his forehead. "It's time, Walt."

Walt rubbed his eyes with both hands and he sat back in his rocker. "I'm sorry," he thought. "I just can't."

CHAPTER 25

John stood in front of Olivia's shack for a few minutes before he had the courage to enter. He knocked firmly at the door and, to his surprise, Evelyn answered. She threw herself into his arms, hugging him.

"Come in," she said. "I have something to show you."

She led him to the cradle in the corner. She pulled back the blanket to reveal Kate where she lay sleeping. John could see how much Evelyn loved her niece. Her face was filled with smiles, and her conversation laden with comments about Kate's daily activities.

He was reluctant to look upon the baby. He had no intention of having anything to do with it. Yet, Evelyn's childlike behavior softened his resolve and made him curious. As he looked at Kate more closely, he was pleasantly surprised to discover that she had all the coloring and facial features of a Ward. "She even looks like me," he thought.

"Evelyn, I have business with Olivia. Where is she?" he asked.

"She's at Flora's doing something with some books. I don't know for certain, but she goes there a couple of nights a week with her Bible. Do you want me to run and fetch her? I can be back in two shakes of a lamb's tail if you want to wait. Besides, it will give you some time to get to know Kate."

"No," he exclaimed. "I'll go out and wait for her by the path." Before Evelyn could comment, he was gone.

Soon, he spotted Olivia as she walked down the path and he approached her. "Olivia, I don't know what my father has said to you, but I was given a letter from him indicating that I am no longer permitted to live at the main house, but that I may live with you and Kate if you would agree." Olivia stared at him blankly.

"That is what he has asked me to do," she said firmly.

"Well, it seems as though you are in charge of my destiny, so I ask. What do you have to say on the matter?'"

"John, your father has plagued me with this notion for weeks and I have exhausted my efforts to change his mind. I have no desire for you to forego college. As far as your hope for a divorce, I have clearly stated how much I would welcome such. Simply put, there is nothing I desire more than to find a way to cut you and your family out of my and Kate's lives.

We don't need you and we surely don't want you."

Olivia's taunt stung John's pride. He was not used to facing rejection. Rather, that had always been his prerogative in a relationship.

"I am capable of taking care of Kate provided I can depend on your father for shelter until I can get on my feet. You are free to get a divorce and get on with your life. I have nothing more to say to you on this matter." She continued along the path to her shack, leaving him standing alone.

"Wait," he said. "We cannot dismiss what my father has asked of us. He has us caught between the 'rock and a hard place.' We need each other, even if it is only for a short while."

"John, I know that you have no feelings for either me or Kate. I accept this, and I have none for you other than disdain for both you and your mother. She is a cruel and evil woman and you are a despicable cad. Do you think that I want to be with a man who has rejected his own flesh and blood? Think again!"

"Alright, Olivia, I agree, but we, at least I, don't have a choice. We must come to an accord here and now. I promise that I'll not expect more from you than your willingness to share the roof over your head and I will stay out of your way as much as possible. Between my bus route and work at the cannery, you will hardly even know that I am around. The ball is in your court and I am at your mercy. What do you say? Can I live here?"

Olivia thought for a moment. To her frustration, it was apparent that Robert had not changed his mind about John's moving in with her. She was left with few options.

"John, although we are married in the eyes of the law, I have no illusions concerning it. I value it only because it made Kate's birth legitimate. Truly, you have given me a precious gift that I suspect I would never have had were it not for you. So, if you need a place to stay, you may move in with us. You'll need to bring with you your own bed and mattress. I expect nothing from you except courteous behavior toward me and your daughter. Do you accept these terms?"

John was relieved and he left to find his father who had just arrived from Dothan. Together, they stood on the porch while John told him of Olivia's consent. He explained that he would need a bed and the information on running the bus route. Robert agreed to lend him a bed and mattress from the house, and provided him with the necessary details for the school bus route.

Robert was pleased that John displayed a mature interest in his approach to his new job. "Perhaps this would all work out." he thought. John had one final request.

"Thank you, Dad. With your permission, I would like to write a letter to explain my absence for the coming term at college. May I use my desk and papers to do so?"

"That will be fine."

After writing Margo to advise her he could no longer see her, he penned a letter to Paul to wish him well in his upcoming marriage. Then, he left the letters in the hall for Flora to post.

With nothing to do and nowhere to go, he meandered to the open stalls where the farm equipment and the old truck were parked. He climbed in the truck and prepared to spend the rest of the night there. It wasn't the most comfortable place he had ever slept, but after all, where else could he go?

.....

The next morning, John was awakened by a farm hand opening the truck door. His bed, mattress, and bedding were loaded in the back and were ready for delivery to Olivia's shack. Upon arrival, they unloaded the bed and set it up in a curtained-off alcove Olivia had made for him. The farm hand left, leaving Olivia and John alone.

"Have you eaten breakfast?" she asked. "I'll be glad to fix something for you, if you like."

"No," he said as he turned and left. She had fulfilled her part of the bargain and she was determined not to waste time wondering where he was going and when, or if, he would return.

.....

Hours later, Olivia was awakened by loud knocking at the door. Dragging herself from her bed, she opened it slightly to find John leaning on the door jamb. He could barely stand upright and he smelled like a whisky bottle. She fought the temptation to slam the door in his face and let him fall to the ground to sleep off his drunken state.

She took him by the arm and together they staggered to the alcove where he fell with a loud thud awaking Kate. Olivia removed his shoes and pulled back the curtain across the opening, leaving him lying in his clothes and snoring loudly in his drunken stupor.

The scene repeated itself over the next two weeks with John behaving the same way. He stayed out all night and slept most of the day while not awaking until he was roused by Evelyn's afternoon visit. Often, he would take time with Evelyn as she related her day's activities. His sister's loving way with Kate did not escape him. Although he and Evelyn talked, he ignored Olivia, and he displayed no interest in his daughter. Olivia's home was not his. Rather it was just a place of shelter; a place where he always could rely on having a meal and clean clothing ready for him.

.....

John's slothful ways did not escape others in High Springs. Upon her return from shopping in town, Flora sought out Olivia and relayed what Janie Green had told her.

"Miss Olivia, Mister John is headed for a heap of trouble. All the menfolk in the Quarters is talking 'bout 'em. He be done hanging out with a rough bunch of no good mens." She paused as she considered whether to let well enough alone, but continued. "My Frank is worried about 'em, and says Mister John don't seem to care what happens to hisself. Frank said he is one of the saddest people he knows."

Olivia frowned. She knew that her pleas to John would fall on deaf ears. "Only he can save himself now," she thought.

.....

Robert Ward entered Kelly's Barber Shop and immediately suspected trouble when the men seated there stopped talking and joking as he entered. They continued in hushed tones and he paid little attention until he realized they were discussing John's nocturnal activities. Because of Robert's position and success, he was envied by most and scorned by others. These men grabbed at any chance to "get his goat" and they raised their voices to ensure that he heard their disparaging remarks.

"Have you heard the latest about John Ward?" one of the men asked loudly. Several of the men then relayed in graphic detail what they either knew or had heard of his exploits with a number of women in town.

"As best I can figure, the Wards have raised themselves a depraved boy. He came home from college a first-class rebel," said one.

Another laughed loudly and snorted as he tried to tell his tale. "Would you blame him for rebelling against being saddled with an old woman and her child?"

"That's nothing," Vincent said. "I look forward to gambling with him. You know he thinks himself to be pretty smart, but I clean him out."

Peter Kelly brushed away the freshly cut hair and adjusted the seat to the appropriate height for Robert. As he did so, he leaned over. "It's your turn. You want to take your seat in the chair or would you prefer to come back when it's a little quieter?" Robert summoned all of his strength of character to respond.

"Yes, I'll take it now," he said as he ignored the men. He would not give them the satisfaction of knowing how deeply he was hurt by their remarks. As he sat back in the Koken chair, he was calm on the surface; but beneath the flowing pinstriped cape, his fingers dug deeply into the leather armrests. His anger grew with every snip of the shears. He was disappointed that his prior talk with John had not worked. He strongly considered giving up on him, but he could not bring himself to do so. At least not yet.

.....

Robert entered Olivia's shack without knocking. He slung back the curtain to the alcove and jerked John out of bed by his collar. As he staggered to wipe away the sleep and maintain his balance, Robert pointed a finger in his face as he shouted.

"You are an absolute disgrace to yourself and to this family. Your gambling and carousing have become the talk of the town and this intolerable behavior will cease immediately. No more nightly visits in town; no associating with unscrupulous men and women; no more illegal drinking. From this day forward, you will report to the cannery on time; stop gambling away your earnings; and conduct yourself as a married man with a wife and child to support. If you cannot abide by these rules, then you will be cast away from here and live your life on the streets. What is your decision?"

John, still coming out of his stupor, struggled to stand up. He was groggy but fully understood the ramifications of his father's words. The air hung heavy as Robert awaited John's decision.

Olivia, hearing the commotion, came in from the garden. Sensing John's plight, she spoke. "You are at a cross roads. If you fail to take responsibility for your actions, you will become like those who have achieved nothing in their lives except the distaste of our community. I hope that you will not come to be regarded as such. While I am powerless to change you, I am committed to one proposition. Kate and I will not continue to live with a drunken man who has no regard for himself or others. Your father made his conditions for your living here known to you at the onset; it is up to me whether or not you stay. Will you abide by his rules?"

As John listened to her words it became abundantly clear where he stood. There was no doubt that Olivia was eager to separate herself from him and his family except, perhaps, for Evelyn. She had no use for him and no desire to share any part of her life with him. He was dumbfounded, and he had difficulty in accepting this. Who was she to reject him? He would accept his father's conditions, and would deal with Olivia's rejection.

"I understand and accept what you ask."

Soberly, he admitted to himself that he, alone, had fashioned his fate into a life of unfulfilled goals and aspirations. He had lost the respect and regard of his father and gained an enforced distance from his mother. Most significant, he forfeited his chance for happiness with Margo Brown. He acknowledged, too, that he had lost the respect of many in his community. He wondered how he could survive.

CHAPTER 26

It was Thanksgiving 1931, and nearly three months had passed since Robert Ward had delivered his ultimatum to John. Throughout these months, John had generally adhered to Robert's dictates by maintaining his jobs on the bus route and working full time at the cannery. But, he did not support his family or change his attitude with regards to Olivia and Kate.

He spent what free time he had at home with Evelyn showing her the love and regard that he withheld from everyone else. In Olivia's mind, she and Kate were better off the less they saw of him and John was happy to oblige. Ann was in college now, and when she came home, he managed to sneak away with her. Their liaisons did not go unnoticed in the community.

.....

The Negroes who worked the farms in and around Geneva County were a tight knit community. Although telephones were not readily available, local gossip could easily be had in High Springs. As in much of the South, in Alabama coloreds were forbidden from sharing public facilities with whites. There were separate public rest rooms, water fountains, and even soda vending machines. Many businesses did not serve coloreds. And many that did serve them, posted signs instructing them to enter their establishments through the rear doors in the alleys and sit in designated areas.

The back alleys and walkways behind the town square served as a meeting place for colored farm workers to share the latest news as they waited for their white landowners to conclude their business. They, in turn, spread the news far and wide as they returned to the countryside. Good news traveled fast; bad news traveled faster.

After chatting with a few of the girls in the Quarters about the goings on in town, Flora felt compelled to share with Olivia the latest gossip in High Springs concerning John. "Miss Olivia, I hates to bring you bad news but Janie Green done brung me some news 'bout John." Olivia knew wild horses could not keep Flora from spilling her news.

"Janie done heard Mr. John has been seen with a mess of hard nose gamblers in the back room of the dry cleaners purty near ever' night. He goes there ever' time he has money in his pockets and those mens gang up on him to cheat him out of his monies. They says that he never catches on to their dealing from the bottom of the deck. He just keeps coming back like a fool to hand over his wages."

Having raised John from a baby, Flora felt bad for him. Olivia was less sympathetic. John was broke every payday and Olivia had long suspected that he was still under the spell of gambling. Although she took no joy in being correct, she was relieved that her suspicions were finally confirmed.

"Flora, all that you said worries me, but Kate and I are fine. We are survivors."

Olivia's sole purpose was to position herself and Kate to escape from the Quarters. Her first objective was to establish Kate's legitimacy by having others recognize herself as a married woman and Kate as the legitimate grandchild of the Wards. Doing so would smooth the road for Kate's acceptance in the community.

Since leaving High Point, Olivia had not attended church. She had once been a faithful member of the Methodist church built on ground donated by her father. It was located only a few miles from High Bluff and, therefore she could walk there in forty-five minutes, weather permitting. She was convinced that church was the place where she could begin Kate's road to acceptance. She was unsure how members of the congregation or her family would receive her, but was hopeful of a warm reception.

.....

On the first Sunday in December 1931, Olivia walked to church with Kate, now seven months old. As they entered the sanctuary, they were greeted by Mr. Adkins who offered to seat them near the back row. Olivia smiled but politely declined his assistance. With her head held high, she ignored the whispers around her as she walked down the aisle toward the Turner family pew.

She feared how Papa would react once she arrived there, but she marched purposefully onward. Few people acknowledged her and as she slid into her seat beside Beth, she prayed.

"God, please touch Papa's heart to accept me as part of our family again and give me the strength I need while I seek to worship and praise you."

Surprised by Olivia's presence, Beth smiled broadly and reached to take Kate. Mama, seated next to Beth, reached across her lap to touch her hand and squeeze it firmly. Papa stared straight ahead with arms crossed and did not acknowledge her.

At the end of the service, he exited from the far side of the pew to avoid contact with her. Beth handed Kate back to Olivia, smiled bashfully, and reluctantly followed him. Olivia had not spoken to him since the scene on the porch at High Bluff more than a year ago, and she was sad that he still bore her ill will.

As she prepared to take the solemn walk up the aisle to leave, Carolyn Gates hailed her. Mrs. Gates, who had once been Olivia's French teacher with whom she shared a warm regard, was now a grade school teacher. Aware of her plight, Carolyn was intent upon helping Olivia weather the rejection of her family as well as the members of the congregation.

"Mrs. Olivia Ward," Carolyn called loudly. "It is good to see you and John Ward's daughter in church. I have been anxious to speak to you about several college-bound students who need tutoring. Are you available?" Carolyn hooked her arm in Olivia's and led her outside to the church yard.

While Olivia was pleased with an opportunity to tutor and make some money, it was more amazing to her that Carolyn was willing to expose herself to criticism for championing Olivia and Kate's cause. After assuring Carolyn that she and Kate were faring well, she shared her plan to move into town as soon as she could locate affordable lodging.

"Olivia," Carolyn asked. "Do you have any suitable prospects for living quarters?"

"No, I don't have any at this time, Mrs. Gates, but I hope to find a room to rent until I can save enough money to purchase a small house. I'm just taking it one day at a time while allowing God's hands to guide me."

"Olivia, I believe God is listening to your prayers. You won't believe this but I just learned that the widow, Mrs. Henry Smith, is confined mostly to a wheelchair and is seeking someone to prepare meals and look in on her in exchange for room and board. She has three rooms at the rear of her house that serve as a housekeeper's quarters. Is this something that you would be interested in?"

Olivia could not believe her fortune. "Mrs. Gates, I would be thrilled to have such an opportunity. I know Mrs. Smith well. In high school, I participated in a church-sponsored program, visiting members of the congregation who were unable to attend services. I visited several times and read 'The Dothan Eagle' to her."

"Excellent! Shall we go see her together today?" Olivia was grateful and agreed. What could she ever do to repay this act of Christian kindness?

.....

The fields rolled by Annie Turner's window in a kaleidoscope of colors. She had ridden the train to Atlanta as a little girl and the loose suspension of the truck coupled with the fence rails rushing by reminded her of the gentle swaying motion of the locomotives and railcars of her youth.

"You're awfully quiet, dear," Walt said.

"I'm just enjoying the view," she responded meekly. "It was a good sermon today. And, it was good to see Olivia back in church."

"Hmmmph," Walt grunted. "It was embarrassing and it will not happen again."

"Walt Turner, surely you do not begrudge your daughter seeking Salvation? What does God tell us about judging others and forgiveness? And, what do you mean it will not happen again?"

Walt sat forward so that his diminutive frame could see over the hood of the truck. "No, of course I do not begrudge Olivia's seeking Salvation. She just needs to seek it somewhere else. As to her association with our family, I have made myself perfectly clear. She has been disowned. My family built that church and she has no place there, especially not in our family pew. I will chalk this up to a stupid girl making yet another stupid mistake; I'll not take kindly to her intruding on my family's house of worship again."

"What on earth do you mean?" Annie gasped.

"I mean exactly what I said."

Annie turned to watch the hills and pastures roll by in silence. She yearned to see her granddaughter again. It hurt her that Olivia had placed herself in such an untenable position. Perhaps Walt would soften his resolve one day. She prayed for God's intervention on Olivia's behalf.

CHAPTER 27

When they arrived at Mrs. Smith's home, Carolyn and Olivia knocked on the front door while Mr. Gates waited in the car. Mrs. Smith greeted them with a broad smile and invited them inside.

"Thank you for receiving us. I hope we have not disturbed you."

"Of course not, dear. I am so pleased to see you and reacquaint myself with Olivia again."

Carolyn continued. "I brought Olivia to see you because I think she fills the bill for the live-in companion that you advertised for." Carolyn then excused herself leaving Mrs. Smith and Olivia to talk.

Mrs. Smith was surprised to hear of Olivia's marriage and the birth of Kate. She remembered Olivia's kind treatment of her and knew she would prove a suitable companion. They quickly reached an agreement whereby Olivia would prepare Mrs. Smith's meals and check in on her during the day in exchange for her use of the housekeeper's quarters.

"Olivia, I am so pleased with our arrangement and I look forward to your moving in as soon as possible."

Not once did Olivia mention John, but Mrs. Smith assumed that he would also be moving with Olivia and Kate. Olivia said that she would return within the week.

On the way home, Olivia and Carolyn discussed all that had transpired. For the first time since Papa had cast her from her home, Olivia dared to hope that her prayers were being answered. She was not, however, without concern. "I am a little worried about moving too fast," Olivia commented.

"Why would you say that, dear?"

Olivia shared her unfortunate dilemma regarding her marriage to John and her agreement with Robert Ward. "Mrs. Smith referred several times to my 'family,' causing me to believe she thinks that John will be moving with us. I never told her that he will not be living with us."

"You are not thinking this through, dear. Because you have the Ward name, parents will agree to have you as a tutor for their daughters. Your respectability and acceptance in our community are tied to your marriage.

The Wards are influential people, and many who would otherwise snub you and Kate will be reluctant to do so. If you decide to exclude John from your home, you will not be accepted anywhere in this community. You need the protection of the Ward name that John and his parents can afford you. You have no other alternative."

Olivia was stunned but acknowledged the truth of her situation. Without John Ward, she could not hope for Kate's acceptance in the community. She was unsure how he would react to news of her impending move; but, no matter, she had to confront him to seek his help.

As the Gates drove away, Olivia looked at the shack and wondered if this place was where she and Kate were destined to remain. The shadows fell, and she looked about, reminding herself to be thankful for Kate. Whatever she faced after talking to John, she would not give up until she found a way to shelter her from the intolerance of those who were disposed to treat her as a "fallen woman" whose child they would not accept.

She dropped down to her knees beside Kate's crib and cried out in her misery. "Heavenly Father, I beseech you to have mercy on me and intervene in such a way that my innocent child does not have to pay for my sin. Grant me understanding of what you have planned for me. I know your Holy Word provides assurance that your plans for me are for my good and I pray that I may regain the respect of those who are so eager to pass judgment. I ask, too, that my faith be strengthened and that I become more receptive to your will for my and Kate's lives. Amen."

Olivia arose, a sense of peace enveloping her. She was no longer dismayed that John cared nothing for her or Kate. She now felt compassion for him as he had no other options either. Could it be that God was already working His will in her life? Now she had to approach John with her proposal.

.....

Olivia faced the monumental task of convincing John to move with her. Approaching him would be no easy job. When he was at home, he rarely uttered more than a grunt to her. Olivia waited anxiously and hoped that he would return home before midnight as was his custom on most Sunday nights. Fortunately, he did so and she arose and met him as he prepared for bed.

"John, there is something of great importance that I need to discuss with you." He sat on the edge of the bed removing his shoes and did not acknowledge her presence.

"You know that my plan has always been to stay here in the Quarters until such time that I could get on my feet. Through a stroke of good fortune, I have found lodging in High Springs. Mrs. Henry Smith is confined much of the time to a wheelchair and she has offered me the opportunity to live in her housekeeper's quarters in exchange for taking care of her. "

John broke his silence. "You may think that I am unaware of what you have gone through because of me. My father has hammered me relentlessly with his assessment of how I have hurt you and the cost you continue to pay with the loss of family, friends, and reputation. Because you tried to steer Ann away from me, I was angry and I wanted to hurt you. For a long time, I have regretted all that happened and although I wanted to tell you so, I never could find a way."

His voice wavered as he spoke and Olivia realized that he had suffered and lost much too. She was tempted to respond but resisted; she could see that he had more to get off his chest.

"Because of my immaturity, I have caused a child to be born and have acquired a wife that I neither love nor want. My reprehensible behavior has robbed me of the future that I once considered bright. You deserve better and I am happy that you have found a way out of these dreadful surroundings. When do you plan to leave?"

"My leaving is not enough. All that you say is true and we are both responsible for the unenviable spot we find ourselves in today. If you are willing to listen, I have a plan."

He nodded in agreement. He had reached the bottom of his miserable existence living in the Quarters among field hands and he doubted there was anything she could say to improve his life. But, he was willing to listen.

"John, if I had behaved as the mature woman I am, you and I would not be here tonight. I was vulnerable to your advances and our precious Kate is the outcome. Because of her, I am unable to harbor any ill feelings toward you. I know you have paid dearly for your part, and I do not wish to extract more. My regret is that you are unable to accept Kate and find love in your heart for her."

Olivia turned to John and touched his arm. Surprisingly, he did not pull away as she continued.

"You may reject my request out of hand, but I must ask you to accompany Kate and me on our move to town. Mrs. Gates has deftly explained what I can expect of the community and our church as I attempt to integrate myself and Kate among them. She has told me that the community will not accept me and Kate, alone. She was clear. To be accepted, I must re-enter society as Mrs. John Ward, your wife and Kate's mother."

John considered all that Olivia said. He had not planned on becoming a father at eighteen or marrying a woman he did not love. He had engaged in many dalliances, but one had ruined his future. No amount of regret could remove that stain on his life.

"I no longer resent Olivia, but I most assuredly don't have any love for her or Kate. What I do have is a grudging respect for this woman; this survivor of the most deplorable of conditions. She is a good woman, even if I do not desire her to be mine," he thought.

John spoke. "Olivia, what I want or do not want is immaterial. I'm in an impossible situation because I can't move back with my parents and I cannot afford to have a place of my own. What choice is left for me? I'll move with you and Kate provided ...."

Before he could finish, Olivia rose from the bed feeling cautious optimism. John stood, placing his hands on her shoulders.

"Let me finish. You must know I do not love you and never will. But, a condition for my agreeing to move with you is that you agree to our sharing a bed as a husband and wife. As distasteful as you may imagine this, you need to consider it carefully for I intend to hold you to your answer. If it is 'yes,' then we shall move together."

Olivia's heart sank. If it meant a better life for Kate, then she could accept a life with him barren of friendship and love. Kate's future was more important than any other consideration, and John was the key to that future. There was only one answer. "Yes."

As he hung his pants on the back of a chair, he said, "Tomorrow evening we'll visit my parents to tell them of our plans to move in the next few weeks. Also, we'll need to find a way to tell Evelyn. Christmas is near and we need to move as soon as possible." Olivia agreed.

.....

The next day, Olivia awakened with a renewed vigor in her step. Having reached an agreement with John about moving to Mrs. Smith's, she was faced with an even more difficult decision: what to do about Evelyn.

Evelyn had bonded with her and Kate, and with little attention from her parents, she was dependent upon them for companionship. Olivia knew once she and Kate left High Bluff, there would be a void no one else would fill. While she knew they could not take Evelyn with them, she hoped Robert would allow Evelyn to visit.

Olivia also knew she had to tell Flora, Frank, and the boys she would be leaving soon. She dreaded this even more than sharing a bed with John. Although Flora was heartbroken upon learning the news, she could not deny that Olivia's escaping the cloud of living under Judy Ward's nose would be a welcome relief. As they parted, Flora hugged Olivia and assured her she could always count on them in her time of need. Olivia hurried home to prepare for their visit with the Wards that evening. After supper, John put on his dress jacket and ushered Olivia up the rutty path to the main house, leaving Kate behind under the watchful eyes of one of the colored girls in the Quarters.

.....

As was his custom after dinner, Robert Ward retired to his study to have a brandy and read 'The Dothan Eagle' newspaper. As he tamped down a fresh bowl of Granger, Flora appeared before him.

"Mister Robert, you and Missus Judy has some callers tonight. It be Mister John and Miss Olivia."

As Robert entered the parlor, John addressed him. "Father, Olivia and I need to talk to you and Mother."

Robert motioned for them to follow him to his office. Flora retreated to retrieve Judy, but Flora returned to report that she was unable to join them. Robert asked John and Olivia to be seated and he excused himself. He was gone only a minute or two before John and Olivia heard Robert's demand that Judy join them immediately.

He returned quickly with Judy following close behind. She waited near the door and did not sit even when Robert suggested that she do so. Rather, she stood propped against one of the chairs and stared at the ceiling while never making eye contact. "What business brings you both here?" Robert asked.

John was silent for a moment while building his courage. "Dad, I wanted you and Mother to know that Olivia will be moving to High Springs in the next week. Mrs. Henry Smith lives alone, and because of her health, she is unable to continue to do so. Olivia will receive lodging in exchange for shopping and preparing meals, light housekeeping, and looking in on her throughout the day."

Before Robert could speak, Judy rushed over to him. "This is excellent news," she exclaimed. "I cannot tell you how relieved I am to hear that Olivia and that baby will no longer be living on Ward property. I have endured a heavy burden with their presence here. I must confess my surprise that an upstanding member of our community such as Mrs. Smith would agree to have them in her home. But that is none of my concern. Tell me, Robert, does this mean John can finally get a divorce from that woman and get on with his life?"

Robert could not believe his ears. He rose from his chair and glared at her. "Will you never give up? John and Olivia are married and have a child, our granddaughter. I have made it clear to both you and John before. There will be no divorce; Kate will have two parents. John, do you remember our agreement?"

Before John could respond, Judy interjected. "I don't want to hear you repeat your 'view' of their marriage again, Robert. It makes me sick; so stop! Why can't you understand that I will never accept this sham of a marriage you forced upon John? And, as to 'our granddaughter,' I'll remind you again for the umpteenth time that we cannot be sure that John is the father. I want nothing to do with either of them and I certainly don't want John saddled with them. So just accept that Olivia has found a way to manage for herself and that baby, and end this tragedy!"

John answered the question that still hung over him. "I have not forgotten our agreement and I don't intend to renege on my promise to you. Olivia and I will move to Mrs. Smith's this week and live as husband and wife. I am also prepared to acknowledge Kate as my daughter and provide the protection of my name. While I have no doubt of Dad's support, I can only request that you, Mother, give yours as well."

Olivia could not believe her ears. She did not think John capable of delivering these words with such sincerity. He did not waiver once in proclaiming his decision to live together as a family with her and Kate. Robert shared his support for their decision and hoped he would be welcome to visit them in their new home.

Judy, not to be outdone, had the last word. "I denounce everything about this move. Nothing will change how I feel about Olivia and that child, and I will not pretend otherwise just because of your sense of right and wrong." With this volley, she hurried from the room.

Olivia was afraid of what was to come from Judy. She understood from firsthand experience how vindictive she could be. Although they would move out from under Judy's nose in the Quarters, she would do everything in her power to see to it Olivia would not be accepted in their community. "So be it! If she fails to heed my warning to her about what I am prepared to do to salvage Kate's reputation, then I am up to the challenge."

Robert moved to shake John's hand, but at the last moment he embraced him, and assured him of his full support. He was proud of his son and respected him for making the "right" decision. He studied John's facial features and in them, he could see Kate's. He hoped as she grew, she would continue to favor his family's coloring and bone structure. "It might help her be accepted in the community if she at least looks like us," he thought.

Robert's attentions turned to Judy. How could she deliberately carry out her hurtful campaign against Olivia and Kate? In his heart he felt cold anger at Judy. It was not a familiar feeling and certainly one he hoped would subside quickly. "Is there anything I can do to assist in your move?" Robert asked.

"No, Dad. Since Olivia has arranged for use of Mr. Gates' truck, there's not much left to do."

Turning to Olivia, Robert added, "You have created a successful business bartering and selling your rugs and aprons. One way I can help is to have my field hands continue to collect feed bags and flour sacks for you. Flora and Joe can drop them off to you on their runs into town." Olivia expressed her profound thanks.

"Before you go, I must ask how you are going to tell Evelyn you are leaving High Bluff. Your move will be hard for her, and we need to find a way to help her understand you are not abandoning her. Perhaps she can visit?" Olivia was touched. She smiled and assured him both would be welcome visitors.

With a heavy heart, Robert waved goodbye. On one hand, John was becoming a man and accepting his responsibility as a husband and a father. On the other, their close relationship as father and son would change forever. Now, John's loyalties would lie with his wife and child. Robert's sorrow was compounded as he considered another significant loss, his loving regard for his wife.

Because of Judy's behavior, coupled with her vindictiveness, he felt his heart harden toward her. "My losses this night have come with high costs. For the remainder of my life, I'll exist without the unconditional love of a son and with a distance toward my wife that I can never close," he thought.

Furthermore, he considered his relationship with Evelyn. She was the result of an unplanned pregnancy and one that Judy deeply resented. From the time of her birth, Judy had as little as possible to do with Evelyn's life. As a result, both he and Judy had an emotional distance from their daughter. Robert was determined to avoid Evelyn's suffering a fate similar to John's. Given the news she was about to learn, he suspected she would need comforting by at least one of her parents.

.....

John and Olivia were relieved that the task of telling his parents about their impending move was behind them. They deeply appreciated Robert's vocal support; however, they dreaded Judy's response. In spite of Robert's stern warnings, they knew Judy would do all she could to make Olivia and Kate's lives intolerable.

CHAPTER 28

The weeks leading up to Christmas 1931 were busy ones for Olivia as she packed and prepared to move her family to High Springs. She managed, however, to always make time for Evelyn. Olivia faced the unenviable task of breaking the news of their move to Evelyn. She asked her to take a walk with her; and as they walked the fence line, Olivia carefully explained that she, Kate, and John had simply outgrown their shack in the Quarters.

"You remember, Rabbit, I told you once that your parents allowed me to live here until such time as I could make it on my own. Now that John is working steadily, we don't need their help like I did when I moved here. One day, you too will outgrow High Bluff yourself and you will go off to college to spread your little wings...,"

Evelyn interrupted, "Rabbits don't have wings, silly."

"You're right, Rabbit, but as I was saying, when we move, your father has promised to bring you to visit us as often as possible. It will be fine. You will see."

Evelyn hugged Olivia around her waist. "I will sure miss you, Cotton. I really will."

Olivia pursed her lips but managed a smile for her beloved Evelyn. "Me too, Rabbit. I really will."

.....

Olivia braced herself against the wooden sides of the 1927 Bluebird school bus as it rocked to and fro over the wagon wheel ruts in the shortcut to High Springs. She held Kate tightly to keep her from sliding off the bench seat beside her. She felt a bout of nausea coming on but she managed to stifle it lest Kate become sick too.

"It's just a little bit further," John said. "This shortcut cuts ten minutes off my trip in to pick up the school children in the mornings. Isn't it great?" Olivia nodded in uncertain agreement.

Soon, they arrived at Mrs. Smith's where he dropped them off and went on to his job at the cannery. Olivia settled Kate in a makeshift playpen; then she and Mrs. Smith developed a timetable for meals and household chores. Later Olivia rummaged through the attic, identifying pieces of furniture she could use. After dusting and placing them in her rooms, Olivia left Kate napping in her playpen while she took care of a few errands for Mrs. Smith.

.....

Olivia had always been well received in High Springs and many ladies remarked that Olivia was the model genteel woman they wished their daughters to emulate. Now, as Olivia made her way around town, she quickly discovered integrating back into the High Springs social setting would be more difficult than she had imagined.

She had several stops to make: Adkins' mercantile, the post office, and Jerrell's drug store. At every stop, she attempted to engage each passersby in general conversation or exchange pleasantries. To her dismay, her attempts were ignored by most or just greeted with cold responses. She had to face it; she met down-right rejection, plain and simple.

As she went from place to place, she realized what had happened and thought, "Judy Ward has beaten me to the starting gate, but this race is far from over. We will see who is left standing in the winner's circle when the dust clears."

True to her determination, Olivia held her head high and greeted everyone she met with a resounding 'good afternoon' or 'how do you do'? Those with malice in their hearts were surprised by her outward positivity, and others were pleased to hear that she would be a regular about town again.

.....

As their moving date approached, Olivia reached the limits of what she could handle by herself at Mrs. Smith's. Flora agreed to stop by while she was in town and she worked to arrange Mrs. Smith's pantry and root cellar to store the jars of canned vegetables, soup, and meat Olivia would bring with her.

"I's got this placed jus like mines at home," she said. "You won't have no problems finding what you needs when you needs it, chile."

"I'll think of you and Frank every time I'm down here, Flora," Olivia remarked. "Once again, you've helped me and I have no way to repay you."

"Them chickens and the vegetables Isaac and Joe gonna be pick'n from you garden in the spring are mo' than enough thanks for us, chile. Besides, you is family to us."

Soon, the time came for Flora to head back to High Bluff. With Flora gone, Olivia was alone with Kate and as she surveyed their handiwork, an unpleasant thought crept into her mind.

"It will be Christmas soon. Surely Papa will relent and allow Kate and me to spend the holidays with my family," she thought. Such was not the case, and she would spend yet another Christmas alone with Kate.

.....

Very early on Saturday morning before Christmas, Mr. Gates' flatbed truck arrived to move their things to their new home. Olivia had everything ready and within an hour, they were loaded and on the road to High Springs.

John and Olivia placed Kate in the bus and prepared to follow when they saw Robert and Evelyn walking down the rutted path from the main house. Olivia wished they had left before Evelyn's arrival. It was hard to witness her acute sadness as she watched them depart.

Robert witnessed the closing of a chapter in his life. His son was leaving to make a home elsewhere and Evelyn's sense of loss wasn't something he could easily change. "How different our lives could have been," he thought. "We could have been a family rich with the blessings of a remarkable daughter-in-law and the birth of a pretty little girl. Judy and I could have been a family in which Evelyn could be happy and grow to mimic the traits that make Olivia the strong and honorable woman she is. But, we have failed our son, our daughter and ourselves."

.....

John remained seated in the bus as the men unloaded their meager possessions. Within an hour, they were finished and took their leave. Olivia served a cold lunch for Mrs. Smith and did not bother John, who remained in the bus for a time, contemplating the events that had transpired to bring him to this point.

While he was relieved to have worked his way back into the good graces of his father, he knew that his decision to move with Olivia had deeply upset his mother. He had escaped the sentence of living in the Quarters, but he still was shackled with Olivia and Kate. It wasn't that he did not respect Olivia. To the contrary, he was amazed at how she had managed to create a livelihood for herself and Kate while living in a shack under deplorable conditions.

This acknowledgment of Olivia's character unnerved him. His shortcomings were magnified and he experienced an acute sense of regret for his part in her predicament. "I've contributed nothing to what Olivia has accomplished. I have an overwhelming feeling of uselessness, but I'm glad my daughter is out of the Quarters."

As he watched Olivia take inside the last few odds and ends from the yard, John's emotions got the better of him. Their entire "arrangement" was awkward, and he began to question how he could spend an evening with her in this strange place. His mind raced and he felt the walls of the bus closing in around him. He had to get out of here before Olivia came looking for him. Surely some of his friends would be out celebrating the holidays and he could find companionship with them. Besides, Ann was home from college and she would probably be among them.

.....

Olivia was not surprised John was gone. She and Kate ate alone, and then Olivia went to help Mrs. Smith prepare for bed.

"Olivia, I have been thinking about your baking and it occurred to me that you could speed up your work if you baked in my two large ovens rather than in your tiny one. Besides, I certainly would enjoy the company of you and Kate."

"That is wonderful news, but are you sure that Kate will not disturb you?"

"Absolutely not," Mrs. Smith chuckled gleefully. "So it is settled?"

"Yes," Olivia said as she rose to leave.

"Wait a moment, dear. I have an untended garden plot behind the shed which my hired man planted and harvested for years. It has lain barren for a while now, but it wouldn't take much to get it ready. I could pay someone to till the plot and we could share the produce. What do you think?"

Olivia lifted her head and silently thanked God for these blessings. She clasped Mrs. Smith around her shoulders, hugged, and thanked her. "We will have the best garden you can imagine. I'll make the arrangements for as soon as weather permits."

Mrs. Smith was overjoyed. She had been lonely since her beloved Henry had died and Olivia's prepared meals and Scripture were just a scratch on the surface of the pleasure she had felt over the past few weeks since Olivia had begun to visit her. Kate's laughter and Olivia's kind smile brought her a sense of optimism and encouragement that had been absent for many years.

.....

It had been an exhausting day. After she put Kate to bed, Olivia sat in her rocker reading her Bible, hoping to gain peace of mind. Her agreement to share a bed with John pierced her thoughts. Exactly what did he have in mind? The idea of his coming home drunk scared her and she had no idea of how she would handle him. She pulled the covers over herself, and moved as far as possible to one side of the bed. Before turning off the lamp, she prayed to God to protect her. She waited.

She thought it was about midnight when she heard John come into their bedroom. She lay very still with her back turned to him, hoping that he would undress and go to sleep without incident. He sat down on the edge of the bed and took off his shoes. The odor of his musky socks was strong but did not overpower the smell of whiskey. He lit a lamp and held it over Olivia's head.

"I know you are not asleep, so don't pretend to be. I have news for you. I saw Ann tonight and we were together until Beth picked her up. She is as taken with me as she ever was and has no qualms about being seen with me in a way not acceptable of a brother-in-law visiting with his wife's sister. Ann said that your father has forbidden any mention of you or your child. Furthermore, he is not going to allow you to sit with them in church. Boy, I thought Mother was unkind, but your father's actions just might take the cake."

Olivia knew there would be no sleep or peace for her for the rest of the night, so she arose to stoke the fire in the sitting room. The light and voices awoke Kate, who cried until Olivia consoled her. John staggered over and stared down at her. She did not fully understand what he was capable of in his drunken state and she was afraid. As he extended his hand toward her, she recoiled and shielded Kate. Instead, he touched Kate's tiny hand, smiled at her, and spoke.

"Olivia, Kate is such a pretty baby. You would be pretty, too, if you made any effort. I have never understood why you were content to remain as an unpaid housekeeper for your family and just let life pass you by."

"John, what I did or did not do is in the past. The life I sought was that of a nurse, but I could not pursue it. I made the best of the situation knowing that no man would marry me when I could not separate myself from the responsibilities of my family." She paused while considering what more to share with him.

"Although it was not of my choosing, it took your actions in the barn to break my bonds of servitude. You seem to pity me now, and I ask you to stop. Because of your actions I have lost my family, my reputation, and my acceptance by most in our community. But God has helped me realize I have gained so much more. I have a precious daughter."

Her words were sobering and caused him to stagger backwards slightly. As he moved away, he turned back. "You know, I could have had Ann in my bed tonight. She was ready and willing but I couldn't. Even for a reprobate such as I, there are limits to what I'll do. I know that you and others consider me a cad, but tonight I was unable to behave as one. Damn it all, I thought of you and Kate and refused what was offered."

His remarks caught her off guard. Did she and Kate really mean something to him? She had no answer. She urged him to go to bed while reminding him that he was expected at the cannery the next morning. Olivia rocked Kate while debating whether to sit up the rest of the night or return to her bed. She had agreed to share it with John as a condition of his allowing Kate and her to live under the protection of the Ward name. Now, it was time to uphold her end of the bargain and she hoped he would be sound asleep by the time she joined him.

Olivia awakened with a sense of relief. John had not moved all night long and she felt a little embarrassed at her preconceived notions about him. Her fears of his behavior the night before were baseless and she took care not to disturb him as she rose and prepared Kate and herself for church.

.....

Although her walk to church from Mrs. Smith's was not as long as it had been from the Ward's, Olivia hurried to avoid being late. Kate squirmed in her arms the entire way, but they still made good time and arrived nearly 15 minutes before services began.

Olivia approached several of the women whose daughters she tutored, but only one, Charlotte Parker, acknowledged her. The other four turned from her while telling Mrs. Parker they needed to be seated before the service began. Carolyn Gates witnessed the scene and came to Olivia's rescue.

"Charlotte, I know how much Mrs. Smith means to your family and you are concerned that she is alone without any help. If you have not visited her lately, you may not know Olivia is taking care of her now." Charlotte responded she knew her friend was desperate for reliable help.

"That is true and don't you agree that Olivia is such a blessing to her?" Charlotte nodded in agreement as Carolyn turned to Olivia.

"Why Olivia, I forgot to tell you, I was in the bank this week and overheard your father-in-law, Robert Ward, going on and on about his granddaughter, Kate. He is so proud of her and was high in his praise of you."

"That is so nice," Charlotte said.

"Yes it is. And according to Robert Ward his daughter, Evelyn, thinks Olivia walks on water. He cannot get over your generosity in permitting him and Evelyn to visit without an invitation."

Charlotte responded, "I was unaware that Mr. Ward held Olivia in such high regard. It seems that the gossip I have heard is untrue. Olivia, come to think of it, I really need some new outfits. Will you have time in the coming weeks?" As Carolyn led her into the church, Olivia assured Charlotte that she would make time to sew for her.

With Charlotte safely out of hearing range Carolyn remarked, "Olivia, a wall does not fall in a day. Rather it crumbles brick by brick over a period of time. So it is with people's prejudicial thoughts and practices."

Carolyn took her seat beside her husband while Olivia settled into the pew directly behind Beth and Ann, on the Turner family pew. Beth was aware of Olivia's presence, but did not turn to speak to her. As they bowed their heads for prayer, Beth dropped her hymnal and pushed it under the bench with her foot. Olivia, careful to avoid attention, picked it up, removed a tiny piece of paper, and pushed the hymnal back under the pew. She discretely unfolded the note and silently read its contents.

.....

Olivia was dejected as she carried Kate outside after church. While most in the congregation knew of her marriage to John, it did not appear to change their stark rejection of her and Kate. Considering these were fellow parishioners with whom she had worshiped for many years, their continued rejection was painful. But it was nothing compared to the hurt of her family's rejection. She could not describe her feeling of isolation.

As Olivia walked toward home, she read Beth's note again. She would visit Olivia after work the following afternoon, but it would have to be brief to avoid Papa's questions should she arrive home from the cannery later than usual. Olivia was elated and she could hardly wait; she had so much catching up to do about each of her siblings.

It took Olivia another ten minutes to reach Mrs. Smith's and when she arrived, Robert and Evelyn were standing with John at the entryway to their quarters. Robert carried a bundle of flour sacks Flora had collected for her, and Evelyn ran to meet them. She wanted to hold Kate but she was too big for her to carry. Instead, Olivia suggested they go inside where Evelyn could play with Kate on the floor.

At seven months, Kate was impatient with crawling and was taking her initial steps. She was rapidly developing both her motor and communication skills. Moreover, she was developing an independent nature. Now that Kate could interact with her, Evelyn expressed her delight in her niece's progress toward becoming a more enjoyable playmate.

Olivia was surprised John was home on a Sunday afternoon. He shared his challenges of managing the older boys on the bus route and listened patiently as his father spoke of his recent business trip to Florida to inspect his cattle herd near Bonifay. Robert was proud of John's new responsibilities he had undertaken at the cannery.

Always the consummate hostess, Olivia listened intently and at the first opportunity she asked if they would like refreshments. They declined the iced tea she was preparing for Evelyn, but readily accepted slices of pound cake. More than an hour passed before Robert prepared to leave. He and Evelyn stopped in the doorway and he turned to his son.

"I would be remiss in leaving without commenting on what a pleasing home Olivia has created for the three of you. I can imagine how proud you must be of what she has accomplished."

John smiled, "I agree with you Dad. I am amazed at all that Olivia had done in just two short weeks."

Olivia listened in wonderment. Surely John was not praising her efforts. At times, she wondered if they could find a way to cope with their situation so that Kate could grow up as part of a real family. Each time, she faced its improbability. John's words were encouraging and for the first time, Olivia allowed herself to consider it might happen. Evelyn clung to Olivia's arm while pulling her down to whisper to her. After listening intently, Olivia smiled and turned to Robert.

"Mr. Ward, when school starts, would you permit Evelyn to ride the bus to Mrs. Smith's some afternoons? I could help her with her homework assignments and Kate and I would really enjoy having her here. You could pick her up on your way home from work."

Unexpectedly, Robert's look turned sour and Olivia wished she had not asked in the presence of Evelyn. "I'll discuss this with her mother, but I am afraid she will not agree to this arrangement."

Evelyn cried, "Please, Daddy. Let me visit with Olivia and Kate."

Robert ushered Evelyn to the car and assured her he would try to work something out. John ran to catch up to them and asked, "Are you headed back through town? If so, may I have a ride with you?"

As she watched John leave without so much as a word to either her or Kate, Olivia was enveloped with an unexpected sadness even the anticipation of Beth's visit could not assuage.

.....

The haze of cigar smoke hung heavy in the room. A wave of John's hand cut through the dense fog like a knife. He tossed four cards on the makeshift table fashioned from an olive oil barrel in front of him. "I'll take four," he said as he swigged from a mason jar of clear liquid.

The dealer, a portly man in his mid-fifties named Wallace, peeled off four cards and tossed them in John's direction. John studied them closely. "Jeepers," he thought. "That's three straight hands in a row I have drawn pairs. This game is easier than I thought." He tossed four chips onto the pile and raised the ante. "I'll bet four," he said with a grin.

"Fold," Jasper said in an exasperated voice. Vincent and Alvin quickly followed suit.

"I'm out too," Wallace said. "You are cleaning us out tonight. I'm going to have to ask one of these boys for a loan just to buy my next stake."

"Sorry about that," John said. "I guess I'm just getting all the cards tonight."

"Yeah you are," Wallace chuckled. "Say, you wouldn't mind if we raised the stakes a little to give me a chance to win back some of my money from these clowns, would ya? I gotta pay your daddy my mortgage tomorrow and he'll be real mad if I'm late. What do ya say pal?"

"Uh…, yeah," John said with a hint of hesitation. "I guess we can do that." He scraped his winning off the table and set about stacking his chips.

"That's a wise decision, young man. Ride Lady Luck while she's hot. That's what I always say," Wallace said as the other four men chuckled. "Shuffle these cards good, Vincent. I feel like my luck is about to change for the better."

Vincent nodded in agreement as he shuffled, cut the deck several times, and dealt the next hand. "What do you say we make deuces wild, Wallace?"

"I love deuces," Wallace said, "almost as much as I like pigeons." The men chuckled as they examined their cards. John had an uneasy feeling.

CHAPTER 29

On Christmas Day 1931, Olivia spent the day alone with Kate. John was nowhere to be found. At first, Olivia suspected he was at High Bluff with his family. Then she remembered the Wards always spent Christmas in Tallahassee with friends. Judy must have felt a sense of victory to have John with her for the holiday without Olivia and 'that child' in tow.

Olivia sat beside her tiny tree with Kate as she opened her presents. Although her baking and sewing businesses were doing well, Olivia had little extra money to spare and she was sad she had only been able to make and wrap a few meager trinkets for Kate. The dark cloud lifted quickly though, as she marveled at Kate's wonderment. She was particularly fond of a stuffed rabbit Olivia had sewn from scraps of velvet material. Kate rubbed the silk lining of its ears against her nose and giggled.

"This, is perfect," Olivia thought. She and Kate would spend many Christmases to come just like this. Her heart was warmed by her vision of their sharing a few happy moments together cast against the backdrop of their continued rejection in the community. Olivia was grateful for what they had and thanked God for Kate who alone was worth more than King Midas' gold.

.....

Within a week, the New Year was upon them. John returned from Tallahassee early to work at the cannery and his routine did not change as he continued to come home later and later every night. She wondered why he even bothered putting up a front to their marriage. It was nearly one o'clock in the morning when Olivia heard John noisily make his way into the bedroom. She was relieved he did not smell of alcohol and she let out a silent sigh of relief. Or so she thought. As he undressed, John spoke.

"Olivia, I know you're awake. I can see your eyes and slight movements in the moonlight."

Without responding, Olivia moved closer to the edge of the bed and away from him "You know, you are not the only one that suffers ridicule in this town. I am reminded by my so-called friends of the pitiful life I have made for myself. I must say, though, Paul has never said a harsh word about you or our travesty of a marriage. He's the only one who behaves toward me as a friend. I saw him this afternoon as he was preparing to leave for college and he spoke of how happy he was at the prospects of his coming marriage. He asked me to be one of his groomsmen. Do you have any idea what this meant to me?"

Olivia was unsure if John expected her to respond or not, so she made no response. "I refused him. Can you believe that? He is my best friend and I refused him."

"Why, John?" Olivia asked weakly.

"I told him my presence there would probably cause him embarrassment, and I could not let that happen."

"John, I am so sorry. I know how close you two have been and it is understandable he would want you involved in this happy time in his life."

"He amazed me this evening by putting everything into perspective. He laid it out as to the harsh gossip others have generated about us. I am the joke of Geneva County; a boy who is stuck, married to an older woman with a child that no one believes is his. To top it off, I was supposed to go to college and return here one day to run my father's businesses. Yet, all I am is a lowly school bus driver who works part time at a cannery to try to make ends meet. I was the valedictorian of my class for God's sake." He leaned forward with his head in his hands.

She was tempted to pat him on the back to console him, but she knew her compassionate touch would be unwelcome.

John continued, nearly in tears now. "You know, Paul was not trying to be unkind to me. As he said, many in this town welcome the opportunity to take me down a notch. He thinks, and I agree, the 'old biddies' in town relish their rejection of you and Kate, and they have made it into some kind of game."

Olivia listened intently. That is what John needed in this moment. In the dim light she saw in his face abject misery. How well she knew the feelings he was describing. He lay back, staring at the ceiling without speaking. His chest rose and fell quickly and Olivia could tell he was becoming more emotional with every waking moment.

"We are both stuck in this so-called marriage neither of us wanted. If

I must endure this public ridicule, then I will at least get something out of it."

Suddenly, John turned toward her and pulled her to him by her nightgown. Olivia felt his dank, stale breath as she found herself face-to-face with him. The moonlight beaming through the curtains cast a soft glow upon his face and she could see his determination.

"John, what do you mean? You're hurting me. Please let me go." She attempted to pull away but he held her tight, putting his arms around her to still her movements.

"What do I mean? Olivia, tonight I plan to show you what sharing your bed means."

Olivia struggled against him while attempting to break his grip on her wrists.

"John, I know you're not drunk and you know full well what you are doing. Please! Release me!" she begged. Her efforts to shed his grasp were unsuccessful so she relaxed and lay perfectly still in hopes her plea had gotten through to him. She thought of Kate who was asleep and kept her voice low so as not to awaken her.

"Yes," he said. "I know what I am doing. I could say I am going to make love to you, but that would be as big a lie as our marriage. You know what my condition was for living with you so I don't owe you any explanation. I'm going to exercise my marital rights tonight and any other night as I see fit. Take off your gown if you do not want it ripped off. Do not resist me."

Hearing this, Olivia renewed her efforts to push John away. But, even with all of her strength, he was too strong for her. As he pulled on her gown, she stopped fighting him and accepted what she knew was to come. As he groped at her, she stayed his hands and removed her gown. Her face contorted with emotion as she reconciled herself to the role of 'unwilling wife.' She only wished the curtains were thicker so she could not see John's face and he had a less vivid view of her body.

As he mounted her, she lay still as he took his pleasure of her. Just as in the barn, it was quickly over and he turned from her and fell fast asleep. Olivia then crept from the bed to the dark kitchen where she went about cleaning and dressing herself. Then, she settled into the rocking chair where she sat for the remainder of the night. She was embarrassed and wondered how she could face John the next morning.

At daylight, Olivia started breakfast before Kate awoke. She was taking a pan of biscuits from the oven when John came in already dressed for the day.

"Good morning, Olivia. Something smells good," he said as if nothing were out of the ordinary.

"Your breakfast is ready," she answered, playing along with his charade. "And, I have fixed sandwiches for your lunch. Here's your coffee. I'll let you eat in peace while I take care of Kate."

Soon, she heard the door open and shut as John left for the day. As she went about her morning chores, she could not get out of her mind the image of what had transpired the night before.

.....

Later that morning as she set a plate before Mrs. Smith, it was evident Olivia had something on her mind.

"Are you alright this morning?" Mrs. Smith asked. "You seem preoccupied, dear."

"It is nothing ma'am. I just have a lot to accomplish today and my sister Beth plans to stop by this evening when she leaves the cannery. I've got a special order for cakes from Mr. Adkins; if you don't mind, I will use your ovens this morning."

"Of course, dear. While you get your things together for baking, why don't you leave Kate in the playpen? I'll watch her and you can work faster without her being under your feet."

Olivia agreed and spent the morning baking and icing the cakes. After she finished, she made lunch for Mrs. Smith and Kate before putting Kate down for a short nap. Once the icings were set, she loaded Kate and the cakes into the pull-wagon and set out for the mercantile. Traversing the muddy road in the cold and damp weather was no easy task, but one Olivia gladly undertook to provide for Kate.

.....

Olivia settled herself in the front room and listened for the sound of

Beth's car. It was not long before she arrived and Olivia opened the door before she could knock. Olivia rushed to hug Beth tightly.

"Beth, I have been anxious all day hoping that nothing would deter your visit. It has been so long since we have been able to share time and I have missed you terribly. Come in and tell me all about our family, especially Mama."

Beth's attention was immediately focused on her growing niece. "She looks like she has grown since I saw her at church last."

"Yes, she is growing like a weed."

As she reached down to hand Kate a toy, Beth was saddened knowing that Mama could not share in the experience of seeing Olivia and getting to know her granddaughter, Kate. "She is so beautiful and you can certainly tell she's a Ward. She has all the coloring and facial features of John and his father. Surely no one can deny that." Olivia shrugged. She only wished Beth's assumptions were true.

Olivia picked up Kate. "Would you like to hold her? I must warn you that she is an eager little thing who likes to explore. She is determined to stand up on her own, and may try to wiggle away from you. Just this week, she has been attempting to walk."

Beth took Kate in her arms and moved to the rocking chair. "Olivia, do you know how much I have missed you? Before seeing you and Kate at church these past two Sundays, I had not seen you since the night I stopped by to deliver the baby items Mama and I had put together for you. The only way any of us knew about Kate's birth was from Mr. Ward who had come to tell Papa.

Papa would not speak of it, but Mama shared with me that you had delivered a baby girl, earlier than expected, and both of you were alright. The only time I have ever heard Mama raise her voice to Papa was when he refused to take her to see you and Kate." Olivia pursed her lips. Hearing that Mama wanted to see her and Kate but had been forbidden by Papa was nearly more than she could handle and her heart hurt.

Beth wanted to know every detail of Olivia's new life so she shared what she had endured while living at High Bluff. Beth was taken aback. The thought of her sister living in the Quarters in an abandoned shack was upsetting to her beyond description. Olivia, typical of her nature, downplayed the hardship and assured Beth all that she had encountered while under the Draconian-style rule of Judy Ward was worth it when she held Kate in her arms. Beth wondered if Papa would be so resolute in his rejection of Olivia if he knew of the obstacles she had to overcome.

Olivia realized that their limited time together was passing quickly and she asked Beth how Ruth, Ann, and her brothers were doing.

"Thomas, Harry, and James continue to improve their farmsteads and increase productivity. James and his wife are the parents of twin boys, and Thomas has added a daughter to his family."

"What about Ann and Ruth?" Olivia asked.

"Not much has changed with Ruth. She and David still live in Florida where he continues to pastor at a thriving congregation. Ruth was unable to teach while she was expecting her son, but from her letters we gather she is stronger now. We don't hear from Jerry often but in his last letter to Mama, he wrote how well things were running with the sugar cane plantation. As for Ann, the only time we hear from her is when she comes home from school on holidays."

"Everyone is doing so well," Olivia responded. "It seems like just yesterday we were all around the Christmas tree as a family. It is hard to believe that it has been nearly two years."

"Olivia, this may come as a surprise to you but I think Papa has come to realize all that you did for us on the farm. Since you left, we've had three different housekeepers. And, in spite of the scarcity of work for them in the community, not one would stay more than a couple of weeks. As for Mama, she is distraught because Papa will not let her see you and Kate. Seldom does she get out of bed, except to go to church on Sundays."

Beth continued. "I have gone on and on about all of us, but I have not learned anything about how you are getting along. I am grateful you and Kate escaped that run down shack and now have this comfortable place, but I continue to hear gossip at the cannery about John's activities and how you are shunned in High Springs. It must be horrible. Tell me, Olivia, how are you?"

"How am I? I am managing as best I can. I have a decent place for Kate and me to live and I have found a way to support us. While I am not optimistic I'll ever be regarded as more than a fallen woman with a bastard child, I have received some well-intentioned support from a few of the ladies in town. Carolyn Gates has been a true friend who has given me sound advice about my situation. Through her guidance, I have come to realize that living with him as Mrs. John Ward under the façade of a happy family is imperative if I am to help Kate. But Beth, you cannot imagine at what cost. I had to agree to share his marital bed and it had not been an issue until last night when...," Olivia stopped. Beth rested her hand on Olivia's arm to reassure her.

"Last night," Olivia continued. "I had to meet his terms and give in to his lust."

Beth was dumbfounded. How could her sister suffer more? "Is there any other way for you?"

Olivia eyes filled with tears. She did not want Beth to be burdened with her troubles. "I am better off now than I was the night Papa dumped me on the lawn at the Ward's. Please assure Mama I am faring better than I could have expected. For now you must go, but please come again whenever you can without incurring Papa's wrath."

With a heavy heart and a face full of tears, Beth rose, handed Kate to Olivia, and left.

If anything, Olivia was a pragmatist and she recognized the futility of wishing for that which would not materialize. Except for 'stolen' visits such as these, she was estranged from her family, and she accepted the finality of her situation. As she readied Kate for bed, another thought persisted. "What was to be her fate with John?"

CHAPTER 30

In the following weeks of January 1932, Olivia worked to establish routines for herself and Mrs. Smith. They had bonded quickly, and taking care of Mrs. Smith was a pleasure. She looked upon Olivia and Kate as the family she did not have, and she enjoyed witnessing Kate's growth as she matured from baby to crawling infant. It wasn't long before she grew into a toddler, cruising around while holding on to furniture.

John continued with his usual activities. He rose early and worked a split shift at the cannery between his bus runs. Then, he hung out at Jerrell's or in the backroom of the dry cleaners where a game was always in progress. He paid little mind to Kate, but did not rebuff her when she wanted his attention. Occasionally, he would share some incident that occurred on the bus or at the cannery with Olivia, but generally remained as distant as ever. The lone exceptions were the times he exercised what he considered to be his marital rights.

The weather was cold and wet causing the dirt roads to become treacherous for travel. Olivia had an increasingly difficult time pulling the wagon with the weight of Kate and the cakes without having it overturn. Mr. Adkins offered to have Ben, a part-time employee of his who lived close to Mrs. Smith's house, pick up and deliver her cakes. This saved Kate from exposure to the bitter cold and provided more time for her sewing efforts. "Things are looking up," she thought. "God has truly blessed Kate and me."

.....

John was in trouble now. He had carried over a debt of three hundred and forty dollars from the night before using an I.O.U. marker. With a chance to recoup his losses, he went 'all in' on a pot while holding two kings and two tens.

Based on Wallace and Vincent's demeanor, heads down and scratching their necks, John had been certain they had nothing and he had a nearly unbeatable hand. At his turn, Wallace tossed four cards face down and had drawn four new cards from the deck. Before him, lay two kings and two jacks. The kings canceled each other out and the jacks trumped the tens. Wallace had narrowly beaten him with a little help from the cards Vincent had dealt.

"How could I have been so unlucky?" John wondered. "And, how am I going to pay my marker?" Around the table, Wallace and the other men smiled coyly as they stacked their chips.

"Tough luck, John," Wallace sneered. "That was a bad beat."

"I guess so. I never saw that coming. I'm nearly tapped out but would you boys mind if I put up another marker and let you give me a chance to win back some of my losses?"

"Well," Wallace said in his Southern drawl. "It's getting late and the boys and me got church tomorrow. It's time to settle your markers."

"But, I'm tapped…," John stammered.

"We'll work something out in good time, Johnny Boy," Wallace chuckled. The other men laughed along and tossed back their drinks.

.....

On the last Sunday in January, Olivia answered a knock at her door and, to her surprise, found Pastor Price. She invited him in and asked him to be seated while she put Kate down for her afternoon nap. Olivia returned promptly to find him still standing near the door.

"Pastor Price, it is a surprise to have you visit. I was unable to take Kate out in the rain these past few weeks, and I truly missed attending services."

He shifted from foot to foot and passed his hat hand to hand while looking as though he would rather be anywhere else. He asked if John were at home and, if so, could he join them? Finding that he was away, Pastor Price revealed the purpose of his visit.

"Olivia, I have known you for years and have always admired your dedication to your family and your work in the church. Please understand that it is with deepest regret that I inform you of a decision made by the elders of the church. After meeting and prayerful consideration, the elders brought before the congregation today a recommendation to withdraw from fellowship with you. The majority of the congregation concurred and it was left for me to deliver their decision. I am truly sorry."

Olivia was stunned and clutched the door frame for support as she felt her knees giving way. How could this be? Had Jesus not died on the cross to pay the debt for all sins? Was there no room in her congregation for forgiveness?

"Pastor Price, did my father cast a vote?"

"Yes. He brought forth the motion to the floor." He took his leave and Olivia closed the door behind him.

Olivia felt defeated and buried her face in her hands and wept. She could stand her rejection in the community, but to be denied the fellowship of her church body was devastating. Adding insult to injury was that Papa had led the way.

"What more?" she cried out. "What more must I endure because of one solitary indiscretion?"

She had never felt more alone as she dropped to her knees and prayed that God would give her the strength she needed to withstand this censure. She also asked for the wisdom to enable her to raise Kate to be strong enough to overcome trials she would face in her life because of her birth. As she lay beside Kate's crib, she suffered silently until she drifted off to sleep.

.....

Olivia wakened to Kate's distressing call for attention. Rising quickly, she changed Kate's diaper and went to check on Mrs. Smith. She found she was not alone. Carolyn had come to share the church body's decision. The elders put before the church body their motion to withdraw fellowship and called for a vote. It was not unanimous. In addition to the Gates and the Adkins, she named Beth and Charlotte Parker among a few others who opposed the action.

"You should be proud of Beth. Her courage was particularly noteworthy in her defiance of your father's lead. As the vote was being taken, she stood and made a resounding denouncement of such actions by so many supposed Christians. She was steadfast in her condemnation of their action by declaring they were voting against a person undeserving of such rejection. All the while she was speaking, your father attempted to pull her down and quiet her. I was so proud of her, but her bravery may have caused repercussions within your family."

Olivia nodded in agreement. He was a proud man used to getting his way without as much as a word to the contrary, and Olivia imagined that he had not reacted well to his being publicly challenged. That the challenge came from one of his children made matters worse. Olivia was thankful to hear Beth had stood up for her and she appreciated Carolyn's visit.

After hearing of the unwavering support of the Gates' and other members of the congregation, Olivia resolved to no longer be demoralized by a bigoted few. The heavy burden of guilt and remorse brought on by Pastor Price's visit was lifted. She might not be allowed to assemble with other church members, but she could spend time each Sunday in the study of His Word and in prayerful thanks for His many blessings. And, most important, she could teach Kate about God.

That night she prayed and asked for His strength to wash away her bitterness. She also prayed that Beth would not suffer greatly at Papa's hands. As she dozed off, her mind was at ease and she had no thoughts of the mean-spirited actions unjustly taken against her that day. She was at peace.

.....

By early February 1932, Olivia's question of "what more?" was answered. She could tell from her symptoms that she was expecting and that her baby should come about the first week of October. Her first reaction was despair which did not last. While she was bereft of but a few friends and family members, she acknowledged how blessed she was in having Kate, a decent place to live, and the means to support them. Her despair quickly turned into joyful anticipation of another child.

As before, Olivia concealed her condition for as long as she could. She determined she would tell Dr. James when she took Kate in to his clinic for her shots in the next few weeks. She certainly did not need a repeat performance of the Ward's kitchen floor this time around. Despite her much improved health compared to her prior delivery, this pregnancy worried Olivia more than her first.

Nothing had changed with John. She was still solely responsible for providing for herself, Kate, and now a third person. Knowing how she had been unable to carry Kate full term and that she would not be able to lessen her work, Olivia carefully planned every activity to maximize her efforts. Fortunately, October was far enough away to allow for this. Isaac had already prepared the garden plot and would till it before March and April plantings. This meant Olivia could establish her vegetable and herb gardens, harvest them, and preserve foodstuffs for the winter before delivering her child.

Even though she was just a few weeks pregnant, she worried about the prospects of future pregnancies. She had been the caregiver for her mother throughout four of her six miscarriages and Dr. James had warned she could not survive another. Since Walt failed to heed his earlier warnings, Dr. James said there were ways she could improve her chances of not getting pregnant again. But before he could explain himself, Mama had sent her from the room.

Just as with Papa, John could not be relied upon to prevent a third pregnancy. Now, Olivia knew she must avoid another pregnancy, but who could she go to for help? Dr. James had the information she sought, but she was modest about her marital relationship with John and was too embarrassed to approach him. She was determined to find a way. There could be no third child.

.....

In the first three months of the year, temperatures ranged at or near freezing from early morning until mid-day. To Olivia, it seemed the whole world was hibernating around her. Ice hung from tree branches and on the shrubbery, creating an eerie scene. Not a hint of green foliage was visible. The low temperatures, coupled with rainfall, caused the ground to freeze. Few stirred outside unless it was necessary, and road conditions were such that Beth made only two visits during this time.

On her last visit, her automobile had become stuck in the ruts making her inordinately late returning home from work. She was fortunate that Mr. Wynn, the owner of the town service station, and his ten year old son, Gus had happened by when they did to tow her to safety. Beth was frightened at the thought of Papa's discovering her clandestine visits and she determined she would not risk it happening again. Due to the inclement weather, John did not drop off Evelyn during the week. Olivia missed her visits and talk of what was happening with her family. Gloom abounded and with no opportunity to see Beth or Evelyn, a sense of isolation quietly crept over Olivia.

Evelyn's love for Kate was apparent. During one of her visits, Evelyn asked Olivia if she and Kate were related. In delicate terms, Olivia explained that Evelyn was Kate's aunt. Several days later, Evelyn told Olivia she had gotten into trouble with her mother when she talked of her joy in being Kate's aunt.

"Olivia, I was afraid of Mama. She took me by my shoulders and shook me until my neck hurt and my shoulders and arms ached. Mama never yelled at me before like she did then. She made me repeat over and over: 'I am not related to Olivia's baby. She is nothing to me.' She said if she ever hears me mention your or Kate's names again, she will not permit me to come here. Why is she so angry?" Evelyn burst into tears and Olivia embraced her to comfort her.

"At times, a parent may be upset about something, and a child just isn't able to understand what or why. Often the parent doesn't even know the cause. From now on why don't we just enjoy our time together and not discuss it with her when you go home? Then she will not be angry with you. Is that okay?"

Evelyn nodded and turned her attention to Kate with whom she played for the next half hour in silence. Olivia was incensed. What a contrast between Judy and Robert Ward! Judy could not abide Olivia and would do all in her power to make life miserable for her, even if it meant being mean-spirited to innocent children like Evelyn and Kate. On the other hand, Robert showed his respect and his kindness for Olivia and his love for his daughter and granddaughter. This strengthened Olivia's resolve to overcome Judy's unkind campaign to ruin her.

.....

Each morning, while Olivia lit the household fires for her and Mrs. Smith, John ate his breakfast and cleared the overnight accumulation of ice from the windows of the bus before starting his route. This had been their routine for the past several months and it did not include much, if any, conversation. This morning, however, was different. After finishing his breakfast, John lingered.

"Do you have a minute? I know that you won't believe this but I need your advice. I'd appreciate it if you could help me with a decision."

"Of course, John."

He explained that Mr. Adkins approached him with a proposition. "Some farmers have asked him to deliver staples to them during the busy planting and harvest times when they can't spare the workers to pick up needed items. He is convinced that a truck outfitted with a variety of goods could be a profitable business. He likened it to a rolling Sears and Roebuck store for famers and the coloreds in their Quarters."

John paused as Olivia considered what he had told her. He then explained why he needed her advice. "Mr. Adkins has offered to partner with me to operate it. If I agree, he will convert an old school bus into a 'rolling store.' He will furnish the vehicle and my part of the partnership will be to pay to stock it at his wholesale cost for the goods. What do you think about this?"

Olivia was intrigued. Having lived on the Turner farm at High Point and in the Ward's Quarters at High Bluff, she knew there would be a substantial demand for a delivery service of items crucial to the operation of the farms and the well-being of their inhabitants.

"It would mean, of course, that I would have to give up my bus route, but I would keep my job at the cannery. After work yesterday, I spoke with my supervisor there, Mr. Anderson, who agreed to adjust my schedule to a split shift with the same number of hours. The bus route won't be a problem as there are several men who can take turns substituting for me until a new driver can be hired."

After getting over the initial shock of John's asking her opinion, Olivia mulled over what he had shared. "The opportunity is ripe for the picking," she thought. "And, more important, John would be going into business with Mr. Adkins who is widely respected in the community as a fair and honest man as well as an astute businessman." If he were not confident both of them would profit, he would not enter into such a venture.

"John, I think you can rely on Mr. Adkins' assessment as to the profitability of the rolling store, but, can you finance your part of the deal and still pay for restocking? If you can, then you should consider it. Have you considered your father as a possible source of start-up capital? If not, perhaps you should discuss the business with him."

John winced at her suggestion. He did not want to involve his father. Obviously put off by Olivia's suggestion, he pulled on his coat and prepared to leave. "Olivia I know my Dad could provide the resources I need. It is not that I am too stubborn to ask for his help."

Olivia could tell with John's refusal to approach his father that there was something stopping him that was not his pride. She waited, and learned what it was.

"You were in the room with me the night my father stated emphatically I could never again depend on him for anything. Don't you recall his telling me I was on my own? Having heard what he said, and knowing him to be a man of honor, do you believe I could approach him?"

Olivia's only response was truthful. "No."

"I don't know why I am even talking to you about this. No matter how good the opportunity seems, I'll never be able to do anything about it. I don't have the thirty dollars that Mr. Adkins says it will cost to stock the rolling store and that is only the beginning. The bus will not run on fumes and I have to have money for gas."

Olivia understood too well his feeling of futility. In spite of his behavior toward her, she felt a keen sense of regret for all he had forfeited. Olivia heard Kate stirring and prepared to go to her but John's desperate plea stopped her.

"Are you willing to lend me the money? You work hard and are frugal and I am not unmindful of how you have undertaken a multitude of jobs and saved every penny you could. As for me, I guess most would label me as irresponsible. Lord knows that I certainly have assumed no responsibility for you and Kate. In spite of these inexcusable shortcomings, will you help me?" he said as his voice cracked with emotion.

After years of flaunting his superiority over her, John was in a position of eating crow. He hated himself for begging Olivia for help when he knew he deserved nothing.

Olivia did not hesitate with her answer. "Yes, I have been as frugal as I know how and have saved all I could for an emergency. I have the thirty dollars you need for initial stocking. While I don't have any extra money for your gas or re-stocking, I should be able to collect enough over the next few weeks to offset your shortfall. But, John Ward, and you hear me now. Before I loan you the money, I need your solemn promise you will not gamble with it."

John could not believe it. "Are you really willing to trust me with all you have saved? I promise the money will be used only for the rolling store and I will not gamble with it." John took her tiny hands in his while she sized him up. She wondered if he were sincere and hoped he was.

"Olivia, for the first time since we have been married, I dare to hope that I may rise above the rank of a lowly school bus driver. This is my opportunity for a better life. When I heard the proposal Mr. Adkins made, I was thrilled beyond words, but my joy was short lived for I did not have the resources to even consider it a reality. With your help, it is now something real. I don't know how to thank you except to assure you I'll make this work." John prepared to leave but Olivia stopped him.

"There is something you ought to know as you consider the upcoming change in your life. You made me pregnant when you last shared my bed and body. I thought you ought to know."

He leaned against the door frame as he absorbed her revelation. Then, he straightened himself and flung his hands in the air. "God, what more?" he said as he stormed out of the house.

Olivia was beside herself. What had she foolishly hoped for? Having persevered this far, she could not give up now. She would get through her pregnancy as she had her first, alone and without the concern of John or her own family. Hopefully, Kate would continue to blossom into the delightful person she was becoming and the baby on the way could be delivered without incident.

MCMURTRY

CHAPTER 31

April 1932 dawned and spring was upon them. Olivia and Kate welcomed the warm breezes that signaled the coming of the flowers and shrubs, and bright sunshine warmed the soil preparing it for spring planting. The promise of new life was all about. Outside her window, two robins hopped from limb to limb and the grass was turning a light shade of green as tiny sprigs and small buds were ready to burst with blooms. The winter of 'hibernation' had ended.

A day like this reminded Olivia of the many springs she had witnessed at Papa's farm. There, farm hands would be preparing the cropland to get plants into the ground with the hope of early crops and accompanying good prices. Similarly, but on a much smaller scale, her vegetable and herb gardens were ready to be planted.

Isaac sent word by Flora he would be by during the week, but Olivia needed to have the plants on hand along with a diagram showing how she wanted the garden laid out. Previously, she had bartered with Mr. Adkins, but Carolyn advised her William would let her have them at a wholesale price from the Feed and Seed. Olivia was elated. Every dime she saved represented money she could put toward her baking and sewing supplies.

.....

While awaiting her turn at the Feed and Seed, Olivia noticed several ladies from the church and not one of them acknowledged her. After Pastor Price's visit, she had not attended church for the past several months. Instead, she embarked on her own journey toward becoming closer to God's Word using materials Carolyn had given her. Every Sunday morning, Olivia reviewed the notes from each lesson and found the corresponding Scriptures in the Bible. Kate proved to be an attentive listener as Olivia read each passage with keen inflection to make the experience interesting and engaging for her.

Although Carolyn was busy pulling stock from the back room, she took time to acknowledge Olivia with a wave and a smile. As soon as she finished, she came over to greet them.

"Olivia, I have missed you on my last two visits with Mrs. Smith. Goodness, Kate is getting to be a big girl. Miss Kate, is what I hear true? You are walking and beginning to talk?" Kate responded with an enthusiastic smile. Carolyn laughed and turned to Olivia.

"Now what can I do for you today, young lady?"

As Olivia rose, lifting Kate on her hip, Carolyn stared at Olivia's midsection.

"My goodness, Olivia, am I seeing what I think? Are you expecting?"

Olivia blushed slightly. Through the winter months, she had successfully concealed her increasing breasts and protruding stomach. Not so today!

"Why yes. I believe you are!" Carolyn exclaimed as she hugged Olivia. Olivia noticed the ladies from church whispering and pointing at her and so she pulled away from Carolyn who realized her gaffe immediately. She felt terrible she had inadvertently exposed Olivia to more ridicule, and now she would be fodder for more rumors and innuendo around town. She took Olivia's arm and led her toward the back room. As they walked, she spoke in an exaggerated stage whisper for the 'busy bodies' to hear.

"What wonderful news, Olivia! William and I will be closing the store shortly for lunch. Could I persuade you to join us at Dallon's Diner? I have some catching up to do with you, my very special friend, and there is no time like the present. Come with me and I'll have Jesse drop the plants by later today."

Carolyn and Olivia stood behind the curtain separating the stock room from the front of the store, and Olivia thanked her for coming to her rescue in front of the other ladies. Carolyn apologized profusely for having exposed her secret and creating new gristle for gossip. Having heard the exchange, William rushed to finish with his customer and joined them.

"I overheard the exciting news. Congratulations to you and John."

The thought of fueling the fires of gossip in town was more than Olivia could handle, and she was eager to be on her way home. Even though the Gates' were well intentioned, she was not ready to bear the barrage of questions she knew would follow. She started to take her leave, but Carolyn cut her off.

"We are happy for you and John, but why did you not tell me? And, does Mrs. Smith know?"

Olivia's anxiety peaked. She was caught now; there would be no clean and hasty exit. With William and Carolyn hanging on her every word, she elaborated on her situation.

"I wanted to be sure. With all of the baking I have been doing, I thought I might have put on a few pounds sampling the wares. And, no, I have not told Mrs. Smith yet. I hoped to have a plan worked out before telling her, but now I guess I need to take care of that before she hears from someone else."

Carolyn and William hugged her and reaffirmed they would help her in any way. Then, Olivia exited through the rear door to avoid coming face to face with any would-be gossipers. A tall colored boy from High Bluff met her in the doorway, holding it for her as she passed.

"Excuse me, Missus Olivia. How is you and Baby Kate doing?"

"Just fine, thank you, Jefferson," she answered as she walked past him without pausing.

"Sump'ns wrong with Miss Olivia," he thought. "I best tellin' Missus Flora when I get home.

.....

As Olivia prepped for an afternoon of baking, she thought about John's partnership in the rolling store. He hoped to be operational by the second week of May to coincide with the planting season. From what she could tell, everything was on track. The carpenter had finished the modifications to the bus and John asked her to review his proposed inventory. She added a few items based upon what she knew farm families needed and would likely purchase. Using the revised stock list, John worked with Mr. Adkins to price each item and come up with a total for John's initial investment. As predicted, the price came to just under the thirty dollar figure he had given John. Now, all they needed to figure out was how to afford gas and John's re-stocking fees. Olivia had been able to squeeze another fifteen dollars from a few last minute orders, and she hoped it would be enough for the gasoline.

"John," she thought, "will have to pay for re-stocking out of his profits." While Olivia was proud of John's newfound maturity and attention to the burgeoning business venture, she was mindful that her contribution meant she would have a shortfall in her household expenses. So, she pushed herself to complete more projects, and maintained a strict budget of her time. Although she desperately needed material to fashion herself a work dress to accommodate her growing figure, she determined that was frivolous if it came at the expense of John's success with the store.

Olivia's thoughts drifted to how she would face the coming months when her ability to work would be curtailed. After deep thought and prayer, she came to a conclusion. "God," she asked, "thank you for providing for Kate and me in our most desperate hours. Please continue to watch over us, and strengthen my faith. Amen."

With a sense of peace, she went off to share her news with Mrs. Smith.

.....

Mrs. Smith was pleased to hear the news from town. After Olivia finished, Mrs. Smith told her that Isaac would come around in the morning to plant. Olivia thought once more of the help Robert provided without having been asked and she wondered how he always seemed to know when she really needed help. She hoped he would be as pleased with his second grandchild as he was with Kate.

"Mrs. Smith, I have something to tell you. I am expecting in the middle of October." Without giving her a chance to respond, Olivia explained that unless something unforeseen occurred, she would be able to continue to meet her obligations until the baby was born. After that, though, she was afraid she would not be able to fulfill her promise to care for Mrs. Smith for a few weeks.

"Oh Olivia...," Mrs. Smith began.

"Please let me finish," Olivia interjected. "Since I will be unable to carry my end, I will understand if you feel our agreement is null and void. I'm so sorry. No matter how hard I have tried, I have not found a solution."

"What? Olivia, do you think that all we have established between us is based upon some 'agreement?' I have known for more than a month you were expecting. You are thin and began to show right way, but I wanted to respect your privacy while I waited for you to tell me in your own good time. Frankly, I am delighted for you. Kate can use a little brother or sister, and I'll have the pleasure of two delightful children filling my mornings and afternoons. So, let us have no more talk of our 'bargain.' I have already made arrangements for you."

"What? How?" Olivia asked.

"Janie Green came to see me several months ago about work for her daughter, Rachel. For the last several years, she has prepared meals for her family and helped new mothers in High Springs. I put her on notice that a 'friend' might need additional help and she is eager to begin working for me. With your baby due the middle of October, we should lessen your workload to conserve your strength. She will be responsible for the care you provide for me as well as looking after Kate and the baby after it is born. You have done well in your baking and sewing business and it is time you have the opportunity to do so on a fulltime basis. This is the least I can do for you after the kindness you have rendered. Now, take Kate and go home with an easy mind."

While Olivia was relieved Mrs. Smith would be taken care of, she could not agree to such an arrangement. "Mrs. Smith, I appreciate all you have offered, but I must tell you I have pledged my savings and financial support to John's business venture. As such, I have nothing left to pay for Rachel's work."

"Olivia Turner Ward! Did I ask for you to pay? I am indeed fortunate my dear husband arranged everything with Jack Gunderson at the bank so that his prudent investments have provided well for me. Now, let me do what my heart desires."

CHAPTER 32

In May, nearly a month had passed since John and Mr. Adkins had reached their agreement to launch the rolling store, and through the intervening weeks, Olivia noticed different behavior in John. Every morning, he followed the same routine with his bus route and part-time work at the cannery. But, instead of meeting with other men after work and rolling in drunk around midnight, he came home sober promptly after his shift. It was a welcome change, but she did not have hopes it would last.

Still, John kept an emotional distance. He did not initiate any conversation, but neither did he withdraw as Olivia worked or cared for Kate. Rather, he worked in solitude at the kitchen table and, occasionally, he interacted briefly with Kate.

Once, Kate fretted while Olivia was busy and John soothed her before she could respond. When Olivia took over, he returned to the kitchen table without as much as a word. "It wasn't much," she thought. "But his helping in small ways and being civil to her could lead to a manageable existence. Perhaps he might be warming up to the prospect of having a daughter, and soon, another child."

.....

A few nights later, Robert visited unexpectedly. "What brings you to visit us, Dad? Is there anything wrong at home?"

John felt a gnawing in the pit of his stomach as Robert placed his coat and hat on the back of a chair and sat down. He visited with Olivia and Kate frequently, but rarely when John was at home. Moreover, his visits with John seldom brought good news and John feared what this visit might mean for him.

"Is Kate already in bed?" Robert asked tentatively. "I've been out of town for two weeks and I really have missed seeing her."

Olivia appeared from the kitchen with Kate in her arms and as soon as she saw her grandfather, she began to wiggle and reach out for him. Her face was aglow with joy at seeing him, and she smiled broadly, showing three teeth that had appeared from nowhere over the past two weeks.

Robert took her on his lap and made cooing sounds for her, causing her to giggle while she entertained herself by exploring a handkerchief protruding from his jacket pocket. After a few minutes, he held her out for Olivia to take her. "It's probably time for this little birdie to go to her nest," he said. Olivia agreed and retired to their bedroom to put Kate down. "How empty he must feel at home," she thought, "being unable to share his love and joy of Kate with his wife."

Their conversation was strained until Olivia returned a short while later. Then, Robert revealed the true purpose of his visit.

"John, there are two reasons I came here tonight. I stopped by the barbershop for a trim and I overheard Mr. Adkins telling everyone about a new venture he is embarking on with you. The men offered speculation as to the odds for success of such a farfetched idea as a 'rolling store.' Some dismissed it as folly while others felt it would meet the needs of many of the outlying farm families. If you would kindly indulge me, I would like to hear more about your plans."

John was relieved his father had not heard about his continued gambling or his occasional snort of whisky with the boys after a shift at the cannery. At the same time, he was equally pleased that his father was open to hearing the plans he had diligently worked on with Mr. Adkins. Olivia prepared to excuse herself, but Robert asked her to stay.

Olivia sat at the table beside them and John carefully laid out the plans for the rolling store. Robert measured John's every word and was impressed with the level of detail both had considered in their planning. Perhaps his wayward son was maturing to some degree.

"You say you have to put up the money to stock, re-stock and operate the bus. How much money did you commit to provide?" Robert asked.

John produced a paper showing the proposed amounts and a timeline he figured for having the money available. Robert nodded in agreement, but looked perplexed.

"Son, as chairman of the school board, I know what a part-time bus driver is paid and I have a fairly good idea of what you take home from the cannery. After you set aside money for your household expenses, there could not be much left over. How have you been able to accumulate the money you need?"

The knot in John's stomach reappeared as quickly as it had gone. He knew there would be no good outcome if his father found out he had depended upon Olivia for financing. He knew if he answered truthfully, his father's approval would evaporate into disappointment. His face reddened and his tongue swelled as he searched frantically for an answer that would appease his father.

"Mr. Ward," Olivia interrupted. "May I answer your question? John shared the details of this incredible business opportunity with me, as his wife, several months ago. Together, we worked out the details of financing John's commitment. We already have the initial capital for stock and operating expenses, and we have a plan to have the balance to sustain its operation shortly."

Olivia turned to John and patted his knee. "Excuse me for interrupting, dear. I guess I was overly eager to set your father's mind at ease and let him know you have thought this out carefully to honor your commitment."

John was relieved, and he was cautiously optimistic his father had bought Olivia's explanation. Meanwhile, Robert listened with an uneasy feeling. While he suspected there was more to all of this than was forthcoming, he had no choice but to accept their story. He rustled in his seat and both John and Olivia started to rise in anticipation of his leaving, but he did not. They could tell something else was bothering him, and he confirmed their suspicions.

"When I was at Gates' Feed and Seed, he asked how I felt about Olivia's meeting with Pastor Price and her discharge from membership there. I did not know how to respond because I knew nothing of the matter. As you know, the Ward family does not place membership in that congregation and ...,"

John interrupted. "Olivia, hell and damnation, is this why you haven't gone to church these past Sundays? I knew something was wrong. Why didn't you tell me? It is a wonder I have not heard of this shame heaped upon you from someone in town or at work."

While John knew he had no standing in the community or in Olivia's church to effect any change, his father certainly did, and his influence might be sufficient to cause the right people to rectify this unmerited action. He turned to his father. "Dad, is there something that can be done about this?"

Olivia shook her head and pleaded. "Mr. Ward, please understand there is nothing you can do that will change how more than half of my church congregation feels about me. I don't doubt you can leverage substantial pressure on the elders to rescind their action. But do you think that I want to be a 'member in good standing' in a congregation that has demonstrated how far they have drifted from God's teachings? No sir, I do not! I am at peace with my situation and I do not have to be in a building to be in His presence. I can worship Him right here at home every day, including Sunday. So, please, please, Mr. Ward, do not approach anyone on my behalf for I tell you it will be a wasted effort. I will not go back into their midst." Olivia braced herself and hung her head in exhaustion.

Surprisingly, news of Olivia's further degradation struck John hard and he wondered if his carnal behavior would ever cease to negatively impact this woman? He felt an urge to reach out to comfort her but found it impossible; it was against his nature.

Robert marveled at Olivia's courage. He felt deep remorse at the way she had been manipulated by his son, tormented by his wife, and rejected by the community. Although he sought to help her, he could not become embroiled in the turmoil of small town gossip at this juncture. Besides, there were more immediate concerns on the horizon.

"Although I am sure you planned to tell me soon, I must confess that William Gates, much to my surprise, inquired of my feelings on becoming a grandfather again. Congratulations to you both. I'll take my leave for now but I'll come back this weekend to discuss how we will all manage when the baby comes."

Robert left and Olivia and John sat speechless as they allowed all that had transpired to sink in.

"You are lucky to have his unwavering support," Olivia noted.

"Yes, I am," John thought.

.....

The dark night reflected how Robert felt while driving home. Thinking about the injustice of the actions taken by Olivia's church community rekindled his anger. She pleaded with him to do nothing on her behalf, but he was not satisfied to leave the matter alone. Somehow, some way, he would see to it that each of the instigators received their 'payback.'

Robert was a modest man noted for his extreme tolerance, but he could take only so much. He knew full well the power he wielded in his corner of the world and vowed to use the full measure of his influence to ensure the offending parties understood anyone with the name "Ward" was off limits. He was resolved that, although Judy would require some convincing, they would unite to convey this message. "Come hell or high water," Robert thought, "everyone will know this baby is a Ward and celebrate its birth."

.....

The '30 Ford's lights pierced the veiled darkness and High Bluff was in sight now. Robert did not understand why Judy could not bring herself to experience the joy of being a grandparent and he was disappointed with her rejection of Kate. To top it off, he detested being made to feel guilty when he wanted to spend time with his granddaughter. He would not go on like this with a second grandchild on the way, and he made the decision to face Judy with an ultimatum: he would no longer tolerate her hostility toward Olivia and Kate and he sure as hell wasn't going to sneak around to spend time with his own grandchildren.

It would be an uphill battle, but getting Judy to retreat from the evil and anger in her heart was essential to their attaining peace in the family. As he pulled around the main house to the side yard and parked, he knew he must make every effort to salvage his family. He would not be thwarted.

.....

John closed the door and turned to Olivia. "You never cease to amaze me. When Dad asked about my arrangements for financing the rolling store, you could have exposed me as irresponsible, but you did not. Why?"

"John, you and I reached an agreement as to how I would help you get your business rolling, and that is between the two of us alone; there is no reason for your father, or anyone else, to be privy to it. He was proud of your arrangements with Mr. Adkins, and we both know he would have been angry had he known you secured your financing from my limited savings. Although I have often been disrespected, the respect that others have for you is important to Kate's and my welfare."

John understood her rationale and he was grateful for her intervention. He wondered how it was possible that she did not sit in judgment of him. Instead, she found it within herself to bolster him.

"I know that it doesn't mean much coming from me, but thank you. I have treated you unkindly for as long as I remember and frankly, I don't deserve your support. I hate my position in life right now and sadly, I have no one but me to blame for where I find myself today. I want to be different, but I have neither your strength nor your nature to overcome the impossible odds stacked before me. My father won't say it but it pains me to know he wishes I were more like you. For that I am embarrassed."

"I keep waiting for John Ward to see the light and mature into the man with the bright future he once had," she thought. "But I'm starting to understand that day may never come."

"Olivia, you have no concept of how fervently I yearn for the freedom to act as others my age. It may seem salacious; but I want to enjoy Ann's company and her gaiety. Does that make me the cad that everyone already accuses me of being? Perhaps I am all that they say I am, undependable, irredeemable, and selfish. Yet, here I stand benefitting from your kindness when I have shown you none."

Olivia understood John's feelings as though they were her own and she recognized he looked upon her and Kate as the root of many of his disappointments. While she had no love for John, she felt betrayed that Ann continued her promiscuous association with him. He was, after all, a married man and it broke Olivia's heart that Ann could not see she was nothing more than a temporary escape. She worried John would be Ann's ultimate downfall. She hoped she was wrong. She would find out soon enough.

.....

Judy and Evelyn greeted Robert at the door. "You're later than usual tonight. What has kept you so long?"

As he removed his hat and jacket, Evelyn ran to hug him. "Daddy, I told Flora I knew why you were late. You went to see Kate and Olivia, didn't you?" Before he could respond, Judy chimed in.

"Robert, have you any idea how awkward it is for me when people see you at Mrs. Smith's? I have made every effort to let our friends and neighbors know how we feel about Olivia and that child; yet you undermine my every effort."

"But Mama," she said hugging him tighter, "Daddy and I love Kate; don't you?" Evelyn remembered Olivia's warning not to discuss them around her mother. But, at eight years old, she could not fully understand the dynamics of her family and was confused. Robert hastened to sooth her feelings.

"Evelyn, of course we care for Kate. You know everyone has a different way of showing their love. Don't worry, dear. I'll take you to visit this weekend. But now, it's off to bed for you. Your mother and I are going to be busy for a while so I will tuck you in later. Flora will help you get ready for bed."

Evelyn was excited she would see Olivia, Kate, and her brother soon and she skipped off in search of Flora. "Flooooora! Guess where I'm going this weekend."

Robert led Judy to the study where he closed the door and turned to her. Before he could speak, she interrupted him in an angry tone.

"What do you mean? I will not put up with your filling Evelyn's head full of ridiculous notions about Olivia and Kate. Olivia and that baby are the topic of gossip everywhere I go and I won't have this, Robert Ward. I have worked too hard to place myself in this community and I will not be outdone by a girl who deceitfully claims our name. Her latest actions are the last straw for me."

"What actions? What do you mean, 'the last straw'?" What on earth are you talking about?"

Judy's face went pale. In her anger she had said too much. Now Robert, like a bloodhound, had caught the scent and was tightening the circle on her subversion. Perhaps she should not have encouraged gossip about Olivia's need for a shotgun wedding. And, it may not have been wise for her to encourage influential members of Olivia's congregation to shun her. Their reaction had been swift and more effective than Judy could have imagined. They went beyond the mere questioning of Olivia's place in their midst to casting her out of their spiritual family. Now, Judy would have to face the repercussions of the mayhem she had wrought for Olivia and Kate.

"Why can't Robert see the situation for what it is?" she thought. "What is wrong with letting people know that I consider neither Olivia, nor her child, to be a part of the Ward family? Besides, Olivia would not have been a proper choice as a mate for John. He would have courted and married a woman more in keeping with the social status of our family name. As it was, he might as well change his name to 'Gulliver' since he had managed to shipwreck himself into marriage with a family of little people."

Robert would not be deterred. "I want an answer. What do you mean by last straw?"

Judy chose her words carefully to avoid lying. "When you were in Dothan before Christmas, unbeknownst to me, Olivia stole away from the Quarters with that baby and attended services at her old church. Apparently, she never considered how her family and other members of the congregation would feel toward her showing up at a house of worship flaunting that baby. Even her father did not welcome her."

Robert bristled at the notion of Judy's continued questioning of Kate's legitimacy but he throttled his tongue to allow her to continue.

"Later that week, some of the ladies at the library committee meeting debated how they, as Christians, should receive her in their midst. While they questioned their right to pass judgment on her, they also recognized their responsibility to shield their own children from the detestable plague of relations out of wedlock. What kind of example of chastity, after all, would Olivia be to impressionable young boys and girls? The mere idea of condoning such activity before marriage could lead to rampant promiscuity in our little community."

Judy paused briefly as she gauged Robert's receptiveness to her rationale. "Now Robert, you must know that I quickly ended their talk by pointing out Christian acceptance is good and not to be taken lightly. I urged them to pray fervently for direction from God and ask Him to what extent it was permissible to let our young people think that wonton behavior, like that exhibited by Olivia, is acceptable in their church."

Robert was furious but he swallowed hard and managed to rein in his emotions for the moment.

"Are you alluding to her congregation's withdrawal of fellowship? Are you telling me you were presented with an opportunity to defend the honor of our daughter-in-law and granddaughter and you did not? It seems as if you not only perpetuated such lies, but you instigated them as well." He fell backwards into his chair in disgust. He knew Judy was a lost cause and no amount of talking to her would change her. "What more," he wondered,

"Could this family do to shame Olivia?"

Robert's demeanor changed from a doting and loving husband to one who viewed her with disgust and strong censure.

"Robert, please don't look at me like that," she pleaded. "You mustn't think me to be responsible for what her church decided about her. They found the influence she could have in their midst made her unworthy to worship with them. Robert…?" The words for the moment eluded her. "I have tried to convince you that she is not the innocent person you believe her to be. You have chosen not to listen to me and you have refused to rid our family of her. You …."

Robert, at wits end, interrupted her. "Stop it now! Stop spewing your hatred and lies. Now, you will listen to me and do exactly what I say. I am sickened by the level of your cruel nature and am appalled that I never recognized it within you until now. Frankly, Judy, I am ashamed at hearing all that you have done to demean Olivia. I wonder how I have been married to you for all these years without recognizing the ease with which you are willing to cause pain in others, especially someone as kind and loving as our son's wife. Tonight, you have one of two choices to make. Once you have made a choice, you will live by it and there will be no turning back."

Judy moved closer to him and reached out to touch him, but she backed away as an icy stare she had never witnessed from him before repelled her. "Robert, dear, I've never seen you like this. Your actions alarm me. What do you mean by choices?"

"I think I can spell it out clearly enough so you will understand the ramifications of each. One is that you continue your behavior toward Olivia and Kate at a cost of your finding yourself alone in this house for as much of the time as I can find excuses to be absent. You will live and sleep alone for I know I can no longer tolerate your malicious ways. Furthermore, Evelyn and I will spend as much time with Kate as Olivia will allow us. And, Evelyn will grow even closer to Olivia, who behaves more like a mother to her than you ever have."

Judy could not believe her ears. Although she and Robert had enjoyed mostly separate lives since his time in France, he had always been warm to her, even when she did not return his affections. Now, he threatened to withdraw Evelyn from her.

"A second choice is that you cease all efforts to discredit Olivia and embark on a crusade with me to change the attitudes of those in High

Springs whom you have poisoned with your half-lies and filthy slurs about her. Henceforth you will refer to Olivia as John's wife, and Kate as our granddaughter. You must also cease chastising Evelyn about her love for Kate. May I trust that you are able to handle both of these propositions with the grace that I know you are capable of showing?"

Judy rubbed her hands over her eyes and lamented that she had revealed to Robert the full measure of her own deceit. It was only behind the shadow cast by Robert's business empire, that she had been able to sway the community against Olivia so easily. Those who went against Robert Ward generally found themselves homeless. Judy understood this and she had used this fear to her advantage.

"There is one other thing," Robert said. "And there will be no negotiation as to its acceptance. But, before you make your choice, there is something you should know."

CHAPTER 33

Robert Ward sat on the edge of his desk. His ultimatum to Judy was without reservation. He had a belly full of dealing with her subversion and John's lack of respect for Olivia. "By any legal definition, John and Olivia are married as husband and wife. However, they do not live as though they are married. John spends as much time as he can away from her either at work, or God knows where. And she cares for Mrs. Smith, bakes for Mr. Adkins, and picks up odd jobs sewing around town."

"Yes, I know, Robert. Is there a point here?"

"Well, I said for the most part. It appears that John and Olivia have been exercising their marital rights."

Judy squinted while she struggled to connect the pieces of the puzzle.

"In short, our family will have a new baby in either late September or early October. Before you say anything, make no mistake, this baby is a Ward. I had best never hear you advance any notion to the contrary." Robert ran his hand through his hair and sighed in desperation as Judy looked at him in stunned disbelief.

"I don't believe you. John despises Olivia."

Robert grinned at her. "That may be but it appears sometime in January our son set aside such feelings. To see Olivia is to know what I tell you to be true," he said with a chuckle. "I think, Judy girl, it is past time for you to give up on the idea that John will be divorced and 'free.' He will not! Since the week Kate was born, you have not laid eyes on our granddaughter who is a Ward in every way." Judy bristled at the notion.

"Judy, put aside your anger, and enjoy our son's children. You might actually find pleasure in doing so." She sensed Robert's deep emotion for his grandchild. She had two choices and wanted neither. How could she?

"I've put my cards on the table. Whichever choice you elect, I am prepared to accept. These past twenty years you and I have made it through both highs and lows. As I drove home tonight, I thought of many of these times. Foremost of these was whether we would grow old together, as I had banked on doing before tonight."

Judy's head swam. Robert appeared as if a stranger to her. His eyes pierced hers and he stood ramrod straight, as rigid in his thought as in his posture.

"It is time to make your choice. What will it be?"

Judy loved Robert and she was saddened at her realization that tonight she had lost something dear to her: his unconditional love. She was certain of this deep within her, and it terrified her. No matter the cost, she had to regain it. She realized she must begin to pay a part of that cost now.

"Robert, when I did not hear from you for months while you were fighting on some forsaken battlefield in France, I prayed daily for your return. When the war was over, I understood your desire to stay two additional years. Every minute of every day, I have wanted to spend my life with you. You may be a grumpy old 'Papa Bear' sometimes, but I love you nonetheless, and more than anything else, I want to grow old with you. This is my choice."

Robert breathed a sigh of relief. From the day he suffered callous needling in the barber shop until now, he had existed under a cloud of anxiety and downpour of dread for John and Olivia. He could not let the night end on these sad notes. It was time to share with Judy some good news.

He took her arm, and together they headed upstairs to their bedroom. He watched Judy brush her hair. Her silhouette reminded him that although she was not the once slender debutante he had left for the war in France, her green eyes and rounded curves of her body stoked a fire within him. As they turned down the covers, he welcomed her into his bed.

"If you'll not object, I'd like to exercise my husbandly rights," he whispered.

.....

Robert awoke to find Judy already up and about. After dressing, he joined her in the kitchen where he found her in front of the stove. "Good morning," she said. "Flora is off today and I'm making pancakes."

"Wow, what is the special occasion?"

"No reason. Can't a wife fix her husband pancakes without having an ulterior motive? You're heading to Dothan today and every time you travel there, you never eat. You're practically skin and bones. Sit down and eat."

Robert ate his pancakes quickly and washed them down with coffee.

"As I said last night in bed, I am very proud of John's work on the rolling store with Mr. Adkins."

"Oh," Judy said, "I still don't quite understand what it is."

"It is essentially an old bus they have outfitted with racks and cabinets full of dry goods. John will make a circuit around the outlying farms and Quarters selling odds and ends to the folks that need them and can't afford to take the time to run into town. It's a real humdinger of an idea."

"And just whose money is being used to promote this venture?" she asked.

"Although John claims to be funding it himself, I suspect Olivia is putting up at least a part of the money for John to undertake this opportunity. When I asked them, Olivia was quick to change the subject."

Satisfied that her money was not being used, Judy turned her attention to understanding the concept of their idea. "So, John is driving another school bus or is it the bus he takes the children to school in?"

"It's a bus Mr. Adkins already owned."

"Well, I guess it is a step up from being a lowly school bus driver. And, a partnership with Mr. Adkins will position him for opportunities later in life. He is very well respected in Geneva County."

She had no idea what the venture cost, but it sounded like a good idea. She knew that they had lost many man hours at High Bluff anytime Flora, Joe, or Isaac was forced to ride into town to pick up minor supplies in emergencies.

"I'm going to get more details on their plan tomorrow."

He hated to broach the subject while she was in a rare congenial mood. There had not been very much of that of late. As he savored the last bite of the salty bacon, he figured now was as good a time as any. She could simmer on it while he was out of town.

"On Saturday, you, Evelyn, and I are going to visit John. It goes without saying Evelyn will be thrilled to see her brother and spend time with Olivia and Kate. I'd also like to learn what arrangements they have made for Kate's care when the new baby comes. They are our family whether you like it or not, and I'll remind you of our agreement. There will be no discussion."

The peace between them had lasted for eight hours. "Do you really think this should be any concern of ours? Olivia will manage without our interfering. Stop worrying. If I have to be dragged to John's on Saturday, I'll go, but I don't have to bother with that baby and I certainly don't have to interact with Olivia." She turned to gauge Robert's reaction and was startled when she found herself alone. The Ford's motor echoed off the barn walls in the side yard and in a moment, he was gone.

"One of these days," she thought. "Robert Ward will learn he needs me and will not be in such a hurry to walk out on me."

CHAPTER 34

It was the last Saturday morning in May 1932 and bright sunshine was visible through the curtains in their sitting room. She hurried to get Kate up, fed, and dressed so they would not be late to Mrs. Smith's. Once there, they found her busy crocheting a blanket.

"Good morning, Mrs. Smith. John's father, Robert Ward, is going to stop by today to learn more about John's new business venture and to discuss Kate's care after the baby is born. With your permission, I'll tell him what you have arranged with Rachel so that he will no longer concern himself with that matter."

"You seem anxious today, child. Are you feeling unwell, or are you worried about something?"

Olivia was worried, but it was not about herself or Kate. She desperately wanted Mr. Ward to maintain his new-found pride in his son, but she could tell he was not sold on her explanation of John's financing his part of the rolling store.

"It amazes me how you seem to know exactly when I am worried. Your instincts about me remind me of Mama. Yes, I am worried that Mr. Ward will quiz John and me relentlessly until he gets details about John's finances. Honestly, I just don't understand why this should bother him."

"Well, he is his son. Of course he is going to worry about him just as your mama would worry about you."

"I know that you are right, ma'am, but I still dread his questioning. Perhaps I am borrowing trouble before it comes, but I can't help it."

Eager to tidy up her home before Robert's arrival, she briefly outlined her afternoon schedule with Mrs. Smith, including a trip to Jerrell's Drugs, and then excused herself.

.....

John was up and had eaten two bowls of cereal by the time she returned. Given her anxiety, she was relieved she did not need to prepare breakfast.

"I knew you were busy so I fixed my own. By the way, do you recall Dad saying what time he would come by today?"

As Olivia placed Kate in her crib with a rag doll she had sewn from scrap linen, she reminded him he had not set any particular time. She usually was content for a little while with this doll, but not today. While her vocabulary was growing, it was still very limited. She had, however, perfected two words, and she used these as Olivia attempted to pacify her.

"No. Out!" she gurgled. Although not the response Olivia wanted, she could not help but smile.

"Kate, you are one determined little girl, but Mama's got work to do."

Olivia retreated to the kitchen with Kate's shrieks trailing behind her. She tried to turn a deaf ear to them and hoped she would tire but she did not. Olivia stopped her sweeping. She had become acutely aware that Kate's whining only served to aggravate John, and neither of them could afford his being off his game today. She hurried into the sitting room and to her amazement, she found John at the play pen with Kate.

"Ok, Little One, you have our attention. We know you won't quit yelling until you are free of this pen. Do you have to be as persistent as your Mama?" He lifted her in his arms and she hushed just as there was a knock at the door. Olivia had disappeared into the kitchen, so John, with Kate in his arms, answered.

Robert and Evelyn stood before him with Judy lingering a few feet back. She stood straight as an arrow with her head down and her purse dangling from her hand to her knees. Kate let out a yelp and reached for her granddaddy. John was surprised to see his mother. She had not visited with them ever before.

"Forgive my manners and please, come in," he said, as Kate squirmed in Robert's hands as Evelyn tickled her.

"Hello, Dumplings," Evelyn said excitedly. "I've come to play with you and brought my mother and daddy too."

"Dumplings?" John asked. "What does that mean?"

"That's my name for her. Olivia is Cotton because of her fine, blond hair. I'm Rabbit because I hop around a lot and have a cute nose. And she's soft and white just like dumplings are."

John hugged Evelyn and turned to his mother who stood outside the doorway taking in the scene before her. She had been astounded at the sight of John holding Olivia's daughter in his arms. "Come in Mother," he said in an encouraging tone. "Welcome to our home."

He breathed a sigh of relief as she entered and took a seat in a chair near the door. "It's going well so far," he thought. "If I can only hold it together for a little while longer, we can be done with the Inquisition that I know   is   certain   to   come."

Judy soaked in her surroundings. She noted that the rooms that comprised the housekeeper's annex were not fancy, but they were tastefully appointed with simple decorations. She begrudgingly acknowledged that, although she did not approve of Olivia one iota, she certainly had made a comfortable home for John. Thoughts pummeled her relentlessly. "What has happened to my world? Why does my son look like a father when he holds Kate?" Here they were, just as Robert had mandated. Now, what was Judy supposed to do?

Olivia entered and greeted them, but before she could finish, Evelyn tackled her while hugging her stocking covered legs. Olivia returned the gesture. Despite her prior confrontations with Judy and the simmering gossip she had served up in town, Olivia remembered her genteel upbringing and was determined to accord John's family hospitality in keeping with honored guests. She might not like doing so, but Mama had raised her to look past the slights one might have had from another and represent the family name with the utmost decorum.

From a side table, Olivia produced slices of chocolate cake, and then inquired if anyone wanted coffee or tea. Only Evelyn took her up on her offer for a glass of milk and followed her into the kitchen. Olivia was relieved as it gave her time to get over the initial shock of seeing Judy Ward at her door.

She had noticed John's expression as she handed him a plate with cake, and he was every bit as puzzled as she. After Evelyn finished her cake and milk, the two of them returned to the sitting room. John was seated between his mother and father, and enthusiastically telling of his plans to initiate the rolling store.

"Olivia, come join us. I'm telling Mother and Dad about the rolling store, and they are eager to hear about the items that will be offered. I've been honest with them; I had no clue what to stock until you took the time to educate me. Come and help me tell them what we have decided to carry."

Olivia fetched a stool and sat down with them to share her thoughts. As she talked about the different items that would be stocked to meet the needs of the farmers as compared to those needed by the coloreds in the Quarters, her mind wandered. She cautioned herself not to place more significance than John's inclusion of her actually implied.

"Mother, you can't appreciate what Olivia's input has meant to Mr. Adkins and me. She has given insightful advice as to what items a farm family needs, and which they will wait to purchase in town. At the same time, she has given us perspective on the best time to start this venture." John paused and smiled coyly at her and she grinned shyly.

"This is good, son," Robert interjected.

"I know, Dad. After going over Olivia's ideas with Mr. Adkins, we both feel we will have a firm grasp over what we can expect in the way of sales and profits. This is due in no small measure to how we have been helped by Olivia."

"I can certainly see that, son. I have watched her build a successful cottage industry with her baked goods, craft projects, and braided rugs. Mr. Adkins shared his admiration for Olivia's keen eye for what people will buy, and her uncanny ability of how to market her goods. Not for a moment do I doubt her contribution to your new business. I hope I'm not putting the horse before the rolling store, son," he chuckled. "But, I will tell you that I am mighty proud of the level of planning and maturity you have displayed in bringing this opportunity to fruition. I must admit that working together, such as you have been doing with Olivia here, is a lot of what has made your mother and me a potent combination. As I have said, without her shrewd business practices while I was away at war, we would not have much of the wealth we possess today. I wish you and Mr. Adkins much success."

As the adults talked, Evelyn turned her attention to the basket of burlap strips which were cut and ready to be braided into rugs. As she had done so often when visiting with Olivia, she mindlessly went about braiding the strips.

Meanwhile, Judy remained silent and disengaged from the conversation. She hoped their time here would be short and she had little interest in adding to the discussion. John was sure, though, that he caught his mother looking at Kate to see if she bore the distinctive Ward coloring and markings. Typically, she could not bring herself to acknowledge the truth of Robert's observations.

"This week," Judy thought, "I've lost my husband's unconditional love, and today I have lost any hope of freeing my son. Olivia has made a home for John. And, perhaps worst of all, based on looks alone that child he cradles in his arms is most certainly a Ward. Olivia is a strong woman to turn a blind eye to the misery and ruin I have heaped on her without bearing visible resentment. Although I cannot ever see our reaching a truce, I am full of respect for this woman. She has won."

Robert turned to Olivia. "I want to tell you again how pleased I was to learn of the baby we are to add to our family. When I got home the other evening, I shared the good news with Judy and she was 'pleased.'" Robert paused to let his words soak in.

"Considering you delivered Kate early and it is a possibility for this baby, may I ask what arrangements you and John have made for the care of Kate during the birthing and beyond?"

Olivia could not enjoy the discomfort she knew Judy felt in the moment and she was compelled to help her. "Mrs. Ward, I know what a busy schedule you have with your volunteer work; however, if you have time, John and I would appreciate suggestions for family names for a boy or a girl. Kate is already so attached to Mr. Ward that I suspect she is going to be somewhat jealous of having to share him with her sibling. I hoped you could plan to spend time with this baby, and there would be enough love in the Ward family for both children."

As much as Olivia hoped her entrée would thaw Judy's cold heart, it obviously had no effect. She could tell Judy was not receptive to any part of what she had suggested. However, Evelyn, "a little pitcher with big ears," chimed in to declare her willingness to help choose a name and she shared her thoughts without prompting.

"Olivia, I know a name for your baby if it is a girl like Kate. I want you to name her Jean. That is the name of my favorite doll, and I am going to love her like I do my doll. Will you name her Jean?"

Olivia smiled and nodded. "That's a great name. As long as your brother approves, it is fine by me."

"Well, I hope it is a girl so Kate and I can include her in tea parties and things that boys don't like." Evelyn turned to her mother who was caught off guard. "Mama, do you like the name I picked? Maybe you and I can help Olivia after school? I'm a big help. Olivia always tells me so. So can we?" Evelyn was exuberant in her anticipation of the coming event and she was eager for her mother to share her delight. Judy remained silent.

Robert broke the uncomfortable silence. "Olivia, could you remind me again of your plans for Kate's care?" Olivia then shared with him the arrangements Mrs. Smith made to have Rachel take care of her as well as to look after Kate. He was pleased and indicated he would find some way to show the Ward family's appreciation for her thoughtfulness.

Judy cleared her throat and Robert acknowledged they had overstayed their visit. As they backed the '30 Ford out of the yard, Olivia observed that John was preparing for a hasty departure. She was right. As soon as they disappeared around the corner, he gathered a light jacket and opened the front door. But he did not exit.

"Olivia, I have found myself in your debt several times lately and this is another. I don't know how Dad persuaded mother to come with him, and I certainly don't understand what we can expect in the future. But right now, I am thankful for your treatment of Mother. I'll see you later tonight. Don't wait up."

CHAPTER 35

May was nearly over and it had been three weeks since the Wards had visited John and Olivia. While Robert had returned with Evelyn every weekend, Judy was conspicuously absent. Robert's initial pride in John's determination to set up and operate the rolling store began to fade quickly as his son became more and more distant from his family. Robert stopped by several times to check on John's progress, but he was never to be found. At first, he came at about the time of day he expected John to be home, but to no avail. Then he prolonged his departure on each successive time as he waited longer and longer without John's returning.

Finally, late one night, Robert asked Olivia point blank, "What is it with John? I stay past what I know to be your bed time, and yet he doesn't appear." Olivia could sense Robert's worry and feelings of defeat.

"Olivia, I suppose I was a fool to think John had matured some and become more responsible for you and Kate. I know now, he has not. Am I to assume he is staying out all night drinking and gambling again?"

"Mr. Ward, John justifies his behavior by blaming it on the ridicule hurled at him from many sources. He was not and never will be strong enough to ignore them." She explained that, in her opinion, John was a defeated man.

As she went on, Robert became more discouraged. "It is my fear that nothing either of us can do will ever be enough to change that. One must be steadfast in rebuffing taunts and ridicule. Trust me, I know of what I speak. Even now, I fight cruel innuendos and criticism about my business practices. I, like John and yourself, continue to endure much of the same in this town." Robert insisted she must know something that would cause John to change.

"I am very sorry, but I have given everything to support John, even when he has been mean spirited and cruel to me. Yet, I have failed to reach him to effect any meaningful change, and now I no longer try." She paused as she searched for the words she was looking for. "Mr. Ward, John is not a bad person. Rather, he is one with demons greater than he can conquer."

"What do you mean he is defeated, Olivia? I don't buy that."

Olivia could feel Robert's frustration. He was approaching an irrational person with rational logic. How could she say what needed to be said without hurting his feelings?

"Mr. Ward, John is not like you. He retreats from those who taunt him. This is true even from his best friend, Paul, who has made known his desire for John to be part of his life upon his return to High Springs. Do you know what he told me? He would not subject Paul's wife to an association with me. He chooses to be with the dregs of this town because they care nothing about the social standing of his wife. They care only for the money they fleece from him every week in a card game."

Robert hung his head in disappointment. He had hoped John had given up his foolish gambling. He hated to admit that he was wrong and the men who made snide comments in Kelly's barber shop were right.

"I'll take my leave now, Olivia. Thank you for your candor. I know it is not easy for you, and I am sorry that you are caught in the middle of the mess my son has made of his life. You can tell John that he can bank on my return." Robert let himself out into the night air. He would be back soon alright. Very soon.

.....

After the threatening clouds cleared, it turned out to be a nice day. The Smith household was abuzz with activity as Olivia and Mrs. Smith planned to celebrate Kate's first birthday. Olivia asked Mrs. Smith to join them in their home. She had baked a special cake and braided a new rag doll to add to the rocking horse that Isaac and Joe had made for Kate. Mrs. Smith marveled at the beautifully crafted gift. Before they served cake, Mrs. Smith produced a tiny package for Kate.

Olivia was surprised and when she opened it, she cried. In the box lay an exquisite cameo on a gold chain. Mrs. Smith went on to explain her mother had given it to her on her sixth birthday and she had treasured it for nearly 80 years. Now, she would pass it on to Kate. Olivia held it up for Kate to admire. Kate pawed at the shiny gold chain and giggled. Olivia said she had best put it away for a few years, but they would both treasure her generous and heartfelt gift. She hugged Mrs. Smith while telling her what a blessing she had been to them both.

By now, Olivia was glowing in her pregnancy and she was happy to have been able to share Kate's day with Mrs. Smith. She only briefly lamented that Beth and Mama could not be with them to celebrate her child's special day, but she was grateful for everything that God had bestowed on them. Mrs. Smith saw Kate was tired and bid them goodbye. Olivia tended to Kate, then set out to put her sitting room back to sorts. Shortly, there was a knock. She opened the door and was overtaken with astonishment. It was Beth.

"Beth, I can't believe you are here. I am so happy to see you."

Beth stared in disbelief. Olivia, whom she had not seen for several months, was wearing a faded, tent-like dress Beth recognized as having been made from flour sacks. It appeared to be as worn out as Olivia. Beth was distressed. How had her once tiny sister been reduced to the unsightly woman she beheld before her? She marveled that her petite frame could withstand the weight she carried. Beth wanted to cry.

"Olivia, Mama and I wanted so much to see you, but Papa has threatened each of us within an inch of our lives if he even hears of our talking to you. Frankly, I don't know what he would do if he knew I actually visited you. Mama sends her love but she was not up to traveling. Besides, she was fearful that her leaving would tip off Papa to my plan."

Olivia took Beth's hands in hers and assured her she understood. "You have no idea what your visit means to me, but I do not want it to cause you suffering because of Papa's wrath. Please don't linger and have him suspicious when you are late getting home."

"I don't care what Papa says. I am here because I want to be. Please tell me how I may help you, for it is plain to anyone that you are worn out."

"Really, Beth, there is nothing you can do. This pregnancy is just like one of Mama's difficult ones. You must not worry about me. I may look ragged but I feel strong and I have many blessings before me such as your visit. When I saw you last, I feared it might be our last time together because I knew it would be foolhardy of you to risk Papa's wrath. Yet, now I see your beautiful face before me and I am happy beyond description. But Beth, right now the best thing you can do for me is to leave and avoid raising Papa's suspicions. Perhaps then, you can find a way to come again soon."

Beth knew Olivia was right. She must continue to be cautious in her efforts to see Olivia and Kate. Papa had proven to be unforgiving for those who betrayed his trust in business and he was even harder on his family. As she prepared to leave, Beth withdrew a small package from her purse and handed it to Olivia.

"Did you think I would forget Kate's first birthday? I may not get to see her as I would like, but that doesn't mean I don't think about her and love her. I ordered her gift and had it delivered to Mr. Adkins so Papa would not discover it in the daily post. I hope you like it."

Olivia opened the small package to reveal a gold bracelet nestled on a blue velvet bed. It was adorned with a tiny spray of rosebuds and Olivia thought it was exquisite.

"I'll make sure Kate understands how special this is, and, Beth, more than the bracelet, the fact you remembered her birthday is what is touching to me. Now, please go."

Beth knew time was flying but she could not leave before she looked in on Kate. "I know she is sleeping, but could I just peek at her? Mama has asked me to describe in every detail how she has grown since she saw her that time at church." As Beth bent over the crib, she marveled at Kate's sleeping peacefully. She thought how sad it was Mama could not see her grandchild. After a quick hug from Olivia, Beth was off to High Point leaving Olivia and Kate to rest from their eventful day.

.....

At four in the morning, Olivia was awakened by creaking pine floorboards and she lay perfectly still. The pungent odor of cigar smoke and sweat crept across the room and reached her nose before John pulled back the sheets and slid quietly into bed beside her. He slept until three o'clock the following afternoon and made no mention of his daughter's birthday. Although Olivia was not surprised, she was heartbroken nonetheless. "Despite my prayers," she thought, "a prolonged change was too much to ask for."

.....

In June 1932, Olivia was busy from early morning until late evening while she tended the gardens and harvested and canned the bounty from the soil. She had to work quickly and efficiently to avoid letting the vegetables and fruit ruin. It was hard, though, to take care of Kate and gather vegetables at the same time. She eagerly anticipated Rachel's help in August. When Flora stopped in to deliver a load of flour sacks, she saw how stressed Olivia was in trying to fit gardening in between Kate's nap times.

A few days later, Joe and Isaac Jackson arrived in Mr. Ward's truck. Olivia waved to them as they backed into the side yard. They removed a few eight foot lengths of wood from the bed and began nailing them together into a square under a maple tree near the edge of the garden. Olivia stopped her gathering and went over to investigate.

"Hello boys. To what do I owe this visit?" She watched as Joe dropped the tailgate to reveal a load of sand which he and Isaac began shoveling into the square.

"Just you wait, Miss Olivia," Joe said. You gonna be surprised. Mama said you were having trouble managing Miss Kate while you were gardening so we brung you a baby sitter." Joe laughed as they continued shoveling sand.

"Joe," Olivia asked. "Gonna? Brung?" Olivia paused and asked, "Really now, is that what we have regressed to?" Joe bowed his head in embarrassment. "It looks like I need to make a trip out to High Bluff to undertake some remedial reading lessons with two young men I know." Olivia smiled at them with a raised eyebrow.

"Not on my account," Isaac added. "I brought you a sandbox and Mama said that you were going to be surprised." He stuck his tongue out at Joe and smiled a toothy grin to Olivia.

Joe waved the shovel at him dismissively. "Brother, how about a little less talking and a little more shoveling? It's gonna' be a long walk home for you if I leave your smart mouth behind." Olivia and Isaac laughed with Joe, and soon the sand was unloaded. Kate now had an outdoor playpen in which to amuse herself while Kate worked.

"There's one more thing," Joe offered. He untied an old beach umbrella from the side of the truck and poked it into the middle of the soft sand. "Mama said that this will provide shade for Kate, and protect her fair skin from the sun."

"Thank you, boys. How can I repay you and your parents for this gift and all that you have done for me?"

"You have already given us a gift that we could not ever have bought for ourselves," Isaac said. "You be done gave … I mean you gave … us the gift of reading and writing. We can't ever repay you for that."

Olivia excused herself for a moment as she went into Mrs. Smith's house. She returned promptly with a canteen of cool water and several slices of chocolate cake wrapped in wax paper. "You may not let me repay you with money but I can fill your bellies," she laughed. "There are two pieces for now and enough to share later at home with your mother and father. You boys better not eat all of this cake before you get home. I'm going to ask your mama if she got some next time I see her."

She looked at the boys with her head cocked and a thin, spindly finger pointed at them. They nodded in agreement and all chuckled. The boys loaded up and headed out, and as she waved goodbye, Olivia heard Kate's cries from inside.

.....

June's temperatures reached the high nineties and Olivia worked overtime to prevent her vegetables from wilting. She tirelessly hauled buckets of water from Mrs. Smith's well and watered each plant. Although there was little time she was not busy, she relented in her schedule to see Carolyn when she paid her weekly visit. From the minute she walked in, Olivia and Mrs. Smith sensed Carolyn's excitement.

"Both of you need to be seated when I tell you my news. I was having my hair fixed today when Judy Ward came in for her appointment. She could not say enough about her and Robert going to be grandparents for the second time early this fall."

Carolyn waited for some response from one or the other of them. "Don't you realize the woman who has told anyone who would listen that John did not have a baby is the same woman broadcasting in the beauty parlor that he not only has one, Kate, but another one to be born soon? I would say that is a major admission to make considering it points out to one and all how she lied about Kate."

Olivia responded that the news was interesting but was far too late to help her or Kate, and only time would tell how her claim of a second grandchild would affect this child.

"And, there is more. She actually referred to your marriage to John. She shared she was preparing to help out with the new baby." Carolyn was so proud to be the one to deliver this news, and continued with a wide smile, "I told William I now believe that 'pigs can fly.'"

Mrs. Smith spoke first, "It is high time Judy Ward behaved herself as a proper mother-in-law and grandmother. She's always been so high and mighty on that boy of hers and yet he is a sot. Here he is married to a fine girl like Olivia, and yet neither Judy nor John appreciates Olivia for the fine rearing she has received in her life. He's a mule and you're a thoroughbred," she said. Olivia grinned. She had often heard Mama say, "My Daddy gave his blessings for me, a thoroughbred, to marry a grade stallion and he never forgave me for not heeding his counsel."

"I think it is progress," Carolyn said. "Or, at least it's a start. With her making a public proclamation, I feel goodwill toward you may snowball around the community."

"I will not hold out any hope for that," Olivia said. "On her recent visit, she showed less than a full measure of enthusiasm for anything you have mentioned. It is more than likely Mr. Ward has issued some demand which she fears ignoring. I urge each of you not to read too much into Judy Ward's rambling. I certainly will not." Olivia wondered if she should share Carolyn's news with John, but she decided against it. "No reason to give him cause to defend her or to justify her actions," she thought.

MCMURTRY

CHAPTER 36

"God answers prayers," Olivia thought as she surveyed the jars of vegetables, soup, and jam in the cellar. It was the first week of July 1932 and she had dedicated herself to canning at a steady pace over the past several days. Her diligence had paid off in the form of an abundant stock to help them make it through the fall and winter months. The task, though, had taken its toll, and she longed for relief.

Standing over the boiling pots for hours at a time had wrecked Olivia's knees and back. She was stiff and almost beyond putting one foot ahead of the other. Now, she had only three months before her baby would be born and it could not come too quickly. Rachel would be her lifeline, but she would not be available until the end of August which seemed a long way off.

John knew she was worn out and struggling. Still, on the rare occasions he was home, he made no effort to help her. Olivia saw telltale signs she might be in for a rough early delivery again when she "spotted" several days in a row. Additionally, she experienced prolonged false labor contractions which were not painful, but were extremely uncomfortable. Although she thought she would have to reach out to John for assistance, she did not. Emotionally, she wasn't willing to expose herself to his rejection of her plea for help.

.....

After the July 4th celebration in the town square, Isaac dropped Flora off at Olivia's. Flora was alarmed at Olivia's untidy appearance. She was more concerned, however at the state of her home. The rooms were in total disarray as was Kate. The stench of dirty diapers reeked throughout the small space.

"Olivia always prides herself in keeping a clean house," Flora thought. "Sumpin' serious be wrong here." Olivia's feet and legs were swollen to almost double their normal size and Flora recognized that she was in dire need of medical care.

"How long has you be done swoll up like dis here and flushed?" Flora asked.

"For a while."

Flora knew none of Olivia's family would see about her, and knowing what she did of John's habits, there was no telling when he would come home or if he would get her the help she required. Something had to be done for her right away.

"Chile, I'm gonna get Isaac to drive you over to Dr. James' so he can sees 'bout you. I'll stay here with Kate. Go on now, and don't you be worryin' none 'bout her."

Although Olivia was in distress, she was reticent to go to Dr. James. "Flora, I don't think he will see me."

"What does you mean, chile? Surely you knows you about to miscarry ifn you ain't hepped? You get youself to that doctor lickety split. Is there something you ain't telling me?"

"You just don't understand, Flora. I've given all of my money to John to finance his rolling store and I have nothing with which to pay Dr. James. I will not accept his charity. I just won't do it."

Flora shook her head in dismay. "I don't be understandin' it none. Not mo than a week ago I overheered Mister Robert telling Missus Judy how well John be doing with his bus store. I knows for a fact dat he still works at the cannery. 'Sides, Joe and Isaac heard he ain't got no money cause he a gamblin' it all away with them boys in the back room of the dry cleaners."

This, of course, did not come as a surprise to Olivia. "Flora, you know how it was when John lived with Kate and me in the Quarters. Nothing has changed. He still regards us as the nuisances in his life."

Flora was disappointed in John. She had raised him from a boy and had hoped things between Olivia and him had changed for the better with the move to Mrs. Smith's house. But apparently, they had not.

"Does you think you can get Mister Robert to hep you with Dr. James' fee?" Olivia shook her head, no.

"Chile, somehow you gonna have to get some hep with this here baby. How 'bout ifn you let me get Janie to come by to see if she can hep? She be ever bit as good as Dr. James and she won't be in no hurry for her money."

Olivia agreed, but she vehemently insisted that Flora not approach Robert Ward. The two hugged and Flora made sure Olivia was comfortable on the settee before she left. "Hold on, chile. We gonna get you some hep straight away."

Once the sound of the truck disappeared, Olivia rose to continue her chores. Each step proved to be a challenge, and she offered a silent prayer to God to strengthen her.

.....

Flora managed to return to High Bluff, finish dinner for the Ward's, and slip out the back door where Joe drove her to Janie's house. As they pulled up in the yard, Flora went inside while Joe parked the truck. As he applied the brake, he noticed Janie's daughter, Rachel standing at the well and he sidled over to her to talk. She was about a head shorter than he and her mocha colored skin was a smooth as corn silk. Joe was smitten with her.

Although he had always had difficulty talking to girls, to his surprise, the words came easy for him. He was sure his work with Olivia on his grammar had made a difference. The two talked until Flora reappeared. Joe wished Rachel a good day and opened the truck door for his mama. As they pulled away, Rachel cast a brief wave with a flick of her wrist.

The next day, Janie appeared at first light. She took one look at Olivia and knew Flora had not exaggerated her feeble condition. Olivia needed help now or her baby would go into distress. Given her prior history with birthing Kate, her present condition was serious for both of them.

"Lord, woman, you sho nuf be in a fix. How far along is you?" Olivia told her the baby should be born in late September or early October. "Miss Olivia, I 'spect unless you get rid of this here swelling and don't have no more spotting, you won't be carrying this here baby too much longer. Is you sure about the time it will come?"

Janie's tone, as much as her words, frightened Olivia and intensified her concern for what would happen to Kate if she did not make it this time. "I know the exact time because of what I know from the times my Mama was pregnant. A baby can come a few weeks early or late."

"It sure enough can do that," Janie agreed. "One thing you can bet on is that there baby you carry won't stand a Chinaman's chance of making it into this world if it be comin' much before the middle of September. I have something here to hep you get rid of the fluid, but you gonna have to change your ways if you wants to delivery this baby healthy. That's the gospel truth. I is gonna brew you a cup of herbal tea now. There's nothing more you can do but stay off yore feet as much as possible and pray to the good Lord."

As Janie stuffed her bags of herbs into her leather satchel, she warned Olivia about side effects to watch out for in the coming days. "Ifn you start having cramps that won't let up after no more than an hour, or ifn you have deep red spotting, then you better get help right away. Find Dr. James or me, Miss Olivia. I'll pray you can carry this here baby another month until Rachel can get here to hep you."

After Janie left, Olivia rocked in her chair and as she wept, a line of prose came to her. 'God helps those who help themselves.' "Well," she thought, "Papa has made it clear I cannot count on family for help and I am bound to abide by his wishes. It is time I helped myself. When he prepared to mete out punishment to one of us children, he always said: 'It's a Meet Jesus Day, ready or not!' John Ward, you need to prepare yourself. It's your 'Meet Jesus Day;' ready or not."

.....

Olivia anticipated John's arrival any time now. He had not told her when or if he would be home, but her deductive reasoning skills had been hard at work. She knew he would not be paid for work at the cannery until Friday so he probably had no money for his poker stake at the nightly game in the back room of the dry cleaners. Whatever time he rolled in she would be ready, as Papa once said, with both barrels loaded.

Around ten thirty, she heard a car sputter to a stop as the exhaust pipe belched a single report as it backfired. John had thumbed a ride home and she rose and met him at the door. She could tell he was sober, which came as a welcome relief. Before he could escape to the bedroom she addressed him.

"John Ward, you have behaved as a boy long enough. It is time you behave as a man."

He ignored her and continued toward the bedroom. Olivia blocked his path while standing firmly with her hands on her hips in the doorway. In a high-pitched voice, she addressed him.

"Look at me and don't you dare turn away! You sit down and listen, Mister."

John was taken by surprise by Olivia's edgy voice and demeanor. "What is it with you woman? I don't even recognize you. What in God's name has happened to the gentle woman who heretofore never raised her voice nor made any demands?" Olivia did not answer. She was determined to wait until he sat down so she had his undivided attention.

"Really?" he thought. "What a twist of fate. He had defended her undemanding personality in front of Ann as they dined at Dallon's Diner earlier that evening. Ann never missed a chance to demean her sister, and tonight was no different. When she had asserted Olivia was bossy and controlling and always thought she knew best when it came to John's life, he inexplicably disagreed with her. Even he was surprised that he challenged Ann so bluntly. Now, he realized, "Boy, was I wrong."

"Don't toy with me like one of your nymphets," Olivia cautioned. "Not tonight. If you do, I promise it will be at your peril. You had best consider I have reached my belly full of you, the Ward's spoiled child who behaves despicably without ever being held accountable for any of his unsavory behavior. Enough is enough, John. I am sick and tired of your horrible attitude and of hearing over and over your moans and groans about your imperfect life. It stops right now. You have come to your 'Meet Jesus Day.' No longer will I tolerate your rejection of Kate or of this baby I carry."

Her outburst was liberating, and now she was nearly out of breath. Olivia stood unflinching while awaiting his response. For so long she had tried to go along with John's childish ways with the hope he would come around to face his manly responsibilities. She had now come to the conclusion he would not.

John was speechless. He had never seen Olivia this angry before. For a moment, he thought she might strike him, but she went on with her rant.

"You regret your unborn baby, yet you conveniently forget that it was your selfish lust that caused me to conceive it. And, I will remind you, I was not a willing party. You declared your intentions to exercise your marital rights and took them without so much as asking me what I wanted. No sir. I was just the unwanted wife who traded her body for your resentful presence in our daughter's life." She paused and John took advantage of the opportunity to get in a word edgewise.

"I am tired, and I'm not going to listen to you ramble on about our tragic union and your notion of 'rejection.' For God's sake, what is different now? Why are you nagging me when you must know I don't give a flip what you think or want?"

He stared at her as if daring her to continue. Could she not see how angry she made him? Did she have to harp on and on about another child he cared nothing about? It was time to end Olivia's little tirade.

"You want me to listen to you. Well, by God, now it is time for you to listen! Frankly, I wish you had never delivered Kate. Now you tell me you have another baby on the way. Surely you must understand I don't want these children or your swollen, fat body in my life. I just want things to go back the way they were on the night we rolled in the hay in your father's barn. That is impossible, so I will make myself clear. I don't want you or any of your brats in my life. Jesus woman, leave me alone. Is that too much to ask?"

John applauded himself as he observed how deeply his cutting remarks wounded Olivia. Maybe now, she would finally get the picture. She had appeared pale and worn out before, but now she looked as if the blood had been sucked out of her body and her face bore the expression of defeat.

Olivia would let him have his say, but she would not let him escape. The smirk on his face sparked a deep emotion in her as if he had touched a match to gasoline. As he stepped around her, she slapped him hard across his face. Surprised, he staggered backward and looked at her in disbelief as he caught himself.

"Finally," she thought. "I have his attention." Olivia had believed there was a decent man deep within John. Why then, was he such a cad to her and Kate?

John hung his head. "God woman, stop trying to control me."

Olivia had said her peace, and realized she had not gotten through to him. At the moment she was ready to give up, she prayed. "Lord, please guide me to know what to do to reach him." An inspiration came over her and she took his hand and led him to Kate's crib where together they looked at their sleeping daughter.

"Just look at your daughter and tell me you cannot see a Ward. She has your eyes, mouth, and coloring. She is undeniably your flesh and blood. Nothing more, and nothing less. No stranger would conclude she is not your child."

A dim lamp cast shadows about the room and John took stock of

Olivia's keen observation. Looking closely at Kate as she slept on her side with one arm resting beneath her dark curls, he was taken back to a time when he had observed Evelyn sleeping in this very same position. Even Kate's patrician nose was exactly like his and his father's. Clearly, she was a Ward and she was lovely.

"Does it affect you, at all, that Evelyn has taught her to call you 'daddy?' You know she prides herself on teaching our daughter about her family. Kate knows you are her daddy and Mr. Ward is her granddaddy. She even recognizes Evelyn as her aunt. It's a double edged sword for me, John," she continued. "I am happy Kate will grow up knowing Evelyn, but I am deeply saddened that she will one day come to understand her father's rejection of her. It will break my heart that I will be unable to comfort her."

Olivia could not continue. She stood and watched John while hoping for some sign he shared her regret but he gave no response. Olivia could not bear to witness John's detachment any longer so she left him standing over the daughter he never wanted, did not love, and would never claim as his own flesh and blood.

John stood over the crib by himself in deep thought for half an hour. He had endured an emotional evening with Olivia having given him both barrels of grief. He soon realized, however, everything she had said was true. Because of his selfishness, he had one daughter he never wanted and yet another child was on the way. He leaned down and touched a ringlet of Kate's hair. He could not deny her any longer.

Simultaneously, he experienced an uncharacteristic sense of regret at his decision to ignore his daughter's birthday. "Thank you, Olivia," he thought. "You have never given up on me as a person who can find redemption. I do not want anything to happen to Kate or to this unborn baby." He knew he would never feel love toward Olivia, but now everything concerning Kate and his unborn child had changed.

John crept softly out of their bedroom to find Olivia. In the bright light of the sitting room, it hit him like a ton of bricks. Olivia was ill and she needed his help.

"Olivia, how can I help? I want our baby to live. Tell me what I need to do."

Olivia covered her face as tears of relief streamed down her cheeks. She could not believe her ears. John had said "our baby." She wiped her eyes and looked him. "You will help me?" John nodded in agreement.

Olivia explained Janie's instructions for the herbal tea regimen and her limited activities. Her biggest obstacle, she said, was minding Kate throughout the day. With John running the rolling store during the week and working at the cannery on the weekends, his time was extremely limited. She had even less time between her caring for Mrs. Smith and meeting the needs of Mr. Adkins for cakes and rugs.

"Fortunately, Kate is content playing for hours in her playpen and she sleeps the rest of the time."

John thought for a minute. He remembered seeing Olivia pulling Kate in the wagon with the cakes and he had an idea. "How do you think Kate would fare if I built her a playpen in the rolling store? Do you think she would do as well as she does in your wagon?"

Olivia thought about it. "I'm sure she would do just fine. She either sleeps or plays six to eight hours a day already and all you would have to be concerned about is feeding her and changing her."

John said he would give it a try. He had found Olivia was an exceptional planner. Whatever she determined was the right method of doing something usually ran smoothly.

Although he rarely showed it, the notion of being a father to Kate had been growing on him. Now that she was able to scoot around the sitting room, he found himself interacting with her more. She reminded him of a young Evelyn in size and looks and it took him back to a simpler, less stressed time in his life. He welcomed that feeling, given all that had transpired over the last two years.

Additionally, he knew interacting with his daughter and demonstrating he could find a way to work with Olivia would go a long way in regaining the confidence of his father. It hurt him to have his father think he was not an honorable man and that he was irresponsible. All he had ever wanted to do was go to college, have some fun, marry Margo Brown, and run one of his father's businesses. Although college and Margo were no longer possibilities, he could still work his way back into his father's good graces by working hard and by showing him he could handle the responsibility of running his business.

John took to heart what Olivia had said. Kate was, after all, a cute little girl. Everyone except his mother seemed to agree on that point. Having her along on his rolling store might mean more sales as he utilized her as a drawing card to bring the women out to sample his wares. He was encouraged that he was finally on the right track. He would give it a try and in the meantime, give Olivia the relief she so desperately needed.

"Okay," John said, "I'm game for this if you are. I'll need you to show me the ropes of feeding and changing her but once I've been schooled on these things, I believe I can manage her."

Olivia was delighted. "Just make sure she can reach her toys while you're away from the bus talking to the customers. Kate is content to play by herself. If she cries, just ignore her. She will stop in a few minutes. I'll pack a bottle and small jar of milk to take with you in the mornings. She holds her own bottle now so you can hand it to her without stopping. I'm betting you won't have any problems at all."

"I'm pretty sure I can handle most of it. My only concerns are knowing when to feed her and what to do when she has a dirty diaper. To be honest, the smell makes me sick. It is all I can manage to keep from gagging. Just write everything down for me. I am no dummy, I'll figure it out."

Olivia had an eerily good feeling about the prospect of John managing Kate by himself. He seemed honestly concerned for her well-being, and although she remained defensive about all things concerning John's behavior, she allowed her heart to thaw and believe his intentions were honorable toward Kate.

She laughed to herself. The image of John having to change Kate's dirty diaper presented a hilarious picture. Her stomach ached and she dared not laugh too hard, but it had been a very long time since she had found anything funny. She enjoyed the fleeting moment of levity. John knew she was laughing at him and imagining him with a full diaper gasping for air. He aped it silently for her as he held his nose with one hand and clutched an imaginary diaper with two fingers of the other. Simultaneously, he pranced around as if looking for a place to deposit the stinking bomb.

At once they both snapped back to reality. For the first time in their lives, they had found a moment in which they both could share something. Laughter faded into smiles which melted into blank faces. John reminded her half-jokingly that he might be the butt of the smelly diaper joke, but that "what comes around goes around." He could not imagine any situation Olivia could not handle with aplomb, but they both sobered quickly as they considered the enormity of a failed outcome to their plan. Olivia could lose their baby.

.....

The following day Olivia rose early, as was her custom, and prepared John's breakfast. He joined her at the kitchen table and dove into his scrambled eggs. "When do you propose I start with Kate?"

"Why don't we attempt it next week? This will give you a chance to figure out your schedule and practice changing one or two diapers to get the hang of it."

"Ahem, I'm going to rough it when it comes to the diapers," John said as he choked on his eggs. "I don't want to change one more than I absolutely have to. Just show me how and I'll figure it out. The worst case scenario is that I can't get the diaper to stay on her and I will use a hammer and some tacks as a temporary fix until I can get her home." John held his breath as he waited for Olivia to process what he had said.

"John Ward, you will not use a hammer and tacks on our daughter. What in Blue Blazes is wrong with you? Did your mama drop you on your head as a baby?"

He let out a belly laugh. He had promised Olivia payback would be fair game and he had set her up masterfully for the joke. He patted himself on the shoulder and chuckled again.

"Seriously though," he said, "I probably should spend a little more time with Kate over the next few days so she gets used to hearing my voice and following my commands. Perhaps I should even bathe, dress, and feed her a few times. I can put her to bed if you think it will help."

Olivia had to admit John was firmly grasping the concept of helping out around the house. Whether it was in general or as a result of the rolling store, she was both at the same time pleased and puzzled over the changes she witnessed in his behavior. But she was going to be careful not to do anything to stifle his involvement. For a moment, she believed he had actual concern for her well-being.

"Olivia, do you think if I help, you can carry the baby to full term? If so, I will gladly do my part to ensure it arrives in good health."

She knew John did not share her steadfast faith that God has a plan for them, and they had to 'wait upon the Lord' for His plan to be known to them.

"You have asked for assurance that the outcome of our efforts will produce the results we desire, John. While I wish I could give you this, I can't. You see, I don't know God's plan for this baby. What I believe is God expects us to do all we can do to give our baby a chance to live. This is not the answer you desire, but it is the only one I can truthfully give. We must take each day as it comes while knowing God will guide us through this difficult time."

John and Olivia shared their bed that night and slept soundly. Hope was on the horizon and they were eager to embrace it together for the benefit of their unborn child.

CHAPTER 37

The next morning, Olivia awoke with improved strength. Janie's herbal mixture had worked miracles in reducing her swelling, and the redness in her face had diminished considerably. She was eager to check in on Mrs. Smith and share with her the arrangements she had made for Kate's care until Rachel was available in August. Mrs. Smith was relieved at the sight of Olivia's noticeable improvement.

Olivia had a full day of baking and errands planned. "Mr. Adkins' man, Ben, will stop by to pick up the cakes and I will ride with him down to Jerrell's to refill your medicine. Janie made it clear to me I am not to pull heavy weight in my wagon until after the baby comes. Thankfully, Mrs. Gates has offered to have Jesse haul me and the groceries back here in their delivery truck. Without my having to walk, I should be back here well before Kate wakes from her nap."

"Don't worry, Kate and I will manage just fine while you are out," Mrs. Smith answered.

"I think you will find this amusing. John and I shared a rare laugh last night." She went on to tell of John's skit of his handling a smelly diaper and desperately searching for a place to dump it. "I fell for his joke which delighted him immensely. I don't know what I am going to do with that man. I've never seen such as that!"

Mrs. Smith laughed as heartily as Olivia had the evening before. The image of John Ward with a dripping diaper was more than she could imagine. She was happy to hear the joy in Olivia's voice and she was glad the struggling couple had found a moment of levity to share together. On the other hand, she had grave concerns about John and his attitude toward Kate, but she did not express them.

However fleeting, it was a start. John had come to the realization he was needed at home in the evenings after work to help with Kate. This relieved Mrs. Smith of some of her anxiety. There was not a day she had not asked God to heal the wounds that plagued John and Olivia's marriage. Perhaps her prayers were being answered.

.....

Later that day, Olivia entered Jerrell's and patiently waited for Mrs. Smith's prescription to be filled. As she left, she heard someone call her name and turned to see Beth sitting with a group of friends. She noticed Ann was among them. As she approached, Beth rose to greet her but Ann pulled on her arm, forcing her back into her seat. Ann turned away from Olivia to talk to one of the girls.

Charlotte Parker called out. "Olivia Ward, come join us. There is plenty of room and you must be anxious to chat with your sisters." Before Olivia could respond, Ann pushed herself away from the table, pulling Beth with her. She then loudly said to Olivia and all within earshot, "My family does not mix with trash. Beth and I will take our leave if you are determined to sit at this table."

Ann continued pulling Beth's arm, but she resisted. Beth turned to Olivia and mouthed, "I'm sorry."

Olivia held her hand up for them to stop while telling the group she was late for an appointment. Before anyone could see her tears, she turned and left the store. Outside, Jesse was waiting for her in the truck. Through Jerrell's front window he saw Ann watching Olivia with a half-crooked smile.

As he pulled away from the curb, Jesse could tell Olivia was upset but he knew asking about it would only make matters worse. They drove silently, and ten minutes later they were in front of Mrs. Smith's house. Olivia opened the door and whispered "thank you" and waddled quickly inside the house, forgetting her groceries. Jesse placed the boxes of groceries on the doorstep and left.

Once inside, Olivia saw that John was asleep on the settee with Kate napping on his chest. It was a good sign and she prayed that in another week, John would be able to manage Kate well enough to take her with him on his route. Her relief could not come too soon. Kate took to her father like 'a duck to water' and every night thereafter, Olivia heard their laughter at bath time. Once, she even heard John's voice as they sang what appeared to be the only song he knew.

That night John put Kate down and went over the instructions Olivia had written out in detail. "I know this is important and I want to get this right." The time was upon them; he would take Kate on his rounds the following day.

.....

It was difficult to tell who was more nervous, John or Olivia. As John loaded Kate into the converted bus turned rolling store, she looked around at the items hanging from the ceiling and cooed at her new experience. Olivia waved uneasily as they embarked on their maiden trip.

Just as he did with his passengers on the school bus run, John spoke over his shoulder to her and Kate responded with incoherent chatter. "As long as she is talking," he thought, "she can't get into anything back there." Soon her chatter subsided and when he reached a stop sign, he turned to check on her, and discovered that she was sound asleep. In fact, she slept through his first and second stops.

By their fourth stop, Kate had found her bottle and was busy sucking the nipple. Then, she serenaded him with another steady barrage of baby chatter. John had not been around her much during her waking hours and was amazed at how many words she knew. "It is an odd feeling," he thought, "hearing her call out to me 'Daddy, Daddy.' She is a determined little one, just like her Mama."

Around eleven o'clock, they made the bend and saw High Point on the horizon. John knew the road well as he had visited there many times. This, however, was the first time he had driven this road since that fateful November night. As he neared the house, he could see there was no activity on the circle track. It lay barren and overgrown. "What a shame," he thought. "Mr. Turner must be in bad shape to let his horse business go to ruin."

As they turned into the driveway leading up to the main house, the converted bus struggled to overcome the steep grade. "I barely made this in my car," he thought, "much less this overloaded bus." He downshifted and floored the gas and the motor seemed to get a second wind as it lurched forward and propelled the bus over the ruts and into the main yard. It swayed back and forth and the sounds of the pots and pans' metal striking metal echoed through the fields like a bell summoning the workers to the midday lunch.

He bypassed the main house and turned left to follow the fence rail down toward the peach orchard and on to the Quarters. As he made the turn, Gussie flagged him down from the back porch at the main house to see what the commotion was all about. He dutifully pulled over. "Hello

Gussie, I'm running this rolling store route with Mr. Adkins now. What can I get for you?"

"Howdy, Mister John. We be hearing that you gonna be stopping by these here farms this week. That sho is a plumb good thing for all us folks here whos can't get no time off to get into town while the sun is up. I 'spect you gonna be real welcome by e'rybody."

Gussie followed John as he stepped inside to get the last two items on her list. There, she found Kate playing in her pen. "Lawdy mercy," she shrieked. "Is this here Miss Olivia's little girl?"

"Yes, it certainly is, Gussie. Meet my daughter, Kate Ward."

"You go on and finish getting my needles. I just 'membered sumpin' I done be forgot inside."

Gussie hurried off the bus and into the main house. Outside, a crowd from the Quarters began to assemble. Each person carried the items they intended to barter for supplies. Since most could neither read nor write, they told John what they wanted and he fulfilled their requests. Without a list to check off, the going was slow. "This is going to take longer than I anticipated," he thought. "I will need to add some wiggle room in my schedule."

In a matter of minutes, Gussie was back and she shoved a few coins in John's hand and quickly disappeared, forgetting her needles. John scanned the crowd until he spotted her walking quickly back to the main house with Kate on her hip. He called out to her but she did not answer. When she reached the porch, she handed Kate to an older woman. "That is Annie Turner," John thought, "Kate's grandmother!"

Given the treatment Olivia received from the rest of the Turner family, John was concerned for Kate's safety and pushed his way through the swelling crowd toward the porch. He was relieved at the sight of Ann, however, who stood next to her mother. She waved to beckon him to join them. As he walked hurriedly toward the house, he noticed she paid no attention to Kate and it angered him. She was rejecting his daughter just as she had Olivia. He could not stand for that.

CHAPTER 38

With the economic slowdown finally hitting the Southeast, Walt found himself traveling less and less to deliver horses and Angus cows. Now with fewer demands on his time, Walt had taken a detour to Louisiana to visit Jerry and his wife. Just like his other sons, Jerry was prospering and Walt was grateful that everyone was holding their own in the dour economy.

Walt thought back to his father-in-law, Michael McGee, who had suffered a heart attack and died a few years ago. In the year before his death, Michael had struggled to keep his mercantile afloat. When Walt visited him, he was alarmed to see that the store was scarcely stocked. It was evident the economy had hit Georgia hard; and with diminished sales, there was little money left to restock shelves. Thus, customers had little reason to shop there.

It was a vicious circle. He couldn't restock because there was nothing to sell and he couldn't sell because he could not restock. They had managed a difficult relationship over the years, based mostly on Michael's efforts to thwart Walt's marriage plans with Annie. But Walt still regarded Michael's memory highly and it had saddened him to see his plight firsthand.

"There's only so much I can take in barter and still stay open," Michael had said. Walt took note of this and decided Michael had failed because he had not planned for any fallback options. "This," Walt thought, "will never happen to my business. I will always be prepared for the unforeseen and be ready to act."

.....

John removed his hat and bowed slightly as he stepped up on the porch. He avoided Ann for the moment in order to pay respects to her mother.

"Hello, Mrs. Turner. It is a pleasure to make your acquaintance again.

Is Mr. Turner around today?" John looked about nervously for the patriarch of the Turner clan. The last time he saw him, Walt Turner and his father had squared off on the front porch at High Bluff and he was not keen about the idea of seeing Walt again.

Before Annie could answer, Ann interrupted. "Papa is away in Louisiana and Mama knows he won't like what she's doing now. He made it clear to all of us that Olivia and that child are not welcome here." She turned to her mother and continued, "I expect he meant on this porch, too, Mama."

Annie paid Ann no attention as she marveled at Kate's good looks and charming demeanor. She hugged her tightly and kissed her forehead. Kate responded with, "Mama, Mama."

Ann had seen enough. She turned to her mother and took Kate's arms, attempting to pry her away. "Gussie, why don't you take this child and put her back where you found her? Do you hear me?" Gussie nervously looked to Annie for approval. Annie smiled at Gussie, turned her back to Ann and walked over to a rocker and sat down with Kate.

Ann was furious. "Gussie, you get whatever it is you need from Mr. Ward and then get yourself back to the kitchen."

Gussie, who had minded Ann since she was an infant, gave her an indignant look. "Miss Ann, I done knowed you since you was a baby and I has changed a heap of stinky diapers of yours, but none of 'em stink as bad as how you been treating Miss Olivia and this here chile. I does what your Mama tells me. Nobody ever allowed as to how you is able to give me orders in this here house. Missus Annie, what you want me to do?"

Before Annie could respond, John reached down and gently pried Kate away from her. "I'll take her," he said. "This talk of dirty diapers has rendered Kate and me temporarily indisposed. And besides, I will not stand here and have my daughter suffer the rejection of a spoiled brat." As he walked back to the bus, he was fit to be tied with Ann.

"Who the hell does she think she is?" he thought. "She is nothing more to me than a tired plaything I have left deserted in the corner. She is crass and desperate, and certainly not worthy of Kate's attention."

Gussie rushed to catch John, and he explained Olivia was in poor health with her expecting a second child in October. He would, therefore, have Kate riding along with him on future runs to neighboring farms.

"Gussie, my daughter doesn't deserve treatment such as Ann just rendered. You need to let your folks in the Quarters know that I'll not be stopping here at High Point again. They will have to meet me out at the main road. I will not expose my daughter to any more of her aunt's mean-spirited behavior."

As the words danced on his tongue, John was surprised at how defensive he was of Kate and how naturally it came to him to speak of her as his daughter. Gussie understood. Tears welled in her eyes.

"Mister John, Missus Annie is not well. She be stayin in her room most of the days now and you won't believes the look she had on her face when I done told her you were here with her granddaughter. I ain't seen her look like that in I don't know how long. Please Mister John. Please don't deny her a chance to see Miss Kate. I will find a way to control Miss Ann ifn you will keep on stopping here."

John was touched by her concern for Mrs. Turner and he agreed.

"Okay. I'll stop again next week, and I will keep stopping as long as there is business to be done here and Kate receives the respect she deserves."

John had underestimated the time it would take to serve the Quarters and he was woefully behind. More important, he needed to settle his disquiet thinking about Ann. Despite their checkered history, he would not meet with her socially again. His pride simply would not allow it. Now, though, he had to get on to the next farm to ensure he met his sales goals. And besides, Kate was nearly due for a diaper change.

CHAPTER 39

John and Kate returned home from their maiden voyage together on the rolling store and were greeted by the smell of beef stew simmering on the stove. Olivia was at Mrs. Smith's so John grabbed a washrag and wiped the dust off Kate's round face. She giggled and cooed as he cleaned her ears. By the time he fed and put her down for the night, Olivia returned.

He hoped there would be signs of miraculous improvement in her condition, but there were none. She was bloated and moved slowly, but she was curious to hear how he had fared with Kate. She asked one question after another to John's dismay.

"Olivia, you are one wound up woman tonight. Slow down just a bit and I'll tell you. First, you should know Kate Ward is a 'charmer.' There was not a place I stopped today where she was not held and played with. The ladies on my route were more interested in her than in what I was selling, but I still had a good day of sales. Once she flashes her big smile, they are hooked."

"That's great. Dare I ask how you fared with her diapers?"

"I didn't have to change a single one. She is so cute that everyone along the way doted on her and several women offered to change her."

Kate had been a model helper riding all over the countryside with him. She not only charmed his customers, she gave him more pleasure than he could describe. Having her along was a real joy and he looked forward to the next day. "Before it slips my mind, your Mama sends her love."

"You spoke to Mama today? How did this happen?"

"Of course. Have you forgotten my route 'rolls' past High Point? While I was stopped there, Gussie heard Kate inside the bus. Before I could bat an eye, she snatched her up and took her to the porch to see her grandmother. I was worried about your father getting angry, but he was away in Louisiana. Your mama adored Kate and asked me to bring her back to visit soon. I thought I would never get away!"

Olivia felt a warm sense of happiness envelope her. "Really? Please tell me what Mama and the rest of the family thought of Kate."

John related how much Mrs. Turner enjoyed her brief time with Kate. But he left out any reference to Ann's antics; he knew it would be too hurtful.

Shortly, they lapsed into what had become their nightly routine. John posted his sales ledger and reconciled his inventory while Olivia worked on finishing a rug. John finished his accounting and was pleased to report their first day sales nearly triple what he and Mr. Adkins had anticipated. John would clearly have no issue with having the money to restock the store when it was required.

John was happy at the prospect of turning a profit. It meant he could finally get on his feet and show his father he had the ability to run his business. A few weeks before, he had seen the movie, "The Gold Diggers of 1933," and he hummed the tune to "We're In The Money" repeatedly as he prepared Kate's bottle for the next morning. Soon, he was ready for bed. Before Olivia joined him, she thanked God for John's change in attitude toward Kate and for her renewed strength. She prayed both would last.

.....

Two weeks passed with John and Kate rolling from High Springs to various outlying farms as he peddled his goods. He was more content than he had been in a long time and his thoughts often turned to Olivia. Spending more time with her had caused him to reconsider his feelings toward her. She had a kind and giving personality and he quickly found he was unable to resent her as he had in the past.

To his dismay, he discovered he possessed a conscience. No matter how his thoughts started out, they always returned to the same issue. Olivia Turner Ward was an amazing woman of many talents, but he just could not love her. This was the crux of the matter. After their baby was born, could he continue to use her to satisfy his needs when he did not love her as a man was supposed to love his wife?

In the meantime, John had shed the shame of being perceived as a washed out athlete and two-bit gambler. His status had changed around Geneva County and he was now a respected businessman. It was time to spread his wings.

.....

Robert's and Evelyn's weekend visits became a ritual; they never missed seeing Kate on either Saturday or Sunday afternoon. After taking care of

Mrs. Smith on Sunday mornings, Olivia set aside time for studying God's Word and she reserved the afternoons for their visits. She had to discipline herself in this regard because she could ill afford to put off work on projects she depended upon for their living expenses. John was doing well with the rolling store but his profits were designated toward restocking inventory and settling John's debt with Mr. Adkins. It was pleasing to her to observe the effort John put into arranging his work schedule at the cannery so that he, too, could be at home for their visits.

From his arrival until his departure, Robert Ward asked many questions about John's experience with the rolling store. He was intrigued and listened intently as John related stories about their adventures. He appreciated his son's maturing business acumen, but he enjoyed more hearing about his travels with Kate. As John related an episode where Kate decided to change her own dirty diaper, Robert bent over double with laughter. Easily the most enjoyable part of his visit was witnessing John's newfound delight in sharing his daughter's escapades.

Evelyn recognized the fun John and Kate had together and she begged him to let her ride along with them. She was eight years old, after all, and capable of taking care of herself. She promised she would be no trouble if allowed to tag along. Besides, she had at least one skill John did not possess: she knew how to change a diaper.

"You're hired," John said enthusiastically as Evelyn smothered him in kisses. He would take her during the week before she started back to school. Evelyn was overjoyed.

Robert's joy was tempered with worry as he observed Olivia's declining health. He wondered why it continued to deteriorate, but he was reluctant to ask her. On his last visit, Olivia thanked him for having Flora continue to deliver flour sacks and she hinted she always delayed Flora's timely departure in order to learn what was happening with Flora's family and her friends in the Quarters. Robert knew this and had played along with Flora's using him as a conduit to her helping Olivia. Now was the time to turn the tables and use her as a reliable source of information on Olivia's health.

.....

Walt had spent the last few days in South Georgia finalizing a deal to sell four Angus bulls. As he crested the hill at top of the driveway, he parked his car near the rusting yellow hulk of Jim's wrecked truck. There, it served as a constant reminder of all that Walt had lost in the last few years. Although he had noticed a considerable improvement in Annie over the preceding weeks, he continued to lament their loss of Jim.

"By now," he thought, "he would be finished with medical school and be on his way to becoming a pilot in the army or a surgeon in Birmingham or Atlanta." Walt pursed his lips in sorrow as he climbed the steps to the porch. There, he found Annie in her rocker soaking in the last few rays of the August afternoon.

"You're looking mighty fine, dear," he said as he clasped her hand and kissed her cheek. "I'm so glad to see you are up and about and feeling better these days." Annie smiled back at him.

"Yes, I'm feeling much more hopeful these days."

"To what do you attribute your improvement? I've not seen Dr. James around. Has he put you on some new medicine or has Gussie concocted you an elixir from the Quarters?"

"No, Walt. It's nothing of the sort like that. I'm just feeling hopeful these days."

Walt noticed the knitting needle and yarn in her lap, but, he could not make out what she was knitting. He was relieved to see she had taken up her favorite past time again. He excused himself to find Gussie and as he picked up his valise, he got a better view of the heap in Annie's lap. There, he distinctly made out the shape of a tiny baby bootie. "Interesting," he thought, "very interesting."

.....

Robert arrived at High Bluff and found Flora. "I've just returned from visiting with Olivia and I am very concerned about her health. Is there anything you can share with me about what Dr. James has said about her run-down appearance?" Flora was full of information.

"Dr. James be done told Olivia he had no use for her and Kate as patients. He be done listened to all that trash gossip about Miss Olivia and figured he sho 'nough didn't be wantin' e'rybodys see'n her in his'n clinic. I guess he figured he couldn't be treating no branded girl at the expense of ticking off the whole town."

Robert became visibly upset.

"Is you alright Mister Robert? You sho be lookin' like you is gonna bust a gut!"

Robert was livid. "How did Charles James have the gall to deny a Ward medical care? That son-of-a-bitch is going to feel my wrath which he could never have imagined."

Flora listened intently as Robert became more incensed. "That idiot. I hold the mortgages on both his home and his office. Additionally, I hold the loan on all of his equipment. At my pleasure, I can call for repayment of all of these, which will surely ruin him. Is he really ready to lose everything over one stupid decision? By the time I am through with that bastard, he won't even be able to treat Evelyn's doll Jean for a cold."

Flora laughed silently and thanked God that she was not Dr. Charles James.

Robert's voice calmed as his cooler side prevailed, and a cardinal principle came to mind. "I'll not act precipitously though, as we might require his medical expertise before Olivia delivers her baby." He figured he could exercise a little patience until he was satisfied Dr. James no longer served a purpose. Yes, he would wait, and then, he would orchestrate his financial ruin.

"Flora, I apologize for speaking so frankly. My temper does not show often; but when it does, it is volatile. I'm afraid I may have gone a little overboard. Please forgive me, and please, don't mention this to anyone."

"Don't you be worryin' none, Mister Robert, 'cause my lips is sealed. Nary a word of what you be sayin' will I repeat. But sir, I gotta tell you whats they is saying in town about Missus Judy. You need to know."

"Go ahead," Robert said as he listened intently.

Flora wrung her hands as she crafted her words. "Missus Judy has done gone and tried to fix all the bad things she done said about Miss Olivia around High Springs, but no one believes her. They be saying she is just putting on a show but don't mean what she be telling 'em. She sho nuf didn't help Miss Olivia with her play acting."

Robert nodded in agreement as Flora confirmed for him what he had heard, but hoped was exaggerated. Now, he knew it was not. It was time he took action to remedy his wife's failure.

"Flora, please find Mrs. Ward and tell her I expect her to be ready within half an hour. You probably should share with her the foul mood you find me in right now. Let her know that it will be best for her if she joins me willingly. I don't want to have to come fetch her."

Flora left not doubting for a minute that Mr. Ward meant business.

"Lordy, Lord," she thought. "I do believe that we be 'bout to have another showdown at the Ward's house." She hurried off to deliver Judy his message.

CHAPTER 40

Robert Ward plotted for Dr. Charles James' destruction and he was reminded how he had paid back Walt Turner for his part in Olivia's rejection from her church. Walt's support of his congregation's withdrawal of fellowship from Olivia had been the last straw for Robert and he had determined to exact his revenge on her behalf. He would hit Walt where it hurt him most: in his pocketbook. As he sat waiting for Judy, he played back the scene of Walt's comeuppance in his mind.

Several months ago, Walt had come to Robert's office with his usual cocksure swagger. "Robert, the rumor in town is that you have poured a lot of money into financing and managing carriage of the Southern Railroad spur to Dothan. With times as hard as they are, I figure you need increased business if you expect to make a profit."

"Is that so?" Robert said as he frowned with displeasure. Walt took a chair across from him without being asked to. Robert lit a cigar without offering one to Walt. As he drew deeply to stoke the smoldering flame, he expelled the smoke into Walt's direction.

Sensing the insult of Robert's action, Walt rushed onward. "I've been thinking since we are relatives, of a sort, I ought to help you out by bringing you my business. I'll accommodate you by letting you haul my livestock and lumber to Dothan where I can get freight delivery from there."

Between puffs on his Churchill cigar, Robert was unable to hold back a smile. "So you think you need to accommodate me? Ha! That's a good one."

It amused him that Walt had the brass balls to suggest Robert's business suffered financially. He knew Walt lost money trucking his lumber and cotton to market. With timelines as tight as Walt required, he knew he needed to use the least expensive way to get his products to the northern markets where there was cash money to purchase his goods. No doubt the cheapest way was shipping via rail.

"Walt, you're full of shit. We both know that you're the one who needs my accommodation. You are financially strapped and we both know it. Don't mistake me for one of those gentlemen farmers you routinely outsmart on your horse trades. To do so is at your peril." As Walt squirmed in his chair, Robert sensed the time was ripe for the kill.

"Apparently you don't realize you have already accommodated me multiple times more than I can ever repay. First, you dumped Olivia on my doorstep. I'll tell you, sir, what a jewel she has been to us. Your second accommodation was leading your congregation in withdrawing fellowship from her. It ended up being a blessing because your action rid her of any association with the hypocrites that make up more than half your congregation. Suffice it to say, the bottom line is this: I don't need your business accommodations. What I do want is for you to get your sorry ass out of my office and never darken my door again."

Walt was stunned. He had seldom endured a verbal beating such as this and he was surprised at the forcefulness Robert displayed. He had underestimated him to be the kind and genteel man the men at the barber shop spoke of. Apparently, there was more to Robert Ward than met the eye. With a newfound respect, he prepared to leave. "My daughter, Olivia, is your problem now," he said. "Deal with her however you see fit. She is no concern of mine."

Robert was appalled by Walt's callous treatment of his own flesh and blood. Could he not realize he was far from the perfect father in his raising of his children? Perhaps he needed a reminder.

"By the way," Robert said. "It would benefit you right much if you paid a visit to Peter Kelly's barber shop and listened to how the men talk of your precious daughter, Ann. On the other hand, you may not want to hear their tales of her wanton behavior while chasing after my married son like a moth to a flame. What is it they call her? Oh yes, a Jezebel. Funny that the daughter you kept in your home ranks below the daughter you tossed out into the street. It would seem that you are as adept at judging your daughters as you are at managing your businesses."

This last shot sunk Walt and he could barely move to open the door. Robert took a long draw on his cigar and snuffed it out in the ash tray on his desk. He exhaled in Walt's general direction and the cloud enveloped the diminutive horse trader. Walt grimaced as he fanned away the gray cloud in front of him. Robert's revenge for Olivia was wrought in spades! "Good day, sir. This conversation, much like my cigar, is done." Walt left in a hurry and did not return.

Now, Robert pushed his encounter with Walt to the back of his mind.

He needed to focus on his plan for dealing with Charles James. He must make certain, though, that Olivia would never learn of his actions with Walt or what he was going to do to Dr. James. He knew that she would not approve. It was her sterling nature to leave judgment and consequences only in God's hands. Perhaps he should subscribe to her view. "But," he thought, "God might need a little earthly help." After all, his motive was good. He would make it clear that he would take care of his own, and by God, she was his own. Olivia was a Ward.

Shortly, Robert heard the sound of Judy's heels approaching. Flora must have relayed his message with the right tenor, for Judy was ready in less than the half hour allotted. She entered his study in a huff.

"What is this all about? Just answer me without yelling. All the colored folks in the Quarters are still gossiping about our last shouting match, and I am not here to put on another show for them."

"I've heard tales about your exhibition in the beauty shop and the general consensus is no one took you seriously. I suspect that is what you intended. Today, though, we are going to remedy your poor performance. Suppose you get a stiff rod for your backbone and some glue to plaster on a convincing smile. We are going calling today and you had better deliver a convincing, if not sincere, act." Robert ushered Judy to his car and they headed toward High Springs. First though, they would stop and look in on Olivia and Kate.

.....

The two people traveling to High Springs were occupied with vastly different thoughts of what was to happen once they arrived. Judy's temper was as hot as the sun's rays upon the car's roof. She would not allow Robert to put her in an embarrassing situation nor would she allow him to undo all her effort to bring Olivia down. He said they were going to set some people straight and she understood his implications.

"Fortunately," she thought, "there won't be many people in town. He's so busy with his idea of straightening people out that he's not considering people are too busy trying to gather their crops to waste time coming to town."

It was the second week of August 1932 and the fields were abuzz with activity. As they drove, Judy noticed farmers and their families working feverishly to harvest their crops which were dying in the fields from the onslaught of heat in the insufferable dog days of summer. Before them lay fields of brown cornstalks and cotton plants heavy with bolls half opened. The scene did not change as they passed from one farm to another.

Uncharacteristically, Judy felt regret. She was mindful of the hard times many farmers were experiencing and she could not take her eyes off the spectacle they made as they fought against the odds of salvaging enough ears of corn, bales of cotton, and gunny sacks of peanuts to repay the loans they had taken to plant and harvest what would be their livelihood for the coming year. She reflected on her deep understanding of hers and Robert's business interests.

It was rare for a woman to have either the interest or the understanding of such matters. Societal norms of the day dictated such. A woman could not even secure a loan without her husband as a cosigner and most did not have their own bank accounts. Rather, they were relegated to child rearing or, if they worked, teaching, retail, or secretarial jobs.

In keeping with this social mandate, few knew Judy Ward was a partner with Robert in his businesses in a time where women simply did not engage in such activity. Even fewer people remembered she had been a shrewd businesswoman who had expanded Ward Enterprises while Robert was in France during and for two years after the Great War.

Of course, she had relied on negotiating the deals via correspondence using his name and accomplished this by forging his signature on key documents. The other parties were none the wiser as she inked one successful business deal after another. Robert returned from France surprised to behold all Judy had accomplished, even if it were on the fringe of being illegal.

Because of the acumen she had demonstrated, unlike most men of their acquaintance, Robert trusted her insights and shared his business plans with her. She wished she did not already know what was going to happen to some of those she saw in the fields when the calendar flipped to 1933.

With no crops to cash out, they would be forced to settle their debts as best they could to whoever held the notes on their properties: either their bank or Ward Enterprises. As the crooked, gray, weathered fence posts clicked by, she predicted with considerable accuracy which of the farms would become Ward properties in the coming year. "How can I feel regret?" She thought. "They gambled and they will lose."

Robert interrupted the silence with a brief reminder of how she was to behave once they arrived at Olivia's. He had no idea how well she had succeeded in her quest to ruin Olivia's chance of ever being accepted by the people who mattered in High Springs. Of course, there were exceptions such as Mrs. Smith, the Gates, and the Adkins. Just thinking about what she had accomplished in sabotaging Olivia eased Judy's mind. Robert could rant and rave till the cows came home and it would not alter what she had already achieved.

Soon, they pulled into Mrs. Smith's driveway and stopped. Although she preferred to wait in the car, she supposed Robert would expect her to accompany him inside. Her desire to avoid this awkward mess was surpassed only by her reluctance to sit in the car in the ninety-eight degree heat. So, she followed him up the stone path and around back to the housekeeper's quarters.

At the door, they were perplexed to hear a scream from inside. Then another scream pierced the air and they knew it had come from Olivia. Robert pushed the door open and ran to the kitchen. Lying on the floor before him, Olivia writhed in pain with blood puddled beneath her. "Oh my God," he thought. "It's a repeat of her incident at High Bluff." Judy stopped in the kitchen doorway, horrified at the sight before her.

Robert rushed to Olivia and knelt beside her, checking her pulse and attempting to determine if she had lost the baby. He yelled to Judy, "Come quickly, I need you."

The urgency of his command mobilized her, and she joined him at his side. Olivia lay before her in abject misery, and all of Judy's thoughts of malice toward her dissipated as she came to understand the gravity of the situation. Olivia was fighting for her life.

"Oh my God, Robert, what can I do?"

Robert had seen many men die in battle and it was no less gruesome or horrifying than here in the kitchen. He knew they must stop Olivia's bleeding quickly or she would die within minutes. "In fact," he thought, "it may already be too late." He motioned to Judy. "Get as many towels as you can find, then, start a boiler of hot water."

He lifted Olivia's clothing enough to determine she had not delivered prematurely.

"So far, so good," he thought. "But we still have a long way to go to get her out of the woods." He checked and found her pulse to be weak and he immediately knew it was from her excessive blood loss. To both his chagrin and relief, he had not yet lashed out at Dr. James. Olivia needed him right now. As Judy returned with towels and stoked the wood burning stove, he turned to her.

"Judy, Olivia needs help only Dr. James can give. Please go for him now and spare no effort to return with him."

Judy rose to go. She frankly was relieved he had asked her as she was afraid to be left alone with Olivia in such bad condition. As she took the car key from Robert, she could not resist poking his strict views on women's rights. "In spite of all your objections to the contrary, aren't you glad I badgered you to teach me how to drive?"

Robert smiled at her feeble attempt to lighten their worry. "Yes, dear. Go then, but promise me that you will bring him back come hell or high water. He has refused to aid her before and he may resist you. You must not take 'no' for an answer."

"You better believe I'll bring him back," she replied. "John's baby is going to live. Olivia, hold on, you are not alone."

Robert heard tires squeal as Judy sped around the curve headed for Dr. James' clinic. He was grateful Judy had an understanding of the dire situation before them and the urgency to get help for Olivia. He realized time was precious and they had little to spare.

Robert's heart was beating in his ears now. It sounded like a drum and he heard muffled noises as if artillery shells were bursting around him. There was blood everywhere and it smelled like spent gunpowder. Olivia's whimpers for help sounded like the cries he had heard on the battlefield. For a moment, he imagined he was in France in the Argonne Forest, September 1918.

Olivia convulsed and Robert came to his senses. Time was rushing by now and Olivia's breathing was becoming dangerously shallow. He pressed the towels against her, trying to staunch the flow of blood. His effort was only marginally effective; but without a doctor, he knew nothing more to do. He had lost a sense of time and wondered, "What in the hell is keeping Judy? I hope to God she isn't taking her sweet time in fetching Dr. James."

CHAPTER 41

Judy steered the '30 Ford Phaeton with reckless abandon. She realized the lives of Olivia and her unborn baby hung in the balance as they relied on her to find Dr. James quickly and convince him to tend to Olivia. As she entered the town square, she blew through the stop sign by Dallon's and cut across both lanes of traffic toward the center of the square. Two ladies leaped out of her path as she jumped the curb and cut across the center of the square. Narrowly missing the gazebo, she exited the other side of the square in front of Dr. James' office. She slid the auto to a stop with one wire-rimmed tire resting atop the curb. Less than five minutes after leaving Mrs. Smith's house, Judy burst through the door of the clinic.

She bypassed several patients who were seated in wooden chairs and rushed to the counter where the receptionist advised her Dr. James was with a patient.

"It's an emergency!" she said. "It is truly a matter of life and death." The receptionist, a heavy set girl of about 19 years of age with a ruddy complexion and wearing a white uniform, told her to take a seat and the doctor would be with her when he was finished.

"The hell, you say. Dr. James is coming with me now or my name is not Judy Ward. You either fetch him this minute or move out of my way and I will get him myself." Her voice must have carried louder than she imagined because Dr. James appeared at the doorway to his exam room followed closely by his nurse.

"Judy Ward, what is the meaning of your outburst in my clinic? You need to calm down." His words had the effect of waving a red flag at a bull. It only made her more aggressive.

"Your clinic?" she challenged him, knowing that her husband held the mortgage to the building and equipment. She thought to mention it but did not waste the time. "Charles James, get your bag and come with me now." Dr. James stood petrified. "Don't stand there like a deer caught in a headlight. Move man, my grandchild's life depends upon it."

Charles James knew all too well of Robert Ward's reputation for destroying anyone who crossed him in Geneva County and Judy Ward's legacy was not far behind. He knew that he had best grab his bag and sort out the mess it would cause in his clinic later. "Did you say life and death?"

he asked. "Nurse, grab my bag and take over for me here today. I'll be back when I can." His nurse seemed to understand the urgency of the matter and handed him his black doctor's case as Judy propelled him toward the door.

"This way," Judy commanded. "I'll drive us there." Dr. James saw the skid marks on the road and the car's tire resting atop the curb and he wondered if riding with Judy Ward was the best idea. It was too late now. She was already in the car and beginning to pull away. He leaped into the passenger's seat just as she released the clutch causing the '30 Ford to lurch forward. A crowd had begun to gather in the square and Dr. James adjusted his hat and managed to pull the door closed about halfway around the square.

Judy was focused straight ahead now. The Ford's motor was screaming mightily as Judy was driving as fast as she could, in second gear. "There is another gear," Dr. James shouted.

"What?" Judy asked over the whine of the engine. Dr. James pointed to the gearshift and motioned for her to pull it down into the next gear. "Okay," she said. "You watch the road!" She slammed her left foot down to mash the clutch, missed, and struck the floorboard. At the same time, she jammed the gearshift into third gear. There was a shriek of metal as the gears engaged and the engine throttled back to a normal range.

"Me watch the road?" he exclaimed. "Oh Lord, please don't take me now," he prayed. "And while you're at it Lord, please don't ever let Robert Ward know that I once refused to care for Olivia."

By his count, she had run three stop signs, narrowly missed a dog on the sidewalk, and sideswiped a mailbox by the time they turned onto Mrs. Smith's street. Somewhere along the way, he had lost his hat to a swerve or a curve. He had no idea which. Although the car was slowing down to turn into Mrs. Smith's driveway, he held on for dear life as she had demonstrated her appetite for taking risks while driving had no boundaries.

As she turned into the driveway, the Ford lurched on two wheels and she used both feet to engage the brakes. The car came to a sudden halt slamming him against the dash board. Dr. James gathered his composure and his bag, and ran inside to find Olivia.

He entered the kitchen to find Robert hunched over Olivia's still body, holding in place the bandage he had made. They acknowledged each other with a nod, and Dr. James moved in to examine her.

"Robert, the pad you used to stop the blood flow may have saved her life. She has lost a lot of blood but she still has a faint pulse. If I am to save her, I have to stop the heavy bleeding but I can't do that unless I take the baby out immediately. I will try to save them both but I make no promises. This baby is nearly two months premature and it's going to be an uphill climb. Can you assist me?" Robert nodded in agreement.

Dr. James moved Olivia into a position so he could examine her. By now, he was kneeling in blood that completely surrounded him and he could feel it soak through his pants. Olivia was almost fully dilated and the baby was in the proper position in the birth canal. Its head was pushing downward and she was having contractions, but she was so weak she was unable to push her baby out. He felt another strong contraction and observed Olivia stop breathing for a few seconds. "It's now or never," he said to Robert with his voice breaking. "We are about to lose them both. She won't survive two more contractions."

Robert's eyes grew wide and they filled with tears. He could not believe what he was hearing. He looked Dr. James directly in the eyes and pleaded, "Tell me what I need to do."

Dr. James did not respond. He mopped his brow with his sleeve and his arm lingered there in thought.

"Charles, what are you doing?" he asked. Dr. James did not respond. "Dammit Charles, what the hell are you doing?"

The doctor turned to him and Robert saw a look of fear and desperation on his pale face. "Perhaps," Robert thought, "saving Olivia is beyond his medical expertise."

He held up both bloody hands and motioned for Robert to relax. "Robert," he said, "it's really bad. If I follow conventional procedure they are both going to die right now."

Robert stared at him in shock and without speaking.

"It is a Hail Mary, Robert, but I'm going to do something I've never done before. It's used as a last resort to save a mother or a baby, and in a few cases, both. Hand me my scalpel. Now!"

Judy looked on from the edge of the kitchen. She normally was squeamish around blood but her concern for both Olivia and the baby surprised her and she could not bear to look away. She had a thought that John needed to be here. He was likely between stops on his route and there were no phones anywhere to call ahead to find him. Her only hope was to have someone telegraph the train platform near the intersection of

Highways 52 and 41 on the southwest side of High Springs. There, they could dispatch messengers in each direction in hopes of intercepting the bus.

Frantic now, Judy ran into the street and flagged down a passing car. The gentleman behind the wheel stared at her blood covered arms and torso and nodded feebly as she gave him specific instructions. Now, after Judy's automobile and blood covered antics, a small crowd was beginning to gather. Believing there must be a real emergency brewing, the motorist agreed to help.

Dr. James hovered over Olivia with the scalpel. There was no time to mix an anesthesia so Robert held her legs as she was too weak to flail her arms or lift her torso. Robert watched intently as Dr. James made an incision into her pelvis. He was surprised that there was little blood and he winced as the incision flayed open. "There's not much blood left," Charles said. "We are working on borrowed time here. If you believe in anything Holy, now would be a good time to call in any favors."

Robert closed his eyes briefly and prayed. Dr. James looked at Robert's hands and shook his head in disbelief. His worried look caught Robert's eyes. By now Judy had rejoined them and she leaned intently over Robert's shoulder.

"I've summoned John," she said. "What can I do to help?"

Dr. Charles answered with a degree of desperation in his voice. "Judy, I have to have help and I can't use Robert because his size will hinder me. Are you prepared to help me save Olivia and your grandchild? This isn't going to be pretty."

"I'm ready," she said. Robert released his grip on Olivia's legs and poured rubbing alcohol on Judy's hands and arms. He told her not to touch anything until Dr. James instructed her to do so and she briefly nodded.

Dr. James took Judy's hands and guided them into position. "No matter what happens, you must not lose your grip. You must not let go." She agreed. He took the scalpel in hand again and began to slit downward toward the baby's skull. He told Judy to move to straddle Olivia positioning herself so she could maintain her hold to allow him to use his forceps to extract the baby when Olivia experienced her next contraction. The contraction came and Charles eased the forceps around the baby's head, gently tugging with the force of the contraction.

Perspiration formed on his forehead and arms; Robert stood behind him and wiped the moisture from Dr. James' forehead and brow before it could drop. With a slow and measured tug, he pulled against Olivia and guided the baby out. Then, working as rapidly as he dared, he firmly slapped the baby's buttocks and gently massaged its chest.

"Water," Dr. James commanded, "I need the warm water now."

Robert retrieved the boiler and held it still for Dr. James who submerged the baby in it for just a second. He then moved the body around in the boiler while holding its head out of the water. He slapped the baby again and brought forth a welcomed cry. Then he cut the cord, and placed the baby in Judy's outstretched arms. She had helped bring her granddaughter into this world on Tuesday, August 22, 1932. Dr. James then turned his attention to saving Olivia.

.....

Meanwhile, a mile or so off his route, John pulled the rolling store off the main road and behind an abandoned barn. There, waiting for him on the tailgate of a rust colored truck sat Wallace and Vincent leaning on two wooden crates full of Mason jars.

"I knew you would make it, Johnny Boy. Old Vincent here owes me two bits because he bet you wouldn't show," Wallace said as he spit tobacco juice at John's feet.

"I got the note from your man at the cannery telling me it was time to settle my marker. What do you want from me all the way out here? Hurry it up; I've got to finish my route."

"Whoa there boy. Settle down. All you've got to do to settle your marker is deliver these here jars to the men on this here list." Wallace unfolded a piece of brown paper and handed it to John. "These boys will be a waitin' fer you. Don't you keep 'em a waitin' too long or they might just get ornery."

John took the list and surveyed the names and the number of jars each man was to receive. "What's in the jars?" he asked, reaching out for a jar and uncapping it. As he sniffed its contents and took a sip, Wallace chortled.

"Fire water, boy. The Devil's Juice. Moonshine. Everything a man needs but Uncle Sam don't want 'em to have these days."

"But…, that's illegal," John stammered as he spit out the acidic clear liquid and recapped the jar. "I can't be hauling moonshine on my route. Mr. Adkins would not approve and I could lose my job. Worse yet, I could get arrested. I won't do it."

Wallace chuckled and turned to Vincent. "You hear that Vincent? Sounds to me like Ole Johnny Boy here is gonna welch on his marker after we were so neighborly and extended him credit to cover that 'winning hand' of his."

Vincent laughed, slapped his knee, and said, "Let me tell you something John Ward. You a gonna to do this here fer me and Wallace cause if you don't, we is gonna have a talk with your daddy. I don't imagine he's a gonna be too pleased to hear about what his little boy has been doing after hours at the dry cleaners and carousing with your wife's sister."

John gritted his teeth in frustration. The Boys had him in a tough spot. He had worked hard to restore his father's trust and the thought of having him find out he was gambling was more than he could bear.

"Okay, I will make the deliveries for you, but only these crates. I can't afford to run afoul with the sheriff. That would make trouble for my father and I cannot risk it."

"Oh, no!" Wallace barked. "You will deliver for us for as long as I tell you to and I'll let you know when your marker is satisfied. And besides, the sheriff is a friend of ours. He's the least of your worries. Your rolling junk yard here is the perfect cover for our operation. As far as anyone will know, you're just making your rounds. You better keep an eye out though; there's some boys from New Orleans and Chicago that might not take too kindly to our cuttin' in on their liquor sales here in Alabamy and Flor'da."

John pocketed the list and quickly loaded the boxes of mason jars into the rolling store. Then, he tentatively tipped his cap to the men, mounted the bus, and pulled back out onto the roadway. He didn't fancy the notion of butting heads with these "Boys," but he liked the thought of becoming acquainted with the "Boys" from Chicago and New Orleans even less. He resolved to do whatever he could to avoid angering either of them.

CHAPTER 42

Peter Kelly skidded to a halt in the soft gravel at the train depot two miles west of High Springs. Just a few minutes before, he had been stopped in the middle of the road by a crazy woman covered in blood and waving her arms frantically. Upon closer inspection, he recognized Judy Ward, the wife of a prominent Geneva County businessman. Reflecting on the gossip he had heard in his shop, he thought, "This family certainly has a flair for the dramatic."

Judy had explained her son's wife was having a baby at that very moment and she needed to locate him on his sales route which extended north from High Springs on Highway 61, over to Highway 41, and down to Highway 52 back into High Springs, completing the circuit.

"John," she said, "is somewhere along this route in a yellow school bus with pots and pans hanging off the side and a one year old child in a playpen in the back. You can't miss him."

"A baby in a playpen?" he thought. Mr. Kelly scratched his head in disbelief but out of respect for Robert, he proceeded without wasting another second.

Now, at the platform, he ran into the lineman's shack to ask the caretaker, Howard Murphy, to wire the depots at Eunola, to the west near Geneva, and Bell Creek, to the north of High Bluff. From there, they could send out messengers in search of the "rolling nursery."

"I'll have to say," Mr. Murphy chuckled. "I've never wired a message to search for a baby before."

"Well I've certainly never been accosted by a crazy woman covered in blood," Peter Kelly countered.

"You got a minute?" Murphy asked. "Come on inside my shack and let me treat you to a cold Coca Cola. You look like you could use one."

"You got anything stronger?" Kelly asked. "It's been one of those days."

.....

Dr. James had no time to lose if he were going to have any chance of saving Olivia. She was fading fast and he had to stop the bleeding by removing the afterbirth without puncturing the lining of her womb. As he removed the tissue and began to suture the slit, he acknowledged the odds were stacked against him and if he managed to save Olivia's life, it would be because of God's will.

Charles James could not imagine more difficult circumstances under which to perform an operation. Kneeling in blood, with dim light, without anesthetic and with only a few supplies in his house call bag, he worked the next two hours to maintain Olivia's blood pressure and breathing. Her loss of blood was great, but there was nothing he could do about it. The nearest hospital with blood for a transfusion was in Dothan, over 30 miles away. She would certainly die before he could stabilize and move her there in the back of a truck.

Olivia was now anything but the image of a strong and determined woman who at one time had been one of the most highly regarded people in Geneva County. Instead, she was now a picture of a dying pixie. The color was gone from her face and, save the occasional groan from the pain, his only indication of life were the piercing blue orbs that peeked out from behind her nearly closed eyelids.

With Judy's help, he was able to manipulate the tiny needle and thread in the right manner to suture the wound. Within a few minutes, her dilation began to reverse and with the use of gauze pads and pressure, the bleeding subsided. "We have done the best we could do," Dr. James said. "It's in God's hands now whether He gains another angel tonight, or not."

.....

It had been a slow morning on the route but John had been particularly pleased to sell three nut clusters on his last stop. "It won't be long now. Everything I touch these days turns to gold!"

The Comet Cookware Company believed in rewarding its salesmen, and to spur sales of their cooking utensils, they provided each with an aluminum pressure cooker filled with caramel and chocolate nut clusters that were to be sold for five cents. John had counted and there were seventy-two clusters in his cooker when he launched the rolling store. Now there were only three left and he was pleased to find himself on the verge of taking home his first premium gift. "I'll start working on the Dutch oven next," he thought. "It will bake a fine turkey at Thanksgiving."

Ahead of him, about a quarter mile away, he saw a young colored boy on a bicycle approaching. He was pedaling furiously and waving at John to slow down and stop. As he drew closer, he recognized the boy as Isaiah, the bicycle messenger from the train depot at Eunola. In his hand was a yellow paper and he signaled John by waving it back and forth over his head.

"Can you believe that, Kate? Not only are we popular on the farms, now we have bicycle messengers stopping us. It looks like he's even got a list. What will stop us next, trucks and cars?"

Isaiah straddled his bicycle in the middle of the road as John stopped the bus to take his order. Before he could speak, Isaiah interrupted. "Mister Ward, I be bringing you a message from Missus Judy Ward from High Springs. Miss Olivia be done having her baby right now and they be needing you there. Missus Judy said don't be wasting no time or dallying."

"Mrs. Judy Ward sent the wire?" he asked.

Isaiah nodded in agreement and John flipped him a dime and a nut cluster as a tip. This one was on him; he was, after all, a new father. John steered the bus to turn around to head back up Highway 41. He would catch Highway 34 and turn east driving past the Turner farm at High Point and make his way into High Springs on the northwest side close to Mrs. Smith's house. As he drove, John could not believe what his ears had heard. His mother had wired him about the birth of his daughter. "Surely pigs are flying somewhere." he laughed. Little did he know his humor would be short-lived.

.....

Dr. James took a minute to wash up and clean the dried sweat and blood from his round, wire-rimmed glasses. He was exhausted from the delicate and mind numbing surgery he had just spent the last two hours performing on his frail patient. He thanked God that he had continued to read up on the latest procedures in the New Orleans Medical Surgical Journal and that he had remembered the relatively untested procedure for suturing inside the womb. Now, he must turn his attention back to the baby.

He had no scale on which to weight this tiny bundle of humanity, but he guessed she was two to two and a half pounds. Robert retrieved a tape measure and they recorded her length as twelve and a half inches. Judy wrapped the baby in a clean pillow case since there were no more clean linens in the entire house. As she swaddled the baby girl, she was unable to take her eyes off her.

As Judy looked into the abyss of her dark ink-blue eyes, she noted that the baby clutched her finger and nuzzled while trying to nurse. "Look, Robert, she is the spitting image of John when he was born and she has Evelyn's curly hair."

Robert peered at the baby who was, indeed, the image of his son and daughter as he mouthed. "You must be hungry, Little One."

.....

Olivia's milk did not come down but this was a minor problem considering the totality of the medical issues surrounding the six week premature baby. They both would require round-the-clock care.

"We are going to have to rig up a country incubator," Dr. James said. "The nearest electric incubator is in Atlanta or Memphis and it would take weeks to get one. This little one doesn't have that long."

"What do you mean?" Robert asked. "What's an incubator?"

Dr. James shared with the Wards a report in a medical journal describing how one physician saved a premature baby. Hot bricks wrapped securely in aluminum foil were placed around all sides of a small wooden box to form a makeshift oven. The box became a substitute for the human womb and tricked the baby's body into thinking it was still inside until it could survive on its own outside. Because the box was never allowed to cool for a month or more, it was an extremely laborious method of treatment. "It's a longshot, but it might work for this baby."

The Wards listened intently to Dr. James' explanation as he continued. "A premature baby such as this one generally does not have strength for several weeks to suckle whether it is the breast or a bottle and you'll need to use a formula. She'll need to be fed every two hours using an eye dropper."

Robert and Judy looked at each other in disbelief. Keeping this baby alive would be a major undertaking, but they were both determined to succeed. Dr. James kept thinking about Olivia's parents, and he asked if Robert were going to get a message to them? Robert nodded; he had already decided what his duty demanded he do.

"Robert and Judy, now that you both understand what will be required if this baby has any chance to live, have you thought of anyone you can get to take on the job?"

Judy stood up while holding the baby. "What do you mean? I am going to take her home with me and see she is taken care of. With the aid of Flora and a few other women from the Quarters to help me, we'll see this baby has the 24-hour-a day care you spoke about. Never doubt this precious baby will live."

Robert stared at Judy in astonishment. He was surprised she was prepared to take care of John and Olivia's child. It was so out of character for her. "Perhaps," he thought, "she has taken my ultimatum to heart." He cast aside the disdain he had felt for her only hours earlier and admitted to himself he was proud of her. On this day, she had regained the deeply held love he thought he would forever withhold from her.

"Judy would do just as she said," he thought. "Now, what about Olivia's care?"

With the flow of blood checked, Robert and Dr. James lifted Olivia onto her bed. She was still in a semi-conscious state and did not resist, although she still must have been in enormous pain.

"Ordinarily I would sedate her," Dr. James said. "But with the amount of blood she has lost, I fear a pain killer will affect her heart and respiration." Turning to Judy, he asked, "Can you locate any clean towels to have ready should she begin hemorrhaging again?"

Judy took the baby and set off in search of anything that would suffice as gauze in an emergency. Shortly after Dr. James elevated Olivia's feet the color began to return to her face.

"We're going to need to get her some blood from Dothan. I'll send the order as soon as we get her comfortable here."

As he talked, Olivia opened her eyes and weakly asked, "Did my baby live? Is it a boy or a girl?" Robert smiled and told her she had a baby girl. "May I see her?"

Judy brought the baby to her. Mustering all of her remaining strength, Olivia raised her head enough to see the baby. She smiled and then she slipped back down onto the pillow beneath her head. "She is so tiny. Can she live?"

Dr. James cleared his throat. By his estimation, the baby had less than a fifty percent chance to survive the evening, but he did not want to alarm Olivia with such news in her weakened state.

Judy did not let him answer. "Of course she will. I'll see that she does. You just don't worry!"

Olivia was beyond exhaustion and could barely get out her words. Robert bent down to hear her frail whisper. "Her name is Jean. Do you hear me?"

"Yes, her name is Jean."

"What will become of ...?" Olivia asked. Before she finished, her eyes closed.

Robert looked at Judy who moved to pick up Jean. "I think she was asking about Kate."

"Don't you look to me," Judy responded. "I'll have my hands full giving Jean the care she must have. If none of the Turners will take Kate, you'll have to hire someone to look after her."

There was nothing more Dr. James could do at this point. He made sure Robert knew how to construct and utilize the crude incubator. Robert took detailed notes and prepared to go fetch bricks right away to begin the lifesaving regimen.

Dr. James said he would place the order for blood for Olivia from his office and he would have his nurse return and administer it intravenously. Robert realized the doctor probably needed a ride back to his office and offered him as much.

"As long as you are the driver," he said sheepishly. "I've had more than my fill of Judy's driving today." As Robert loaded the blood soaked towels into the car for washing, Dr. James jotted down written instructions for the formula and the frequency to feed the baby. As he wrote he remarked, "She will be too weak to suckle a bottle for possibly a month or more. You're going to have your hands full. Good luck."

"What about Olivia?" Robert asked.

"Once the nurse administers the plasma, she should begin to come around. But, if she begins to bleed again, there is no use calling for me. I will not be able to alter the inevitable. The only hope I can give is if she does survive tonight, Olivia will still only have a slim chance for recovery."

"Thank you, Charles. I sincerely appreciate all you have done to save our Olivia and her baby."

"It was a challenge," Dr. James replied. "And, we are not out of the woods yet. I'll make my rounds out to High Bluff tomorrow to check on Judy's progress with the baby. Get that incubator built and going tonight."

"I will. You can count on it."

Just as they were preparing to leave, they heard a rumbling noise on the road in front of Mrs. Smith's house. They turned to see John's rolling store pulling up onto the lawn. John climbed down and placed Kate on his shoulders as he approached the men.

"Am I a father again yet?" he called to them with a bit of glee in his voice. The men waited for him to get closer before they responded. Noticing their hesitation, he stopped. "Dad, Dr. James, what's going on?" He shifted Kate from his shoulder and positioned her on his hip.

"John, go on into the house. Your mother is in there and she'll fill you in."

John could not believe it. His mother was actually present for his daughter's birth.

"Dr. James has been here to help Olivia deliver a baby girl, and I'm taking him home." Robert spoke rapidly and then just stopped with his hand on the car door. "Son, I don't know an easy way to tell you, but Dr. James doesn't think Olivia will survive and the baby's chances are slight. Go on in. Maybe Olivia will come around enough to see you and know you are with her."

The car engine was running and still Robert did not move. Instead he opened his door and stood on the running board while calling to John. "Do I need to take Kate with me? I can manage her."

John hugged his daughter tightly and held her close to him. "No, Dad, Kate needs to stay with me. You go on ahead."

Robert waved and set off to deliver Dr. James to his office. As he drove, he thought of stopping by the Gates' to see if Carolyn could look after Mrs. Smith for a few days. He would do so after he dropped Dr. James at the clinic. His mind was awhirl with all that had happened and all the things he needed to do. "Take one step at a time and you'll cover all of the bases," Robert thought.

.....

John entered and found his mother sitting in Olivia's rocking chair, holding a baby who was small enough to be held in one hand. As he looked at her, Judy straightened the kitchen towels around her. He took Kate and drew her near. "Kate, this is your baby sister." Kate looked on in wonderment, but quickly turned her attention to her mother.

"Mama, Mama," she cried out and wiggled to go find her.

"I'll tell you everything after you settle that child," Judy said.

His mother's off-handed referral to Kate as 'that child' pained him and he reacted. "She's not 'that child' Mother. She is your granddaughter."

He picked up Kate and headed to the bedroom fearing what he would find. "How was it this morning Olivia was fine and now she may be dying?" he thought.

As he faced the possibility of losing Olivia, he experienced an awareness that had escaped him before. "My wife is a special woman," he thought. "She has accomplished so much with so little and without her ever hearing one word of praise or even a thank-you from me."

John felt small and unworthy of her labor for him and Kate. He held Kate up to the bed where she could see Olivia and he reached down and felt her cold hand. Her eyes were closed and he did not want to wake her but he did not want to squander an opportunity to speak to her if her time was short.

"Olivia, your eyes are closed, but can you hear me?" There was no response. He squeezed her hand and bent down saying in her ear "Kate needs you, and Olivia, I need you."

Kate tried to touch her mother and in restraining her he pushed against the bed. Olivia opened her eyes and tried to speak. A bit of a smile appeared on her face as she murmured "I'll fight. Take care of Kate and Jean." Her eyes closed again.

"I will," he said softly. He felt cold chill bumps rise on his arms and neck, and what he experienced frightened him. Something unexplainable had occurred: Olivia had garnered the last of her strength to open her eyes to reassure him of her will to fight and live.

Kate whimpered while reaching out for Olivia. He took her from the room and put her into her play pen. He was ready to hear what his mother could share.

.....

Robert continued on his way to drop Dr. James at the clinic downtown. He would then stop by Carolyn Gates' home and proceed to High Point. He was so deep in thought as to how best to approach Walt Turner with news of Olivia's dire situation and the birth of her baby that he ignored the shout from the passenger's seat.

"Watch out!" Dr. James yelled as he reached to grab the steering wheel. Robert had almost sideswiped a parked car in front of the mercantile.

"Well, Judy cleared out the center of the square today. I guess it is Robert's turn to hit every stationary thing on the outside of it. God," Dr. James thought, "these Wards are going to be the death of me today."

"I'm terribly sorry!" Robert responded. "I am a little preoccupied here." The near miss scared him, too, and he needed no prompting to slow down, stop wool gathering, and pay attention to the road. As he slowed, he became conscious of his surroundings and realized he had lost track of time. Lights were already visible in most of the homes he passed and he needed to turn on the car's lights.

As Robert fumbled with the switch on the dash, Dr. James alerted him that they were in front of the clinic now. Otherwise, he would have passed right by it. As he pulled to a stop, Charles opened the door, and Robert heard a distant thunderclap. Only then did he notice how agitated Charles was as he gathered his bag. Robert suspected he must have frightened him with his inattentive driving, excessive speed, and near misses.

Standing in the door, Charles spoke, "Robert, forgive me for delaying you further, but I can't let you go until I admit and apologize for how unprofessionally I have behaved toward Olivia these past several months. I violated my Hippocratic Oath to 'do no harm,' and I am embarrassed." He would have gone on but Robert interrupted.

"Stop, Charles. I know all about your behavior and you can forget it. After today, all is forgotten and forgiven."

Charles James knew this was totally uncharacteristic of the way Robert Ward handled any slight to him or his family. "Are you sure?" Robert nodded and urged him to drop the matter for good. Charles obliged.

Robert shifted gears and pointed the '32 Phaeton toward High Point. He noticed a grinding noise between second and third gears. "Hmmm," he thought. "I've never noticed that before."

He drove for several miles as he recounted his history with Walt Turner. He vividly remembered Walt's anger the last time they had met in Robert's office. Although small in stature, Walt Turner's temper was colossal. Robert had witnessed it firsthand when Walt realized he had been bested at his own game. "Perhaps," Robert thought, "blowing smoke in the 'Little Man's' face was a bridge a bit too far?" Now Robert needed Walt's help and he dreaded the coming encounter. He had to do it though, for Olivia.

.....

Judy took charge when she heard the faint whimper of the hungry baby. "Son, do you hear her? Olivia has no milk but even if she did, Jean is still too weak to suckle. I have to get her home where Flora can prepare her formula and begin feeding her with an eye dropper. The sooner I get her home the sooner I can get her fed."

John was confused. "Aren't you and Dad going to stay with me tonight and help with Kate and Olivia?" Judy understood the fear she heard in her beloved son's voice and it was hard for her to refuse him, but he would have to manage on his own unless Robert could get help from the Turners. "Answer me," he said. "What do you mean about taking the baby with you?"

Judy recounted the difficulty with which she and Dr. James had delivered Jean. She went on to explain any chance this baby had to survive depended upon constant care and staying warm in the makeshift incubator for an extended period of time. Given Olivia's precarious health, she would be unable to meet all of Dr. James' specific instructions. With Olivia estranged from her family, Judy was the only one left to care for Jean until she was strong enough to survive on her own. "I'm going to take care of this baby as if she were my own," Judy said.

John could not believe his ears. Had he journeyed outside the realm of reality? "This is my mother. She is the woman who never has time for Evelyn or to do her own grocery shopping and errands. Yet, she proposes to take over the care of my baby 24 hours a day for Lord only knows how long?" It was beyond him. "What do you propose to do with Kate during this time? She needs care as well."

"John, you know I have never taken a liking to that child." Judy could tell John was tense as she spoke, and she could see her answer was not going over very well. "Jean is different, son. When I first looked upon her, I knew she was a Ward. She looks exactly like you did when you were born. I know one hundred percent this baby is your child. Why, I even helped bring her into this world. Let that sink in for a moment, John. I delivered my own granddaughter. How could I trust her care to anyone else?" John listened intently.

"And, given the care that Jean must have, how can you expect me to manage that child too? No. It is final. I can't be saddled with Kate. You'll have to get someone else."

John's gut wrenched. He finally understood the pain Olivia felt at his mother's rejection of Kate. He knew his mother would never change. Without a word, he lifted Kate out of her play pen and headed across the lawn to Mrs. Smith's.

John navigated the stone path from his and Olivia's home to the main house in front of them. As he entered through her kitchen door, he found Carolyn Gates fixing Mrs. Smith's evening meal. She explained that she came as soon as Robert had alerted them about Olivia and the baby. She promised to care for Mrs. Smith until Janie's daughter, Rachel, was available the middle of the following week. He gathered Kate, and prepared to return to their home. Before he could leave though, Carolyn called to him.

"Why don't you leave her here with us?" she asked. Carolyn hoped Mrs. Smith's anxiety over Olivia would lessen with Kate being there to distract her. John agreed and as he was putting her in her playpen, Mrs. Smith reminded him she had hired Rachel to relieve Olivia of her care as well as to watch after Kate in the afternoons.

"Tell Olivia although her baby came a little early, nothing has changed. Rachel will handle Kate whenever you or Olivia need her."

"What a relief," John said. "Once again, Olivia and I are in your debt."

As John walked back to check on Olivia, he thought, "Kate is so loved by Mrs. Gates and Mrs. Smith who are no relation to her, but she is so despised by my mother. I will never understand that."

CHAPTER 43

Robert heard another loud thunderclap and he leaned forward looking up at the dark clouds gathering overhead. Without warning, a deluge of rain hit his windshield. A thunder storm was upon him. The wind was fierce, causing trees on either side of the road to bend. A few had their branches snapped off as they fought against the tempest. He barely missed a long thick limb in the road when he jerked the wheel just in time to avoid it.

"Damn, if I am not careful I am going to get myself killed before I ever face Walt Turner. He debated pulling off the road but he could see lights atop the butte at High Point and he continued. By his estimation, the sky had dumped two to three inches of rain in the last half hour. Runoff water snaked its way down the driveway from the main house and Robert down-shifted the Ford and said a brief prayer as he attempted to ascend the quagmire that was formerly the driveway. By the time he pulled into the main yard and made his way to the front door, the storm had significantly abated.

Through the glass panes Robert could see lights on both floors. "Thank goodness," he thought, "someone is still up." He knocked and braced himself for what he knew was to come. For a moment, he thought he saw a shade rustle and Walt's face appear in a window to the far left of the front door. He waited for a moment and since there was no activity inside, he knocked again, this time more forcefully.

Annie and Walt were in their sitting room when Walt arose and peered out a front window. Recognizing Robert, he grunted and returned to his chair. Soon, Annie heard the repeated knocking and when Walt made no move, she rose to answer the door, but he stopped her.

"Let the bastard knock and wait just as I did when I delivered Olivia to his doorstep. I have no business with him. He made that perfectly clear the last time I saw him. Either hell will freeze over or he'll get tired and leave. It makes no matter to me which happens first."

"Walt Turner," Annie exclaimed, "you may have been raised to be a

271

stable horse but I was reared to be hospitable to guests, invited or not. Your uncouth behavior is unbecoming of the prosperous businessman you have become. You should be ashamed."

Annie had indeed been raised differently and she would not tolerate his disrespectful behavior toward a guest in their home, even if it were Robert Ward. She pushed past him and opened the front door.

"Good evening Annie, Walt. I apologize for calling unannounced but I have urgent business with you both. May I come in?"

Annie moved aside and motioned for him to enter. Walt stormed to stand in front of him actually pushing him backward. In a loud voice he let Robert know he was not welcome in his house despite Annie's invitation. Hearing Papa's raised voice, Beth and Ann appeared at the head of the stairs to investigate the source of the commotion downstairs.

Walt turned and yelled up to them, "Get back to bed. Nothing is the matter other than an uninvited person is at our door. Go on."

Robert stepped forward toward the stairs and suggested Beth and Ann should probably come down to hear what he had come to say. A visitor at this hour and in this weather surely meant trouble.

"I bet we are at war with the Germans," Beth surmised.

"Or maybe those Japs; John says we can't trust those little buggers," Ann added.

Annie sensed something was wrong. "Robert, I can tell you have bad news for us. Please disregard Walt and the girls' insufferable behavior and tell me." Walt stood in abeyance of his wife's censure. While he would have reveled in returning Robert's snub from their prior meeting, he would hold back a bit for now because it would displease Annie. He was, however, the man of the house and he certainly had the right to ask what this nonsense was about.

"Well, say what you came to say and be off with you Robert Ward." Annie stepped forward and placed her hand on Robert's arm. "Please, won't you be seated?"

Robert cast a sharp look at Walt and spoke, "Mrs. Turner, I have come with grave news, and I need to return to Olivia's side as quickly as possible. She delivered a premature baby a few hours ago and I am sorry to inform you Dr. James doesn't think Olivia will make it through the night. He is equally concerned about the baby, a girl, who is your granddaughter. If you wish to see either of them, I would encourage you not to dally but to do so now, before it is too late."

Annie broke into sobs and Beth and Ann moved to comfort her. "Yes, Mr. Ward, I will go now with no lack of haste."

Walt was enraged, "Annie, you know what I have decreed about Olivia. She is already dead to this family. Why would you even consider going to her now? Nothing has changed with her status, baby or not."

Ann chimed in, "Mama, how could you consider being under the same roof with her? Think about what I have gone through with people gossiping about her shotgun wedding and how she ruined John's future. Maybe this is God's punishment of her. Do you deny that all of us would be better off if she were truly dead?"

Everyone, including Walt, looked at Ann in disbelief. What kind of person would wish her sister dead and without any remorse? Annie looked at Walt. "We have reared a selfish beast. This child spoiled by you beyond redemption is so heartless as to wish such a fate on her own sister. And you are no better. You condemn our daughter who is nothing but goodness in all she is and does. Hear me, Walt. I am going to Olivia, and I am not going to waste precious time listening to your sanctimonious drivel about why I should not."

Walt and Ann stood with mouth agape. Annie turned to Beth and asked, "Will you take me or shall I go with Robert?"

Beth hesitated before she answered. Walt had engaged her with his brooding eyes and she was paralyzed in fear.

"Remember what I have said, child," he warned. "Olivia is dead to us and you will not go to her aid."

Beth grimaced, "To hell with your decrees. If Olivia can't count on us now in her greatest time of need, then we are not much of a family, and I am even less of a sister. I will take you, Mama."

Beth challenged Papa and it felt good. "Mama we'll leave in a minute as soon as I can dress. And, Papa, if you want to toss me out tonight, then so be it. But hear me now, after tonight you will never again prevent me from sharing my life with Olivia and her children."

Ann was astounded at Beth's defiance of Papa, but she was even more astounded at his lack of pushing back on her. "What about me, Beth, who'll take me the places I need to go if Papa kicks you out? You're just being selfish choosing Olivia over this family."

Beth stopped and turned at the head of the stairs, "Go kick rocks,

Ann. Find your rides into town with someone else from now on."

Ann ran upstairs after Beth yelling out to her about how unfair she was, and Walt left the room stoically. Robert followed him knowing he still had unfinished business with Walt that would be settled here and now.

.....

Evelyn sat at the top of the stairs at High Bluff waiting for her mother and father to return. She was supposed to be in bed already but the hard rain pelting the tin roof and the accompanying thunder and lightning had chased away the Sandman. As she waited, she found a measure of comfort in listening to Flora singing hymns from the kitchen. They echoed down the hallway and the reverberations tickled her ears.

She scooted down to the middle of the stairs so that she could hear them more clearly. By Evelyn's estimation, Olivia and John were about the most favorite people in her life. She would count Flora as a close third though. Evelyn was confused about her feelings at times and she wondered if any of the other girls at school had three families as she did.

Her first family was her mother, father, and John. Although they really didn't have much time for her, she still loved them and held out hope one day when they weren't so busy, they would pay more attention to her.

Her second family was Flora who had cared for her since she was a baby. Evelyn didn't understand why, but she thought of Flora as her second mother. There was no doubt in her mind Flora loved her. She told her as much daily when she referred to her as her "sweet baby."

Evelyn had heard that coloreds and whites didn't get along a lot of times and she was at a loss to understand why. "Although her skin is dark," she thought, "she is just the same as me inside. She loves me, and I love her. The color of our skin doesn't make any difference to me."

Finally, Evelyn's third family consisted of Olivia and Kate. Evelyn had come to understand she and Olivia were related by marriage and she was Kate's aunt. Olivia was a sister to her, but she seemed to be more like a mother that anything else. Whether it was by marriage or by blood mattered little to Evelyn, she had felt close to Olivia since she had seen her from the porch on the night Olivia had come to live with them.

Although she didn't understand everything that was happening, Evelyn knew that Olivia's daddy had abandoned her that night. She had been tossed on their doorstep like a sack of garbage and left to rot. Evelyn imagined that it was a lonely feeling for Olivia, much like she herself felt at times.

Now, there would be an addition to their family and she was anxious to meet Olivia's new baby. "I hope," Evelyn thought, "that I can grow up to marry someone just like my brother, John, and bake cakes and braid rugs just like Olivia. That is my wish."

Evelyn heard Flora's footsteps approaching so she scurried up the stairs and hopped back into bed. Her parents may not have made much time for her, but they certainly found time when she misbehaved. As the rain and thunder subsided, she drifted off to sleep.

.....

Robert hurried to catch Walt; their difference in height allowed him to close the distance faster than he expected, and he found himself nearly on top of him before he knew it.

"Walt, wait up and listen to me. It may be worth your while."

Walt halted. "What do you mean 'worth my while'?"

Robert threw up his hands in resignation. "I'll put all my cards on the table. Olivia means everything to me as does Kate, and I suspect her baby Jean will too, if she lives. Olivia means so much that I am willing to accept your earlier offer to 'accommodate' me. If you still want to haul your freight to Dothan using my railroad spur, you may."

"What's the catch?" Walt asked suspiciously.

"You are right, Walt. There is a catch." Robert proceeded to lay it out for him. Walt would have to take Annie and Beth to John and Olivia's house now and let them see Olivia and the baby.

"If Olivia and Jean survive, you have to agree to allow Annie and Olivia's siblings to visit with her as often as they choose. As long as you uphold this agreement I'll haul your freight for free. Agreed?"

Walt Turner was a businessman before he was a righteous one. He offered his hand and said, "Agreed. How soon can I start?"

Walt hurried back to the foyer and stood by the front door waiting for Beth and Annie to return from dressing. "Annie," he said, "you know I can't let you face this alone. You ride with me. Beth, you take your car because as soon as we learn how Olivia fares, I'll leave to get word to her brothers."

Annie smiled and placed her hand on his arm. "Walt, I knew one day you would figure out how to make me so very, very happy again. Thank you."

Walt turned to Robert and, as their eyes met, he said, "No, dear. Thank Robert."

CHAPTER 44

Beth was the first to arrive at Mrs. Smith's house, and Walt and Annie showed up a few minutes later. They made their way to the housekeeper's quarters and to their surprise, John greeted them at the door. He ushered them into the tiny sitting room and motioned toward the bedroom for Annie and Beth to go to see Olivia. Walt took a place on the settee to wait for some update from Annie. Shortly, Robert entered and turned to Judy as he inquired about Olivia.

"Olivia appears to be no better and perhaps a little worse."

Judy made no effort to acknowledge the Turners. Now that they had arrived, she and Robert could take Jean and go home. She could not waste any more time. This beloved granddaughter had to eat after all. "Robert, can we go now?"

Robert responded, "I understand the urgency to situate Jean and get her feeding schedule underway. Do I need to pick up anything to make her formula from Jerrell's on my way home?"

Before Judy answered, Beth entered the room. "Mama won't leave Olivia. She hopes she will open her eyes and realize she is not alone. Papa, do you want to go in and be with Mama?" Walt shook his head. Beth turned to Judy. "Mrs. Ward, is it alright if I hold my niece Jean?"

"No, it is not alright," Judy snapped while turning to shield Jean from her. You should know she is too fragile to be jostled around and handled by everyone." Beth recoiled in surprise and Judy smiled sheepishly as she realized she had overreacted. Surprisingly, she was mildly ashamed of her abrupt manner with Beth and turned and extended the bundle for Beth's inspection.

"Oh, just look at her." Beth said as she moved the towels and looked at Jean. "Everything about her resembles John. She is most assuredly a Ward."

Judy beamed her approval. "Beth, you are right. Thank goodness she is not going to be short like you Turners."

"Mrs. Ward, would you wait for a moment until I can bring in Mama to see her granddaughter? It would break her heart if she did not get to see Jean before you left." Still feeling abashed from her outburst, Judy nodded in agreement and Beth went to fetch Annie.

Annie carefully approached Jean and stood quietly over her. Walt moved closer to stand beside her. He pulled Annie tightly to him while whispering for her not to fret. "Let Mrs. Ward take this baby and do what she can for her. Right now our daughter Olivia needs us and we'll take care of her."

Annie wondered how she could convey what his presence and loving words meant to her? They released her from the dark despair that had abated her joy for far too long.

Soon, John returned with Kate. She was reluctant to leave her daddy as he passed her to Beth who reached out for her.

"John, I think Kate is going to be all right now, so go ahead and do what you need to. She and I are going to get along just fine."

As John entered the sitting room, he noticed Walt and extended his hand to greet him. Walt grunted and ignored him while leaving John's hand hanging for a moment. Then, without commenting, John withdrew it and turned to follow his parents out to the car as they were preparing to leave with Jean.

"Mother, do you have any idea how hard it is for me to watch you take Jean? Don't try to justify what you are doing. I understand, but this does nothing to lessen my sadness as I think of how Olivia will feel if she awakens enough to realize she is gone. It pains me greatly to consider that our baby may die without Olivia or me with her."

As he spoke, he took Jean from his mother and held her tightly against his chest. He placed a gentle kiss on her forehead and then handed her back to his mother who had taken her seat in the Ford.

Robert cast a brief wave to his son and backed out of the driveway. John watched the tail lights dim in the distance until he could see them no more. As he walked back inside, he was unable to understand how he, who had given so little thought to the baby Olivia carried these past months, could hurt so deeply.

Kate's chatter and Beth's laughter greeted him as he entered. Walt paid him no mind and continued his pacing back and forth in front of the hearth. Walt obviously did not want to be there, and John could not imagine who could have persuaded the stubborn Scotsman to come.

Nonetheless, he was hungry and set off to the kitchen to prepare something. As he rummaged through the cabinets, he realized that the Turners had likely not eaten as well. To his dismay, the cupboards were bare. "Great," he thought, "yet another reason for Walt Turner to find disappointment in me."

Returning to the sitting room, he found Walt still pacing and John made no attempt to engage him in conversation or acknowledge his presence. The image of his hand hovering in midair as Walt rejected his handshake was still fresh in his mind and he was not prepared to subject himself to more of the same. He thought it better that he look in on Olivia. As he entered the bedroom, he noticed Annie had turned up the lamp light, and the room seemed less dismal. He remarked upon this to her, and she smiled.

"I wanted Olivia to see light and not darkness as she opens her eyes. Her breathing is stronger and it seems she is trying to rouse herself. Several times, I've been able to get her to take spoons of water. I believe she is improving and if she continues this way, I think we can give her broth by morning."

As he looked over Annie's shoulder at Olivia, she opened her eyes and weakly exclaimed, "Mama!" Annie squeezed her hand and John moved so Olivia could see him. She smiled at him before closing her eyes. John considered her smile.

"Mrs. Turner, did you see her smile? Even in her semi-awakened state and with her life hanging by a thread she sought to reassure me. She is the most caring person I have ever known."

Annie observed her daughter's tender look at John and she felt a sense of dread for Olivia. Her daughter telegraphed her care for this man who had brought her so much unhappiness.

"Oh, Olivia," she thought, "if you survive, I fear you will experience only more hurt. It appears you have gained your husband's respect, but you will probably never win his love."

Silently she prayed Olivia might find some measure of comfort in her children as a substitute for John's lack of love for her.

.....

The status quo of the Turner family no longer existed. Too much had happened since Robert Ward knocked on their door a few hours ago. Annie hoped that she might enjoy a renewed relationship with Olivia and John. Throughout the evening and night, she had witnessed John's deep concern for Olivia and she found herself unable to maintain her ill feeling toward him.

"How is it that all I feel now is sorrow for him when I admit that his predicament is as hopeless as Olivia's? What a tragedy!" she sighed. There was nothing she could do to change either of their lives. She knew she could only lighten their load.

Having ensured her daughter knew that she was not alone in her desperate state, Annie set out in search of Walt. She wanted to discuss his thoughts on Olivia, Kate, and Jean's care. "Jean," she thought, "was the least of their worries because the Wards would take care of her. Kate was a concern though. Who would care for her?"

John lingered outside the bedroom. With Olivia now under her mother's watchful eye, avoiding Walt had become his primary mission. As she passed him, Annie spoke to John.

"Walt is waiting for me to let him know if he can leave. I will send him on his way back to High Point so he can notify the boys of Jean's birth. Olivia seems to be holding her own and there is nothing more for him to do here tonight."

John nodded pensively. She touched his arm to relieve some of the worry she saw etched on her son-in-law's face. "We'll get through this. Walt is figuring out the problem of Kate and Olivia's care. Give him time. He will work out how best we should proceed."

"Do you really think Olivia has improved?"

Annie nodded in agreement but her encouragement did little to allay his fears. "She is not feverish so I do not think she is getting worse. Fortunately, she has not suffered another hemorrhage. That would be devastating for her. There is nothing we can do now but watch and pray."

John hung on Annie's words as he felt a sense of desperation creep over him. "What will I do?" he thought. "How will I manage to look after Olivia and babysit Kate at the same time? What will become of the rolling store and my job at the cannery?" He felt an odd awareness about everything around him. The walls of the hallway seemed a little closer together and the ceiling seemed shorter. He felt trapped. "I cannot lose my job. It would be the end of me."

There were no easy answers. As his anxiety rose, he remembered what his father had said many times. "Where there is a will there is a way." He had the will and he would find a way. A good start, he rationalized, would be to stop gambling away his weekly pay. The money would cover their basic needs but they would have nothing left over. There must be other ways, and he was determined to find them.

Meanwhile, Annie found Walt and asked, "Walt, did you mean what you said? Will we take care of Olivia and Kate?"

Walt drew her to him and wiped away the tears she could not hold back. "Annie, my dearest, is it not your heart's desire to do so? Yes, we'll see to our daughter." He hesitated and Annie broke in to urge him to go and let their sons know about Olivia and to look in on Ann.

"I've been thinking," Walt said. "How would you feel about my getting Gussie's daughter, Florabell, to stay with Olivia and watch Kate? I know she is capable, but she has another job that will keep her in town for another week."

Annie agreed that would solve the problem if they could just hold on for another week. She also remembered Beth was set to begin a two week vacation the next week, and perhaps she could care for Olivia and Kate during this time. "What do you think Walt? Will you allow it?"

Walt smiled with amusement, "Why ask me? Don't you recall what that feisty daughter of yours told me this evening? She is of age and will make her own decisions from now on. It seems to me we best let her start now. You talk to her while I head out to let the boys know about their sister. I'll be back as soon as I can to take you home. I can't let you wear yourself out."

Annie approached Beth about helping with Olivia, and she was delighted to spend her time off with her sister.

"Mama, of course I'll take care of them. There is nothing I wouldn't do for her. I am punching the clock right now," she said as she held up an imaginary time card and made a 'dinging' sound. "I'm on duty," she smiled. "I guess I better start by putting this little girl to bed," she said as she scooped up Kate and carried her away.

As Beth carried Kate past John, she reached for her father and cried for him to take her. Kate's cries awakened Olivia and she opened her eyes. John placed Kate beside her and, although she was weak, she was able to speak and tell Kate that she loved her. Kate reached out and touched

Olivia's face and attempted to snuggle beside her to go to sleep. John took her and placed her in her crib where she turned to her side away from him and went fast asleep.

He wondered how his mother was faring with Jean. It had been some time since she had managed a baby and even then, the lion's share of Evelyn's care had been delegated to Flora. He knew his mother, if nothing else, understood how to marshal the troops to accomplish any task. With everyone settled, he found a comfortable chair to catch a few winks. "This baby business is exhausting," he thought.

CHAPTER 45

Judy Ward burst noisily through the front door at High Bluff with Robert nipping at her heels and Rufus barking from the porch. Her campaign to save Jean had begun. Flora heard the commotion and hustled from the kitchen to meet her in the foyer. She was eager to hear all that had happened with Olivia and the birthing. To her surprise, Judy was carrying the baby with her, and she imagined the worst. "Oh Lawdy, what done happened with Miss Olivia? Did she pass giving birth to this here young'un?"

"No, she did not die, but Olivia is of no concern at this moment. We have a very sick baby here and under my watchful eye, we will nurse her to health." Flora was lost as to what was happening before her, but she knew it was serious.

"Yes ma'am. We be gonna take care of Miss Olivia's baby."

"We," Judy said sternly, "are going to take care of my granddaughter."

Judy barked orders and Flora nodded in agreement. She did not know what Missus Judy meant by 'incubator,' but when she heard 'bricks and fire;' she knew Frank was the man for the job. She woke him and set off to gather the women of the Quarters. "Missus Judy gonna need a heap of hep," she thought.

Frank wiped the sleep from his eyes and set out to find Missus Judy who explained the construction of the incubator. Frank then began gathering the bricks and placing them in a spare bedroom near the kitchen which would serve as a makeshift nursery. Once he had a stack about the size of a traveling trunk, he carefully arranged them into the shape of a crude oven. On the bottom was a "hot box" to hold the warmed bricks and above it was an area that could capture and retain the heat.

As the shape came together, Frank began to understand how the incubator worked. The heat from the warm bricks would radiate and were captured by the oven. Baby Jean would lie inside the oven which would keep her warm as though she were still inside her mother's womb. Once the incubator was completed, Frank set out to find his sons. He followed the dull scrubbing sounds of hand saws to the yard where he found Joe and Isaac building a wooden box to hold Jean's tiny body.

"Almost done," Joe said. "We'll bring it inside directly."

By now, three colored women had assembled in Flora's sitting room where she filled them in on what was expected from them throughout the night. They would need to fire up their stoves and provide a steady supply of warm bricks every half hour to the nursery. Then, she returned to the main house to find Judy so they could go over Dr. James' instructions for mixing the formula.

Flora found Judy in the kitchen standing over one of the drawers from the dining room buffet. Inside Jean was nestled in some linen. Flora felt something brush against her backside and turned to find Evelyn who had heard the commotion and had come down to investigate. She hovered around her peeking at what she could see of the baby.

"Mama, is this Olivia's baby?

"You should be in bed dear," Judy lamented.

"I'm sorry, Mama but …."

As had been the case throughout her short life, Evelyn was pushed aside. Judy had so much to see about for Jean, but she knew the child would persist. Turning to Evelyn, she answered, "This is our baby girl and her name is Jean. Are you satisfied?"

Evelyn was thrilled. She finally had a real baby she could love and care for. Still, she wondered why she was there. "She really isn't our baby is she? Why do we have her?"

Exasperated, Judy wondered why she never noticed Evelyn's astute nature. Why couldn't she be like other eight year old children and just accept her answers? "Evelyn, can't you understand this, for Heaven's sake?"

Evelyn stared blankly. While she didn't understand what was going on, she understood she better 'hush up' considering her mother's frenzied mood. Thankful that she did not ask more questions, Judy told her to go fetch Flora and then go back to bed. Evelyn thought to herself, "This is my brother's baby and I will take care of her."

Shortly, Flora appeared with a teacup of formula and an eye dropper. She tried to feed Jean with no success. Jean was weak and nearly choked on the single drop. Although she had experienced birthing early babies and was not surprised Jean had difficulty swallowing the drops of formula, Flora was sad to think this little thing might not survive for long. She hugged Jean closely against her bosom and swayed her side to side, while singing softly as she did.

Judy observed Flora's concern and shouted, "Whatever bad thoughts you have, don't you think them again. Do you hear me, Flora? All you are to think is how we are going to keep my granddaughter alive. Now, put another drop in the side of her mouth and massage her throat with your fingers to move the liquid down." A few minutes later they both were relieved to see Jean had begun to take a little of the liquid from the dropper.

"Flora," she said, "is Frank ready to go with the incubator? We are going to need it sooner than later."

"Yes'um," Flora responded. "He's ready and I done took care of everything jus like you said. The womens is on them bricks and they knows what to do." She continued to feed Jean one drop at a time. "You want me to be bringin' back a girl from the Quarters to take over this here feeding?"

Judy was exhausted from the events of the day but she was not trusting Jean's care to anyone else at this critical juncture. "No, it looks like it will be you and me tonight. I will work out a schedule in the morning."

Flora excused herself. She knew Evelyn was probably awake in her bed and was worried about Olivia and Kate. She poured a glass of milk and headed upstairs to comfort her. Meanwhile, Judy held Jean's swaddled body. "I will not be denied," Judy thought. "This Ward will live."

.....

When Walt arrived at High Point, Gussie met him at the door alerting him to Ann's foul mood. Walt was not surprised. Ann, he had learned, always considered herself before others, even with her sister and niece lying on the verge of death.

"How's Miss Olivia and her baby?" Gussie wiped away tears as she bowed her head and asked, "Sir, yore visit is a heap of surprise. They ain't dead, is they? We ain't be had no way of findin' out 'bout her, but I done figured I'd stay here so ifn you be needin' me I'd be on hand."

"The baby and Olivia are alive, barely, and they have a rough road ahead of them. Her name is Jean, and she is a beautiful little girl. As soon as I check on Ann, I'm headed out to the boys' farms to let them know and then back to High Springs to pick up Mrs. Turner."

Gussie headed back to the kitchen. "Do you want me to fetch Miss Ann?"

Before he could reply, Ann appeared at the top of the stairs. She had heard her father arrive. "Papa, what took you so long? Surely Mr. Ward exaggerated his tale about Olivia?" Looking about and not seeing her mother or sister, she asked why they were not with him. It did not escape Walt that Ann had asked nothing about Olivia and the baby.

"Beth and your mother remain with Olivia, and, depending upon her condition, I aim to pick your mother up later."

"Oh," Ann yelled down without any indication of worry about her gravely ill sister, "I'll be in my room, reading."

Walt considered taking Ann to task for her uncaring attitude about her sister, but he held himself in check. He would discuss with Annie exactly how they would handle her. But, he knew one thing was sure: Ann would not be returning to college in the fall.

CHAPTER 46

Walt steered the Model T stake-bed truck carefully in the early morning haze. The sun would be up soon and he knew animals often congregated on the roadway at this time of the morning. He had updated Ann and her brothers on Olivia's condition, and was now on his way back to Mrs. Smith's home. He hoped Annie could return to High Point soon. As he drove, he thought of Ann's behavior. "Maybe she did not intend to wish Olivia dead," he thought. But, he could not ignore the truth he had come to realize: Ann was a mean spirited and hateful person.

Recalling her look as she wished Olivia harm repulsed him and he agonized over his failure to recognize this facet of Ann's personality. Could anyone fault him for not wanting to believe his favorite child was capable of such hate for her own flash and blood? Olivia had tried to warn him, but he had refused to listen. While he had managed to ignore Olivia, he had been unable to disregard Robert Ward's taunts. To his vexation, Walt had confirmed each of Robert's accusations and nothing made him as angry as he was to have to admit that the bastard Robert Ward was right.

As he investigated each of the allegations against Ann's character, he discovered her behavior was worse than he could have imagined. Some acquaintances now prohibited their daughters from associating with her or including her in their social circles. She had become a pariah whose shameful conduct had placed her beyond the pale. He learned even at her college campus, she was regarded as little more than white trash.

He had yet to reveal any of this to Annie, just as he had hidden the impact of the Depression on those outside of Geneva County from her. He knew it would break her heart. The time had come though, to tell her how miserably they had failed to raise a chaste and charitable daughter. Sadly, they knew they would not be able to reverse the damage Ann had inflicted upon herself. Society was not kind to young women of breeding who chose to ignore the strictures of their families and social circles.

As the fields rushed by, Walt's thoughts drifted back to his discussion with his father-in-law when he was pursuing Annie. Michael McGee had warned Annie to abandon any thought of marriage to Walt. He had insisted that nothing good would come from her being yoked to a grade stallion. He had gone on to say that the bloodlines never mixed well and the result was always disastrous. Considering how Ann had turned out, he wondered if Michael had been right. Had Walt's unrelenting desire to marry his thoroughbred Annie resulted in an untamable filly in the personage of Ann?"

As the sun pierced the morning fog, the trees glistened with dew and the forest came alive. It was a new day in Geneva County and it would soon be a new day for the Turner family, especially for Ann.

.....

Having seen about Ann and the boys, Walt returned to Olivia's and was pleased to hear she had improved. Annie and Beth were exhausted and ready to return to High Point; but before they left, Walt pulled Annie aside. After several minutes, she nodded in agreement and Walt asked John to step into the kitchen with Annie and him.

There, Walt and Annie outlined their proposal for the care of Olivia and Kate. To his amazement, their plan was more than he could have expected, and solved most of his problems.

"Don't worry about Olivia, I'll watch over her throughout the night," John assured them.

Hearing their conversation coming to an end, Beth stuck her head in the kitchen door. "I'll be back around noon tomorrow. You should have time to contact your boss at the cannery and still make an afternoon rolling store run with Kate," she said.

As they all stood to leave, Walt abruptly asked Beth and Annie to wait for him in the sitting room. "John," he said, "May I have a moment with you to talk man to man?"

John's heart leapt into his throat, and for a moment, he felt he would suffocate. "Yes sir, of course you may."

.....

After a half hour, Walt and John emerged from the kitchen. For his part, John looked no worse for the wear. As Beth and Annie rose from the settee, Walt turned to John and shook his hand while placing his other hand on John's shoulder.

"We may bring this family together yet, boy." Turning to Annie he said, "Let's be on our way Mama. John's got work to do to take care of our daughter and granddaughter."

John closed the door and went in to lie down beside Olivia, taking care not to disturb her. He lay still watching the odd shapes the slivers of moonlight made on the shades. The semi-darkness of the room was as foreboding to him as were his thoughts of how he could possibly meet their needs. Aside from his financial worries, John was concerned about Jean and how she had fared on the trip to his parent's house. How would his mother manage? "Thank goodness for Flora," he thought.

.....

Walt and Annie lounged in the sitting area of their bedroom at High Point. Walt sipped a brandy and was pleased at the notion that he and Annie had solved the issue of Olivia and Kate's care. By his estimation, that equated to solving all of their problems, but he would soon learn that the fallacy in his thinking came from his lack of understanding of how Olivia and John lived. She, alone, supported herself and Kate; without her income, John could never pay their bills.

Oblivious to this, Walt and Annie turned their attentions to the issue which had been ignored for far too long. What would they do with Ann? They agreed she could not continue to live with them. She was out of control and they held no sway over her. She must, therefore, be sent away. Aside from where they would send her and with whom, the larger problem lay in their convincing her she must leave High Springs at all. Both knew as long as she held her infatuation for John and had a connection to him, she would never leave.

Annie's lip trembled as she asked, "Walt, how do we impress upon Ann her dire predicament? How can we paint a picture of her future that she cannot ignore?"

"Our daughter is not stupid and this fact frustrates me. She knows the cost she incurs with her behavior but she doesn't seem to care. She is already rejected by her circle as undesirable, yet she persists in wallowing in an unreal expectation for a life with John Ward. My God, woman, you would think she would run away from a fate like Olivia suffers. She does not want to change, and because of this attitude, there is nothing you and I can do to change her. There is only one person who can help her see her folly, and that is John."

Annie looked at Walt in disbelief. "John?"

"Yes, John. You may think I have lost my mind but I said as much to him tonight. Annie, Have you thought about what has brought Ann to this point? First, she was in love with Paul Gunderson who she thought had abandoned her. As it turns out, Paul was serious about courting her."

"How do you know this?" Annie asked.

"John told me earlier tonight Paul told him he cared for Ann deeply and wanted to pursue her as a love interest, but his parents made him break it off. He still loves her to this day. So even when he brought home that girl, Sandra, from college his heart has never been far from Ann all this time."

"Oh my, that poor boy," Annie cried.

"There is more," Walt continued. "Once Ann decided Paul was out of the picture, she pursued John. Then, she learned John was the father of Olivia's unborn baby and she felt betrayed. Finally, she suffered the ridicule of her friends over losing both suitors to other women. It was the ultimate social embarrassment."

"Are you saying John did not encourage their association?"

"I know for a fact without any encouragement from John, Ann threw herself at him. I learned that on more than one occasion when Ann met him at Jerrell's, he tried to fend off her brazen overtures to him. She could not handle the truth. Being ostracized, Ann created her own reality and continued to fantasize about rekindling a relationship with John. It may be hard to understand, but I suspect his rejection amplified her bizarre behavior. She abandoned reality and embraced her fantasy of one day becoming Mrs. John Ward no matter the cost or who was hurt."

Walt paused. It pained him to realize the depth to which his beloved Ann had sunk.

Annie realized he had not finished. "Go on," she said.

"If there is anyone who can affect a change in Ann, it is John Ward. She will never be Mrs. John Ward and she must understand that. Tonight, I asked John to forbid her to initiate any further contact with him and he has agreed."

Annie's eyes filled with tears at the thought of Ann's likely reaction. She knew her daughter would suffer greatly if John followed through on

Walt's request.

"You may be right, Walt. She will be crushed but perhaps her sorrow will be enough to make her realize her social life is that of a pariah and she will agree to our offer to start over somewhere else. She might embrace the chance to wipe the slate clean and begin anew."

Annie wiped her eyes, grasped Walt's hand, and sighed. "Although I know it will hurt Ann, I wish John Godspeed in his mission. I am grateful John is willing to do this for us. Let us pray for him."

"Yes," Walt answered. "And let's pray Ann makes the choice to start fresh on her own. Otherwise, we will have to make the choice for her."

.....

The next morning Walt and Annie arose, had their breakfast and laid out the possibilities for Ann's relocation in the anticipation that John would succeed in his quest. It had to be one where it was unlikely that people would have heard about her indiscretions. Finding a place, they suspected, would be much easier than finding a person who could manage her and not be easily swayed by her conniving ways.

Another concern was the financial resources such a program would entail. For the first few years of the Great Depression, Walt, like most of his business associates in Alabama, had not suffered greatly. But as the Depression lingered, its effects were far reaching and all parts of the United States were suffering to some degree or another. Now, Walt was experiencing ever decreasing demands for his thoroughbred trotters and Angus cows.

Their options were limited. Ruth lived far enough away the gossip would not be a factor, but they discounted sending her there because of Ruth's health and the fact she, as a schoolteacher, had no entrée into society.

Neither was Jerry a possibility. Although he was situated ideally due to the wealth and social position of his wife's family in Louisiana, Annie pointed out their daughter-in-law would know of Ann's reputation due to her father's business dealings in High Springs and it would be a barrier to their accepting her.

"It is unfortunate your father is no longer with us! I have no doubt he could have handled Ann's strong will and deceitful ways."

"That may be, Walt, but my mother was equally strict. Perhaps my mother Amelia and my oldest sister Pearl are an option instead?"

Remembering how her mother had ruled their household and held an iron fist over her three daughters, she had no doubt that she was equally equipped to handle Ann. Amelia McGee was a woman of excellent background and breeding who was well received throughout the county. Not one of her three daughters was allowed any leeway in learning proper behavior and etiquette; all three had gained successful entry into society as debutantes.

Amelia McGee would prove a formidable match for her granddaughter. The McGee home was far enough away to be isolated from the gossip of a small town in Alabama and, coupled with Amelia's capability to reform Ann, it was obvious how they should proceed. But the question remained: would Amelia agree to take in Ann?

"Walt, do you really think we could persuade Mama to take Ann?"

Walt considered her question while knowing that Amelia McGee still harbored regrets that Annie had brought him into their family when she could have had the cream of the crop of upstanding young men in their county. How could he deal with someone who refused even now, thirty years later, to accept him? Likewise, Amelia would not be receptive to Ann solely because she was her granddaughter. There must be some compelling reason he and Annie could find to cause Amelia to take up their cause. But if salvaging her granddaughter were not reason enough, what would be?

"I think I have it. Your sister Pearl was widowed within a few months of your father's death. As best I could learn from your father, her husband had no aptitude for making good business decisions and left Pearl nearly destitute when he died."

"Well, being destitute doesn't sound promising to me."

"No, that is just it. Your father realized Pearl's husband Cecil was inept and did the exact opposite of what he recommended. When stock values dropped and Cecil encouraged Michael and others to buy, Michael got out of the market before it crashed. In doing so, he managed to hoard a significant reserve of cash sufficient to provide a modest living for your mother. Unfortunately, he had not planned for the maintenance of your sister. Does that make sense?"

"That makes sense. From Pearl's letters I have learned she and my mother live a frugal but genteel life and yet have managed to remain accepted in the 'right' social circles. Do you think assisting my mother and sister financially is an entrée to approach her?"

"I do, but I suspect that she may still resent having a stable horse like me as your husband. I don't believe she is in any position to refuse my money though. Your mother and Pearl are exactly what Ann needs. Now, I must convince them of that."

"You must," Annie urged. "If Ann continues on her current bent, she will bring down our family and your business. I don't know how long John can resist Ann's charms and I cannot imagine Robert Ward would continue his agreement for your using his railroad line if his son were to abandon his daughters for their aunt."

"Aye," Walt grunted. "I will convince your mother if it's the last thing I do."

EPILOGUE

As he drove through the Georgia countryside, Walt rehearsed the lines he would use to convince his mother-in-law, Amelia McGee, to take in his wayward daughter. Knowing the truth was the wrong play, Annie's poor health and her resulting lack of community involvement provided an ironclad reason why Amelia was the better choice for instructing Ann in the ways of becoming a genteel woman.

She had many questions, but she quickly found that none of the answers were as easy to accept as the bundles of cash Walt carried in the carpetbag on the seat beside him. She agreed to take Ann in.

.....

Annie watched from her bedroom window as John Ward fulfilled his promise to Walt to cut ties with Ann. She drew no pleasure from seeing her daughter humiliated, but Annie realized nothing short of that would ever bring Ann to the place where she would turn her life around.

Within two weeks, Walt returned and Ann was on her way via train to Georgia to live with Amelia and Pearl. Only time would tell if Amelia's strictures, which were in line with those of Walt, were stronger than Ann's will. She and Walt had nearly lost one of their daughters and they were desperate to do what was necessary to avoid the same with Ann.

.....

Walt was pleased with where his family stood. Having resurrected a relationship with Olivia and her daughters made Annie happy which, in turn, warmed Walt's heart. While his cattle and equine business lulled, his sawmill business held steady. Even in a flailing economy, people always needed lumber. The real gem of his business dealings however, was the privilege Robert Ward had afforded him to transport his lumber, horses, and cattle free of charge on the Southern Railroad spur he controlled.

Furthermore, Walt's political contacts in Montgomery felt strongly that if the civil unrest in Europe continued, the United States Army might seek to build a training area in the Southeast. He hoped the money he had spent cultivating favor and influence among the political elite would land him lucrative government contracts. Surely he would profit from the need for lumber for building and horses for mounted cavalry. As was his motto, Walt would be prepared for his own 'Meet Jesus Day'.

.....

After Olivia's near-death experience, she and John entered a period of peace in their relationship. Previously, they were two people who barely spoke to each other and had no history of sharing intimate aspects of their lives.

As Olivia recovered, John worked with her to share a home and raise their daughters. At supper one evening, John had referred to himself as Olivia's 'husband' for the first time and it brought a smile to her face.

He proved to be a capable father to Kate and after a few weeks, he did not have to rely on the ladies on the route to change her diapers. More important, he bonded with her and marveled at all she seemed to learn. It saddened him to think how much time he had wasted denying her and to realize she would suffer similar treatment from many in High Springs throughout her life.

Olivia's faith continued to grow as she spent every spare minute reading His Word. "You may doubt what I am going to tell you, John, but it is the truth. While I lay near death, every time I waked, I sought God's care. More than once I felt His presence beside me and He seemed to beckon me to go with Him. Although I felt I was slowly leaving this earth, you whispered in my ear you wanted me to live, and it gave me the strength to clutch this life."

Her confession proved sobering for John, but he knew he could not reciprocate her unselfish love. As he struggled to find a way to make ends meet without her income, he became more and more frustrated as he arrived at the same conclusion. Because he still owed his markers for gambling, they did not have much money and it was upon him to find a means to make them soluble. He only hoped he could find a way to do so legally.

.....

Life could not have been better for Robert Ward. His businesses were steady and in particular, the agreement with the Southern Railroad was a cash cow. His was an unusual situation. Because he had cash money to lend as the economy continued to falter, he was able to acquire numerous properties from those who could not satisfy their mortgages. In exchange for allowing them to live in their homes and cut him in on the profits from their crops, he continued to flourish. To top it off, he had two beautiful granddaughters, and Judy and he had reached a peace regarding the love and care of at least one of them.

While Judy continued to tacitly deny Kate and Olivia, Jean was the apple of her eye. Having been nursed to health after her premature birth, Jean enjoyed the love and constant attention Evelyn could only have dreamed of.

Evelyn grew more beautiful as she aged. Her talents in science, music, writing and poetry manifested themselves in her studies. Olivia, ever her guardian angel, encouraged her to apply herself so she could attend college. Evelyn had long admired Olivia's efforts to become a nurse and she hoped one day she could help people as well. Perhaps a nursing career awaited her; she would certainly try her best.

.....

The Turners and Wards established themselves as families of note in Southeast Alabama. Walt Turner had moved his genteel bride from Georgia to Geneva County, Alabama, with the promise of riches. To his word, he had achieved much of what he had promised. In doing so, they planted the seeds of a bloodline which would grow and prosper beyond his expectations.

Michael McGee may have regarded him as a grade stallion undeserving of Annie's love, but Walt made sure their children grew up with every opportunity to achieve their goals.

Annie's health was precarious at best, but as she and Walt sat on the porch at High Point, they marveled at all they had.

"I wish I could live long enough to see what our grandchildren will accomplish."

"I know, Annie, but we must be content to know strong seeds and careful tending lead to deep roots and continued growth. We've planted our seeds and tended them as best we knew how. They are strong, these roots, and I expect they will grow stronger than either you or I could possibly imagine."

"You may be right, Walt. I have that feeling."

EVELYN'S RECOLLECTIONS:

We lived in a house until I was seven. I remember that the details I remember are these: the front of the house faced east, looking across open fields at a distance wooded area and a neighbors – a tenant house just across the garden. It was on a northwest corner at a cross roads and a neighbor lived on the southeast corner - my father's family home in earlier years. North of our house was a tenant house that belonged to our farm.

Between home and the tenant house sat the barn and tool shelter. I remember climbing to the top of the barn roof to see the pigeons' nests – the pretty eggs and watch their flight. I remember climbing the rafters of the barn and finding bottles of bluing as a later reminder that the barn had once been my father's country store.

I remember pomegranate trees that stood near the kitchen window on the north side of the house and the pump and wash shelter. The "battlin' blow" and stick. The black pot for boiling clothes. The wood pile out back and the smoke-house and car shelter (now called garage) and the old Buick that ran no longer but was housed there.

The car in current use was always parked in the south yard under massive oak trees. From there to the road on the south was a wooded area that I rambled in – had a "June bug" tree and which served as a nesting place for Easter bunny rabbits which each Easter laid eggs in a nest there, or so my father said. It was also the place my father's bees were kept. I remember his gathering honey and the honeycomb which I always ate or chewed the wax for gum.

I remember riding the cultivator as my father or a tenant plowed the fields. I remember going along as the cows were carried to the pasture a ways west of the house. I remember maypops (passion flowers) each summer and sitting on the front steps pushing my toes in the damp earth on the first day of summer each year – that was the first barefoot day of the year. I remember dew of early mornings and the Gardenia that grew on either side of doorsteps of the side porch which was on the south side of the house – the thrill of jumping off what seemed at the time to be a high porch.

–Evelyn Ward captures her memory of High Bluff in her journal

<u>COMING MAY 2018</u>

"THE COTTON CHRONICLES VOLUME TWO:
A GROWING SEASON"

BUY YOUR COPY AT:
WWW.THECOTTONCHRONICLES.NET

PLEASE LIKE US ON FACEBOOK AT:
BETTY COTTON MCMURTRY – AUTHOR

PLEASE RATE AND REVIEW "A PLANTING
SEASON" ON AMAZON.COM

ABOUT THE AUTHORS

Betty Cotton McMurtry was born in Hartford, Alabama.

After high school, she attended Auburn University. After college, she began a life of civil service with the United States Department of Agriculture.

In 1997 she became a certified National Football League Players Association agent where she helped a number of players sign professional contracts in the NFL, Canadian Football League, and Arena Leagues.

Betty resides in Auburn, Alabama where she enjoys writing, cooking, studying God's Word, and spending time with her two grandchildren and five great-grandchildren.

****

Ford McMurtry was born in Columbus, Georgia.

After high school, he attended Auburn University where he was a member of the football team.

In addition to becoming a successful coach at the high school, college, and professional levels, Ford's career included stints as an NFL agent, sports journalist, business owner, and auto insurance claims director.

Ford resides in Auburn, Alabama where he enjoys Auburn University sports and spending time with the family and dog, Missy.